OCEANSIDE PUBLIC LIBRARY
330 N. C
Oc

D0575746

OCEANSIDE PUBLIC LIBRARY

3 1232 00536 6861

Q
301.4157
MAC

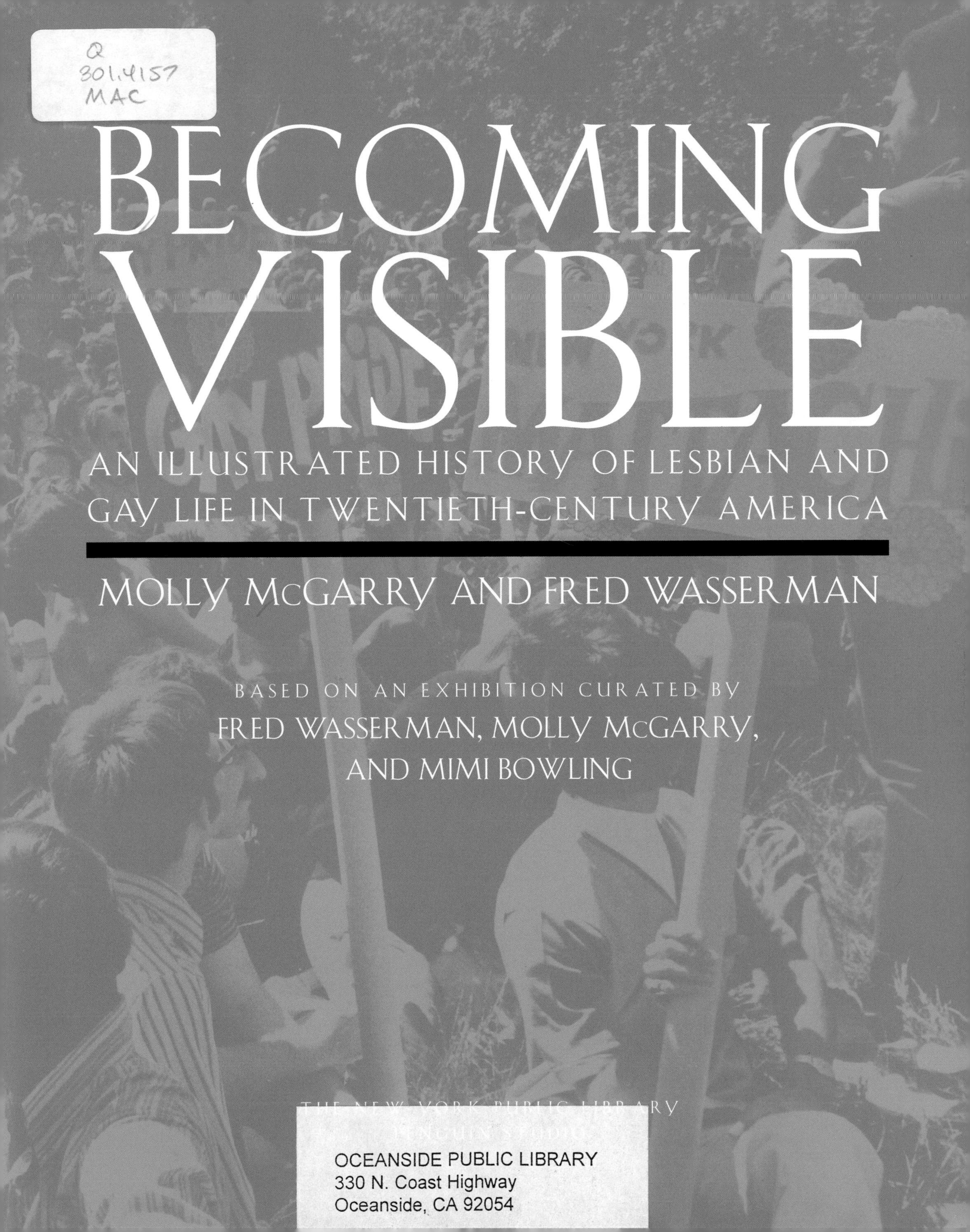

BECOMING VISIBLE

AN ILLUSTRATED HISTORY OF LESBIAN AND GAY LIFE IN TWENTIETH-CENTURY AMERICA

MOLLY McGARRY AND FRED WASSERMAN

BASED ON AN EXHIBITION CURATED BY
FRED WASSERMAN, MOLLY McGARRY,
AND MIMI BOWLING

THE NEW YORK PUBLIC LIBRARY
PENGUIN STUDIO

OCEANSIDE PUBLIC LIBRARY
330 N. Coast Highway
Oceanside, CA 92054

In memory of my father,
Shepard Wasserman,
and my dear friend Ron Jacobowitz
—F.W.

In honor of the lesbian and gay community historians who made this work possible.
—M.M.

PENGUIN STUDIO
Published by the Penguin Group
Penguin Putnam Inc., 375 Hudson Street,
New York, New York 10014, U.S.A.
Penguin Books Ltd, 27 Wrights Lane,
London W8 5TZ, England
Penguin Books Australia Ltd, Ringwood,
Victoria, Australia
Penguin Books Canada Ltd, 10 Alcorn Avenue,
Toronto, Ontario, Canada M4V 3B2
Penguin Books (N.Z.) Ltd, 182-190 Wairau Road,
Auckland 10, New Zealand
Penguin India, 210 Chiranjiv Tower, 43 Nehru Place,
New Delhi, 11009 India

Penguin Books Ltd, Registered Offices:
Harmondsworth, Middlesex, England

First published in 1998 by Penguin Studio,
a member of Penguin Putnam Inc.

10 9 8 7 6 5 4 3 2 1

McGarry, Molly.
    Becoming visible: an illustrated history of lesbian and gay life in
        twentieth-century America / by Molly McGarry and Fred
        Wasserman.
    p.   cm.
    "Based on an exhibition curated by Fred Wasserman, Molly
        McGarry, and Mimi Bowling."
    Includes bibliographical references and index.
    ISBN 0-670-86401-3
    1. Homosexuality—United States—History—20th century.
    2. Gays—United States—History—20th century. I. Wasserman,
    Fred. II. Title.
HQ75.16.U6M37   1998   97-49124
306.76'6'09730904—dc21   CIP

This book is printed on acid-free paper.

∞

Printed in Singapore
Set in Bembo
Designed by Jaye Zimet

Without limiting the rights under copyright reserved above, no part of this publication may be reproduced, stored in or introduced into a retrieval system, or transmitted, in any form or by any means electronic, mechanical, photocopying, recording or otherwise, without the prior written permission of both the copyright owner and the above publisher of this book.

Copyright © 1998 The New York Public Library, Astor, Lenox and Tilden Foundations

The name "The New York Public Library" is a registered mark and the property of The New York Public Library, Astor, Lenox and Tilden Foundations.

The Library gratefully acknowledges the museums and archives, authors, photographers, agents, and publishers for their permission to use copyrighted material in *Becoming Visible*. Every reasonable effort has been made to obtain all necessary permissions. Should any errors have occurred, they are inadvertent, and every effort will be made to correct them in subsequent editions, provided timely notification is made to the Library in writing.

"Café: 3am" by Langston Hughes: From *Collected Poems* by Langston Hughes. Copyright 1994 by the estate of Langston Hughes. Reprinted by permission of Alfred A. Knopf, Inc.

"B.D. Women's Blues": Words and Music by Clarence Williams and W.R. Calaway. © Copyright 1935 by MCA MUSIC PUBLISHING, A Division of UNIVERSAL STUDIOS, INC. Copyright Renewed. International Copyright Secured. All Rights Reserved.

"Prove It On Me Blues": Words and Music by Ma Rainey. © Copyright 1927, 1928 by MCA MUSIC PUBLISHING, A Division of UNIVERSAL STUDIOS, INC. Copyright Renewed. International Copyright Secured. All Rights Reserved.

Excerpts from the radio documentary *Remembering Stonewall* used with permission of Pacifica Radio Archives, North Hollywood, California.

Additional credits for the images used in this book appear on pages 269–270, which constitute an extension of this page.

Title page photograph: **Gay Be-In, Sheep Meadow, Central Park, New York, June 28, 1970.** © DIANA DAVIES

DEC 2 4 1998

CONTENTS

PREFACE

Of the many expressions of wonderment uttered during The New York Public Library's landmark exhibition *Becoming Visible: The Legacy of Stonewall* in 1994, perhaps no sentiment was more prevalent than "How did this get here?" How did it come to pass that the stately Beaux Arts halls of the Library were packed to the rafters with queer history? It was a good question.

It is widely acknowledged that mainstream repositories, particularly museums and research libraries, neglected the field of gay and lesbian history for most of this century, and in many respects The New York Public Library was no exception. Paradoxically, from the time of its founding in the 1890s, the Library methodically acquired an extensive collection of relevant monographs and periodicals and amassed an impressive representative sample of erotica, too. But it did this collecting from within its own closet. Until the 1970s, when automated cataloging mandated adherence to external standards of terminology, the subject headings "Homosexuality," "Lesbian," and "Gay" did not appear in the Library's catalog; researchers had to know to look up "Sexual Inversion" instead. And while the Library may have from time to time acquired collections of personal papers and organizational records containing documentation of lesbian and gay lives and culture, until 1983 none was sought specifically because of such content.

In the 1970s, as the gay liberation, lesbian feminist, and gay rights movement gained momentum, a series of discussions took place among senior Library management and trustees regarding the importance of seeking gay and lesbian historical collections. These discussions led to the acquisition, in the 1980s, of two collections. First came the papers of Howard Brown, a former New York City health commissioner and founder of what is now the National Gay and Lesbian Task Force; several years later the Library acquired the records of the lesbian/feminist poetry journal *Thirteenth Moon*. More important than these two acquisitions per se was the fact that a fundamental shift in policy was under way, and was openly articulated.

The groundwork was thus laid for negotiations in the late 1980s regarding the International Gay Information Center Archives (IGIC). This collection, comprising approximately eight hundred linear feet of organizational records, personal papers, periodicals, books, audiovisual material, and ephemera, was the offspring of the Gay Activists Alliance History Committee, and other organizations no longer extant. Several dedicated volunteers struggled for some years to keep the collection independent, growing, and accessible, but were unable to rally the financial, physical, and human resources needed to run an archive. (Interestingly, the IGIC experience stands in contrast to two New York community-based repositories that have remained independent for many years, the Lesbian Herstory Archives, and the National Museum and Archives of Lesbian and Gay History. In 1988, the directors of the IGIC Archives gave the collection to the Library.

The acquisition of a collection this large, unique and important resulted in an instant critical mass, drawing new collections and researchers alike. The IGIC Archives have attracted several dozen new acquisitions since 1988, including the papers of historians Jonathan Ned Katz and Martin Duberman, writers Doris Grumbach and Karla Jay, and activists Morty Manford and Craig Rodwell. The numbers of gay and lesbian archival collections are continually expanding. For their part, researchers began arriving to use IGIC almost as soon as the collection was off the loading dock. In the space of one short decade, hundreds of books, articles, dissertations, documentaries, and exhibitions have been written or created, based on research in IGIC and related collections.

Just as it had acknowledged the importance of gay and lesbian history a decade earlier, at the end of the 1980s the Library realized that chronicling AIDS—the effect of the pandemic on society and society's response, or lack thereof—should be one of its most urgent missions. To that end, the Library acquired the records of Gay Men's Health Crisis, the People With AIDS Coalition, ACT UP/NY, and Gran Fury (the artists' collective associated with ACT UP). Through its partnership with the Estate Project for Artists with AIDS, the Library has also acquired the papers of a number of writers and artists with HIV and AIDS.

Given these resources, it was inevitable that the Library should figure prominently in what was initially envisioned as a citywide network of exhibitions observing the twenty-fifth anniversary of the 1969 Stonewall Riots. The Library recognized this anniversary as an ideal opportunity to share its treasures with a wide audience and mounted a major exhibition on gay and lesbian history, focusing primarily on New York City in the last one hundred years. The exhibition, on which this book is based, proved hugely popular, and propelled the continuing acquisition of lesbian and gay collections into a whole new dimension as people began to realize that much of the memorabilia in their attics (and closets) was historically important.

Like those new donors, we have come to realize the changing nature of archival materials. Archives were once thought to consist of works on paper, then perhaps photographs, and eventually recorded sound, moving images, and computer-generated media. For marginalized people and radical organizations, the records of human activity may exist as much in a T-shirt, a bar ad, a button, a physique magazine, or a lesbian pulp novel as they do in the more traditional forms of letters, diaries, and legal documents.

Acquiring and managing gay and lesbian archival collections is not without challenges, including the balancing of individuals' rights to privacy against the considerable societal benefits of open records. Institutions holding gay and lesbian material must learn to navigate the shoals of community politics—"Who speaks for the gay and lesbian community?"—and to recognize that in fact there are many communities. And homophobia still exists: Not everyone is happy that these collections are here. These challenges occasionally put the Library out on a limb. But the work is too important not to do: There is a hole in history—everyone's history—that needs filling in. And besides, out on a limb can be a good place to be—we can see a lot farther from there.

—Mimi Bowling
Curator of Manuscripts
The New York Public Library
January 1998

ACKNOWLEDGMENTS

This book is based on the exhibition *Becoming Visible: The Legacy of Stonewall* organized by The New York Public Library in the D. Samuel and Jeane H. Gottesman Exhibition Hall, June 18–September 24, 1994.

The exhibit grew out of the Stonewall History Project, a collaborative effort by the Library and several other cultural institutions to commemorate the twenty-fifth anniversary of the Stonewall Riots. We would like to thank David M. Kahn, then Executive Director of The Brooklyn Historical Society, for initiating the collaboration, soliciting the Library's participation, and inviting Fred Wasserman to serve as Project Curator for collaboration. In that capacity Fred developed the preliminary concept for the Library's *Becoming Visible* exhibition.

As guest curators and co-authors, Fred Wasserman and Molly McGarry are most grateful to Mimi Bowling, the Library's Curator of Manuscripts, who was our co-curator for the *Becoming Visible* exhibition. A very special colleague and collaborator, Mimi brought wonderful ideas, stupendous knowledge of the Library's collections (and bureaucracy), and great vision to the project. During the course of producing this volume, she read the manuscript and helped in other ways too numerous to list. While Mimi was unable to join us in writing this book, her hand and spirit are evident throughout.

We received tremendous support from the scholarly community while organizing the exhibition. We especially appreciate the assistance of George Chauncey. We are also indebted to Martin Duberman, Barbara Smith, Joan Nestle, Jonathan Ned Katz, John D'Emilio, Alice Echols, Lillian Faderman, and Kendall Thomas. Curatorial consultants Robert Rosenberg and Deb Schwartz provided their research and writing talents and exhibited enormous grace under pressure. Thanks also to research assistants David Gips, Tracy D. Morgan, and Laura Wernick, and photography coordinator Scott Sensenig.

Many individuals at The New York Public Library were critical in bringing the *Becoming Visible* exhibition to fruition. The strong backing at the outset from the late Timothy S. Healy, S.J., then President, was crucial. Dr. Paul LeClerc, President, and Paul Fasana, the former Andrew W. Mellon Director of The Research Libraries, were particularly supportive of our efforts to showcase the Library's collections in this subject area. We are also grateful to Rodney Phillips, David Cronin, and Bonnie Levinson for the important roles they played in the exhibition project.

We were most fortunate to work with the talented staff of the Library's Exhibitions Program Office who helped us realize our vision in an endless number of practical ways: Susan Rabbiner, Myriam de Arteni, Jeanne Bornstein, Tracy Edling, Caryn Gedell, Jean Mihich, and Philip Mrozek. We owe a special debt to our exhibition designer, Lou Storey, who brought it all to life with color and style and imagination. Thanks also to Barbara Bergeron, Doug Clouse, and Mark Dunn for their efforts. Special thanks to Doug McKeown and Randy Wicker for creating a videotaped record of the exhibit.

We particularly appreciate the cooperation of the chiefs, curators, and staff of the following New York Public Library collections who assisted in the identification of materials for the exhibition: Center for the Humanities: Henry W. and Albert A. Berg Collection of English and American Literature; General Research Division; Manuscripts and Archives Division; Map Division; New York Public Library Archives; Rare Books Division; U.S. History, Local History and Genealogy Division; Miriam and Ira D. Wallach Division of Art, Prints and Photographs. The New York Public Library for the Performing Arts: Rodgers & Hammerstein Archives of Recorded Sound; Billy Rose Theatre Collection. Schomburg Center for Research in Black Culture: Art and Artifacts Division; General Research and Reference Division; Manuscripts, Archives and Rare Books Division; Photographs and Prints Division. Science, Industry and Business Library.

We thank all of the sponsors of the *Becoming Visible* exhibition. The show was made possible by Pinewood Foundation and the Stonewall Community Foundation Inc., with major gifts from the David Geffen Foundation, Michael D. Palm, Michael A. Recanati, Jeff Soref, Ira Statfeld, Fred Hochberg, Steven Kossak, and James Pepper. Special thanks to Louis A. Bradbury and Douglas W. Jones, William F. McCarthy and Jonathan F. Burleson, the New York Community Trust, the Paul Rapoport Foundation, Adam R. Rose and Peter R. McQuillan, the Streisand Foundation, Henry van Ameringen, Terrance K. Watanabe, Wheelock Whitney III, and Louis. Additional support was provided by Edith Dee Cofrin, Mario M. Cooper, Cynthia J. Dames and Tamar C. Podell, the Honorable Thomas K. Duane, Stephen E. Herbits, Aaron Lieber, Mary T. Nealon and Vivian H. Shapiro, Timothy J. Sweeney, and an anonymous donor.

We gratefully acknowledge the generosity of all of the many individuals and institutions who lent or donated items for the exhibition and this book. In particular we would like to thank the lesbian and gay community-based archives and their volunteers, who collected, preserved, and exhibited gay and lesbian materials long before mainstream repositories were interested in the subject: the International Gay Information Center Archives, which was donated to The New York Public Library in 1988 by John Hammond and Bruce Eves; the Lesbian Herstory Archives/Lesbian Herstory Educational Foundation, Inc.; and the Lesbian and Gay Community Services Center's National Archive of Lesbian and Gay History (Center Archives). We are especially indebted to the coordinators of the Lesbian Herstory Archives and to Richard Wandel of the Center Archives.

Transforming an exhibition of some six hundred items into a book has been a formidable project. We had the good fortune to work closely with Karen Van Westering, The New York Public Library's Manager of Publications, on the process of expanding the exhibition into a book. Her professional expertise and careful attention greatly facilitated the realization of this enormous project. Publications assistant Alexa Sanzone did an outstanding job organizing the visual materials and obtaining releases. Xan Mazzella helped with many important details in the crucial last months of the project. Chris Alksnis helped arrange additional photography.

Many individuals helped make the book a reality. Our agent, Jed Mattes, was enthusiastic about the project from the beginning. Our attorney, Kenneth P. Norwick, offered sage advice. Working under less than ideal conditions, Peter Bittner of Spring Street Digital, Inc. effectively photographed the many artifacts and documents included in this book. At Viking, our editor, Sarah Scheffel, focused extraordinary attention on our manuscript and made many important suggestions; Jaye Zimet created a powerful design for the book; copy editor John Jusino smoothed our rough edges; and Christopher Sweet was a strong advocate for the book and lent full support through the many phases of the project.

We especially would like to thank Lisa Duggan and Jeffrey Escoffier, who read the entire manuscript, offering insightful comments and suggestions throughout. Jeffrey Escoffier also went beyond the role of scholar and editor, providing advice on a host of book-related matters large and small.

Fred Wasserman would like to acknowledge a gay men's history study group in which he participated in San Francisco in the early 1980s and thanks the group for providing his introduction to the subject. I deeply appreciate the efforts of many friends and associates who read parts of the manuscript and made valuable suggestions, assisted with research, proffered advice, or were simply there with much-needed encouragement: Steven Amarnick, Bert Hansen, Jane Holzka, Eric Gabriel Lehman, Jeffrey Escoffier, Allen Ellenzweig, Keith Mascheroni, Robert Rosenberg, Eve Sicular, Carl Morse, Stephanie Wilson, Peg Byron, Mimi Bowling, Tina Martin, Roberta New-man, Marshall Weeks, and Richard White. My mother, Selma Wasserman, always had heartening words and helped me keep things in perspective. My brother, David Wasserman offered emotional support and a fine sense of the absurd during the rougher moments. Finally, a note of gratitude to two special people whom I lost during the course of the project, my good friend Ron Jacobowitz and my dear father, Shepard Wasserman.

Molly McGarry would like to thank advisers at New York University, especially Tom Bender, Lisa Duggan, Richard Sennett, and Danny Walkowitz for supporting this public history work. Special thanks to Paul Gabriel and José Sarria, who found and sent fabulous material at the eleventh hour. Many friends and colleagues have read (or talked through) various chapter drafts, offering editorial advice, historical help, and endless encouragement; for their friendship, humor, and/or help with footnotes, I thank Adina Back, Pennee Bender, Nan Boyd, Jeffrey Escoffier, Elizabeth Freeman, Terence Kissack, Kevin Murphy, and Deb Schwartz. My parents, Frank and Sylvia McGarry, gave their consistent support while always asking when I would finish "the other paper." Finally, my deepest thanks go to Regina Kunzel, who read multiple chapter drafts and, throughout this sometimes arduous process, provided nuance, insight, and perspective.

INTRODUCTION

This book had its first life as an exhibition entitled *Becoming Visible: The Legacy of Stonewall,* which opened at The New York Public Library in June of 1994 in conjunction with the commemoration of the twenty-fifth anniversary of the Stonewall Riots. With Mimi Bowling, the Library's Curator of Manuscripts, we curated what was the largest and most extensive exhibit on lesbian and gay history ever mounted in a mainstream American museum or gallery space. More than one hundred thousand people from more than forty states and thirty-six countries had the opportunity to see the show. In the comment book, alongside literally hundreds of pleas that the show travel to other cities, one woman from Los Angeles simply wrote, "I wish I could take it home with me." This book is our attempt—and the Library's—to give the exhibit a permanent home.

The exhibition was not only a comprehensive look at a century of lesbian and gay life—it was also an event. And if for only a brief moment in time, The New York Public Library's marble-columned, Beaux Arts exhibition hall was transformed into a very queer space. Amidst photographs of fierce gay liberationists and sepia-toned Victorian couples, a sound system played eight decades of music important to gay men and lesbians, including show tunes, disco, women's music, and the blues. Gloria Gaynor must have sung "I Will Survive" a hundred times a day that summer as

The New York Public Library's very first disco ball shimmered above.

The celebration in New York City of the twenty-fifth anniversary of Stonewall, slated to be the occasion of an international march as well as the Gay Games, seemed like the perfect opportunity to showcase the rich holdings of the International Gay Information Center Archives (IGIC), which had been donated to the Library in 1988. This vast collection, assembled in New York's gay community beginning in the 1970s, included some eighty feet of organizational records and personal papers, more than three hundred audio- and videotapes, approximately two thousand periodical titles (tens of thousands of pieces) from forty-seven states and twenty-seven countries, an estimated four thousand books, and hundreds of feet of ephemera (posters, buttons, flyers, newsletters, etc.) from approximately four thousand organizations worldwide. Additionally, many other divisions of The Research Libraries of The New York Public Library had significant holdings related to gay men and lesbians.

On the occasion of this anniversary, we sought to contextualize the Stonewall Riots so that visitors would appreciate that this event, while a critical turning point, was part of a century-long history of community building and resistance. Because Stonewall had long been enshrined as the genesis of modern gay life—a notion reinforced by the anniversary celebration—we were very conscious of the need to underscore the richness and tenacity of lesbian and gay communities and political movements in the decades before Stonewall. In order to adequately tell this story, we expanded our purview well beyond the holdings of The New York Public Library, ultimately drawing on material from more than eighty archives and private individuals.

This book builds and expands upon the exhibition. While it necessarily reflects the show's emphasis on New York City, in our text, as well as with selected additional photographs, we have tried to include more material about other parts of the country. The resulting volume demonstrates the vibrancy of the visual record of gay and lesbian history, not only in photographs but also in a wealth of documents and ephemera. From gay liberation buttons and posters to a turn-of-the-century photograph of women kissing, we have collected material representing the most public and private aspects of lesbian and gay lives. "High" culture abuts "low" here as well; we include a 1918 Charles Demuth watercolor of a gay bathhouse and "Gay Bob," a kind of clone Ken doll; an 1891 Alice Austen photograph, and a flyer from the Lesbian Food Conspiracy. Much of the material in this book, and virtually all of the vintage photographs and artifactual material (i.e., letters, diaries, posters, flyers, buttons), has never before been published.

The book maintains the exhibition's basic organization and is arranged thematically rather than strictly chronologically. We begin with "Stonewall," an account of the riots, as well as an appraisal of the event's symbolic and historical significance. Stepping back in time, "Sodomites, Perverts, and Queers" traces the changing meanings of and prohibitions against same-sex desire. Moving from the Bible to Colonial American laws to the late-twentieth-century Supreme Court, this section chronicles society's attempts to define and police (homo)sexuality through religious, legal, and medical strictures. The two largest sections of the book are "Social Worlds" and "Organizing." "Social Worlds" documents the emergence and growth of lesbian and gay subcultures and social institutions from the turn of the twentieth century to the present. "Organizing" explores the formation of the gay and lesbian political movement from World War II to the present, emphasizing developments of the last three decades.

The book, like the exhibit, is a collaborative project, though each of us wrote separate sections of the book: Fred Wasserman wrote "Stonewall" and "Organizing"; Molly McGarry wrote "Sodomites, Perverts, and Queers" and "Social Worlds." The book was shaped, and we hope enlivened, by the different perspectives we each bring to this history. Nevertheless we worked together closely, reviewing and commenting on each other's chapters, and the completed manuscript represents a joint effort.

Throughout the book, we have attempted to utilize terms most appropriate to the period that produced them. Thus, we do not use *homosexual, heterosexual, gay,* or *lesbian* prior to the late nineteenth century. When discussing same-sex acts or identities throughout the twentieth century, we have tried to employ the terms most widely used by homosexuals, lesbians, gay men, or queers themselves. Of course, this is not a precise science. Terms coexist and overlap; those embraced by some are disdained by others. And today as in the past, same-sex desire spills over the categories that attempt to contain and name it.

The history we are trying to tell is not an easy one to name or to unearth. Despite our title, a one-hundred-year history of homosexuality has not been a simple forward march toward visibility. Indeed, in the twentieth century, periods of relative openness often have been followed by repressive backlash, and visibility has not automatically, or even typically, led to historical progress. Nor has visibility been desirable for many homosexuals. Throughout most of this period, and still for many today, invisibility has been not only the norm, but, an absolute necessity as a strategy for survival. For many, selective visibility was optimal—gay people wanted to be able to find each other, though they might not have wanted to be recognized by everyone else.

Uncovering a visual record of people who often did not want to be seen posed a particular challenge. Especially in the decades prior to World War II, material is scarce. As we approached the mid-twentieth century, it was still difficult to find a visual record of the private social lives of lesbians and gay men, but increasingly we found publications and archival records of the homophile movement that emerged in the 1950s. Stonewall, almost universally heralded as a political turning point, is also a critical divide for those doing historical research. After 1969 the visual record suddenly grows exponentially, and we were faced with a very different challenge. While the paucity of documentary evidence for the earlier years was frustrating, the extraordinary amount of material for the post-Stonewall decades required careful selection.

Nonetheless, for all periods we have been constrained by what kinds of activities get photographed, who allows themselves to be photographed, which diaries and documents survive, and what kinds of organizational records are preserved. In the past, as in the present, the visual record is skewed toward those who can afford to be openly gay or lesbian. Middle-class gay white men have been, and continue to be, much more visible in the photographic and archival record—as they are in the media and in the streets—than lesbians, people of color, and working-class people.

Despite these constraints, the visual evidence in this book depicts an extraordinarily rich and complex gay and lesbian past. In making this material available to a wide audience, we hope to make a contribution to a larger documentary project. Our work is made possible by the community historians who first realized that our story *is* history, the archivists who preserved these documents of queer lives, and most important, those lesbians and gay men who have known for decades that their lives mattered, and that their memories, photographs, and scrapbooks would have meaning to those of us who have followed. As one man wrote in the exhibit comment book, "The past comes back to inspire us." It also serves to remind us that our power is in the present, and that by taking our memories into our own hands, we can build a different future.

—Molly McGarry and Fred Wasserman
January 1998
New York City

BECOMING VISIBLE

STONEWALL

A crowd gathers outside the Stonewall Inn the weekend of the riots, New York, June 1969.
© FRED W. McDARRAH

"THERE'S A RIOT GOIN' ON"

That night in some very deep way we finally found our place in history,
not as a dirty joke, not as a doctor's case study, but as a people.

—JOAN NESTLE

In the early hours of June 28, 1969, New York City police officers launched a raid on the Stonewall Inn, a well-known gay bar in Greenwich Village. Such raids were routine and the police had little reason to expect trouble. But it was to be no ordinary night. The atmosphere was tense and nerves were strained. Many gay men were distraught over Judy Garland's death—her funeral had taken place the morning before—and they were fed up with

Judy Garland shaking hands with fans during her legendary performance at Carnegie Hall, New York, April 23, 1961. In the 1950s and 1960s, Judy was an icon for homosexuals, many of whom experienced her death as a tragedy. Their feelings of grief, loss, and anger may have contributed to the defiance of the crowd when the police raided the Stonewall Inn on the night following Judy's funeral.

the harassment of gay bars in recent weeks. Surprising both the police and homosexuals themselves, this routine raid turned into a riot. As history would prove, not just any riot, but one that took on significance as *the* preeminent symbol of gay and lesbian resistance.

New York had a lively and extensive gay scene in the late 1960s, with more than forty bars and clubs serving a clientele that included college students, leathermen, drag queens, and the "elegant" set. Three or four bars catered to lesbians. The Stonewall Inn at 53 Christopher Street was one of the city's most popular gay bars at the time.[1] Opened in 1966 by three owners with ties to the Mafia, the bar was operated as a "private" club to circumvent the need for a liquor license. The Stonewall's nondescript brick facade had blackened windows and a large wooden door. When patrons knocked, a bouncer surveyed them through a peephole and decided whether they could enter. After paying admission—three dollars on weekends, a dollar on weeknights—the select had to sign their names in a guest book so that the owners could prove that it was a private club. Few used their real names, preferring ever-popular aliases such as "Elizabeth Taylor," "Judy Garland," and "Donald Duck."

The Stonewall crowd was eclectic, typically ranging in age from those in their late teens to early thirties. In the mix were underage street kids; the "sweater set"; college students; drag queens in full female attire; "flame queens," dressed in men's clothing with makeup and coiffed hair; and a small number of hippies. Few women attended, though occasionally a lesbian would visit the bar. As with so much surrounding Stonewall, descriptions of the crowd are also contradictory: "We were Street Rats," recalled Thomas Lanigan-Schmidt, one of the bar's regular queens. "Puerto Rican, Black, Northern and Southern whites. 'Debby the Dyke' and a Chinese queen named 'Jade East.' The sons and daughters of postal workers, welfare mothers, cab drivers, mechanics and nurses aids (just to name a few) . . . We all ended up together at a place called the Stonewall." Jeremiah Newton, another regular patron, has a different recollection: "The Stonewall was not without very serious problems. If you were black, Puerto-Rican or even Chinese, it was next to impossible to get in. To be a woman or a drag queen was as bad. That peephole would open and close like the shutter of a lens and that was that."[2]

The Stonewall had two rooms, painted black and dimly lit, with a large dance floor, one of the few places in the city where gay men could dance together. Behind the bar, lights provided a bit of color to the smoky haze. Watered-down drinks were available and drugs—particularly uppers and acid—could be bought on the premises. In 1969 the jukebox blasted Motown hits by the likes of Marvin Gaye and the Temptations, as well as the romantic theme from Zeffirelli's *Romeo and Juliet,* the Beatles's "Get Back," and Elvis Presley's "In the Ghetto." A go-go boy in a flesh-colored posing strap danced on the bar on weekends.

The place engendered strong emotions. One patron interviewed by the *New York Post* the week following the riots observed, "You felt safe among your own. You could come down around here without fear of being busted or of being beaten up by some punk out to prove his masculinity to himself. Around here, we outnumber the punks."[3] Writer and activist Vito Russo, a college student when he visited the Stonewall, captured the ambivalent fondness many felt for the bar:

> It was a regular hell hole. The pits. It was also one of the hottest dance bars in Greenwich Village. It was a bar for people who were too young, too poor or just too much to get in anywhere else. The Stonewall was a street queen hangout in the heart of the ghetto. A place everyone loved to hate. Seedy, loud, obvious and heaven.[4]

However, some in New York's gay community, like activist Craig Rodwell, decried the deplorable sanitary conditions and exploitive practices of Mafia-run bars and considered the Stonewall to be the worst offender. In fact, Rodwell suspected that the Stonewall had been responsible for a hepatitis outbreak in the gay community in early 1968.

In being tied to organized crime, the Stonewall was not unusual. Indeed, New York City's gay bars were a Mafia franchise in the 1960s. The

New York State Liquor Authority (SLA) had long considered establishments that served homosexuals to be, by definition, "disorderly houses" that encouraged "unsavory conduct." Licenses were frequently revoked on such grounds, and the threat of closure—and the concomitant need to pay off the corrupt authorities—had forced gay bars into the hands of organized crime. Typically, these owners operated without liquor licenses, demanded a high cover charge for admission, and served overpriced, watered-down drinks.

(above and opposite) **Stonewall Romances.** *Flower Beneath the Foot Press, New York, 1979.*

COVER BY DANIEL ABRAHAM

By 1969 the legal situation in New York State had changed. The year before, the Appellate Division had ruled that "close dancing" between same-sex couples was legal and that merely serving homosexuals did not make for a "disorderly house." Despite this ruling the status quo persisted, and New York City's gay bars were still in the hands of the Mafia at the time of the Stonewall Riots. "The SLA refuses licenses to operators of gay bars, then has gay clubs closed because they don't have licenses," reported one homosexual organization following the riots. "Even legitimate, licensed bars are harassed by cops and SLA investigators."[5] Indeed, the Stonewall Inn, like all of New York's gay bars, was still under surveillance, and routinely made payoffs to the police and SLA officials in an effort to avoid periodic raids.

At around two A.M. on June 28, New York City police officers launched a routine raid on the Stonewall Inn as part of a campaign against unlicensed gay bars with ties to organized crime. New York was in the midst of a mayoral race—typically a time when the current administration cracked down on gay bars and gathering spots to prove that it was "tough on vice." At least five gay bars had been raided or closed in the preceding two weeks, including the Snake Pit, the Sewer, the Checkerboard, the Tele-Star, and the Stonewall, which had been raided once earlier that week. Arriving on the scene early Saturday morning, the police had a warrant to search for the illegal sale of alcohol. They anticipated no problems as patrons rarely put up resistance during bar raids.[6]

As the eight officers, including two policewomen, most in plainclothes, entered the bar, white lights on the dance floor flashed, signaling the arrival of the police—whom the patrons campily called "Lilly Law," "Patty Pig," "Betty Badge," or "Devil with the Blue Dress On." The revelers stopped dancing as the music was turned off. Following standard procedure, the cops ordered the two hundred or so customers to line up for identification inspection. They detained those without proper IDs, drag queens (for cross-dressing was still illegal), and several employees. Most of the patrons were simply escorted to the door after being checked. As they exited one by one, some struck poses and camped for a growing crowd of curious onlookers who enjoyed the antics, cheering and applauding their favorites.[7]

When a police wagon pulled up Christopher Street the celebratory mood outside the bar grew more agitated. As the police escorted the arrested into the van, cheers turned to boos and catcalls, and the rapidly growing crowd closed in on the wagon. Tension filled the air. Sylvia Rivera, a queen on the scene, recalls that, "You could feel the electricity going through people. You could actually feel it. People were getting really, really pissed and uptight." From this point on, accounts of what happened vary. Deputy Inspector Seymour Pine, the officer who led the raid, remembers that one drag queen was hauled into a waiting police car, escaped out the other side, was chased and caught and loaded back into the car, and was finally handcuffed after another attempted escape. Robert "Birdie" Rivera, another drag queen, saw "one particularly outrageously beautiful queen with stacks and stacks of Elizabeth Taylor–style hair" attack a cop with her high heel, steal the keys to her handcuffs, and free herself and other locked-up queens. However, Craig Rodwell, who was in the crowd, is emphatic that drag queens were not in the forefront. "That's another myth about the Stonewall," he protested. "The drag queens did not lead the Stonewall Riot. There were few drag queens around at the time and hardly any went to the Stonewall."[8]

Others on the scene, including Lucian Truscott IV, reporting for the *Village Voice,* observed that a struggle with a particularly tough lesbian started the riot. Yippie activist Jim Fouratt similarly recalls a "bull dyke" who "invigorated" the crowd when she escaped from a police car and threw a rock through the Stonewall's window. Still others believe that the "first blow" was thrown by one of the many gay men in the crowd. In all likelihood, the "truth" lies in Rodwell's observation that "a number of incidents were happening simultaneously.

There was no one thing that happened or one person, there was just . . . a flash of group—of mass—anger."[9]

Whatever the trigger, once the melee started, all hell broke loose. As the *Daily News* reported: "Without warning, Queen Power exploded with all the fury of a gay atomic bomb . . . New York City experienced its first homosexual riot."[10] As the cops herded people into the police wagon and patrol cars, the crowd taunted with cries of "Pigs!" "Police Brutality!" "Gay Power!" and "We Want Freedom!" Members of the crowd threw pennies and beer cans, bottles and bricks at the eight officers, until the police retreated into the bar, locking the door behind them. But the throng—which had grown to hundreds of Villagers and nighttime visitors—was not to be quelled. A parking meter was uprooted and used as a battering ram to storm the door of the Stonewall until it gave way.

"The door crashes open, beer cans and bottles hurtle in," wrote *Village Voice* reporter Howard Smith, who had taken cover in the bar along with the police. The cops grabbed one of the protesters, pulling him kicking and screaming into the Stonewall, and beat him up. "We'll shoot the first motherfucker that comes through the door," threatened one of the officers. Under siege, the cops took a firehose and aimed it out a crack in the door, spraying the crowd with a weak stream of water. "By now," wrote Smith, "the sound filtering in doesn't suggest dancing faggots anymore. It sounds like a powerful rage bent on vendetta." Deputy Inspector Pine called for reinforcements. "Everybody was frightened, there's no question about that," the officer remembered. "I've been in combat situations and there was never any time that I felt more scared than I felt that night. There was no place to run."[11]

Outside, the mob was in a fury as it swelled to at least four hundred—by some accounts a thousand—as word spread. "I was in the Village at a women's bar on West Fourth Street called Bonnie & Clyde," recalls black lesbian activist Candice Boyce. "Somebody came in and said, 'There's a fight on Christopher Street' . . . After a while we got ourselves together to go see the fight. But when we got there, we knew that this was more than a fight." One protester threw a trash can at a plywood-backed window, shattering the glass. Someone else threw lighter fluid through the window, then matches, and flames went up in the bar. "I remember someone throwing a Molotov cocktail," recalled Sylvia Rivera. "And I just said to myself in Spanish, 'Oh, my God, the revolution is finally here,' and I just like started screaming freedom, we're free at last, you know, and it felt really good."[12]

Pine and the others pointed their guns at the crowd, prepared for the onslaught. But then sirens were heard by rioters and cops alike as vehicles arrived with units of the Tactical Patrol Force (TPF), a special riot-control squad that had been created to deal with anti–Vietnam War protests. Decked out in helmets with visors, and armed with billy clubs, tear gas, and other weapons, two dozen TPF troops, linked arm in arm, moved in on the furious mob. "That's when we saw people getting beat up," recalled Mama Jean Devente, who came upon the melee after leaving Kooky's, a nearby lesbian bar:

> I remember one cop coming at me, hitting me with the nightstick in the back of my leg. I broke loose and I went after him. I grabbed his nightstick. I wanted him to feel the same pain I felt. I kept on hitting him and hitting him. I was angry. At that particular minute I wanted to kill him.[13]

In short order, the TPF dispersed the crowd. The siege on the bar had lasted only forty-five minutes and the entire raid and melee from start to finish had lasted about two hours. The police confiscated twenty-eight cases of beer and nineteen bottles of liquor. A total of thirteen people were arrested, seven for the unlicensed sale of liquor, the others for assault, disorderly conduct, harassment, or resisting arrest. Ironically, the "protester" who the police had dragged into the bar and beaten turned out to be folk singer Dave Van Ronk, a heterosexual who had left another watering hole down the street to see what was happening. Two, three, or four police officers were injured, depending on the report. One of the cops had broken his wrist, an injury that many gays appreciated as a bit of divine justice, given the stereotype of the limp-wristed homosexual.

News of the riot spread quickly by word of mouth. Saturday, a short article ran in the *New York Post* and the story was also carried on local radio and television stations. With unwitting irony, the horoscope in the paper that morning read: "General Guide—Full moon tomorrow, so this can be a lively weekend with people on the go but rather aimlessly, as recent friction in the atmosphere has been very distracting generally. People tend to seek activity as an escape from thinking."[14] During the day, the windows of the Stonewall were boarded shut and covered with graffiti: THEY INVADED OUR RIGHTS; SUPPORT GAY POWER—C'MON IN, GIRLS; GAY PROHIBITION CORUPT$ COPS FEED$ MAFIA; INSP. SMYTH LOOTED OUR: MONEY,

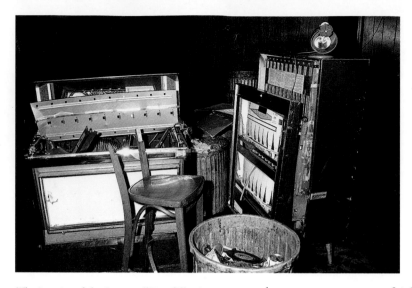

The interior of the Stonewall Inn following the raid, New York, June 1969. The damage didn't prevent the bar from reopening for business the following night.

© FRED W. McDARRAH

JUKEBOX, CIGARETTE MACH, TELEPHONES, SAFE, CASH REGISTER, AND THE BOYS TIPS; and LEGALIZE GAY BARS AND STOP THE PROBLEM.

Thousands of protesters chanting "Gay Power!" filled the streets on Saturday night. "The amazing part of Stonewall," recalled Candice Boyce, "is how many people started coming down there as word spread. People came from every borough, people who never came to the Village were there. And if you were there, you were part of it."[15] The Stonewall Inn, which had been cleaned up during the next day, reopened for business Saturday night, serving only soft drinks. Protesters blocked traffic along Christopher Street and the police spent the night trying to clear away the crowd in front of the Stonewall. But the mob would not be quelled as protesters threw bottles and bricks and lit small fires in garbage cans, all the while chanting "Gay Power!" On this night, however, violence was also accompanied by another kind of resistance—defiant public displays of affection as many, for the first time, engaged in open kissing and hand holding in the streets.

Acclaim for the confrontation in the streets was far from universal. Some homosexuals, viewing the second night of rioting, were appalled by the protesters and the threat they posed to a comfortable, if not perfect, status quo. Noting this "generation gap," Truscott wrote, "Older boys had strained looks on their faces and talked in concerned whispers as they watched the up-and-coming generation take being gay and flaunt it before the masses."[16] Many gay people simply ignored or dismissed the events in the Village.

TPF units (some accounts placed the number of police to be in the hundreds) arrived on the scene around two-fifteen A.M. Linking arms and forming a human chain, they swept up and down Christopher Street to clear the protest. But as the TPF marched toward the crowd, groups of rioters circled around via side streets, reappearing minutes later to charge from the rear. When the police looked back, they were confronted with a dancing chorus line of drag queens kicking up their heels and chanting,

We are the Stonewall girls
We wear our hair in curls
We have no underwear
We show our pubic hairs![17]

Confrontations between rioters and the police continued until around four A.M. when things finally quieted down. According to the *Village Voice,* the TPF busted one head and made several arrests.

On Sunday longtime homosexual activists went into action. Members of the Mattachine Society, a "homophile" organization that since the 1950s had worked to urge societal acceptance of homosexuals, tried to calm the rebellious atmosphere. They painted a sign on the windows of the Stonewall, imploring those inflamed by the riot to "help maintain peaceful and quiet conduct on the streets of the Village," and scheduled a public meeting for later in the week to discuss the riots. Many of the group's members were incensed at the antics of the rioters, including Randy Wicker, who felt that the sight "of screaming queens forming chorus lines and kicking went against everything that I wanted people to think about homosexuals . . . that we were a bunch of drag queens in the Village acting disorderly and tacky and cheap."[18]

However, other activists welcomed the turbulence and tried to harness this newly manifested gay power. Some Mattachine members distributed a flyer condemning the State Liquor Authority and the police. And

A plea from the Mattachine Society, hand-painted on the window of the Stonewall Inn the weekend of the riots, New York, June 1969. © FRED W. McDARRAH

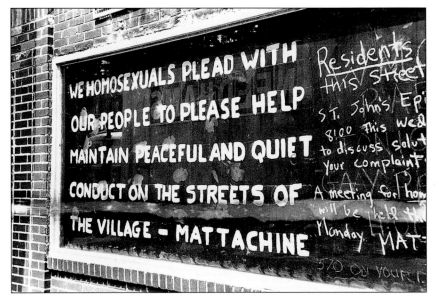

Craig Rodwell, continuing his long-standing campaign against Mafia control of gay bars, produced and distributed thousands of copies of a flyer that exhorted lesbians and gay men to "Get the Mafia and the Cops Out of Gay Bars."[19]

Sunday night, the streets of the Village were still tense and confrontations continued between gays and the police. People hung out on Christopher Street and in the park across the street from the Stonewall, and some of the "stars"

"THE HAIRPIN DROP HEARD AROUND THE WORLD"

Although the Stonewall Riots have taken on great significance since 1969, most of the coverage at the time was quite modest. The *New York Post*'s short piece on page 4 was the only coverage of the riots in Saturday's papers. On Sunday the *Post* ran an almost identical piece to Saturday's; the *New York Times* ran a story on page 33; and the *Sunday News* had a story on page 30 that featured the only known photograph of the initial Friday-night riot. The *Times* ran another brief story on Monday and the *Post* had one on Wednesday. The *Village Voice*'s front-page coverage, also published on Wednesday, was far and away the most comprehensive. The dailies ran follow-up stories a week later and accounts of the riots also appeared in the alternative press, including pieces in the *Rat,* the *East Village Other,* and *Screw* in New York, and the *Berkeley Barb* in California.

In the gay press, word crept out slowly over the next few months. The *New York Mattachine Newsletter* ran a special supplement on the riots in their July issue, while the *Mattachine Midwest Newsletter* also briefly mentioned the riots in July. The *Advocate,* a gay paper in Los Angeles, reprinted the story "The Hairpin Drop Heard Around the World," from the July *New York Mattachine Newsletter* (with the byline of New York Mattachine president Dick Leitsch). *Vector,* published in San Francisco by SIR, ran a short notice in its October issue, and the Daughters of Bilitis's *Ladder* had a notice in its October/November issue.

The national newsmagazines first reported on the riots in late October when *Time* published its cover story "The Homosexual: Newly Visible, Newly Understood," and *Newsweek* published "Policing the Third Sex." *Esquire* also ran a story titled "The New Homosexuality" in December 1969, which discussed the riots.

Photographic coverage of the riots was extremely limited. The *News'* grainy photograph of Friday night's riot was the only one published.[20] Fred W. McDarrah shot several photographs, two published in the *Village Voice,* of protesters posing outside of the Stonewall later in the weekend, graffiti on the exterior of the bar, and damage to the interior of the bar. Diana Davies also photographed the exterior of the Stonewall after the riots. Craig Rodwell had a camera at the riots, but the film did not come out when he had it developed.

The search for photographs of the riots began early. Gay Liberation Front's *Come Out!* published "A Plea to the Community" in the January 10, 1970 issue imploring, "Anyone owning or having access to photography of the Christopher Street–Stonewall Riots of last summer" to please call. Since then journalists, curators, filmmakers, and the gay community have continued the hunt, but to date no other images of the riots have come to light.

of the previous night made return appearances. The police made a sweep of the area around one A.M. Poet Allen Ginsberg, who stopped in at the Stonewall Inn late that night, noted that "the guys there were so beautiful—they've lost that wounded look that fags all had 10 years ago."[21]

Only scattered incidents occurred in the Village on the following rainy Monday and Tuesday nights, but on Wednesday crowds—possibly prompted by the *Village Voice*'s front-page coverage of the riots that morning—returned to the Village, and an estimated thousand people filled the streets. Outside the Stonewall, hundreds threw bottles and lit garbage cans on fire, while sporadic incidents were happening throughout the Village. The TPF swept the area for more than an hour, arresting five people in an extremely violent and retaliatory attack:

> At one point, 7th Avenue from Christopher Street to West 10th looked like a battlefield in Vietnam. Young people, many of them queens, were lying on the side walk, bleeding from the head, face, mouth, and even the eyes. Others were nursing bruised and often bleeding arms, legs, backs, and necks.[22]

It was the last night of the riots.

While no more than a couple of thousand gay, lesbian, and transgendered New Yorkers had participated in the riots, their impact would ultimately be profound, reaching far beyond Greenwich Village. Most participants could not have known or even imagined that they were part of a truly historic event. But some immediately proclaimed the significance of what variously came to be called the Christopher Street Riots, the Stonewall Riots, the Stonewall Rebellion, the Stonewall Uprising, and ultimately, simply Stonewall. The Mattachine Society's July newsletter called the riots "The Hairpin Drop Heard Around the World" [gay argot for dropping hints that one is homosexual] and trumpeted, "The 'Christopher Street Riots' marked a first in the history of homosexuals." "The word is out," hailed an article in the countercultural *East Village Other*. "Christopher Street shall be liberated. The fags have had it with oppression. Revolution is being heard on Christopher Street." And in their "Homosexual Citizen" column in the sex tabloid *Screw*, Lige Clarke and Jack Nichols declared that "last week's riots in Greenwich Village have set standards for the

Mattachine Society flyer, New York, 1969. The Mattachine Society, implored by radicalized gays to make a public response to the Stonewall Riots, established an Action Committee and sponsored a community meeting for July 9th.

Gay Be-In, Sheep Meadow, Central Park, New York, June 28, 1970.
© DIANA DAVIES

(above, top) **Official poster from New York's first gay and lesbian pride march, June 28, 1970.**

(above, bottom) **Permit for a "Gay Be-In (happening)" to celebrate the first anniversary of the Stonewall Riots, New York, 1970.**

rest of the nation's homosexuals to follow."[23] The change of attitude was seen not just among activists. One nineteen-year-old man interviewed the following week in the *New York Post* commented, "All my life, the cops have sneered and pointed at me and my friends. We've been harassed for doing nothing more than having our fun; not hurting anybody else. Well, the 'gay riots' mean we're not going to take it any more."[24]

In the days and weeks that followed, a rash of meetings were held where the radical concepts of gay liberation and gay power took center stage, challenging the more moderate homophile aim of seeking societal tolerance. By late July, these early discussions led to the founding of Gay Liberation Front (GLF), a radical organization that sought to align the struggle of lesbians and gay men with those of other oppressed groups. Within a couple of months, a GLF had been started in Berkeley, California, and, within two years, dozens of gay liberation organizations were active in cities and on college campuses around the country.

Stonewall was hailed as the birth of gay liberation and recognized as a potentially powerful catalyst for organizing lesbians and gay men. In the fall of 1969, several activists formed the Christopher Street Liberation Day Committee to plan a commemoration of the first anniversary of the Stonewall Riots and to encourage other groups around the country to do the same. On Sunday, June 28, 1970, several hundred lesbians and gay men gathered at Washington Square in Greenwich Village and marched up Sixth Avenue to a "Gay-In" in Central Park. By the time they arrived at the park, the crowd had grown to thousands, in what was the largest and most visible gay power demonstration to date. Recalls activist Arnie Kantrowitz:

At last we came to the Sheep Meadow, our feet hot and tired. I got to the crest of a small knoll before I turned around. There behind us, in a river that seemed endless, poured wave after wave of happy faces. The Gay Nation was coming out into the light! There was hardly a dry eye on the hill. What had begun as a few hardy hundred had swollen all along its route, until we filled half the huge meadow with what the networks and newspapers estimated as five to fifteen thousand people, all gay and proud of it![25]

Lesbians and gay men in other cities commemorated the first anniversary of the Stonewall Riots simultaneously, as more than a thousand marched in Los Angeles and hundreds gathered in Chicago and San Francisco. Celebrating the first anniversary of the riots, the Chicago-based *Mattachine Midwest Newsletter* observed,

> Although the beginnings of Gay Liberation had already been seen in Berkeley and San Francisco, the single historical event of the Christopher Street riots has come to be seen as the "official" start of Gay Liberation, a movement that has since spread to Kalamazoo and Carbondale, Kansas City and Milwaukee, as well as Los Angeles, Chicago and points in between.[26]

Indeed, the riots have assumed mythic significance since 1969. Gay men and lesbians have variously likened Stonewall to the storming of the Bastille, the Boston Tea Party, Independence Day, and various boycotts and sit-ins of the black civil rights movement. Enshrined as *the* watershed event in gay history, Stonewall has served as a rallying cry for lesbians and gay men as they confronted adversity and injustice. Above all, Stonewall's abiding symbolic power has come to be honored and renewed in dozens of lesbian and gay pride parades held every June in cities around the nation and the world.

Implicit in this celebration is the idea that Stonewall was a spontaneous event that suddenly transformed gay consciousness as well as the position of homosexuals in society. The distance of three decades, however, calls for an examination of the ways in which the riots have been mythologized, obscuring the history that came before and after. While the first night of riots may have been spontaneous, the activism it triggered did not happen in a vacuum. Contrary to the Stonewall myth, which seems to suggest that lesbian and gay communities came into existence as a result of the riots, New York, Chicago, San Francisco, and other large American cities had highly organized and extensive lesbian and gay subcultures that date back to the late nineteenth century. Early gay liberationists did not invent a community wholesale but drew on the resources of an existing one that they, in turn, politicized on a mass scale.

Gay Pride posters from London, 1979, and Berlin, 1981. International commemorations of Stonewall have flourished since the 1970s when London, Berlin, Paris, Barcelona, and Toronto first mounted celebrations.

Nor did gay and lesbian political activism begin with the Stonewall Riots. A small but courageous gay civil rights movement had been in existence for almost twenty years prior to Stonewall, and had achieved some modest legal successes. They had also challenged the medical profession's view of homosexuality as an illness, and promoted media coverage of homosexual issues. Although these moderate homophile organizations, notably the Mattachine Society and the Daughters of Bilitis, had emphasized the education of society and the assimilation of homosexuals, as the 1960s progressed some of their members became increasingly militant and staged public marches at the White House and Independence Hall in Philadelphia. In the months before Stonewall, homophile activists adopted "Gay Is Good" as their motto, a gay liberation-type group—the Committee for Homosexual Freedom—started in San Francisco, and at least one gay publication featured an article heralding the "gay revolution."[27]

These developments, as well as the Stonewall Riots themselves, were part of a widespread questioning of the status quo in the late 1960s. As *Newsweek*

(above) **Lesbian/Gay Freedom Day Parade, San Francisco, June 27, 1982.**

(right) **Sticker, Gran Fury, New York, 1989.**

observed in its reporting of the riots the following October, "It began on a balmy June evening with a police raid on one of Greenwich Village's homosexual bars. In summers past, such an incident would have stirred little more than resigned shrugs among the Village's homophile population—but in 1969 the militant mood touches every minority."[28] Indeed, the early gay liberation activists—and some of the rioters themselves—drew on the militant tactics and radical rhetoric of the New Left, the counterculture, and the black, women's, and antiwar movements, in which many of them had been (and continued to be) involved. Furthermore, as products of the sexual revolution that had swept the country in the 1960s,

they naturally extended their critique of the system to the oppression they experienced as homosexuals. For many of the early gay liberationists, Stonewall embodied the notion—and the reality—that they could fight back as gay people. As yippie and GLF activist Jim Fouratt observed, "They didn't have to put anyone else's revolution before their own."[29]

In the service of their new vision, the gay liberationists enshrined Stonewall, but in the process they delegitimized the lives and strength not only of their homophile activist forbears, but of all homosexuals who lived before Stonewall. By touting Stonewall as the beginning, the new generation devalued or ignored the creative and courageous ways that gay men and lesbians struggled to live and love in a deeply homophobic society prior to 1969. As Donald Vining, whose published diaries chronicle his gay life beginning in the 1930s, wryly comments:

> Many gay men of my generation are amused when we hear younger gays claim that after the Stonewall uprising closet doors all over America swung open and thousands of us suddenly emerged after long years of hiding there. In reality closets were where some of us stored our drag, others our porn pictures, laboriously collected in those days before they were available in newsstand magazines. Few of us had ever spent time in the closet ourselves.[30]

Despite all of the ways the celebration of Stonewall tends to skew the actual history, Stonewall has been an extraordinarily appealing—and useful—creation myth for lesbians and gay men trying to define themselves as a community. The riot has become the symbol of a common shared heritage that has deep meaning for many gay people. Given this enduring significance, it is not surprising that the story of Stonewall has been contested over the last three decades. Some of the original participants, and others, still fight over who sparked the riot. And the role of drag queens, people of color, gay street kids, and butch dykes—people on the margins who fought back because they had little to lose—has frequently been downplayed or written out of the story.

Stonewall Was a Riot. *International Gayday/Gaywalk for Freedom, New York, 1979.*

(right) **Original participants in the Stonewall Riots marching in the Lesbian and Gay Pride March, New York, June 30, 1991.** *Left to right:* Ivan Valentin, Nori Nke Aka, Sylvia Rivera, Jim Fouratt, and Marsha P. Johnson. © JOSEPH CAPUTO

(opposite) **Stonewall 25 March, New York, June 26, 1994.** More than one million lesbians and gay men descended on New York for the Gay Games and an international march on the twenty-fifth anniversary of the riots. The march featured a mile-long rainbow flag, one of the symbols of the gay rights movement.
© RICK MAIMAN/SYGMA

Meanwhile, legions of people, far more than seems likely, claim to have been at the riots. All of this suggests the extent to which people want to own a piece of this critical event in lesbian and gay history.

A generation has passed since the Stonewall Riots of June 1969, but Stonewall retains enormous power as a symbol of collective resistance and a beacon of hope for lesbians and gay men around the world, as evidenced in this statement issued by a group of Chinese bisexuals, lesbians, and gay men in June 1995:

> On the twenty-sixth anniversary of the Stonewall Uprising in New York, we are in our own way joining the people of New York and those all over the world celebrating this day. Twenty six years ago the trumpet call of the Stonewall Uprising allowed many nonheterosexuals to bravely stand up against discrimination . . . At this moment in time, whether we are in Christopher Street in Greenwich Village, New York, or at the foot of the Great Wall in Beijing, hand in hand and heart to heart we move forward to strive for all we deserve.[31]

Why the Stonewall, and not the Sewer or the Snake Pit? The answer lies, we believe, in the unique nature of the Stonewall . . . It catered largely to a group of people who are not welcome in, or cannot afford, other places of homosexual social gathering . . . When it was raided, they fought for it . . . They had nothing to lose other than the most tolerant and broadminded gay place in town.

—*"The Stonewall Riots: The Gay View,"* New York Mattachine Newsletter, *August 1969*

I don't know if the Stonewall riots will ever be recorded in history books but I do know that my world—my safe, smug, little world has not been the same since. I learned something this past Summer, something I can't put into words yet, but whatever it is, it helped me to stand in front of the *Village Voice* on a Gay picket line and say Fuck You to the Closet Cases and Straights who looked at me aghast for standing up to be counted.

—*Bob Kohler, Gay Liberation Front activist, 1970*

Mama Jean Devente (left), one of the original rioters, and a friend place a bouquet at the site of the Stonewall Inn, Christopher Street Liberation Day March, June 30, 1974. © FRED W. McDARRAH

I was escorting two women from Boston around Greenwich Village, taking them on a tour of the bars . . . While we were walking around, we saw these people . . . throwing things at cops. One of the women turned to me and said, "What's going on here?" I said, "Oh, it's a riot. These things happen in New York all the time. Let's toddle away and do something else."

—*Martha Shelley, President of the New York chapter of Daughters of Bilitis in 1969 and one of the founders of Gay Liberation Front*

No, this wasn't a 1960s Student Riot . . . This was a ghetto riot on home turf . . . Nobody thought of it as history, herstory, my-story, your-story, or our-story. We were being denied a place to dance together. That's all . . . The mystery of history happened in the least likely of places.

—*Thomas Lanigan-Schmidt, a participant in the Stonewall Riots*

Stonewall meant I wasn't alone, I wasn't isolated. I wasn't just with one other person. That there was a "we" out there to get to know, a "we" out there to become a part of, a "we" out there to make some contribution to. To make that "we" ever larger, ever wider, ever more diverse, ever stronger. And I think that's what we're about.

—*Virginia Apuzzo, activist*

I wasn't impressed by Stonewall, because of all the open gay projects we had done throughout the sixties in Los Angeles. As far as we were concerned, Stonewall meant that the East Coast was finally catching up.

> —*Harry Hay, founder of the Mattachine Society*

In 1969 I was in the U.S. Army in Vietnam. I was having lunch in the army mess reading the Armed Forces news summary of the day, and there was a short paragraph describing a riot led by homosexuals in Greenwich Village against the police, and my heart was filled with joy. I thought about what I read frequently but had no one to discuss it with, and secretly within myself I decided that when I came back stateside, if I should survive to come back stateside, I would come out as a gay person, and I did.

> —*Henry Baird, soldier*

For those of us in Public Morals, after the Stonewall incident things were completely changed . . . They suddenly were not submissive any more.

> —*Seymour Pine, deputy inspector in charge of public morals, First Division,*
> *New York City Police Department*

Stonewall was a spark. It was Rosa Parks. Rosa Parks was not the beginning of the black civil rights movement but somehow she was unifying. She was something that you could rally around. And Stonewall, for some reason, was the rallying point. There had been raids before but nobody had fought back. And all of a sudden it was the straw that broke the camel's back. It had to happen.

> —*Renée Vera Cafiero, homophile and gay rights activist*

After Stonewall sex was different. Not only was there less guilt and less anxiety, but the promise of Stonewall was, in a very real way, the promise of sex: free sex, better sex, lots of sex, sex at home and sex in the streets . . . This sexual energy fueled the movement. It filled us with fervor and desire—not only for one another, but to change the world.

> —*Michael Bronski, writer and activist*

Stonewall was a messy situation, never made for myth. It was a polyglot of most of us and who we are as gay people. Stonewall was more of a bad trip than the stuff of dreams. Yet there it is. Spontaneous generation of the demand for equality, made not by the suited middle-class respectables but by the late-night habitués of a sleazy mob-run clip joint.

> —*Jewelle Gomez,*
> *writer and activist*

Protester at a demonstration demanding that President Jimmy Carter condemn Anita Bryant's antigay campaign, New York, June 23, 1977. © BETTYE LANE

ACT UP participating in the "alternative march" commemorating Stonewall 25, June 26, 1994.

SODOMITES, PERVERTS, AND QUEERS

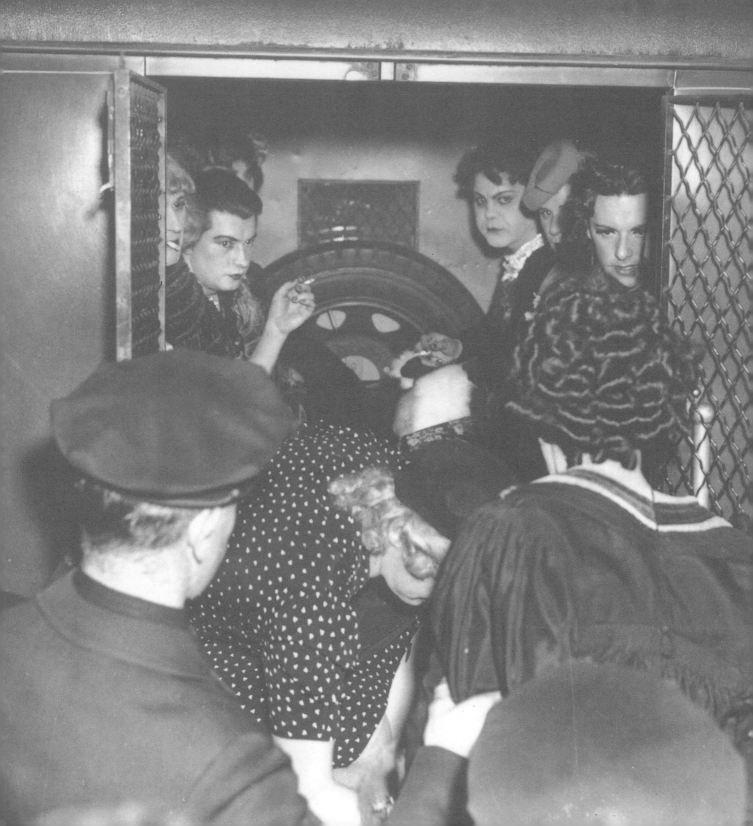

Police raid masked ball and arrest ninety-nine men on "masquerading" charges, New York, October 21, 1939.

LABELING AND POLICING

"The infamous crime against nature" is an offense of "deeper malignancy"
than rape, an heinous act "the very mention of which is a disgrace
to human nature," . . . "a crime not fit to be named."

—CHIEF JUSTICE WARREN BURGER,
BOWERS V. HARDWICK, 1986

Early one morning in August of 1982, Michael Hardwick was in bed with another man when he heard a noise outside his bedroom door. The door squeaked, opening a crack, but Hardwick assumed it was only the wind. He turned back to the man beside him and continued having sex. A moment later, Hardwick realized that there was in fact someone standing in his room. It was a police officer, who identified himself and announced: "Michael

Hardwick, you are under arrest." The officer, who had let himself into Hardwick's house, arrested both men for having oral sex, charging them under a Georgia State sodomy statute. As he placed Hardwick in a holding cell, the arresting officer proclaimed to the gathered prisoners that Hardwick was in there for "cocksucking." Under Georgia law, this offense could have brought a sentence of up to twenty years in jail.[1] However, Hardwick's lawyers fought the charge, and the case *Bowers* v. *Hardwick* made its way to the Supreme Court in 1986. In a five-to-four decision, the Court upheld the Georgia sodomy statute, allowing states the right to outlaw private, consensual homosexual sex. This ruling remains the law of the land.

Chief Justice Warren Burger wrote a separate concurring opinion in the case, in which he invoked "the history of Western civilization" as legal reason to outlaw "homosexual sodomy" in the late twentieth century. Quoting from the Bible, colonial American sodomy statutes, and eighteenth-century English jurisprudence, Burger concluded that "to hold that the act of homosexual sodomy is somehow protected as a fundamental right would be to cast aside millennia of moral teaching." Justice Harry Blackmun's powerful dissent that "it is revolting to have no better reason for rule of law than so it was laid down in the time of Henry IV," and that the law "simply persists from blind imitation of the past," was a pale defense against the weight of Burger's imagined millennia of precedent.[2]

Burger's moral certainty stands in stark contrast to sodomy's vexed and complicated history. Sodomy, which French theorist Michel Foucault termed "that utterly confused category," has historically encompassed a multitude of sexual acts, including bestiality, as well as oral and anal sex, between men, between women, or between men and women.[3] Throughout history, sodomy has often been unnamed and unspoken; since the inception of the term, there has been a refusal to name acts of sodomy, to define them, or to distinguish among them. This historic

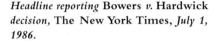

Headline reporting **Bowers v. Hardwick** *decision,* **The New York Times,** *July 1, 1986.*

"crime not fit to be named" was, in practice, a class of crimes, and the distinctions among them were often collapsed or ignored by both the Church and the State.[4]

Although the Supreme Court in 1986 was relying on a tradition of law structured by this convoluted history, the Justices declared that it is only "homosexual sodomy" that is unprotected by a right to privacy and only homosexuals who are marked by this "criminal" sexuality. The Georgia statute upheld in *Hardwick,* like the majority of state sodomy laws, makes no mention of either homosexuality or same-sex acts, defining sodomy as "any sexual act involving the sex organs of one person and the mouth or anus of another." The judges chose to ignore the language of the law itself, ruling on the sodomy law *only* as it applied to "homosexual" sex.[5] As critic Jonathan Goldberg has argued: "The Supreme Court decision tacitly upheld the right of heterosexuals to perform sodomitical sex and denied that right to homosexuals. Yet, it also defined homosexuals as those who perform that act, and several post-*Hardwick* decisions have affirmed that homosexuals now are by definition a criminal class."[6] In 1998 gay men and lesbians still can be selectively prosecuted under existing sodomy laws in more than twenty states.

This chapter details the history of sodomites and sodomy laws, sinners and criminals, and the ways in which "millennia" of religious, legal, and medical interpretations and codifications continue to have a profound impact on lesbian and gay lives today. The terms used to name same-sex practices and the people who engage in them have changed over time. Sodomite, one who commits a "sin" or a "crime against nature"—these designations encode specific histories of societal prohibitions and suggest that the "labeling" of same-sex practices is inextricably linked to their "policing." Dominant understandings of same-sex desire have shifted from sin to crime to sickness, each layer adding to but not supplanting the one before. In spite of this history of forbiddances, inverts and perverts, homosexuals and queers, have also claimed and celebrated these labels, in the face of a society that continues to police the boundaries of a "proper" sexuality.

■ IN THE BEGINNING, THERE WAS SODOM . . .

The roots of Judeo-Christian proscriptions against homosexuality can be traced to a few passages in both the Old and New Testaments. These Biblical prohibitions were inscribed into canon law in the late Middle Ages and later translated into civil legal codes prohibiting almost all nonprocreative sexual activities, usually under a vaguely defined rubric of "sodomy." These activities might have been engaged in by couples of the same or opposite sex; the gender of the participants was historically less important than the fact that the acts took place outside the bounds of procreative marriage.

Sodomites first appeared in print in the Book of Genesis, in the story of the destruction of the city of Sodom. From this story comes the word *sodomy*. Yet the act of sodomy is named nowhere in the Genesis story. The Sodomites committed a grave sin, for which their city was destroyed by fire and brimstone, but no specific sexual act or acts are either described, prohibited, or named as that sin. Both the word and the act of sodomy are missing from its founding text.

Demonstrators march up the front steps of the Georgia State capital building, protesting the state's sodomy law, Atlanta, 1990.

Other Biblical forbiddances are clearer. Leviticus is the Old Testament passage typically cited to prove religious prohibition against sex between men. Leviticus 20:13 calls for death as the punishment for the sin: "If a man also lie with mankind, as he lieth with a woman, both of them have committed an 'abomination': they shall surely be put to death; their blood *shall be* upon them."[7] This prohibition is one of more than 600 rules, the purpose of which was to set apart the Israelites from neighboring cultures and to regulate and codify a wide range of everyday practices. In the late twentieth century, people tend to selectively choose which of these 613 rules are still relevant. For example, many who point to Leviticus in their condemnation of homosexuality have no compunction about eating shellfish or extracting interest on loans, other prohibitions in this ancient set of regulations.

New Testament condemnations of variously described "abominations," "sins against nature," and acts contrary to "natural use" are relatively larger in number than Old Testament laws. St. Paul's letter to the Romans (1:26–27) is often invoked as the most direct condemnation of what we would today term "homosexual acts," and is the only passage in either the Old or New Testament that includes a direct reference to women:

> For this cause God gave them up unto vile affections: for even
> their women did change the natural use into that which is against
> nature: And likewise also the men, leaving the natural use of the
> woman, burned in their lust one toward another; men with men
> working that which is unseemly, and receiving in themselves that
> recompense of their error which was met.

Biblical proscriptions became the basis for Church teachings and canon law beginning in the Middle Ages.[8] Scholars of the medieval church have detailed the shifting meanings of "unnatural acts," attempting to untangle proscriptions against same-sex acts from the more general prohibitions of a variety of behaviors that contradicted the procreative aims of marriage. Changes over time and contradictions in various medieval interpretations raise questions as to how equal sins like fornication, adultery, bestiality, masturbation, and sodomy were considered in the eyes of the Church. Historical confusions about the nature and moral seriousness of sodomy or "sins against nature" were enshrined in canon law and translated into civil code. "Sins against nature" became the equally ambiguous "crimes against nature" that would eventually be inscribed in English and, later, American law.

■ CRIMES AGAINST NATURE; OR, THE BEGINNING OF BUGGERY

It was not until 1533, under the reign of Henry VIII, that a sin against nature became a crime against nature, and against the State. Until that time, sodomy was not considered a crime under English law, but a matter for the Church to deal with in ecclesiastical courts. In 1533, however, the British Parliament enacted a statute making "the detestable and abominable vice of buggery committed with mankind or beast" a felony punishable by death. (*Buggery* was the preferred English-language civil law term for the Biblical crime of sodomy.) Although the legal language of "mankind" could technically include both men and women, women were rarely convicted under sodomy or buggery laws. There are, however, scattered historical examples from the thirteenth through the eighteenth centuries of sodomy laws being used against women, though they are relatively few in number.[9] Sodomy and buggery laws were frequently mobilized against those who posed political as well as sexual threats to the sociopolitical

Two men respond to a Christian counter-demonstrator during an anti-Bush protest at the Republican National Convention in Houston, August 16, 1992.

order; in England at the time these included papists and other traitors to the Crown.[10]

English law, as the received legal tradition of the American colonies, eventually provided the framework, and often the language, for many U.S. sodomy statutes. At the nation's founding, each of the thirteen colonies either had its own sodomy law or was governed by common law under England's 1533 statute.[11] In all of the colonies at the time, the official criminal penalty for sodomy was death. Although enforcement varied, all fifty states had sodomy laws on the books until 1961. In that year, Illinois was the first state to adopt the Model Penal Code, which decriminalized "adult, consensual, private sexual conduct." Beginning in the 1970s, more states followed suit, and today more than half of the country's states have decriminalized sodomy. However, as many states repealed their sodomy statutes in response to changing sexual mores, several others rewrote their statutes to expressly criminalize oral or anal sex between persons of the same sex. Currently, eight states—Arkansas, Kansas, Kentucky, Missouri, Montana, Nevada, Tennessee, and Texas—specifically outlaw "homosexual sodomy."[12]

■ POLICING THE PUBLIC SPHERE

Sodomy laws are just one way that the State has sought historically to regulate, control, and police the lives of homosexuals in this country. In addition to prohibiting specific sexual acts, sodomy laws have provided the legal reasoning for a host of laws and ordinances regulating the public and private lives of homosexuals on the basis of a presumed criminal sexuality. For lesbians and gay men, federal, state, and local laws and regulations have resulted in exclusion from jobs and military service, entrapment and arrest in public gathering places and private homes, bans on the adoption and raising of children, prohibitions on immigration, and surveillance of political activity. In the 1960s and 1970s, the lesbian and gay movement and a more liberal judiciary effected the overturn of a number of these policies. But a growing conservative movement has fought these changes and, over the last few years, a host of initiatives on ballots across the country have sought to deny lesbians and gay men equal protection under the law.

Lesbian and gay bars have been frequent sites of police surveillance.

Although levels of harassment and the frequency of arrest of patrons have varied over time, bars have often been dangerous, semilegal places. Beginning in the 1920s, gay commercial establishments formally became a target of state control, although they had existed in large American cities like New York since the late nineteenth century. New York State, for instance, passed a law in 1923 criminalizing as "disorderly conduct" any "solicitation" for a "crime against nature or other lewdness." Over the decades, municipal courts interpreted this statute broadly to prohibit homosexuals from assembling in public, often deeming gay gathering places "disorderly" by the mere presence of homosexuals. State liquor authorities oversaw bar licensing in many states, and typically threatened to revoke the liquor license of any bar or restaurant that served homosexuals or simply allowed them to congregate. While hundreds of gay bars opened in major cities across the country between the 1930s and the 1960s, relatively few survived police and liquor authority scrutiny for any significant duration, giving lesbian and gay nightlife a nomadic quality. In some cities, the semilegal nature of gay bars pushed them into the hands of organized crime, and it was not until the late sixties that gay and lesbian bars began to be legalized across the country.[13]

The policing of bars, parks, and cruising areas were state and local actions, outside the purview of the federal government. Homosexuality first became a federal issue in the 1940s, when the government, for the first time, banned homosexuals from the military.

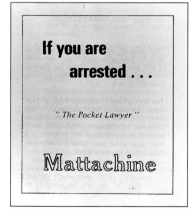

■ GAYS IN THE MILITARY

Prior to World War II, the U.S. armed forces had no formal mechanism for excluding homosexuals as a group. While the service had long treated acts of sodomy as criminal offenses punishable by court-martial or expulsion, during the Second World War, homosexuality *per se* became cause for exclusion or discharge.[14] The Selective Service System began to rely on psychiatrists to detect homosexuals during the preinduction screening process, asking male recruits if they "liked girls" and searching for "effeminate looks or behavior and . . . by repeating certain words from the homosexual vocabulary and watching for signs

The Pocket Lawyer, Mattachine Society Inc. of New York, circa 1969. So serious was the risk of entrapment and arrest that the Mattachine Society distributed booklets that advised homosexuals of their rights. "You are not required to give any information except your name and address. Do not make any statements or sign any statements, no matter how insistent the police may be. Plead NOT GUILTY and follow through. Behave with dignity and insist that the police treat you with respect."

of recognition."[15] Some watched for signs that WACs and WAVES might like girls too much. While women who volunteered for the newly established female military auxiliaries were not subjected to screening procedures comparable to those endured by male recruits, female soldiers' choice of a seemingly "masculine" pursuit exposed them to intense scrutiny.

The military's reliance on "psychiatric expertise" represented a larger trend in American society, and was part of a new interest in scientifically delineating the "normal" from the "abnormal." Dr. William Menninger, the chief psychiatric consultant to the surgeon general of the U.S. Army, lamented that the psychiatric screening was not more effective at catching homosexuals, concluding that "for every homosexual who was referred or came to the Medical Department, there were five or ten who were never detected."[16] Thousands of gay men—patriotic, willing to serve, and not wanting to be stigmatized as homosexual—found their way into the ranks by simply lying at induction interviews. Some recruiters were happy to look the other way during a time when official military policy was at odds with the growing need for personnel. In fact, at the height of the war, as large-scale troop buildups were required, the War Department ordered induction centers to relax the screening procedures.

Once admitted into the services, lesbians and gay men who were discovered typically were discharged under an army regulation for "undesirable habits or traits of character." From 1941 to 1945, nearly ten thousand enlisted men and women received "blue discharges," so named because of the distinctive blue paper on which they were printed. Prior to 1943, these discharges were officially classed as neither honorable nor dishonorable, though their meaning was widely known. In 1943 the military policy shifted, allowing the army to discharge homosexuals whether or not they had engaged in "undesirable behavior," effectively excluding homosexuals as a group from the armed services. Blue discharges, in use until 1947, stripped soldiers of their hon-

"South Post Office Gang," Fort Oglethorpe, Georgia, 1943. This group includes lesbian WAC Private Dorothee "Sarge" Gore (*third from left*). A year after this picture was taken, army officials at Fort Oglethorpe launched an investigation into the presence of lesbians in the military.

ors; denied them GI benefits; stigmatized them as gay, crazy, or both; adversely affected their employment prospects; and jeopardized their standing in their hometown communities.[17]

Although only 275,000 women served in the armed forces during World War II, the Women's Army Corps, or WACs, gained a reputation as "the ideal breeding ground" for lesbianism.[18] And though WAC officers were instructed to root out service women for homosexuality only in "extreme cases," the war years did see some exhaustive investigations into lesbians in the military. Pat Bond, a lesbian who served in the WACs during World War II, remembered one such purge at a base in Japan: "Every day you came up for a court martial against one of your friends. They turned us against each other . . . The only way I could figure out how to save my lover was to get out. If I had been there, they could have gotten us both because other women would have testified against us."[19] At the end of the war, the army instituted antilesbian purges coinciding—not coincidentally—with the army's decreasing needs for female labor. During World War II and up to the present, lesbians have been discharged because of sexual orientation at rates proportionately far higher than gay men: The navy releases twice as many women on grounds of homosexuality than it does men; in the Marine Corps, the figure is seven times higher for women than for men.[20]

The United States military is one of the last government employers that continues to maintain an explicit policy of discrimination against lesbians and gay men. The regulation enacted during World War II, which stated that "homosexuality is incompatible with military service," remained in effect and relatively unchanged for a half century. From World War II to 1992, the armed services imposed the policy with varying degrees of harshness, enforcement shifting with the military need for bodies and the changing political climate of the country. During the Reagan and Bush years, regulations were aggressively enforced, resulting in over fifteen hundred dismissals of lesbians and gay men from the military each year.

The debate over gay men and lesbians in the military has intensified in recent years. In his 1992 presidential campaign, Bill Clinton pledged to remove the ban on gays in the military, but instead compromised with ad-

"Blue discharge," 1943. The soldier who received this discharge in 1943 because of his homosexuality only recently won his long campaign to upgrade it to a general discharge. Over a half century since the end of World War II, he is finally eligible for veterans' and disability benefits, but still feels the need to remain anonymous.

(right) **Poster by Bureau (Marlene McCarty and David Moffett). To Die For: Allen R. Schindler and Terry M. Helvey. New York, 1993.** A graphic response to the murder of a gay sailor, Allen Schindler, who was beaten to death by his navy shipmates on October 27, 1992 in Sasebo, Japan. The navy allowed Schindler's chief attacker, Terry Helvey, to plead guilty to reduced charges.

(below) **Grave of Sgt. Leonard Matlovich, Congressional Cemetery, Washington, D.C., April 25, 1993.** Leonard Matlovich was a sergeant in the U.S. Air Force and the first serviceman to initiate a challenge to the military's policy of excluding lesbian and gay men from their ranks. He designed his tombstone before he died in 1988, at the age of forty-four, of AIDS.
© FRED McDARRAH

versarial military and congressional leaders who opposed allowing homosexuals in the service: The current policy of "Don't Ask, Don't Tell" was born. Recruiters may no longer ask individuals about their sexuality, but lesbian and gay soldiers are still prohibited from disclosing it, and homosexual conduct, in or out of uniform, remains forbidden. Since the institution of Clinton's "Don't Ask, Don't Tell" policy, dismissal of lesbian and gay service members has actually increased; 1996 saw the highest rate of discharge of gay soldiers in a decade.[21]

The policy barring homosexuals from the military, begun in the Defense Department during World War II, was echoed throughout the federal government in the 1950s. The Cold War and domestic anticommunism created a political climate in the United States in which "subversives" of all stripes were seen as a threat to national security. "Containment," the foreign policy aimed at controlling the Soviet communist threat abroad, had its domestic corollary in the hunt for dissidents within U.S. borders. Communists real or imagined, traitors and those who passed secrets, and Americans who strayed from the nuclear family and its proscribed gender roles all became increasingly suspect. In this ideological context, homosexuals were seen as a particularly dangerous enemy within.

In 1950, after Senator Joseph McCarthy and other political leaders charged that homosexuals in the State Department threatened the nation's security, a senate committee undertook an investigation of homosexuals in the government. The Republican national chairman, Guy George Gabrielson, proclaimed that "perverts who have infiltrated our Government . . . are perhaps as dangerous as the actual Communists."[22] The senate committee's report became a landmark document of the deeply homophobic 1950s. The language of 1950s homosexual panic had at its core the contradictory fears that homosexuals were weak, but at the same time constituted a serious threat in their immense power over other susceptible Americans. The Senate report was filled with assertions of the emotional instability of "the pervert" and his particular susceptibility to blackmail and foreign espionage.

On April 27, 1953, newly inaugurated president Dwight D. Eisenhower signed Executive Order 10450, which revised President Harry Truman's loyalty and security guidelines. The new order made "sexual perversion" (widely interpreted to mean homosexuality) grounds for exclusion from federal employment. The campaign against homosexuals in government fomented by Joseph McCarthy and his aide Roy Cohn took on the force of law. During the next two years, homosexuals were fired from an average of forty government jobs per month, a rate eight times higher than that of 1950. The federal government's policies had wide-ranging effects, as state and local governments and private industry modeled their employment policies on those of Washington.[23]

The federal government's ban on the employment of homosexuals

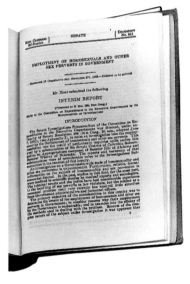

This 1950 Senate report warned that even one "sex pervert in a government agency" can pollute an entire office.

(right) **Senator Joseph McCarthy and Roy Cohn, Washington, D.C., 1954.**

(below) **"Are Homosexuals Security Risks?" One, October 1960.** The 1960 defection to Moscow of William Martin and Bernon Mitchell, both National Security Agency mathematicians and presumed homosexuals, sparked a new round of investigations into homosexuality among government employees.

remained in force throughout the 1960s. During this period, gay and lesbian employees of the U.S. government—or of any company with a federal contract—faced the constant threat of investigation. In the 1970s, the Carter administration's overhaul of the civil service system and a series of judicial decisions began to reverse this policy, which was formally nullified in 1988.

The Federal Bureau of Investigation's infiltration of homosexual organizations and surveillance of gay men and lesbians began in 1954. FBI officials later acknowledged that for decades the agency had pursued such probes for the purpose of excluding homosexuals from government and military service, targeting what the agency deemed "subversive" organizations. Although the agency states that it ceased surveillance of gay and lesbian organizations in 1978, the FBI continued to infiltrate groups such as the AIDS activist organization ACT UP in the 1980s and 1990s.[24]

That the U.S. government would continue to infiltrate gay organizations, formally ban gay men and lesbians from its workforce until the late 1980s, and persist to this day in excluding homosexuals from the military if they dare admit their sexuality are facts that belie any simple notion of progress toward greater tolerance of difference in this country. What is so striking about the history of state regulation of homosexuality in the twentieth century is the way in which it has become so recently virulent. Looking back on the last half century, one would think that homosexuality always has been policed or prohibited. Yet there were no bans on homosexuals in the military until the 1940s. The fear and threat of "sex perverts" in government is a particular invention of the 1950s. And although sodomy laws have existed for hundreds of years, they were not frequently enforced in this country until the late nineteenth century. In fact, the very notion of sexuality—homosexuality or heterosexuality—as a defining aspect of a person is in itself a relatively new concept.

■ "THE HOMOSEXUAL WAS NOW A SPECIES"

Same-sex behavior has had a long, rich history, with a legacy of scattered communities constructed around same-sex desire, from classical antiquity through the seventeenth and eighteenth centuries. The very terms *homosexuality* and *heterosexuality,* however, date only as far back as the latter decades of the nineteenth century. The word *homosexuality* made its first public appearance in an 1869 appeal for the reformation of German sodomy laws, preceding the term *heterosexuality,* which followed eleven years later in an 1880 published defense of homosexuality.[25] By the turn of the century, medical doctors in the United States began to employ the terms *heterosexual* and *homosexual* to name a "normal" and an opposed "abnormal" sexuality. It took much longer for the terms and the ideas they conveyed to move into common parlance, although the people who would come to be called homosexuals were already visible "types" in the public life of large American and European cities as these categories were making their debut.

Sodomy was significant, historically, mainly as a set of acts, forbidden by religious and civil laws, in which anyone might conceivably engage. The sodomite was seen as a sinner or a criminal, but no more a distinct type of person, with a particular psychology or physiology, than was an adulterer, fornicator, thief, or liar. As homosexuals became an object of study for doctors, homosexuality became a medical condition. The homosexual became a case history and a type of person with a possibly deviant brain and body that could, it was thought, be mapped, described, categorized, and potentially cured. As Foucault summarized this shift: "The sodomite had been a temporary aberration; the

O. S. Fowler and L. N. Fowler. "Symbolical Head" in The Illustrated Self-Instructor in Phrenology and Physiology, 1855. Phrenology, a popular science of the mid-nineteenth century, postulated that discrete areas of the brain governed specific human characteristics, which could be read through the shape and texture of the skull. Long before the first psychiatric case studies of homosexuality were published, phrenologists found a region at the base of the brain that was said to govern "amativeness" (area 3). Individuals in whom this area was underdeveloped experienced "little conjugal love" or "desire to marry" and "were cold, coy, distant and reserved toward the opposite sex."

Walt Whitman invoked another area on the phrenological chart, "adhesiveness," when he used the term "adhesive love" to describe the attraction and "fervid comradeship" he felt for other men. Scientists over the next hundred or more years have continued to search for that place in the brain that marks or determines homosexuality.

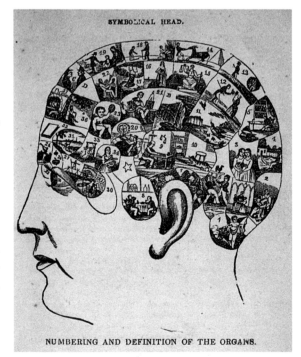

SYMBOLICAL HEAD.

NUMBERING AND DEFINITION OF THE ORGANS.

Pictures of Life and Character in New York (detail). *New York: G. W. Averell & Co., 1878.* An 1870s tourist guidebook pictured this limp-wristed caricature situated in a lower Manhattan neighborhood known to have housed several taverns catering to "fairies," as they were popularly called at the time. While the medical profession was defining the "homosexual" as such, this effeminate type was already a widely recognized figure on the streets of American cities.

homosexual was now a species."[26] This new medical attention, and the resultant construction of homosexuality as a sickness joined, rather than replaced, the older classifications of sin and crime.

The entrance of the term *homosexuality* into the Euro-American lexicon can be traced to Hungarian author and sodomy law reformer Karl Maria Benkert (writing under the pseudonym of Kertbeny). In 1869 Benkert argued that "homosexuality"—his newly minted term—was an innate characteristic of a group of people, among which he counted himself.

"Sexual deviance" and "gender deviance" have always been linked in medical discussions of homosexuality; this was all the more true in the early part of the century. Havelock Ellis, writing in England at the turn of the century, employed a concept of "sexual inversion" in an effort to explain homosexuality. In his 1903 study *Sexual Inversion,* Ellis linked athletic ability, a low voice, and a "decided taste and tolerance of cigars" to female "sexual inverts," writing that "the brusque, energetic movements, the attitude of the arms, the direct speech, the inflexions of the voice, the masculine straightforwardness and sense of honor . . . will all suggest the underlying psychic abnormality to a keen observer."[27] In sexual inversion-based theories, transvestites, masculine women, and effeminate men were often grouped in one category. Feminine women who were sexually attracted to other women, and masculine men who desired men remained a puzzle to doctors who posited a singular homosexual "type." These other individuals were often not considered "real" homosexuals by doctors, merely weak and susceptible (or failed) heterosexuals. By the turn of the century, the conceptualization of homosexuality began to undergo a shift, with same-sex object choice rather than "improper" gender behavior taking on increasing importance as a defining feature of homosexuality. Nevertheless, gender deviance and sexual deviance would remain entangled in medical studies throughout the century.

Within dominant medical models, homosexuality was seen as a sickness—either innate or acquired—that could be "treated" by medical attention. A few doctors began to move away from this orthodoxy, arguing that medicine could not and should not attempt to "cure" homosexuality in their patients. Magnus Hirschfeld, a German physician and homosexual, departed radically from the psychiatric mainstream of the time by claiming that homosexuality was an innate variation, not a sickness. In his 1914 book, *Homosexuality in Men and Women,* he maintained that homosexuals need not be changed, but rather "set at ease" with their sexuality,

Questions prepared by (Long Island "Rest" Home - Amityville, N.Y.) Dr. Titley
Wed. Dec. 17, 1937

1. Examination — thorough, internal, for embryological development.
2. Hormone test — ovarian examination
3. Determination of whether or not a pseudo-hermaphrodite.
4. What is Dr. Fox's analysis? Is she willing to experiment? With male hormone?
5. Does she want me to stay out here?
6. Possibilities of a job here, or like guarding weight, and burning trade; leaving the race question in the open, etc. They tried to palm me off as a Cuban.
7. Where do you think is the seat of conflict — in the brain, the body, the glands — or where?
8. Where could I go to get an answer? What fields are doing experimentation and have the equipment?
9. Why this nervous excitable condition all my life and the very natural falling in love with the female sex? Terrific breakdowns after each love affair that has become unsuccessful? Why the willingness to fight instead of running away in this instance?
10. Why is that my greatest attractions have been toward extremely feminine and heterosexual women?
11. Why cannot I accept the homosexual method of sex expression, but insist on the normal first?
12. Why is it that I believe that psychiatry does not have the answer to true homosexuality, but that experimental science does? (Don't know)
13. Why are you so interested in my gaining weight, unless you attach some importance to my case?
14. Why do I desire monogamous married life as a completion?

Dr. Titley
Wed. Dec. 17

15. Why do I prefer experimentation on the male side, instead of attempted adjustment as a "normal woman?"
16. Question of pseudo-hermaphroditism with secreted male genitals.
17. Do you think this conflict is an ego drive, or any organism (this one human) fighting for survival?
18. If this is merely an ego drive, why wouldn't I be satisfied with the splendid treatment I got here and the kindness of people to me everywhere? This would not be sufficient satisfaction for the ego?
19. If it is a question of race conflict, submission to authority, being hemmed in by restrictions, why is I am proud of my negro blood, that I do submit to authority as far as I am able, until I am proven wrong, or my point of view is accepted; also that I do a capable and efficient job in spurts until this conflict becomes too great for me.
20. Why do I have periods of extreme energy when I must be doing something, then periods of extreme weariness.
21. Question of what hospitals, fields or medical institutions experimentation is being carried on, in this an other countries.

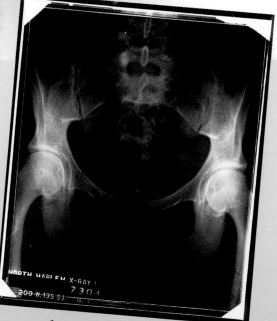

The case of "P.M." exemplifies the ways in which the medical concept of homosexuality as a sickness and as a physical difference was internalized by some lesbians and gay men, often with severely damaging consequences. "P.M." committed herself to mental institutions on several occasions, explored hormone therapy, and even demanded that X-rays, pictured here, be taken to determine whether or not she possessed internal male organs. (She didn't.) As a well-educated African-American woman born in 1910, she worried that her lesbianism compromised her potential as a leader of the race. Her anguished relationship to her sexuality, and her continual efforts to change, led to a painful break with a girlfriend, who wrote ending their relationship because of "Miss M.'s" avowals to leave "the life."

Questions prepared by "P.M." for Dr. Titley, Amityville, N.Y., December 17, 1937. "4 P.M." Pelvic X-rays, New York, July 30, 1942.

and that "homosexuality is an innate drive incurred through no fault of the patient, and is not a misfortune in and of itself, but rather becomes so as a result of the unjust evaluation which it comes up against."[28]

Sigmund Freud, unlike many Freudians, similarly argued that homosexuality was a variation of sexuality and not an illness. In a 1935 letter responding to an American mother who questioned the doctor about her homosexual son, Freud stated that "homosexuality is assuredly no advantage, but it is nothing to be ashamed of, no vice, no degradation, it cannot be classified as an illness; we consider it to be a variation of the sexual function."[29] Freud was also pessimistic about a cure for homosexuality, arguing that "in general, to undertake to convert a fully developed homosexual into a heterosexual is not much more promising than to do the reverse."[30] Despite this caution, many doctors and psychiatrists, including Freud's own followers and popularizers, sought to do just that, building careers out of treating and attempting to "cure" lesbians and gay men.

Psychiatric treatment for homosexuality has ranged from traditional psychoanalysis, with the aim of reorienting a patient to a heterosexual object choice, to aversion therapy and shock treatment. Lobotomies to treat homosexuality were reported as late as 1951.[31] Throughout the twentieth century, many lesbians and gay men have been forcibly incarcerated in mental hospitals. Others have sought out psychological treatment themselves, as they struggled to come to terms with their sexuality. "Many of us cursed our fate, longed to be straight," historian Martin Duberman remembers of his own odyssey of cures. "And as part of its missionary fervor, Western science has pursued the causes and cures of homosexuality with a zeal that has been almost comic—were it not for the tragic number of lives destroyed in the process."[32]

As some doctors searched for the cause of homosexuality in psyches, others turned to the body itself. This search for visible difference in the bodies and brains of homosexuals has a long history. Since science's earliest interest in homosexuality, doctors have attempted

Women reading of Kinsey's findings on female sexuality, August 20, 1953. Like the earlier work on male sexuality, *Sexual Behavior in the Human Female* (1953) startled the American populace. The researchers found the incidence of female homosexuality to be lower than male: 1 to 3 percent for women as opposed to approximately 10 percent for men. Over 70 percent of the lesbian respondents said they had no regrets regarding their sexuality.

to link excess body hair or "hypermasculinity" to lesbianism and effeminacy or lack of virility to gay men in a desperate attempt to discern who is and who is not a homosexual. Growing out of a nineteenth-century notion that criminality or deviance can be sited in head shapes, body types, or discovered in the brain, scientists continue to look for innate physical markings that might cause or characterize homosexuality. From phrenology—the nineteenth-century "science" that sought to connect bumps on the head to a person's character—to researcher Simon LeVay's forays into the gay male brain in search of the "homosexual hypothalamus" and Dean Hamer's efforts to isolate a "gay gene," scientists continue to probe the physiology of lesbians and gay men for the "cause" of homosexuality and signs of sexual difference.[33]

A skeptical response to a 1993 study, which asserted that only 1 percent of American males are homosexual.

For more than one hundred years, psychiatric orthodoxy held that attraction to one's same sex was pathological, a view that has had profound personal effects on generations of gay men and lesbians. A few maverick practitioners throughout the last century countered this mainstream view, postulating that there was nothing inherently sick about homosexuality. But it was not until 1973, after much pressure from gay liberationists as well as from within its own ranks, that the American Psychiatric Association removed homosexuality from its Diagnostic and Statistical Manual of Psychiatric Disorders.

From sodomitical sin to crime against nature to psychiatric illness, homosexuality has been labeled and policed. The very word *homosexual* is an invention of the medical profession, and terms such as *sodomite* or *pervert* telegraph the constructions of homosexuality as sin or sickness. But words begun as epithets take on very different meanings when used in the first person. The power to name is also the power to claim an identity, to declare oneself a part of something larger.

A few weeks before his death in 1993, Craig Rodwell, a pioneer of the gay rights movement, described a ritual familiar to thousands of gay men and lesbians:

> My high school had one of those big dictionaries on a stand. And
> I would go to it, again and again and again, and look up *homosexual*. It meant I existed.

SOCIAL

WORLDS

Alice Austen. **The Darned Club.** *Staten Island, New York, October 29, 1891.*
Left to right: Alice Austen and friends Trude Eccleston, Julia Marsh, and Sue Ripley.

EARLY WOMEN'S COMMUNITIES

Using little or no make-up or jewelry, these women wore ties, high stiff collars,
mannish suits and hats and simple short hair styles. They looked unflinchingly
at the camera, full-face, with just a trace of a smile around the corners
of their mouths. They looked like women with a secret
they dared the viewer to discover.

—JUDITH SCHWARZ,
THE RADICAL FEMINISTS OF HETERODOXY

The inexorable pull of a photograph and the feeling that the image carries with it some knowable secret about the past is a response familiar to many. Historian Judith Schwarz describes this as her own reaction in coming upon an album of photographs of a group of Greenwich Village feminists compiled in 1920. Their "mannish suits" and short hair as well as the direct gaze of these remarkable-looking women drew her to them. Eventually, she went on to

Myran Louise Grant, pictured in the **Heterodoxy to Marie** *photograph album, 1920.* Grant was a denizen of Greenwich Village in the teens and 1920s, a librarian at the Peace Conference at Versailles, a lecturer for the New York Board of Education, and the owner of at least one very flashy tie.

document their history, but her initial link to the women was an emotional one, produced by the photographs themselves. She found something in the faces of these women—in their manner, stance, and dress—that made them feel to her like "ancestors" such that, as a radical feminist writing in the 1980s about a club convened over a half century earlier, Schwarz would title her book *The Radical Feminists of Heterodoxy.*[1]

Photographs, unlike traditional historical documents, literally render the past visible. They seem to offer the promise of faces that can tell secrets, of clothing that holds meaning, of visual clues that allow the viewer to create a historical lineage linking *us* and *them.* Especially for lesbian and gay viewers who are so accustomed to looking for bodily and sartorial signs of homosexuality and who bring a kind of privileged intuition to the streets as well as to the archives, there is an often unquestioned assumption that "we know it when we see it." Because of the particular power of photographs to function as visual "proof" of lived reality, historical images seem to provide an unusually clear window into the lesbian and gay past.

French theorist Roland Barthes has written that "every photograph is a certificate of presence."[2] We might ask of this point: Presence of what? What kind of evidence do historical photographs provide? What can we divine from a photograph of two Victorian women holding each other close and looking into each other's eyes? What meanings do a "mannish suit" confer? Does a photograph of a woman with cropped hair and a tie signify lesbian desire, (hetero)sexual liberation, or attention to style? And what of the woman who does not enter the frame of vision either in a mannish suit or with another woman wearing one? Photographs—especially of faces and of fashions that feel somehow familiar to us—at once provide unique access to the past at the same time that they stubbornly withhold their meanings.

Nevertheless, what we do know is that in the late nineteenth and early twentieth centuries, growing numbers of women created communities and forged lifetime partnerships with other women. Predominantly white and middle class, these women frequently found one another at women's colleges. In some cases they lived and worked in women's-only

The Women's Trade Union League marches into Washington Square Park, Labor Day parade, New York, circa 1912. Founded in 1904, the WTUL was a coalition of working-class and upper-class women that fused feminism and trade unionism through its campaigns to regulate factory conditions and hours, and to unionize female laborers. Many of the founders and members of the league spent their private lives as well as political lives in a community of women: Mary Dreier and Frances Kellor, Helen Marot and Caroline Pratt, and Pauline Newman and Frieda Miller were among the long-term couples.

137th Street YWCA, Harlem, New York City, circa 1940s. The Young Women's Christian Association provided boarders and long-term staff members alike with a women's-only social, living, and work space. YWCAs were desegregated nationally in 1946; the Harlem Y, however, remained an African-American institution long after that date. © MORGAN AND MARVIN SMITH

spaces of YWCAs or settlement houses, organizing for protective legislation for women and children to limit abuses in factories, and providing education for immigrants. Many worked steadily for women's suffrage. Some combined feminism and unionism in organizations like the Women's Trade Union League, and created valuable networks in social organizations such as Greenwich Village's Heterodoxy Club. They forged their closest emotional bonds with other women and often had lifelong female partners with whom, in some cases, they raised children. They loved each other and built lives together.

This chapter focuses on a particular segment of women who formed these early women's communities and, crucially, happened to leave a visual record. Working-class white women and most women of color did not have the same economic options and freedoms to create women-centered communities. That a few middle-class white women in the late nineteenth and early twentieth centuries *could* carve out personal lives beyond the confines of the heterosexual nuclear family is testament to the emergence of a historically new structure of middle-class life. New kinds of relationships were made possible by complex changes in the American economy and in society as a whole.

During the Colonial era and well into the nineteenth century, the majority of American life was organized around the agrarian household economy: the family farm. Men, women, and children labored as part of a self-sufficient household unit, and all of their labor was necessary for the production of food and household goods. Children were vital as workers and very few adults remained unmarried or lived outside of the family. The family was, above all, a unit of production.

With the advent of industrialization, more and more Americans began to work as wage laborers outside of the household economy. As work was separated from home, the family came to function less as a unit of production than as an "affective unit," the place for a private life and a haven from the world of work.[3] As children became less crucial to family support and survival, birth rates dropped and women began to be freed from a life devoted solely to childbearing and housekeeping.[4]

The advent of wage labor profoundly altered the daily lives of all Americans, men and women alike. These economic changes were—among other things—transformative of heterosexual family structure and crucial to the creation of a homosexual identity. Single adults, especially adult men, could now sustain a life and livelihood outside the nexus of the family. As historian John D'Emilio has argued: "Only when *individuals* began to make their living through wage labor, instead of as parts of an interdependent family unit, was it possible for homosexual desire to coalesce into a personal identity—an identity based on the ability to remain outside the heterosexual family and to construct a personal life based on attraction to one's own sex."[5] By the turn of the century, a small group of men and women began to construct their lives with members of the same sex and build communities to make that possible.

Living outside the family remained a more viable option for men, who had greater freedom of movement and access to work than did women. Class structured these life decisions as well. Well into the twentieth century, many working-class men and women remained part of a family economy, which was "both a strategy for survival and a working-class cultural ideal."[6] Because of an economy in which most unskilled and semiskilled jobs were low paying, men's wages typically needed to be supplemented with the earnings of wives, sons, and daughters, which reinforced the interdependency of working-class family members.

Some middle-class daughters, however, had entirely new options. By the late nineteenth century, more and more women of the prosperous

"New Women," circa 1910. At the turn of the century, as middle-class American women fled small towns, attended college in larger numbers than ever before, and organized for rights and reform, some people worried that these women were forming a new breed of "female inverts."

classes were seeking higher education and pursuing careers after college. Although more women attended college beginning in the late nineteenth century than ever before, they still remained a small percentage among women in general. For women, selecting college often meant *not* selecting marriage. Between 1889 and 1908, 53 percent of women educated at Bryn Mawr College, for example, remained unwed. For women who pursued postgraduate degrees, the figures were even more telling: 75 percent of women granted Ph.D.s between 1877 and 1924 remained unmarried.[7]

But for many college women, remaining unmarried did not preclude other kinds of partnerships, ones that were often more nurturing of their life choices than were traditional marriages. Girls' boarding schools and women's colleges had long been places where women and girls got mad crushes on each other, courted, and developed love relationships. In 1873 a Yale student newspaper described these affairs as "smashes" in ways that suggest they barely raised an eyebrow: "When a Vassar girl takes a shine to another, she straightway enters upon a regular course of bouquet sendings, interspersed with tinted notes, mysterious packages of 'Ridley's Mixed Candies,' locks of hair perhaps, and many other tokens, until at last the object of her attentions is captured, the two women become inseparable, and the aggressor is considered by her circle of acquaintances as—*smashed*."[8] It is not surprising, then, that women's colleges would become home to intimate relationships between women in later decades, though the once-ubiquitous smashes became largely a relic of the Victorian past.

In women's colleges, settlement houses, and reform organizations, a growing number of women began to live together as lifelong partners, passionately committed and devoted to each other. They were accepted as couples and moved among networks of women with similar commitments. As historian Estelle Freedman has aptly described it, "Here was a female world of love and passion, different from the same-sex ties of the mid-nineteenth century in that its participants were freed from the bonds of matrimony, able to work and live independent of men."[9]

"Separatism as strategy" and life choice was almost exclusively the province of middle-class, white women. As Freedman has argued, this "reflected the societal racism of the time."[10] Many African-American women—who were either unwelcome or uninterested in female-separatist organizations—turned their attention to the social and legal problems confronting both black women and men in organizations like the National Association of Colored Women and in various female-led antilynching campaigns. Countless more forged ties with other women out of the public eye.

Historians have heatedly debated whether these independent women, these "lifelong companions" and "romantic friends," can or should be termed "lesbians." Historian Lillian Faderman has drawn a direct lineage connecting her own lesbian-feminist community to the "romantic friends" of a century ago. In lesbian feminism, Faderman found "a contemporary analog to romantic friendship in which two women were everything to each other and had little connection with men who were so

Mary Dreier (right), president of the Women's Trade Union League, out for a drive with her partner of fifty years, social investigator Frances Kellor, New York, circa 1907.

alienating and totally different . . . I venture to guess that had the romantic friends of other eras lived today, many of them would have been lesbian-feminists; and had the lesbian-feminists of our day lived in other eras, most of them would have been romantic friends."[11] Although Faderman has been adamant about claiming romantic friends as "lesbian-feminist ances-

Alice Austen. **Trude and I Masked, Short Skirts, 11pm, August 6th, 1891.**

tors," she has been equally insistent upon erasing overt sexuality from their lives in an effort not to impose current sexual standards on women of other eras. This historical caution has often led to "an ahistorical prohibition against reading sex between women in history."[12]

Although we rarely demand "evidence" before conferring the label *heterosexual* on historical personages, this is often the standard of proof when documenting the lives of those who were involved in same-sex relationships in the past. Many traditional historians have dismissed the entire uncomfortable discussion. Arthur Schlesinger Jr., writing in the *New York Times Book Review,* found the question as to whether Lorena Hickok and Eleanor Roosevelt were "lovers in the physical sense" an "issue of stunning inconsequence."[13] Yet sexuality could only be of "inconsequence" in a society in which all forms of sexual and familial relationships were seen as equal, granted equal respect, and calmly documented.

Sexuality is clearly a matter of great consequence, but it is also one that eludes easy analysis. Lesbian and gay history is a history of categories that don't fit, of labels that do not and cannot encompass the complexity of many people's lives in the past or, for that matter, in the present. What we are left with are fragments from letters, some old photographs, and archives filled with documents that offer glimpses into a not simply visible, or always legible, past.

Alice Austen, a turn-of-the-century Staten Island photographer, documented the domestic life she shared with her small circle of female friends and her companion of more than forty years, Gertrude Tate. Austen was a woman of independent means whose estate "Clear Comfort" was the backdrop for many of her photographs. Her catalog of work richly captures the late-Victorian world of female friendship, but without the prim propriety one might expect from a woman of her class and era.

Supportive and loving female relationships and radical causes structured the lives of many of the early twentieth century's New Women. However, both the causes they championed and the relationships in which they lived, violated the traditional social and gender order, opening these women to attack. Beginning as early as the mid-nineteenth century, but reaching fruition in the Freudian-steeped 1920s, women's relationships were increasingly tarred with the brush of "deviance." As historian Carroll Smith-Rosenberg has documented, European and American sexologists began to brand certain women "unnatural," insisting that "unmarried career women and political activists constituted an 'intermediate sex.'"[14] Writing in 1901, British sexologist Havelock Ellis linked female emancipation and homosexuality, suggesting that women's choice of feminism, and rejection of traditional female roles, placed them on a slippery slope toward lesbianism:

S. Josephine Baker, pictured in **Heterodoxy to Marie,** *1920.* Baker was the renowned head of the New York Bureau of Child Hygiene.

> Having been taught independence of men and disdain for the old theory which placed women in the moated grange of the home to sigh for a man who never comes, a tendency develops for women to carry this independence still further and to find love where they find work . . . This . . . is due to the fact that the congenital anomaly [homosexuality] occurs with special frequency in women of high intelligence who, voluntarily or involuntarily, influence others.[15]

Female institutions like boarding schools and settlement houses began to be seen with a newly jaundiced eye.

Sexual arrangements of all kinds were receiving increased public attention in the early twentieth century. The period between 1890 and 1920 ushered in a new, "modern" sensibility in regard to sex: A growing public discourse emphasized female sexual liberation and heterosexual pleasure at the same time that homosexuality became increasingly noticeable on the American scene. In urban enclaves like Greenwich Village, where bohemians, artists, and free-lovers flouted bourgeois convention, an incipient lesbian subculture flourished. Greenwich Village had long held a reputation as a place for people with little regard for middle-class propri-

Elisabeth Irwin, pictured in **Heterodoxy to Marie,** *1920.* Elisabeth Irwin was a psychologist, progressive educator, and founder of Greenwich Village's experimental Little Red Schoolhouse. She and her longtime partner, and fellow Heterodoxy member, Katharine Anthony, raised several children together.

ety. One observer commented at the time that those who flocked to Greenwich Village were "men and women taunted by their biologically normal companions in the small towns that ostracize those who neither eat nor sleep nor love in the fashion of the hundred percenters."[16] Fortunately, there were few "hundred percenters" in the Village.

Heterodoxy, the Village social club for women, self-consciously styled itself in opposition to orthodoxy of all kinds. Members were involved in utopian social, cultural, and sexual experiments. Indeed, as the writer of a satirical description of the "customs" of the Heterodites put it: "There is the strongest taboo on taboo. Heterodites say that taboo is injurious to free development of the mind and spirit."[17] Because the only taboo was *taboo,* the group was freed to express a wide range of opinions and to live their personal lives in a variety of ways. Among the "unconventional women" of Heterodoxy, schooled in female institutions and raised on the tenets of suffrage and reform, lesbianism was one of the societal taboos they refused to recognize as such. Most members granted the same respect to the lesbian couples among them as they did to women in traditional (and nontraditional) heterosexual couplings. According to Judith Schwarz, "Anniversary dates were recognized and the lesbian couples received strong emotional support from most Heterodites when one of the partners was sick or died."[18] At least ten and perhaps twenty-four of the more than one hundred members were lesbians, many in long-term relationships with other Heterodites.

This social club, which one member dubbed, "a little band of wilful [*sic*] women, the most unruly and individualistic females you ever fell among," gave home to some of the most prominent feminists, social reformers, writers, and artists of the early twentieth century.

Heterodoxy to Marie. *New York, 1920.* This photograph is the frontispiece to a photo album, given as a Christmas gift in 1920 to Marie Jenny Howe, founder of the Heterodoxy club (seated facing the camera).

The group was a lunch and social club, founded in 1912 and presided over by Unitarian minister and suffrage leader Marie Jenney Howe. At biweekly lunches held at Polly Holladay's venerable bohemian haunt, women sat at long trestle tables, discussing the art, politics, and culture of the day with the women who were shaping it. Feminist writer Charlotte Perkins Gilman, labor radical Elizabeth Gurley Flynn, *saloniste* Mabel Dodge Luhan, and activist Crystal Eastman were among the club's members during its almost forty-year history.

Heterodoxy housed many remarkable and unconventional women who were grateful for such a club. In 1920 they presented the club's founder, Marie Jenney Howe, with a photograph album filled with pictures of each of them with handwritten inscriptions. In the preface they wrote to Marie:

> "It is the aim of women not to hate, but to love one another." To realize the spirit of these words is one of the emotional treasures of life which all women desire, many of them fear, some of them seek, and a few of them find. We owe it chiefly to you that we may count ourselves among the fortunate finders. Like Lysistratum, Aspasia and Sappho, you have "started something."[19]

Times Square, New York, 1938 (detail).

OUT ON THE TOWN

*The world of sexual inverts is, indeed, a large one
in any American city, and it is a community distinctly organized—
words, customs, traditions of its own; and every city has its numerous
meeting-places: certain churches where inverts congregate;
certain cafes well known for the inverted character of their patrons;
certain streets where, at night, every fifth man is an invert.*

—HAVELOCK ELLIS,
HOMOSEXUALITY IN AMERICAN CITIES, 1915

O nly in a great city," observed one man who arrived in New York in 1882, could an invert "give his overwhelming yearnings free reign *incognito* and thus keep the respect of his everyday circle . . . in New York one can live as Nature demands without setting everyone's tongue wagging."[1] The city, yesterday as today, offered freedom from small-town stares and the possibility for single men and women to live outside the strictures of family.

This openness and anonymity, as well as the employment opportunities offered in the city, has created an environment in which same-sex communities thrive. For more than one hundred years, New York City has been home to established lesbian and gay social worlds. Some were quiet and intimate; others were public spectacles that *did* set tongues wagging.

In the late nineteenth and early twentieth centuries, extensive gay worlds took shape in the streets, bars, cafés, and tenements of New York, and lesbians and gay men played a central role in the social life of many city neighborhoods. As early as the 1890s, the Bowery was home to "fairy resorts," where "fairies"—flamboyantly dressed, campy, rouged men—drank with sailors and entertained neighborhood bar-goers. In Harlem in the 1920s, men danced together, decked out in tuxes and drag at fabulous balls, and mixed at speakeasies and cabarets. Downtown, lesbian couples were among the throngs who flocked to Greenwich Village's Webster Hall for costume balls and joined other "lady lovers" in cafés and bars. The early thirties saw a "pansy craze" in New York's Times Square, followed by a clampdown on public gay life. During the 1940s, as World War II brought single men and women to port cities like New York, gay men and lesbians found bars, cheap cafeterias, and elegant restaurants filled with their own.

The very existence of these numerous public worlds catering to "same-sexers" in the early and mid-twentieth century belies a notion that lesbian and gay life burst from the secrecy and closetedness of the past into liberation and openness today. In fact, as historian George Chauncey has documented, gay social worlds were actually more numerous and open in the early part of the century than they would become in later decades. It is, in part, *because* of the very visibility of gay life in New York during these years that it was eventually forced underground and further from view. The laws enacted during the 1920s and 1930s censoring representations of so-called sexual perversion in theater and film, and regulating homosexual meeting places, were a response to the growing efflorescence of queer culture and to a perception that things had gone too far in the Roaring Twenties.

Throughout the decades, gay nightlife and gathering spots came and went, alternately prospering and closing down—often due to periodic police crackdowns or citywide "cleanup" campaigns. Yet, in the face of ever-

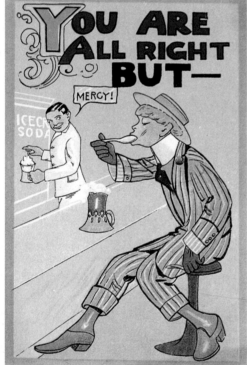

Postcard, circa 1910. At the turn of the century, a red tie was a clear signal to those in the know. One man recalled that he could proclaim himself a fairy to working-class boys in the 1890s simply by wearing white kid gloves and a "large red neckbow with fringed ends hanging down over my lapels."[2]

present policing, in the public spaces of bars and balls, cafés and restaurants, gay men and lesbians still managed to meet others like themselves, forging shared communities long before organized political movements gave them voice.

The extraordinary panoply of urban nightlife during these years was often referred to by its participants simply as "the gay world."[3] The term *gay* was used in the 1920s as an insider term, to refer first to men, and later to women. The usage can be tracked earlier still; in the mid-nineteenth century, some male prostitutes in London called themselves "gay ladies," a designation borrowed from female prostitutes.[4] Terms like *queer* and *fairy* were used for and by homosexual men in the teens and the twenties to distinguish among various effeminate types. *Lesbian* and *lady lover* were used for homosexual women in the same period, with *mannish lesbian* signifying a specific, gendered type, while *Uranian, invert,* and *third-sexer* crossed over from contemporary medical literature. *Faggot* and *bulldagger* had lasting appeal and, like today, were not always used as terms of opprobrium.

The meanings of same-sex sexuality, as well as the terms, have changed over time. Men who lived together in boarding houses in Times Square in the 1930s or cruised the docks for sailors may not have considered themselves "gay" in the modern sense of the term. Women who formed lifelong partnerships while living and working together in settlement houses in the teens may never have considered or called themselves "lesbians." On the other hand, there may have actually been more freedom of sexual movement in the past than in today's world of identity politics.

If the past cannot be understood in exactly the same terms as the present, neither should it be imagined as a wholly foreign place. As early as the late nineteenth century, sources like memoirs and vice reports document distinctive milieus in New York and other major cities—worlds that were recognizably "queer" to insiders as well as outsiders.

In many large cities the subjects of the contrary sexual impulse form a class by themselves and are recognized by the police. The men have their balls, where they dress as women even to the de-

X'MAS ON THE HIGH SEAS.

Postcard, circa 1918. This postcard of sailors dancing aboard ship was distributed by the navy YMCA during World War I. Even at that time, "experts" worried about the special conditions of war. One, blaming foreign influence and cramped quarters, commented that "American boys undoubtably become familiar with perverse practices while in France or at sea."[5]

tails of their dainty underwear . . . The female pervert or Lesbian rarely differs from others of her sex, except that the active agent is gross, wears mannish attire and cultivates masculine habits.[6]

In 1893 another outside observer attended a "colored" drag ball in Washington, D.C., and was horrified to discover men "lasciviously dressed in women's attire . . . feathered and ribboned head-dresses, garters, frills, flowers, ruffles." The most shocking sight for this guest was the centerpiece of the ball, "the naked queen (a male), whose phallic member, decorated with a ribbon, is subject to the gaze and asculations [sic] in turn, of all the members of the lecherous gang of sexual perverts and phallic fornicators."[7]

Lower Manhattan, at the turn of the century, boasted a number of gathering places well known at the time as "fairy resorts." They included Columbia Hall (often called Paresis Hall, after the term for a venereal disease–induced insanity), Manilla Hall, and Little Bucks, all on the Bowery; the Palm Club on Christie Street; and the Slide and the Black Rabbit on Bleecker. A city vice investigator in 1899 described the denizens of Paresis Hall, "a well-known resort for male prostitutes," in the following way:

A Greenwich Village ball at Webster Hall, New York, 1920s.

"They act effeminately; most of them are painted and
powdered; they are called Princess this and Lady So
and So and the Duchess of Marlboro, and get up and
sing as women, and dance; and ape the female character; call each other sisters and take people out for immoral purposes."[8] The "manly men" that the fairies
took out for "immoral purposes" were not considered
fairies themselves, and sex with these effeminate
"third-sexers" would not have compromised the sexual identity of the "normal" men who engaged in it.
Bowery fairies, like female prostitutes, were just one
among many offerings of early-twentieth-century
urban nightlife in this working-class, immigrant neighborhood.

Walhalla Hall, a Lower East Side social club, held
dances during the same years attended by, among others, many same-sex couples. One observer commented on the spectacle, noting " 'quite a few
masculine looking women in evening dress' dancing
with other women."[9] By the 1920s, such sights would
become, if not commonplace, at least an expected slice
of New York nightlife, particularly in areas like Greenwich Village and
Harlem.

The Village was known for its cheap housing for single people and as
a safe haven for artists, bohemians, and other unconventional sorts. Lesbians and gay men also made their mark, ensuring that homosexuality was
as much a part of 1920s' Village life and lore as bohemianism. A song from
the era included the line *"Fairyland's not far from Washington Square."* Indeed, a gay world flourished below 14th Street during these years, with
clubs, cafés, and speakeasies catering to "fairies" and "lady lovers." A 1925
Variety article noted as many as twenty Village restaurants, cafés, and clubs
playing host to the "temperamental" element during the era.[10] Prohibition, which forced all establishments serving alcohol behind closed doors,
actually created a protected space for gay clubs. Proprietors needed only to
pay off the police like other speakeasy owners, a practice in gay bars that
outlasted Prohibition.

During the twenties, there were drag shows in Greenwich Village at
the Jungle on Cornelia Street, featuring the ever-popular "Rosebud" and

Reginald Marsh. **Chop Suey Dancers
(#1).** *Etching, New York, 1929.* This print
is one of a series in which Marsh depicted
couples of the same sex dancing together
in a New York nightspot. While the gender
of the couple is ambiguous (are they
women? men in drag?), the image is sug-
gestive of "gay life" in New York in the
1920s.

WHEN LIFE IS VERY STRENUOUS AND SPIRITS ARE WAY DOWN
YOU'D BETTER GO TO POLLY'S IN LITTLE GREENWICH TOWN
FOR THERE THE CLANS ARE GATHERED - ITS THERE YOU'LL FIND 'EM ALL
THE ARTISTS AND THE WRITERS RANGED ALONG THE WALL
MISS POLLY TAKES THE MONEY AND MIKE SAYS HE JUST CAN'T
WAIT ANY FASTER ON THE FOLKS IN POLLY'S RES·TAU-RANT
J.T.B.

24

GREENWICH VILLAGE - NEW YORK

©JESSIE TARBOX BEALS

Jessie Tarbox Beals. **Postcard of Polly's Restaurant.** *New York, circa 1918.* Polly's was a dining and gathering place for Village artists, writers, and freethinkers. Djuna Barnes remembered seeing Eugene O'Neill there "every night at dinner," where "Polly was drunk and served rather drunk dinners which we all ate."[11]

the "Countess," and pansy acts at Paul & Joe's nearby. The Flower Pot, run by Dolly Judge at the corner of Christopher and Gay, was a popular speakeasy, as was the Red Mask, operated by gay impresario Jackie Mason. A contemporary account described another Prohibition-era club only as that "ultra-ultra speak" on Charles Street, "which isn't Ireland even if the fairies may be seen there."[12]

Because many Village denizens lived in crowded quarters, much socializing took place in public. Tearooms and neighborhood restaurants provided public kitchens, complete with interesting company and easy credit. These intimate restaurants were often run by charming hosts whose own intellectual, artistic, and sexual involvements set the tone for the place. The gathering spots functioned as salons or "personality clubs," where customers were entertained as guests. Polly's on MacDougal Street, run by Polly Holladay and her husband, was the premier gathering place of this kind for the Village intelligentsia during the teens and early twenties. Following the success of Polly's, lesbians and gay men began their own personality clubs, usually catering to a mixed—gay and straight—clientele.

Eve Addams (formerly Eva Kotchover) was among the most famous of the Village hosts. The so-called queen of the third sex, she ran the Black Rabbit, a tearoom on MacDougal Street. A 1926 blurb in the *Greenwich Village Quill* described "Eve's Hangout" as a place "where ladies prefer each other. Not healthy for she-adolescents, nor comfortable for he-men."[13] Popular with the after-theater crowd, the Black Rabbit was less popular with police, who raided it in the summer of 1926 in the midst of a poetry reading. Eve Addams was convicted on disorderly conduct and obscenity charges (her collection of short stories, *Lesbian Love,* was judged obscene), and sentenced to one year in the workhouse. Addams was later deported, and landed conveniently on the Left Bank in Paris. But while they lasted, places like the Black Rabbit and the Flower Pot provided art, artistry, and refreshment, presided over by hosts who were often, themselves, the biggest draw.

Another hallmark of twenties gay life was the extravagant costume balls held at Webster Hall on East 11th Street. The balls were spirited soirées, attracting free-thinkers from the Village and the curious from Uptown. Originally conceived as lucrative fundraisers for organizations like the bohemian Liberal Club, these events were more often purely social affairs, and gay men and lesbians organized their own Webster Hall galas during the 1920s. Participants came both to dance with "whom they liked," as well as to enjoy the spectacle of rouged men in expensive gowns and short-haired women in tuxes. An invitation to a 1926 ball dropped the titillating tidbit, "Unconventional? Oh, to be sure—only do be discreet!"

Grumpy pundits groused about the exceeding *lack* of discretion in the Village. One guidebook from the period lamented the "changed Village," complaining that "Bohemianism covers a multitude of sins" and that "the interesting people who once frequented the better-known Village favorites have been supplanted by long-haired men and short-haired women."[14] Although some felt that sexual nonconformists—hetero and homo—were overrunning Greenwich Village, the gay world was often discernible only to those in the know. An outsider, even one looking for the community, may have been hard-pressed to find it. "It was quite a handicap to be a young guy in the twenties," lamented one gay man who arrived in New York from the Midwest during the era. "It took an awfully long time to learn of a gay speakeasy."[15]

Advertisement, New York, 1926.

The Pirate's Den, New York, 1920s. In Sheridan Square in the 1920s, waiters often provided the best entertainment in the house. Don Dickerman's Pirate's Den on Christopher Street advertised "clanking chains, clashing cutlasses, ship's lanterns, and patch-eyed buccaneer waiters."

Uptown during the 1920s, Harlemites "in the life" built a gay world that surpassed its Greenwich Village counterpart in size and in scope. Harlem had become a major metropolis and the cultural capital of black America in the years following World War I, when tens of thousands of African Americans migrated from the South to take advantage of the North's booming industrial economy in a mass exodus known as the Great Migration. This demographic transformation, particularly its influx of single people, also made Harlem a gay mecca. Bruce Nugent, a writer known for his work during the Harlem Renaissance, remembers the era:

> "Male" and "female" impersonation was at its peak as nightclub entertainment . . . The Ubangi Club had a chorus of singing, dancing, be-ribboned and be-rouged "pansies," and Gladys Bentley who dressed in male evening attire, sang and accompanied herself on the piano; the well-liked Jackie Mab[ley] was one of Harlem's favorite black-faced comediennes and wore men's street attire habitually; the famous Hamilton Lodge "drag" balls were becoming more and more notorious and gender was becoming more and more conjectural.[16]

Gender was bent most freely at Harlem's drag balls, which Langston Hughes called "spectacles in color." The largest were hosted by the Hamilton Lodge and held at the Manhattan Casino (which later became the Rockland Palace) and at the Savoy. Whereas *hundreds* had attended the balls Downtown, *thousands* attended the Harlem balls. The events were frequented by neighborhood denizens as well as white tourists from Downtown, and were covered as cultural happenings in the popular press. A 1937 *Amsterdam News* headline shrieked: "PANSIES CAVORT IN A MOST DELOVELY MANNER AT THAT ANNUAL HAMILTON LODGE 'BAWL.'" A 1928 surveillance report, written by a group of city reformers investigating the spread of prostitution and "commercialized amusements," had this to say about one Harlem ball, held at the Manhattan Casino on 155th Street:

> About 12:30 A.M. we visited this place and found approximately 5,000 people, colored and white, men attired in women's clothes, and vice versa. The affair, we were informed, was a "Fag/(fairy) Masquerade Ball." This is an annual affair where the white and colored fairies assemble together with their friends, this being attended also by a certain respectable element who go here to see the sights.[17]

James VanDerZee. **Beau of the Ball, 1927.** The highlights of the Rockland Palace drag balls were the beauty contests in which the men, who "looked more like ladies than the ladies themselves," vied for the title of Queen of the Ball. Photographer James VanDerZee created this portrait of one of the Queens. COURTESY OF DONNA VANDERZEE

While seeing the sights held some attraction for Harlemites, it was the major appeal for white Downtowners who flocked north to experience Harlem nightlife. A 1929 *Variety* article declared that Harlem's "sizzling cafes, 'speaks,' [and] night clubs" had created a scene in which Uptown "nightlife now surpasses Broadway itself."[18] Harlem's clubs boasted world-class entertainment, the titillation of "the exotic" for some, and for others, a place to be openly gay. A gay character from white author Blair Niles's 1931 novel *Strange Brother* expresses this particular appeal: "In Harlem I found courage and joy and tolerance. I can be myself there . . . They know all about me and I don't have to lie."[19] Though Harlem may have felt like "freedom" to some whites, not all Harlemites celebrated their neighborhood's newfound popularity. Langston Hughes lamented the way whites were "flooding the little cabarets where formerly only colored people laughed and sang, and where now, strangers were given the best ringside seats to sit and stare at the Negroes—like amusing animals in a zoo."[20]

Famous for spots like the glamorous (and segregated) Cotton Club, Harlem also housed a number of lesser-known clubs. Speakeasies like the Clam House, the Drool Inn, and the Hot Feet provided wild entertainment in which performers like Gladys Bentley flirted with double entendres in their songs and played with gender in their acts. Bentley was costumed in a top hat and tuxedo, backed by a "full pansy chorus line."

Blues lyrics of the era included wordplays on the transgressive sexuality that was acted out in clubs and city streets; they also included unabashedly open references to homosexuality. The song "Sissie Man's Blues," recorded and performed by a number of male blues singers in the twenties, included the line *"If you can't find me a woman, bring me a sissie man."* Of course, songs like "Sissie Man's Blues" or "Freakish Man Blues" were hardly paeans to queer culture. The sissie man and the freakish man were positioned outside the proscribed boundaries of African-American masculinity, but the frequent invocation of these figures in songs of the era does speak to their presence—however problematic to some—in urban life.

Lesbian themes were even more common in the blues of the time. Bessie Jackson's "BD [Bulldagger] Women's Blues" sang of the problems with men and the possibility of something better: *"Comin' a time, BD women, they ain't gonna need no men / Oh, the way they treat us is a low down and dirty thing."* Ma Rainey, Bessie Smith, Alberta Hunter, and Ethel Waters were among the female performers of the era known—or thought to be—lesbian or bisexual, a fact Ma Rainey toyed with in her 1928 song "Prove It On Me Blues." The lyrics include the lines: *"I went out last night / With a crowd of my friends / They must been women / Cause I sure don't like no mens / Cause they say I do it / Ain't nobody caught me / You sure got to prove it on me."*

If the blues lamented "lowdown" gay life, there was also high living to be had in Harlem during the era. The most lavish parties were thrown by the heiress A'Lelia Walker, daughter of Madame C. J. Walker, a self-made millionaire who earned her fortune developing and marketing hair-straightening products. Madame Walker left much of her fortune to A'Lelia, who used it to entertain extravagantly, hosting a salon for artists, writers, minor royalty, and

Gladys Bentley. *New York, circa 1930s.* Bentley was a much-discussed local celebrity, known for her risqué lyrics and for having married her white girlfriend in a civil wedding ceremony.

twenties celebrities at her residence in Sugar Hill, an affluent section of Harlem. Her get-togethers usually included a sparkling collection of her lesbian lovers and gay male friends.[21]

Although Harlem was best known for its glamorous nightlife, Harlemites, many of whom could not afford, nor were allowed to enter, the famed venues, also socialized in less-flashy spots. The area was dotted with corner saloons and basement speakeasies, and alive with parties in apartments and tenement flats. "Rent parties" not only gave the landlord his due but provided inexpensive all-night entertainment, complete with music, dancing, and liquor for sale in the kitchen or bathtub. Buffet flats, which first opened in the late nineteenth century to provide accommodations for

UBANGI CLUB, 131st STREET and 7th AVENUE, featuring GLADYS BENTLEY and a cast of 40.

Postcard, New York, circa 1930s. One reviewer described the Ubangi Club revue as featuring "Gladys Bentley, who wears trousers, and a sextette of boys who shouldn't."

African-American travelers denied service in white-owned hotels, were private apartments that tenants opened to paying guests. Buffet flats became famous in the 1920s as wild speakeasies, often featuring drinking, gambling, drag acts, and live sex shows. "It was an open house, everything goes on in that house," recalled Ruby Smith of a Detroit flat she had visited with her aunt Bessie Smith in the twenties:

> They had a faggot there that was so great that people used to come there just to watch him make love to another man. He was that great. He'd give a tongue bath and everything. By the time he got to the front of that guy he was shaking like a leaf. People used to pay good just to go in there and see him do his act . . . That same house had a woman that used to . . . take a cigarette, light it, and puff it with her pussy. A real educated pussy.[22]

All of this took place during a period known as the Harlem Renaissance, a term that named both a flowering of Harlem's urban life as well as an artistic and literary movement of profound importance. Langston Hughes,

Wallace Thurman, Countee Cullen, Aaron Douglas, Alain Locke, Angelina Weld Grimké, Alice Dunbar-Nelson, and Claude McKay were a few of the writers and artists who called Harlem home during the period. Irreverently dubbed the "Niggerati" by African-American novelist Zora Neale Hurston, this extraordinary group of black artists was also disproportionately—if rather quietly—queer.

In the summer of 1926, the leading lights of the Harlem Renaissance edited and published the first (and only) issue of a literary magazine, *Fire!!* Aaron Douglas designed the cover, Langston Hughes and Countee Cullen contributed poetry, Zora Neale Hurston wrote a short story, and Carl Van Vechten backed the project. The magazine included (Richard) Bruce Nugent's "Smoke, Lilies and Jade," an erotic narrative poem that was probably the first published work about homosexuality by an African-American author. Written under the pseudonym Richard Bruce, Nugent's thinly veiled autobiographical piece tells the story of a Harlem artist who finds love in the arms of a Latin, "Beauty":

> Alex turned in his doorway . . . up the stairs and the stranger waited for him to light the room . . . no need for words . . . they had always known each other . . . as they undressed by the blue dawn . . . Alex knew he had never seen a more perfect being . . . his body was all symmetry and music . . . and Alex called him Beauty . . . long they lay . . . blowing smoke and exchanging thoughts . . . and Alex swallowed with difficulty . . . he felt a glow of tremor . . . and they talked . . . and slept.[23]

In the 1920s, queer culture flourished, not only in Greenwich Village and in Harlem, but also on the Broadway stage. For a public intrigued with unconventional sexuality in general, lesbianism seemed to hold a particular fascination. Three plays about lesbianism opened and closed within a short period during the decade. In 1923, Sholom Asch's *God of Vengeance,* one of the earliest plays with a lesbian theme, opened on Broadway to this review: "A more foul and unpleasant spectacle has never been seen in New York." The producer, director, and the cast of twelve were hauled off to court on charges of obscenity. Another play on the theme, *Sin of Sins,* opened in Chicago in 1926 and closed after a three-week run and a series of scandalized reviews. Edouard Bourdet's *The Captive,* about a young married woman seduced by lesbian love, created a similar stir. Though the

Café: 3 am
  by Langston Hughes

Detectives from the vice squad
With weary sadistic eyes
spotting fairies

  Degenerates,
  some folks say.

  But God, Nature,
  or somebody
  made them that way.

Police lady or Lesbian
over there?
  Where?

production ran on Broadway in 1926 to large audiences and some very positive reviews, it also garnered other more censorious pronouncements. The influential theater critic George Nathan considered *The Captive* "the most subjective, corruptive, and potentially evil-fraught play ever shown in the American theater . . . nothing more or less than a documentary in favor of sex degeneracy."[24] In the same year, Mae West attempted to bring the play *The Drag* to Broadway. The play, which ended with a raid on a drag ball, was filled with a cast of gay chorus boys recruited from downtown speakeasies. In the increasingly chilly climate, *The Drag* opened and closed in Bayonne, New Jersey, never reaching Broadway.

After this brief and fractious Sapphic theater craze, the New York State Legislature snapped into action. In 1927 it passed the Padlock Bill, which prohibited plays from "depicting or dealing with the subject of sex degeneracy, or sex perversion." Any play that included lesbian or gay characters, or even broached the subject of homosexuality, was effectively banned from Broadway. This law remained on the books until 1967.

The gay presence on Broadway was not confined to its stage. Whether cruising Bryant Park, camping it up in the cafeterias and Automats along Broadway, or working in the neighboring theaters, gay men were a significant presence in Times Square in the 1930s. Though less well remembered as a gay neighborhood than either Greenwich Village or Harlem, the blocks stretching down Broadway through the West 40s and 50s were home to a sizeable working-class gay male community. The location of much of the city's housing for single men, this neighborhood also sheltered more than its share of gay bars, including many former speakeasies.

Many gay men were employed in the area's entertainment industry, in both legitimate theater as well as in the burlesque shows and nightclubs that featured "pansy acts," stage shows that were all the rage during the 1930s. Pansy entertainer and master of ceremonies Jean Malin brought the camp wit of Greenwich Village to the Club Abbey on Broadway, introducing Midtowners to Downtown drag. The New York tabloid *Broadway Brevities* reported that after Malin's theatrical success "the pansies hailed La Malin as their queen!" The pansy craze lasted until the early 1930s, with

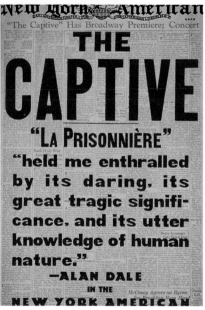

(above, left) **Fire!!** *New York, Joseph Leventhal, printer, 1926.*

(above, right) **The Captive. New York, 1926.**

pansy clubs featuring New York stars appearing as far west as Los Angeles. However, by the fall of 1932, New York City officials began cracking down on the "Nance and Lesbian amusement places in town," as well as enforcing ordinances against the wearing of drag offstage.[25]

The Automats and the Child's chain of cafeterias were gathering places for the men who lived in boardinghouses around Times Square. "Cafeteria society" had none of the opulence of café society, but offered all of the camaraderie. One man remembers going to a Child's cafeteria during the era: "After hours—you might say after the theater, which brought hordes of people together—Child's was a meeting place for gays and they would congregate and yak-yak and talk until three and four and five o'clock in the morning . . . I was always there with my friends, that was the social thing to do."[26] For gawking tourists, the cafeterias provided a place to watch parading pansies. Having one's picture taken with a "fairy" on 42nd Street was another favorite, if short-lived, pastime for tourists.

The Depression era saw a general quieting of urban nightlife, and a growing sense that the excesses of the twenties—cultural as well as economic—had caused the Great Depression. Homosexuality stood out as an easy target for those wanting to punish "excess." Suddenly, what was quietly tolerated in the 1920s became "immoral and illegal" by the mid-1930s. Film and theater censorship codes were inaugurated during this period for the first time, curtailing representations of sex on stage and screen. The Catholic Church's National Office for Decent Literature, founded in the 1930s, placed homosexuality on its long list of topics deemed indecent and began to pressure Hollywood to do the same. In 1934 the Motion Picture Production Code officially banned all references and depictions of homosexuality from the movies.[27]

At the same time, public gay life on the street was increasingly regulated. In 1933 New York State's highest court upheld regulations that prohibited gay men and lesbians from congregating in licensed bars. The State Liquor Authority began to enforce these new regulations, threatening to revoke the license of any bar or restaurant serving homosexuals or simply allowing them to congregate.[28] Regulations differed from state to state, but many had similar laws on the books, often dating from the post-Prohibition period. The new laws did not eradicate public socializing or eliminate gay

Brevities, *May 15, 1933.* The Broadway *Brevities,* a New York tabloid, featured regular gossip and news about the city's "queers," including this report of the takeover of Times Square: "Emboldened by the tolerance of the public and police alike, New York's hordes of third sexers have descended upon Broadway and Times Square with a whoop and are making life intolerable for normal passers-by." COLLECTION OF THE NEW-YORK HISTORICAL SOCIETY

venues, but they did drive many further underground and often into the hands of organized crime.

Access to public socializing was never granted equally. Largely because of men's higher wages and greater independence from family life, gay male subcultures have been larger and more visible throughout the twentieth century. Racial stratification in the larger society has reinforced similar divisions in the homosexual world: Lesbians and gay men of color have had access to far fewer commercial establishments than have white gay males.

Because many bars and restaurants refused to serve homosexuals, and those that did were regularly raided by the police, much of gay social life took place at parties held in apartments and private residences, as well as in the less-easily regulated parks, streets, piers, and beaches of the city. However, as historians Elizabeth Kennedy and Madeline Davis have noted, "open spaces like parks or beaches, commonly used by gay men, were too exposed for women to express interest in other women without constant male surveillance and harassment."[29] Bars, too, have historically been considered "men's dominion," posing dangers for women in general and for lesbians in particular.

Nevertheless, many remember the thirties and forties in New York as a time of active neighborhood social scenes for lesbians as well as gay men. Greenwich Village housed a number of clubs, like the 82 Club and the 181 Club, featuring floor shows where both men and women performed in drag. The Moroccan Village, on West 8th Street, was billed in the forties as "the Gayest spot in the Village." Third Street was remembered by one lesbian as *the* street of lesbian bars, with the venerable Howdy Club on one end and Willie and John's, El's, the Welcome Inn, MacDougal's Tavern, Tony Pastor's, the Ptown Landing, and Ernie's nearby.[30] Remembering the 3rd Street strip, the same woman recalls:

> I've heard that femmes congregated in one bar while butches started out the night in another. That older women stuck pretty much to one bar and younger women to another. That you could check your coat in one place and go off down Third Street to an-

WeeGee. **The Gay Deceiver.** *New York, 1941.* Because of their visibility, drag queens were the most frequent targets of police crackdowns in New York. This photograph of a drag queen camping her way out of a paddy wagon was taken at the Harbor Precinct near Battery Park, a popular cruising area during the 1930s and '40s.

other, then come back and pick it up later. They tell me that before women wore pants on the street, which wasn't until World War II, the dykes had three-piece suits made with a skirt and slacks to match the jacket. They'd wear the skirt on the street and change into the slacks when they got to the bar.[31]

Times Square remained a haven for gay men: both for the working-class men who worked in its streets and theaters and the middle-class men who came to play in this amusement district. One man remembers Times Square's Astor Bar, "tooling up for its wondrous wartime years in the Thirties," as "always good for a short cruise on the way to or from the theater."[32] Also beginning in the 1930s, a vigorous male prostitution industry heated up in the streets, bars, and movie houses of Times Square. Fairies and more masculine "rough trade" sold their services in the district, moving when necessary to avoid police sweeps and periodic "cleanups."

Middle- and upper-class gay white men had access to easier cover and more options for socializing in public than did either working-class gay men or lesbians. The toney and manly Oak Room at the Plaza and the King Cole Room at the St. Regis Hotel, where single businessmen drank together, were also well known as gay haunts.[33] Indeed, as historian Allan

Howdy. *New York, 1940.* The Howdy Club, a lesbian bar on 3rd Street in the Village in the 1930s and '40s, had its own football team, pictured here.

Times Square, New York, 1938. The Automat and legendary Child's Cafeteria are at left.

Bérubé has pointed out, there existed discreet male bars in elegant hotels across the country that functioned in this way beginning in the 1930s. They included the Astor Bar in New York's Times Square, the Top of the Mark at the Mark Hopkins Hotel in San Francisco, and the bar at the Biltmore Hotel, off Pershing Square in Los Angeles.[34]

Harlem during the thirties and forties was, according to one woman, "a thriving Black Lesbian and Gay community within a thriving Black community. Harlem was alive with the life of her people. We lived there, played there, and worked there . . . But on the weekends, we jumped at the Savoy, went swinging at the Rennin, after hours at Wells, show time at Jock's, Red Rooster and the Yea Man before B and C's, Cookie's, La Femme, Bagatelle and the Duchess."[35]

World War II marked a turning point in gay and lesbian public life. Soldiers flooded into port cities during the war, exploring urban nightlife while on leave. Los Angeles and Chicago were filled with GIs, Market Street in San Francisco teemed with sailors, and New York's Times Square was a throng of men in uniform. New Yorker Leo Adams remembered the Astor Hotel as "one of the great hang-outs for all the military people," and the Shelton Hotel as having "a bar that could be so gay . . . that they finally had to decline to serve anyone in uniform." He continued: "My heavens, the gaiety was so flagrant, it was astonishing. It was as open then, from about '44 to '47, as it is now . . . Anybody in uniform seemed to be available at that time. I guess guys figured they had a short life ahead of them.[36]

BUTCH-FEMME BAR CULTURE

*Oh, we had our styles—our outfits, our perfumes, our performances—and we could lose ourselves
under the chins of our dancing partners, who held us close enough to make the world safe;
but we walked the night streets to get to our bars, and we came out bleary-eyed into the deserted
early morning, facing a long week of dreary passing at the office or the beauty parlor or the telephone company.
I always knew our lives were a bewildering combination of romance and realism.*

—Joan Nestle

In the forties and fifties, in waterfront dives and neighborhood bars in the shadows of factories, women who loved other women found respite from an often hostile world in bars filled with their own. The 1940s witnessed an unprecedented boom in bar life that, especially in the case of lesbian bars, has not been surpassed to this day. Buffalo, New York, is typical of many cities in which there were approximately the same number of lesbian bars operating in the 1940s as there are in the 1990s.[37] Following World War II, in cities around the country, the local tavern became an increasingly central part of lesbian social life for many women. Historically located in "marginal" areas of cities, lesbian bars were often found in waterfront or industrial districts, making them neighborhood spots for many working-class dykes.

For many the bar *was* home. It was the place to drown out "the hating voices" of the McCarthyite fifties, providing a sustaining network of friends to replace the lack of acceptance many lesbians felt in the larger society and in their own families. However, gay and lesbian bars were hardly utopias. They were often violent and semilegal places, subject to periodic police raids, as well as to the occasional angry or jealous brawl between patrons. In spite of their drawbacks, bars functioned as places to turn to at the end of a long day. There many lesbians could find affirmation for queerness in a society that increasingly characterized homosexuality as sickness. Many lesbians recall finding "home" or "sanity" in the bars. One woman, after spending time in a mental hospital because of her "suspected homosexuality," remembered, literally, finding sanity when she discovered her first lesbian bar in Lynn, Massachusetts, in the mid-1950s:

I was sitting right there in the hospital on the bed and she came up to me and said, "Alice I know you're gay" . . .

And she goes, "as soon as you get out of here, I'll be there, and you'll find all kinds of people just like you." And I'm looking at her and I thought, oh god let me go now, please I've got my sanity now.[38]

Bars were also places to find love and sex, and lesbian bar culture in the 1940s and 1950s had its own unique social and sexual styles. Butch-femme was the reigning erotic system: a play of gendered dress and stance, with a charged sexual pull. In the 1950s, lesbian communities were made visible by butches in ducktails and loafers and femmes in bouffants and high heels, by women who passed as men with "wives" on their arms, and by thousands of women who knew exactly what they wanted sexually at a time when the larger culture was working overtime to deny it to them. "Sexual courage in the 1950s" is what Joan Nestle called the butch-femme relationships marked by a "deeply Lesbian language of stance, dress, gesture, loving, courage, and autonomy," an "erotic partnership serving both as a conspicuous flag of rebellion and as an intimate exploration of women's sexuality.[39]

With many men overseas, groups of women socializing together attracted little attention during the war years. One Buffalo lesbian remembers cracking, "Here come the war brides," when groups of straight women would enter her neighborhood lesbian bar.[40] Moreover, the expanding war industries allowed larger numbers of women than ever before to enter the previously male domain of heavy industry. In munitions factories and pink-collar offices, World War II created new opportunities for women to live independent lives and to work and socialize exclusively with other women. For lesbians, who were already leading women-centered lives, the war provided a protective covering, giving them new latitude to dress (pants were just becoming acceptable for women) and behave as they saw fit. Lisa Ben, who was living in a women's boardinghouse in Los Angeles during the war, was introduced to lesbian nightlife in bars like the If Club and the Flamingo in Hollywood.[41] The war changed gay public life in smaller cities as well. In the wake of World War II, gay bars opened for the first time in cities such as Kansas City, Missouri; Richmond, Virginia; Worcester, Massachusetts; and San Jose, California.

By the 1950s, gay and lesbian nightlife had gone national, although larger coastal cities like New York, Los Angeles, and San Francisco still had the most extensive social scenes. One lesbian remembers the marked contrast of New York in the 1950s to her native Chicago: "There were lesbians in the streets in droves. Women that looked like men, men that looked like women, women with the hair slicked back, femmes with the beehive . . . They were there to pick and choose from."[42] In New York there were gay and lesbian bars, mostly concentrated in the Village with a string of men's bars, including the famous Bird Circuit, on Manhattan's East Side. Garnering its appellation for obvious reasons, the Bird Circuit included the Blue Parrot, the Green Cockatoo, Faisan d'Or, and the White Swan bars. Harlem still had a lively nightlife, and a 1951 article entitled "Harlem's Strangest Nightclub" described Lucky's, a bistro on St. Nicholas Avenue: "Steeped in the swish jargon of its many lavender customers and sharpened by the wit of the intellectuals and artists of both races who are attracted to the place like iron filings to a magnet. If Harlem has a café society set, it can be found at Lucky's."[43]

Beatnik bohemia sheltered more than its share of queers, both in San Francisco's North Beach and New York's Greenwich Village. Poet Audre Lorde recalled the Village at the time: "The women I ran with, we knew we were outside the pale. We lived in the Village. We were out-

(opposite) **Ira Jeffries (far right), with her arm around her girlfriend, Snowbaby, her mother, Bonita (standing), and friends at her sixteenth birthday party at the Celebrity Club on 125th Street in Harlem, New York, 1949.**

Police raid masquerade ball, New York, October 26, 1962. Although drag balls were fixtures in New York City nightlife for decades, they were not immune to raids. Dozens were arrested on charges of masquerading and indecent exposure following a raid on the 1962 National Variety Artists Exotic Carnival and Ball held at the Manhattan Center.

siders. We were dykes . . . Now this, of course, was the fifties. It was like the gay girls' version of the beatniks."[44] The beats themselves—Allen Ginsberg, William S. Burroughs, and Gregory Corso among them—were living in New York and San Francisco at the time. Allen Ginsberg remembers the "cultural scene" of late nights at the Automats and the streets of Times Square: "Herbert Huncke, then a hustling junkie on Times Square, was working with Dr. Kinsey as Kinsey's informant for the floating population of Times Square, so that Burroughs and myself, and Huncke, and many of my friends are integrated into the first statistics of the Kinsey Report."[45]

The Kinsey report, which announced that there were roughly twenty million homosexuals in the American population, was greeted with a range of responses. For many gay men and lesbians, it had the liberating effect of confirming that, even if they were isolated, they were not alone. Kinsey's findings had a different effect within the larger context of McCarthyite America, inflaming popular fears of a subversive and ever-growing homosexual conspiracy. Popular fears, as historian John D'Emilio has argued, gave "local police forces across the country a free reign in harassment."[46]

In gay and lesbian bars, as well as in cruising areas like parks and beaches, harassment and arrests of homosexuals rose dramatically during this period. In the District of Columbia alone, arrests numbered over one thousand a year during the early 1950s. New York, Miami, Memphis, Baltimore, Pittsburgh, Wichita, Ann Arbor, Minneapolis, Boise, Seattle, and Pasadena all witnessed sudden upsurges in police actions against homosexuals.[47]

Following a crime wave in the summer of 1959, New York City police closed down virtually every gay bar in the city by revoking liquor licenses. "One by one they all closed. Mary's was the first to go. After fifteen or twenty years as the symbol of the Gay Life on Eighth Street, it was snuffed out of existence. Next went the Old Colony. The Main Street held out a little longer, but it too succumbed after a few months. Lenny's, Ce Soir, Mais Oui, The Grape Vine, the 415, the Annex, not to mention the Bagatelle for girls—all disappeared." Police also raided cruising areas in Central Park repeatedly that year, and leaned on the West Side YMCA to "clean house."[48]

Novelist Leslie Feinberg recounts the relentless harassment, arrests, and abuse that were part of of bar life in the late 1950s and early 1960s. She describes a typical police raid on a Niagara Falls, New York, gay bar during this period:

> When the music stopped and it was the cops at the door, someone plugged the music back in and we switched dance partners. We in our suits and ties paired off with our drag queen sisters in their dresses and pumps. It's hard to remember that it was illegal then for two women or two men to sway to music together. When the music ended, the butches bowed, our femme partners curtsied, and we returned to our seats, our lovers, and our drinks to await our fates.[49]

David and Johnny, New York, 1960s.

Some homosexuals had it easier. Remembering his own safeguarded social world of the fifties and sixties, one middle-class gay man remarked: "Discreetly making their sexual and romantic contacts at parties, on beaches or in the protected bars . . . few I knew were very conscious of needing liberation."[50] For other lesbians and gay men, the experience of police harassment, combined with the lived knowledge of a vital community built in gay and lesbian bars over the decades, created an explosive mix— one that would erupt in a 1969 bar riot that changed the face of gay and lesbian life in this country.

Gay Guide, 1968.

"I LOVE THE NIGHTLIFE"

A special effort has been made to help you find New York
a really gay place to visit. We hope you find what you're looking for . . .
The bar scene in N.Y.C. is groovie, but watch out for trouble
to come in the private clubs.

—GAY-WAYS '69,
NEW YORK CITY DIRECTORY

Long before gay liberationists first shouted "Out of the bars and into the streets!" lesbians and gay men fought for public space and created vital social institutions. Especially when turning to the West Coast, the history that emerges is one of a homosexual rights movement arising directly out of the bars, and doing so years before Stonewall.

With a reputation as a "wide open town," dating back to the Gold Rush, San Francisco has been home to a collection of multiethnic, nonconformist, and rough-and-tumble subcultures for over a century. Bohemian neighborhoods have abutted ethnic enclaves, each sitting fairly comfortably side by side, sharing space—and even some neighborhood institutions—for years. San Francisco's North Beach has long been one such area. Once a quiet working-class Italian neighborhood, by the late 1950s North Beach had been transformed into what *Look* magazine termed "the international headquarters of the so-called 'Beat Generation.' "[1]

Just a few blocks from the center of North Beach stood the Black Cat bar. A venerable bohemian haunt, it provided a backdrop for a segment of Jack Kerouac's *On the Road.* It also functioned as a cruising ground for gay men in the post–World War II era. Allen Ginsberg described the Black Cat as "the greatest gay bar in America. It was really totally open, bohemian, San Francisco . . . and everybody went there, heterosexual and homosexual. It was lit up, there was a honky-tonk piano; it was enormous. All the gay screaming queens would come, the heterosexual gray flannel suit types, longshoremen. All the poets went there."[2]

José Sarria as "Carmen." From an original oil painting by Alexander Anderson, which hung at the Black Cat in San Francisco.

This North Beach bar became the site of a crucial battle in the burgeoning homosexual civil rights struggle. Sol Stoumen, the owner of the Black Cat, was tired of paying off the police and went to court to protect his right to serve alcohol to homosexuals. In a 1951 landmark decision, *Stoumen v. Reilly,* the California State Supreme Court ruled that bar owners could serve homosexual clientele with impunity "so long as they are acting properly and are not committing illegal or immoral acts."[3] The definition of what constituted an illegal or immoral act, however, was still left up to the vice squad to decide, and it continued its surveillance of "resorts for sex perverts," searching for incorrect behavior.

One of the sights surveyed by the San Francisco vice squad was José Sarria, whose Sunday afternoon, high-camp performances drew standing-room-only crowds to the Black Cat. He sang parodies of popular torch songs, dripping with political satire, and at the end of his pointed pageants, Sarria would lead the crowd in a round of "God Save Us Nelly Queens," sung to the tune of "God Save the Queen." A frequent patron from the early 1950s recollected:

You must realize that the vice squad was there . . . They used to come in and stand around and just generally intimidate people and make them feel that they were less than human. It was a frightening period . . . But Jose could make these political comments about our rights as homosexuals . . . to be able to stand up and sing, "God Save Us Nelly Queens"—we were really not saying "God Save Us Nelly Queens." We were saying "We have our rights too."[4]

Sarria would eventually launch a historic (though unsuccessful) bid for a seat on San Francisco's Board of Supervisors in 1961, running under the slogan "Equality." Sarria's campaign—the first ever by an openly gay candidate—garnered 6,000 votes, which suggested to many the potential of a gay voting bloc. San Francisco bar owners organized into a Tavern Guild and proved themselves a political force to be reckoned with by the mid-1960s. As testament, the number of gay bars in the city rose from fewer than twenty in 1963 to fifty-seven by the beginning of 1968, surpassing much larger cities like Los Angeles, New York, and Chicago. By 1964 *Life* magazine had proclaimed San Francisco "the gay capital" of America.[5]

Other states followed California's lead in loosening legal regulations on gay bar life. By 1967 state courts in New York, New Jersey, and Pennsylvania all upheld the constitutional right of homosexuals to assemble in a licensed bar. Still, there remained provisions against "solicitation" and such vague crimes as "lewd and indecent behavior," all of which remained open to interpretation by the courts. The New Jersey State Supreme Court, which laid out both the historical antecedents for the prohibition of gay bars and the legal reasoning for the overturn of that precedent, stipulated that it would uphold "the rights of well-behaved apparent homosexuals to patronize and meet in licensed premises."[6]

As modest gains were being made in the courts establishing the rights of "well-behaved" homosexuals to congregate, the nation was exploding in a new era of liberation. College campuses erupted in protests over the Vietnam War. The civil rights struggle moved from nonviolent civil disobedience to militant Black Nationalism. And the hippie heirs to San Francisco's beat tradition transformed their city into a rapturous happening. Across the country, young people broke away from the trappings of their stultifying pasts and began to imagine new ways of living. If

City & County of SAN FRANCISCO City Election, Tuesday, Nov. 7th 1961

Elect

JOSÉ JULIO SARRIA

Supervisor

"Equality!"

Campaign poster from José Sarria's 1961 run for the San Francisco Board of Supervisors.

1967's Summer of Love was still mostly about heterosexual love, it was of an entirely new kind. Breaking down monogamy and bourgeois notions of propriety, the counterculture pushed at the boundaries of 1950s gender roles. Long hair for men, once a sure marker of homosexuality, became a banner of the age. And if the Left and the counterculture were still predominantly straight boys' clubs, in which "faggot" was often hurled as an epithet to discredit those without the proper revolutionary credentials or the "guts" to act on them, both the Movement and the counterculture managed to push the country toward questioning a generation of received values.[7]

A 1966 statement from San Francisco's anarcho-radical group the Diggers summed up a sentiment that an entire generation was beginning to act on: "Throw it all away. The system has addicted you to an artificial need. Kick the habit. Be what you are. Do what you think is right. All the way out is free."[8] All the way out is where the gay movement would go, and many in it would point to the hippies and the counterculture as charting the way. One woman remembered: "When the hippies came it was a real liberating thing because they started wearing anything they wanted to. And that made gay people freer to do likewise."[9]

The cultural changes wrought during the 1960s, including legal challenges to the suppression of sexually explicit material and a growing openness to unconventional sexuality in general, created a climate in which lesbian and gay culture could begin to thrive. Gay sexuality was expressed in an increasingly frank manner in print and in public. Moviegoers in 1968 could find theaters showing independent films like Andy Warhol's *Chelsea Girls* and Kenneth Anger's *Inauguration of the Pleasure Dome,* replete with queer characters. Hollywood would begin a new flirtation with filmic depictions of gay and lesbian life, with such offerings as *The Killing of Sister George, The Fox,* and *Midnight Cowboy* all released by 1969. And if cinematic gay life was still pictured as seedy, tragic, or both, it *was* pictured. The decades-old blackout on homosexual life was lifting.

As the sixties wore on and legal restrictions on lesbian and gay bars loosened, more commercial establishments opened across the country, and access to gay social worlds became easier for those seeking them for the first time. In San Francisco in 1967, there were more than thirty gay bars affiliated with the Tavern Guild. Chicago boasted an excess of forty gay bars that same year.[10] In 1968, one year before Stonewall, a New York City "Gay Scene Guide" listed over one hundred bars, clubs, restaurants, coffeehouses, and bathhouses catering to a varied "gay crowd." There were listings for bars for "girls only," clubs for "the leather set," and venues catering specifically to college boys and "sweater queens." In fact, at least for lesbians in New York City, there were more bars immediately *before* Stonewall than after.[11]

As gay liberation took hold following Stonewall, the new political movement was accompanied by a dramatic social and cultural transformation. The gay liberationist impulse was translated into utopia building—or at least ghetto formation—as thousands upon thousands of young lesbians and gay men left their small towns and went looking for gay communities. Many left the interior to flock to the cosmopolitan cities of the coasts. They went to Greenwich Village in New York, San Francisco's Castro, and Los Angeles's West Hollywood. Chicago, New Orleans, Atlanta, and Houston marked other destinations, as gay ghettos were settled across America. No reliable statistics quantified the number of people who migrated to these burgeoning enclaves, but the development of new communities was clearly a national phenomenon.[12]

Student Mobilization Committee, New York, 1968.

New larger gay neighborhoods developed where they had, to some extent, already been. But there was a critical difference. "Liberated" lesbians and gays were not content to build on the existing institutions of the homosexual past. Quite the contrary. To these young liberationists, older homosexuals were closeted, self-hating, and abject—everything the new "out," "proud" generation stood against. In the sweeping judgments typical of the newly politicized, movement activists accused their homosexual forbears of being shrinking "Uncle Toms," living straight lives by day, cowering in gay bars by night. "At day's end they have only a few fleeting hours to be with others like themselves," wrote activist Randy Wicker in 1969; "they are hypocrites by day and social refugees by night."[13] Allen Young, writing in the 1972 movement anthology *Out of the Closets,* was typical of many young gay liberationists who understood "old gay" institutions—especially gay bars—to be as tainted as the generation who frequented them. Moreover, many activists saw bars as the products of the sexist, capitalist system they were striving to eliminate: As Young put it: "The gay bars are the focal points of conflict between our new spirit of liberation and the forces which would keep us in our place."[14]

The forces that would keep gay people in their place did not disappear with gay liberation. Bar owners soaked their patrons; tales of watered-down, overpriced drinks were legend: " 'It usually costs $3 to get in and a dollar for every beer. Who can afford to be gay at those prices?' asked one lesbian."[15] The role of the Mafia in New York's gay nightlife was so well known that by 1970 even the *New York Times* could casually comment that "gay bars" are "often run by disreputable characters, some by mobsters, who charge exorbitant prices."[16] In New York in the sixties and early seventies, gay bars were still heavily policed and patrolled. Although court battles had been waged since the fifties—and gay bars were in fact legal in New York after 1967—sporadic police actions still took place throughout the seventies, often, it was rumored, when the police were not properly paid off. Targeting bars without licenses and shadowy after-hours clubs, police continued to raid gay gathering places on various legal technicalities. None of this changed in the immediate aftermath of Stonewall, but what *did* change was the response of the patrons.

In March of 1970—less than a year after the Stonewall riots—the same cop who had led the raid on the Stonewall bar, Police Deputy Inspector Seymour Pine, arrived at the nearby Snake Pit to serve papers for liquor and fire code violations. He hustled more than 160 people, including customers, bartenders, and management, out of the packed bar and over to the nearby police station because, as Pine explained, "We didn't want a loud, riotous crowd milling around outside. Our purpose in the arrests was to get them out of there."[17] Pine was on shaky legal ground to be sure. Nevertheless, it was not uncommon for police to arrest customers first and management second. At the Snake Pit, everyone was arrested.

The disorderly conduct summonses that police handed out to patrons that night would not hold up legally and were eventually dismissed. But those arrested were unaware of that fact. Packed into police wagons and dragged to the precinct station in the middle of the night, some began to get nervous. One of the arrested men, Diego Vinales, an Argentine national in the country on a visa, panicked. Fearing the consequences of arrest—at this time, a person could be denied a visa and entry into the United States for being a homosexual—he attempted an escape from the police station. Hurling himself out of a second-story window, Vinales missed his target and impaled himself on a fourteen-inch spike of the wrought-iron fence surrounding the precinct. Officers were overheard saying, "You don't have to hurry [with the ambulance], he's dead, and if he's not, he's not going to live long."[18] Diego Vinales lived. In critical condition and fighting for his life, he was charged with resisting arrest.

It was less than a year after the Stonewall riots, and the response from the community was immediate. Within hours, hundreds of gay men and lesbians flooded the streets, marched to the station house and then over to St. Vincent's Hospital, where Vinales lay in a hospital bed with two police officers stationed outside his door. A Gay Activists Alliance flyer distributed at the demonstration read: "Any way you look at it—that boy was PUSHED!! We are All being pushed."[19]

Many in the gay community felt that they had been pushed too far and were ready to fight back, as lesbian and gay activists began to target the bars that were profiting from the community. Kooky's, a lesbian bar on West 14th Street in New York City, became the site of a number of protests in 1970 and 1971.[20] Along with

Lesbians picketing Kooky's bar on West 14th Street, New York, July 30, 1971.
© BETTYE LANE

the usual overpriced drinks and bad service, Kooky's made it known that lesbians working for gay liberation were not welcome there. When a group of women from Gay Liberation Front attempted to advertise their Spring All Women's Dance, Kooky—the bar's owner and namesake—and her burly helpmates tried to stop them. GLF women responded with a demonstration, demanding that lesbians run their own bars and refuse to "cooperate in being exploited."[21]

One of the ways in which gay liberationists refused to cooperate was by creating new community institutions that could serve as alternatives to bars. Gay coffeehouses, which were usually nonprofit, collectively run, and short-lived, sprang up in many major cities. Hartford's Kalos Society established one in 1970 with dancing and food. Berkeley had its Five-Squared, Four-Squared; and New York's Gay Liberation Front briefly hosted a night at the People's Coffee Grounds.[22]

In New York, gay liberation groups began to raise funds to start community centers almost immediately upon their founding. Gay Liberation Front opened its center in the winter of 1970–71 in the Village, and the Gay Activists Alliance established its new headquarters in an abandoned firehouse in SoHo in 1971. The Firehouse was a major alternative to the city's commercial offerings and provided a site linking the gay liberationists with the larger lesbian and gay community. Although GAA's membership typically hovered around three hundred, some dances at the Firehouse were attended by more than fifteen hundred people. GLF also hosted dances at the movement center, Alternate U., which consistently drew many more people from the community than did typical GLF actions. GLF dances had strobe lights and go-go boys like the bars, but were

All Women's Dance, organized by Gay Liberation Front Women, May 9, 1970.

considerably more affordable, and had none of the bars' hassles and strictures. As one happy attendee commented: "At a dance, the vibrations are certainly a lot better than at a bar."[23]

The women attending GLF dances —always predominantly male—were picking up different vibrations. Some of the women described the ambience as "oppressive . . . an over-crowded, dimly lit room, where packed together (subway rush-hour style) most human contact was limited to groping and dryfucking."[24] Because the dances were originally conceived as an alternative to the bars, a place where people might have conversations rather than cruise, dance alone or in a group rather than wait to be picked up, this environment was particularly disturbing to some. Moreover, many of the women felt alienated by the overwhelming male atmosphere, protesting that they were being "lost to each other in a sea of spaced out men."[25] In response, a group of GLF women and others who would go on to form the group Radicalesbians, decided to host their own all-women's dance in April of 1970. One woman who attended that spring dance wrote: "The response to this first All-Women's Dance was in fact mind-blowing. At peak there were somewhere near 250 women dancing together, in circles, in lines, in twos, in threes, laughing, playing, talking, hugging, kissing and just loving each other."[26]

The dance represented a kind of turning point in the post-Stonewall gay liberation movement in New York. Some lesbians active in the movement were becoming convinced that the gay liberation movement, like the term *gay* itself, intended to include both gay men and women alike, but in practice, spoke only for men. For other lesbians, politicized by the women's liberation movement, the issue was larger than not being listened to or failing to have their needs met in the mixed gay groups: Many became increasingly convinced that their interests as gay women were antithetical to those of gay men. Radical women's liberationists saw men and women as radically different and radically opposed *by their very nature*. And gay men were, after all, men.

Gay Liberation Front Women (some of whom would later form Radicalesbians) prepare for the first All Women's Dance at Alternate U., New York, April 3, 1970.
© ELLEN SHUMSKY/IMAGE WORKS

If the male dances were filled with "groping" and "dryfucking," the women's dances could be "an environment of women rapping, drinking, dancing, relating with fluidity and grace."[27] The women's dances were also a bridge to the wider radical women's community. Advertised as women's—as opposed to specifically lesbian—events, these dances marked a turn toward the creation of spaces and institutions structured (or unstructured) by feminist design, and open to all woman-identified women. One woman who attended that first GLF dance with her women's liberation group, although she had never identified as a lesbian, found in that all-women's space a new practice for her feminist theory: "The atmosphere was warm and close and for the first time publically [*sic*] those of us from women's liberation who attended realized a fuller more expanded meaning of what we have been referring to in the women's movement as 'Sisterhood.' "[28]

Duchess Bar, New York, August 23, 1974.
© BETTYE LANE

This expanded meaning of sisterhood began to be articulated as lesbian feminism. Beginning in the early 1970s, some women began to create a woman-centered way of life. Dedicated to the ethos that women could build their own separate women's culture untainted by the "male" values of violence, competitiveness, and greed, lesbian feminists established women's coffeehouses, bookstores, and music concerts, as well as credit unions, living collectives, and presses. While there were still lesbian bars in major cities, no lesbian nightlife boom occurred after Stonewall to rival the explosion of gay male bars and clubs. This was due in part to the fact that women in general, and lesbians in particular, have never been a very economically powerful group.[29] Moreover, in the 1970s, many lesbian feminists spurned patriarchal values and capitalist culture, crafting alternatives like women's music festivals, which showcased female performers as well as providing jobs for women who may have otherwise been shut out of the mainstream entertainment industry. Well into the 1980s, "women's culture" provided *the* lesbian social space in many communities. However, by the early 1980s, fault lines were appearing in the Lesbian Nation. Urged by critiques from women of color, sex radicals, as well as by generational fractures, many called into question the viability of a single lesbian culture.

Lesbian feminists fashioned alternative social worlds in the decade and a half after Stonewall, which were feminist, separatist utopias.[30] During that same period, gay men imagined and built their own separatist utopias, though they bore little resemblance to their sisters' creations. Whereas lesbian feminism was dedicated to an "anti-style," which was, in cultural theorist Arlene Stein's words, "an emblem of refusal, an attempt to strike a blow against the twin evils of capitalism and patriarchy, the fashion industry and the female objectification that fueled it,"[31] gay male subcultures, by the early 1970s, were paralleling the consumerist values that had already made sex a highly marketable commodity. However, lesbian feminist and gay male subcultures had certain corollaries: Both enforced and created cultures of gendered homogeneity. The ideal lesbian feminist was an anti-style androgyne—neither butch nor femme—female-identified and wholly dedicated to living her politics. The gay male "clone" was a hypermasculine, mustachioed, gym-toned, tanned Marlboro Man who *loved* the nightlife. And while few lesbians or gay men could—or did—live up to these ideals, the "types" set the tone for their respective communities.

Writer Andrew Holleran recalled the march of the clone:

> They come down Christopher Street like an army, in ranks and ranks, and (here's the nightmare) they're all your physical ideal. It's the doom of Don Juan: must I go to bed with all of them? A friend looking at this homogeneous mob one Sunday afternoon moaned, "It's like an invasion of the body snatchers."[32]

But activist Michael Callen contended that, despite the rise of this new uniformity, "there were still many different ways to be gay":

> Long hair was out. Crew cuts were in . . . Because of the way the gay media and mainstream media marketed the clone look as the insignia of the gay revolution it seemed like more people were into the clone look than I think actually were. There were still hippies. There were still people who wore cardigans and nice slacks.[33]

Dancing at the Gay Activists Alliance's Firehouse, New York, 1971. © DIANA DAVIES *(right)* ***Gay Bob, created by Harvey Rosenberg, Out of the Closet, Inc., 1978.*** Gay Bob is the unofficial, unlicensed boyfriend Ken always needed. He is anatomically correct and dressed up here in perfect clone fashion for a night on the town.

(below) ***The Village People.*** The Village People, formed in 1977, consisted of six singing, masculine gay archetypes: the leatherman, the cop, the sailor, the construction worker, the cowboy, and the Indian. (The Indian never really caught on as a look.)

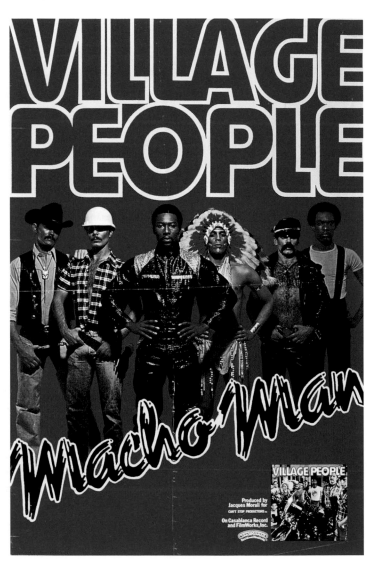

The Christopher Street–Castro Street clone was the poster boy of post-Stonewall gay male culture. As one observer of the scene noted, the very style, "whether they know it or not," was "a militant act, broadcasting the statement 'I am gay' not only to gays (we could always recognize each other) but primarily to the straight world."[34] The visibility—and recognizability—of these gay men was a message that at least some of the gay community was now "out" in public.

Gay male nightlife became increasingly visible in major cities across the country. In New York in the early 1970s, gay male bars and clubs flourished, notable for their openness, their sexual action, and their specialized clientele. Those into leather, Levis, or clones could all find their particular niche. As the straight world was drifting toward androgyny in the 1970s—with unisex hair salons and fashion—many gay men began to reclaim traditional masculinity with leather, Levi's, flannel shirts, mustaches, and weight lifting. Bars and clubs characterized by a "new masculinity" opened; and many of these had their antecedents in the leather and S&M culture.

The earliest gay male leather bars and "motorcycle clubs" began in the 1950s in New York, Los Angeles, and Chicago.[35] San Francisco's first leather bar, the Why Not, opened in 1960, but the scene really took off with the opening of the Tool Box a few years later. Although New York had its share of leather bars and clubs in the late sixties—including Keller's, P.M., and the N.Y. Motorbike Club—they were far outnumbered by more traditional gay bars.[36] By the mid-seventies, however, muscles and swagger were replacing limp wrists and swish. Certain bars

and clubs attempted to strictly enforce the new rules of fashion in order to weed out any "sissy" holdouts from their ranks.

The Mineshaft, which opened in 1976 and thrived until it was closed in 1985 in the heat of the AIDS epidemic by the New York City Department of Health, was considered by many to be the preeminent leather sex establishment in New York. The Mineshaft was a members-only club, which—according to its membership rules—required that a man "be known to us and have no problem with our rules and Dress Code, which is designed for our kind of guy":

> Dress Code approved items include cycle leather and western gear, levis, T-shirts, Uniforms, Plaid and Plain shirts, Cut-Offs, Club Patches and Overlays, and *just plain sweat.*

835 WASHINGTON STREET, NEW YORK, N.Y. 10014

No Colognes, Perfumes or Designer Wear
No Suits, Ties, Jackets or Dress Pants
No Rugby-Style Shirts or Disco Drag
No Heavy Coats in the Back Playground
No LaCoste Alligator Shirts[37]

One Mineshaft patron described the entrance ritual: "I climb the narrow flight of stairs to find myself

*(left) **Advertisement. Scene and Machine: National Levi / Leather Monthly. Washington, D.C., 1973.***

(below) Bodybuilding boomed in gay culture in the 1970s and the gym became a major social venue for gay men. The "gym bod," with its pumped pectorals and bulging arms, quickly became *de rigueur* in the new hypermasculine gay male culture.

(left) **Mineshaft.** *New York, circa 1980.*

being inspected by a black body-beautiful bouncer in matching leather. His job is to make sure the clientele is wearing the necessary denims and/or leathers. He sniffs me. If I were wearing Aramis, I'd be out in the street again. No colognes allowed. If I were wearing a Pierre Cardin suit, I'd either have to take it off or leave the premises."[38]

Dancing at the Crisco Disco, New York, 1970s. © BILL BERNSTEIN

The Mineshaft was less a bar than a sex club, but many gay male bars opened in the 1970s with "backroom" spaces specifically designed for sexual play. While bathhouses that catered to homosexual patrons had existed for decades, in the early 1970s a large number of bars—such as the Strap and the International Stud—opened that explicitly targeted gay men and made no pretense of serving anything other than a sexual purpose. Many clubs included fantasy elements that harkened back to an older, more furtive, hazardous era: Man's Country bathhouse had a truck installed inside, and New York's Glory Hole boasted rows of bathroomlike stalls. The new clubs created the dangerous atmosphere of classic cruising spots likes parks and piers, but within a relatively controlled environment:

> Before back room bars, men were being erotic with each other in trucks and alleys, on deserted hills, and in warehouses. Amidst all these glorious, sweaty entwinings, there was always the possibility of being hurt by someone or something. A loose floorboard. A lonesome nail. A screwy sailor. So why not open up a place with loose floorboards, lonesome nails, and screwy sailors? Serve beer. Have a jukebox. It will take very low overhead to supply all that dangerous eroticism of the old hangouts, and the profit will be huge and quickly gathered.[39]

The seventies witnessed a boom in gay male dance clubs. Same-sex dancing was no longer illegal, as it had been in the pre-Stonewall era, and clubs flourished. Disco,

We would not stop dancing. We moved with the regularity of the Pope from the city to Fire Island in the summer, we danced until the fall, and then, with the geese flying south, the butterflies dying in the dunes, we found some new place in Manhattan and danced all winter there. We lived only to dance.

—ANDREW HOLLERAN
DANCER FROM THE DANCE,
1978

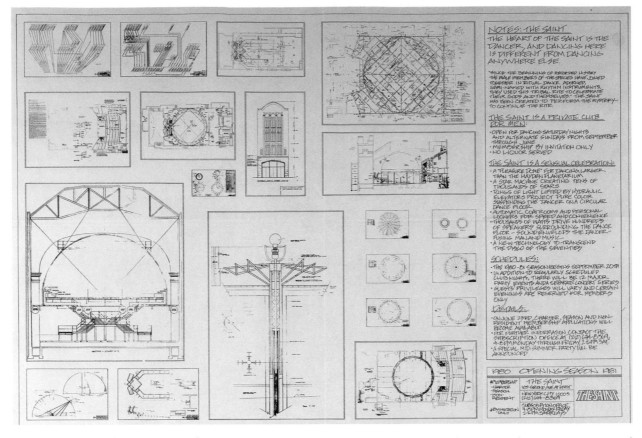

The Saint, New York, circa 1980. The Saint was the largest, most exclusive dance club built and run for a primarily gay male clientele. It attracted a self-defined "A-list" of gay men, most of whom were white, summered on Fire Island, did designer drugs, and took dancing seriously.

the backbeat of this new gay culture—born in African-American and Latino gay male dance clubs—crossed over into the American musical mainstream and left the nation dripping in glitter and sweat.

"It's hard to pinpoint the exact beginning of the disco movement," remembered an early participant, "but the clubs that come to mind as being part of the transition in the '60s from nightclubs to discotheques were the Cheetah, the Roundtable and Arthur."[40] Dance clubs like the Sanctuary, the Loft, 12 West, the Paradise Garage, and the Tenth Floor created gay disco culture in New York in the seventies. By the middle of the decade, gay discos had opened from coast to coast, packed with boys bumping and sweating to a throbbing bass beat. With more than thirteen hundred discos flourishing across the country, and dance hits lodged in the nation's Top 40, the gay magazine the *Advocate* declared 1975 "The Year of the Disco."[41]

In May 1974, Studio One opened in Hollywood. Billed as the "disco to end all discos," it quickly established itself as L.A.'s premier gay nightclub.[42] In 1977, Studio 54 opened in New York, gaining the national spotlight as *the* celebrity disco where men and women, if they were beautiful enough to gain entrance, could bump shoulders with Liza Minnelli, Calvin Klein, and Halston. In the meantime, the private gay dance club was born in clubs like the Flamingo, where promoters created invitation-only gatherings, filled with the "A" list of Manhattan dancers. These men, described in loving detail by novelist Andrew Holleran, "formed a group of people who had danced with each other over the years, had gone to the same parties, the same beaches on the same trains, yet, in some cases never even nodded at each other. They were bound together by a common love of a certain kind of music, physical beauty and style—all the things one shouldn't throw away an ounce of energy pursuing, and sometimes throw away a life pursuing."[43]

And at least some gay men were pursuing it hard. In September of 1978, the Saint opened in New York, and within a few short weeks, nearly three thousand men had paid their $250 membership fee to dance in what quickly became the apotheosis of exclusive, gay male clubs. The Saint was an architectural extravaganza in which thousands of gay men partied under a massive planetarium projection dome, soaring seventy-six feet over the dance floor. A nearly inexhaustible waiting list was established for those hoping to get in.

The Saint closed in the winter of 1987–88, the same season the Paradise Garage closed, two years after the Mineshaft was shut down. The AIDS epidemic had inalterably changed the fast-paced world of gay male nightlife. Although clubs and bars still flourished in the late eighties and into the nineties, and some lesbian clubs adopted their own "backroom" spaces for sex, New York nightlife would never be the same. As Gayle Rubin has commented about the dying of a certain scene: "AIDS will not last forever. The gay community is already recovering its balance and its strength. There will be a renaissance of sex. There will be new clubs, new parties, and new horizons."[44]

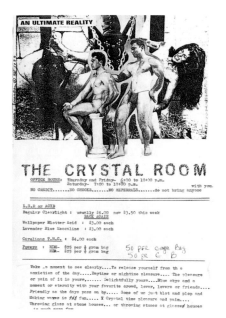

Drug menu, The Crystal Room, New York, 1979. Drug use, popularized by the 1960s counterculture, became an essential part of the fast-track gay male world of discos, backrooms, baths, and private parties that marked the "liberated" 1970s and early '80s. Private services provided an array of trendy drugs to those heading out for a weekend of all-night partying and club hopping.

Charles Demuth,
Turkish Baths

CRUISING

New York provides its citizens with unlimited sexual possibilities,
much as any great city does. But what is unique to New York
is the cruising . . . What I'm singling out are the scanning eyes
that lock for an instant, the cool and thorough appraisals of someone's person
and apparel—the staring, in a word.

—EDMUND WHITE,
STATES OF DESIRE

Cities offer endless possibilities for cruising. They grant anonymity and provide streets filled with crowds to be searched and surveyed for eye contact that might signify something more. The sheer numbers of urban denizens extend the promise of a world of potential partners for sex or romance. New York street life has a theatricality, a sense of display that, coupled with the existence of its well-known and well-traversed cruising areas, has

(clockwise from above) **Cruising spots, New York, circa 1950s.** Central Park West, two images of The Ramble, Bryant Park, and Rockefeller Center.

(below) **Cruising. The Gay Board Game.** *Created by John Chatterton and Saul Love, 1980.* This whimsical adult board game captures in miniature the cruising rituals of gay men. Players move their pieces "out of the closet," play "rounds of tricking," "proposition" one another, and attempt to win by making their way to the "I'm just resting, thank you" square.

made the city one of unique erotic opportunities. As one gay man remembered of his early forays into New York's gay underworld: "From the 'gay side' of the Astor Hotel bar to the bushes behind the Forty-second Street library [in Bryant Park], to the public tearoom right outside of Fordham University (where I was once arrested by entrapment), . . . and on and on and on, New York seemed to be one big cruising ground, especially to this teenager."[1]

Of course, cruising is not unique to New York nor is it an exclusively urban phenomenon. Gay men—among others—have long sought each other for sex, sometimes anonymously, in a wide variety of public places: in the foliage of wooded parks, the steam of communal baths, and in the darkness of city streets. This "cruising," the search for a willing, desirable partner for sex or romance is available to any amenable participant; but it has, and continues to be, a hallmark of gay male life. Women—gay or straight—both because of societal strictures as well as the very real threat of physical danger, have not had the same access to public space as have men. Moving freely through lonely streets, parks, and abandoned alleys in ways that few women safely could, men have often found each other.

Danger, in the

form of criminals, the police, sexually transmitted diseases, or the "trick" himself, is part and parcel of the cruising game. Over the last quarter century, more of this cruising has taken place in commercial establishments such as bathhouses, movie theaters, bars, and clubs. However, cruising in the great outdoors continues to hold an appeal both for men who relish the sport's danger and excitement and for those who favor the occasional gay pleasure in their lives but who do not identify as gay. In addition to sex, cruising spots have always been places for less intimate social contact and for the construction of what could rightly be called community.

Cruising, and the sex that typically follows it, is both widely practiced and widely disavowed by those who publicly present themselves as the "gay community." Although bathhouses, as well as certain piers, parks, and public toilets, function in many instances as long-standing community institutions, they rarely get recognized as such or accorded their due status as landmarks. Cruising is about staking a different kind of claim to space—to the edges and the unused areas of the city. It is a remaking of the territory of the everyday into a site of erotic possibility. Cruising is also a singularly democratic process. Unlike bars, clubs, or bathhouses, public sex is not circumscribed by the standard barriers to admittance; looks and desirability take precedence over economic and social status, and sexual identity itself can metamorphose or melt away with the right offer.

Holiday Time at the Park-Miller. *New York, 1968.* The Park-Miller Theater on 43rd Street was one of the first New York theaters to offer explicitly homoerotic films marketed to a gay male audience.

Many in the gay and lesbian community distance themselves from public sex, arguing that it is a vestigial byproduct of an earlier, furtive era. Others see it as just plain dangerous. But to many, the draw of cruising is quite straightforward. As one man wrote in a letter to a 1968 homophile magazine:

> O.K., here goes—no self-respecting homosexual in his right mind should condone sex in public places, but let's face it, it's fun . . . The danger adds to the adventure. The hunt, the cruise, the rendezvous, a great little game. Then more likely than not, "instant sex." That's it.[2]

Tearooms are public men's rooms . . . and everywhere they exist—I'm speaking empirically now—they are used for sex. Don't balk. Some of these shrines are quite popular, even legendary, and are known to those who care to know such things. More men than you might think, both straight and gay, make a pilgrimage as part of their daily routines—though categories like "straight," "gay" and "indifferent" don't hold up for long in tearooms.[3]

—Stephen Greco, 1982

Searching for the key to the hidden mysteries of the homosexual argot, sociologist Laud Humphreys, in his classic study *Tearoom Trade,* suggests that "like most other words in the homosexual vocabulary, the origin of *tearoom* is unknown," but that urine has been called "tea" in British slang and is sometimes used as a verb, "meaning 'to engage with, encounter, go in against.' "[4] It is also likely that the "*t*" in toilet, coupled with the very unladylike goings-on in "t-rooms," made for a nicely arch inversion of the gastronomic rituals of genteel propriety. Tearooms were also referred to in some quarters in the early part of the century as "sunken gardens." In fact, if one considers the genealogies of the terms *tearooms, gay ladies,* and *coming out,* it becomes clear that the Anglo-American upper crust has given more to the homosexual argot than they would probably like to know.

Sexual activity in tearooms has a long history. One man, asked in the 1960s about his knowledge of the history of "tearoom trade," commented: "I suppose there has been such activity since the invention of plumbing."[5] Indeed as early as 1899, a librarian at the New York Public Library logged a record of such an encounter when two men filed a formal complaint over an unsolicited friendly offering they received from a stranger in the library's "men's Toilet Room."[6] Men's rooms in public buildings—libraries, park pavilions, subways, train and bus stations, department stores— have been easily accessible and available to a large cross-section of men. In areas where people drive to and from work, tearooms have developed roadside. As one man remembered of his experience, which began in the 1920s: "I first started out in one of those pavilion

Letter concerning tearoom incident at The New York Public Library, March 28, 1899.

The New York Public Library
Astor Lenox and Tilden Foundations

ASTOR LIBRARY BUILDING
40 LAFAYETTE PLACE.

New York, Mch 28 1899

(310 East 13th St N.Y.C.)

H. Hofman, reader, during this month (March, 1899) has made obscene and immoral propositions to us in the mens' Toilet Room.—

F. S. Wilson
John Black.

The above statement made in our presence, March 28/99

J. Ferris Lockwood, Business Dept.

C. H. A. Bjerregaard, Librarian

places. But the real fun began during the Depression. There were all those new buildings, easy to reach, and the automobile was really getting popular about then . . . Suddenly, it just seemed like half the men in town met in the tearooms."[7] Another man associated World War II with his own tearoom experience. He remembered: "The toilets were marvelous during World War II with all the sailors. Those 13 buttons. I think we enjoyed unbuttoning the buttons more than anything."[8]

Gay Lemonade Party. *Gay Revolution Network, New York, 1972.* In an unusual intervention, gay liberation activists spent one evening distributing lemonade and radical literature to men hanging out in an area under the old West Side Highway, which doubled as an overnight storage site for trucks and a popular spot for public sex.

Perhaps the biggest draw of public toilets, unlike gay bars or bathhouses, is that they provide patrons with a built-in excuse for being there (aside from seeking sex with other men). Yet precisely because tearooms are *public* toilets, they are necessarily frequented by the uninitiated and initiate alike, and always present the danger to participants of getting caught in the act. The biggest danger for tearoom participants is not from the unaware person who happens into the men's room—and typically notices nothing—but from police and the ever-present threat of arrest.

Public sex, whether categorized and criminalized as indecent exposure or sodomy, has been and remains illegal across the country. Raids, entrapment, and arrests have been endemic to cruising areas. Public bathrooms have, historically, been favorite targets of police crackdowns. In New York City in 1921, for example, 38 percent of the arrests of men for homosexual activity occurred in subway men's rooms.[9] In 1953, as historian John Howard has documented, Atlanta police staked out the men's room in the Atlanta Public Library (at the request of library officials), installing a one-way mirror in order to survey and arrest men engaging in "homosexual acts." Twenty men were arrested over the course of eight days in September of 1953. Charged under state statutes, they faced heavy fines and maximum sentences of ten years in prison. News of the arrests was publicized in Atlanta's two daily papers. Dubbing it the "Atlanta Public Library Perversion Case," both newspapers printed all of the names and addresses of the accused on at least six different occasions. With the sole exception of one man, all were fired from their jobs.[10]

The 1950s was the high point for these sorts of elaborate State crackdowns on homosexual activity. Not coincidentally, this period saw an expansion of space for heterosexual public sex at the same time that homosexual public sex was being increasingly policed. In the 1950s, as heterosexual institutions like "parking" and "make-out lanes" were becoming a hallmark of American teenage life, homosexuals were arrested for their expressions of public sex in record numbers. Policing public sex continues to this day and remains a timeworn means for politicians to "clean up" cities and garner "law and order" votes.

■ BATHHOUSES

Baths vary in character, from the Wall Street Sauna, where businessmen get their rocks off during the lunch hour (it's called "funch"), to the Beacon, where the East Side executive pulls his socks down after cocktails. St. Mark's in the East Village is frequented by older men and Third World gays. Students prefer Man's Country, on West 15th Street. Mount Morris is an all-black bath in Harlem. People on their way up go to the Club Baths. Those who dally in sadism and masochism prefer the New Barracks on 42nd Street. And total masochists are advised to visit the Continental, only because this once-great countercultural pantheon has turned into a pit.[11]

—Arthur Bell, 1978

Brevities. *New York, November 23, 1933.* This 1930s New York scandal sheet "exposed" the takeover of steam baths by the "pansy men of the Nation," warning the unsuspecting bather of the "diabolic cupidity" of "joyboys on the make." COLLECTION OF THE NEW-YORK HISTORICAL SOCIETY

The late seventies marked the heyday of gay bathhouses throughout the country. Writing in 1984, historian Allan Bérubé estimated that there were approximately two hundred gay bathhouses across the United States, "from Great Falls, Minnesota, and Toledo, Ohio, to New York City, Los Angeles, and San Francisco."[12] New York and San Francisco alone had enough variety to satisfy any connoisseur. But, one by one, city by city, these community institutions were closed down—often to much criticism and controversy—as a response to the AIDS epidemic. Sometimes the closures were mandated by city health departments, as in New York City; in other cases the decisions were made by the owners themselves. These institutions had been sustaining forces for gay men for more than one hundred years.

Turkish baths, typically located in hotels or Midtown office buildings, were favorites of many gay men and, by the 1920s, there were fifty-seven of these types of baths in Manhattan. Though not established as specifically "gay baths," a number of these bathhouses had developed reputations as

Booklet advertising the facilities of the original Everard Baths, New York, 1892.

"favorite spots" for homosexual men. In New York, Stauch's and Clar-idge's were infamous for homosexual tête-à-têtes. One 1933 New York scandal sheet referred to the "gay bath" phenomenon, screaming: "The pansy men of the Nation—New York, Philadelphia, and San Francisco—are just nuts about Turkish bathing. Steam joints of the aforementioned cities are the gathering places of perverts."[13] In a perhaps more reliable—or at least less sensational—account, a German correspondent, writing in 1929, referred to the Lafayette Brothers Turkish Baths as "very well-known . . . especially as a place where like-minded people meet."[14] The Lafayette Baths were also depicted in a series of paintings by early-twentieth-century artist (and homosexual) Charles Demuth.

"Gay baths" were no different in structure or design from other such steam and electric baths, except for the closed cubicles provided in some in which men met to have sex. Owners and managers of these bathhouses may not have been fully aware of the uses to which their es-tablishments were being put, but it was alleged at the time that "not a few

of the places which cater to the public demand for steambaths are glad to enjoy the patronage of pansies provided their actions do not result in police proceedings."[15] The assumption was that managers were tipped to look the other way.

Despite payoffs, baths were not immune to raids. An eyewitness, writing in a European publication, described this 1929 raid of New York City's Lafayette Baths:

> At about ten-thirty I go up to the dormitory and look for a bed. Chance brings me together with a young, racy Sicilian. Unfortunately, we hadn't noticed that there were eight detectives among the customers of the baths . . . Now it's midnight, and I'm already asleep, my friend at my side. All at once there's a whistle, someone yells "Hallo," and everyone has to go to the front room. The bath is locked shut. Various people were struck down, kicked, in short, the brutality of these officials was simply indescribable. A Swede standing next to me was struck on the eye with a bunch of keys, and then he got hit in the back so that two of his ribs broke.[16]

Despite the risks patrons faced in frequenting gay bathhouses, these establishments remained important in many men's lives. One man had a whole circle of friends centered at the Lafayette Baths in the 1910s, though he also regretted that the baths were his *only* contact with the gay world, lamenting: "It always angers me that one cannot meet these people anywhere except there, but they always seem to be afraid."[17] Additionally, George Chauncey attests that many men snared in bathhouse raids in the early part of the century were married, a fact that could have only added to their fears. But for others, bathhouses were among the sole venues in the city where they could be surrounded by other men, and issues of sexual identity could vanish in the steam.

By the 1950s, according to Allan Bérubé, bathhouses began to develop across the country as "explicitly gay institutions." A mimeographed guide to San Francisco's gay bars and baths handed out at a May 1959 Mattachine Society meeting listed Jack's Baths, the Club Turkish Baths, the Palace Baths, and the San Francisco Baths on its roster.[18] In cities like New York, baths were long-standing institutions that often outlasted bars by decades. The Everard Baths, opened in 1888 by James Everard, "a prominent financier, brewer, and politician," was the longest-running

(opposite) **Charles Demuth. Turkish Baths. *Watercolor, 1918.*** Charles Demuth painted a number of watercolors of bathhouses in the 1910s. This one reportedly depicts the Lafayette Baths. The figure in the center foreground is purported to be a portrait of the artist.

(below) **A Night at the Baths for McGovern.** *Man's Country, Brooklyn, New York, 1972.* Getting out the "gay vote" began in earnest in the early 1970s, as activists organized potential voters in a variety of gay venues. Nixon campaign workers are not known to have followed suit.

gay-oriented business in New York City. The bathhouse initially catered to an all-male, upscale (presumptively heterosexual) clientele, but by World War I the Everard was known as a meeting place for gay men. It was hit by a deadly fire in May 1977 in which nine men were killed, and was finally closed by the New York City Department of Health in 1985 in the wake of the AIDS epidemic.

The opening of New York's Continental Baths soon after the Stonewall Riots signaled a dramatic break with the past. The Continental was one of the first bathhouses established as an explicitly gay club, and it was comfortable, clean, and anything but seedy. As one man remembered:

> The Continental when it was new was wonderful. I had been to baths before but they were grubby. When the Continental opened up it was as if someone opened up the Waldorf in the middle of some flop houses. Although we were doing the dirtiest things imaginable, it felt innocent. It felt fresh. It felt comradely. They had singers who were working shows on Broadway and you would sit around in your towel, eat the buffet, watch the show, talk, and then get laid. It was ideal.[19]

Continental Baths sign, New York, 1970s.

The Saturday night performances in the early seventies (including appearances by the then-unknown Bette Midler) attracted the attention of the mainstream media and brought in more than one heterosexual tourist. As Richard Goldstein wrote in *New York* magazine in 1973: "In response (and sensing, perhaps, that its gay clientele might provide just the draw a New York pop audience requires these days), the Baths began admitting straights on Saturday nights. It was a surefire formula for notoriety: and in the past year, the Baths have emerged as New York's most Weimarian nightspot, a sort of City of Night *a gogo,* where straights may move among gay people without necessarily feeling gay."[20]

But the public delight with gay bathhouses was a short-lived phenomenon. As the AIDS crisis reached epidemic proportions in the mid-eighties, people both inside and outside of the gay community pointed to bathhouses, and other clubs where sex took place, as contributors to the spread of the AIDS virus. Others argued that bathhouses were community institutions that must be protected, and that closing them was part of a long tradition of state surveillance, harassment, and criminalization of gay gathering places. The latter group often suggested alternatives to closing the bathhouses such as community policing, arguing that the baths were ideal places from which to disseminate safe-sex information.

In 1985 the New York City Health Department closed down many gay bathhouses. Though some have since reopened, the mass closures dramatically changed the culture. As old institutions like baths have faded away, new institutions have emerged. Phone sex was born and boomed at a time when advances in telephone technology coincided with social change. As the owner of one of Los Angeles's many suddenly flourishing phone sex lines rhapsodized: "It's the ultimate mind fuck, in some ways even better than reality. It's what I call wash-and-wear sex. It doesn't require small talk, or putting your trick in a cab afterwards. You get exactly what you want. It's like television; you can turn it on and turn it off, in the privacy of your own home at any hour of the day or night."[21] A similar phenomenon has developed on the Internet over the last few years. And virtual reality can sometimes be better than the real thing.

Corner of Christopher and West streets, New York, 1982. Photograph by Richard C. Wandel. At this all-important intersection, Christopher Street, the commercial center of the city's gay male culture, joins up with the Hudson River's piers, one of the city's more famous cruising and hustling spots.

Valerie Taylor. **The Girls in 3-B.** *New York: Gold Medal, 1965 (detail of front cover art).*

LESBIAN PULPS

Darling, Lesbian love doesn't have to be brief or heart-breaking, just because it's a love between two women. I want to teach you that. I want to live with you and do things for you and even let you do things for me.

—Ann Bannon, *Beebo Brinker*, 1962

In the 1950s and '60s, while the Mattachine Society and the Daughters of Bilitis promoted an image of the "nice" homosexual, one palatable to mainstream America, thousands of lesbians searched for a very different sort of girl and found her in the pages of the lesbian pulp. Termed "pulps" after the cheap, wood-pulp paper they were printed on, these novels covered territory untouched by the Sapphic Modernism of such writers as Virginia

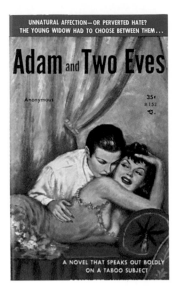

Woolf, Gertrude Stein, or Djuna Barnes. Far from Woolf's Bloomsbury and distant from Natalie Barney's Parisian salon, the world of the pulps was both urban and working class, peopled by protagonists who were more likely to be elevator operators or former housewives than globe-trotting artists or heiresses. Pulps treated readers to glimpses into smoky Greenwich Village gay bars, shadowy underground cellars rife with triangulated love affairs, violent jealousies, and scandalous sex.

Despite their subcultural subject matter, lesbian pulps were primarily mainstream marketing ventures, pitched to what was presumed to be a predominantly heterosexual, male audience. And in the postwar years, lesbian pulps sold remarkably well, indicating the existence of a large readership located well beyond the white, urban, gay communities the books documented. Indeed, Reed Marr's *Women Without Men* was one of the ten best-selling paperbacks of 1959 among *all* books.[1]

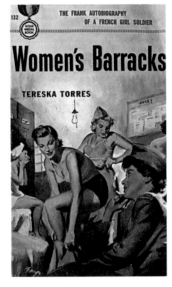

Lesbian pulps even found their way onto the floor of Congress. Tereska Torres's *Women's Barracks,* billed as "the frank autobiography of a French girl soldier," was hauled before the U.S. House of Representatives Subcommittee on Current Pornographic Materials in 1952. Bearing a cover illustration of a leering lesbian officer and two scantily clad service girls, the book was declared by the Subcommittee to contain "passages not quotable in a public hearing." The publisher defended the book on the grounds that "its treatment of homosexuality was milder than Plato's *Symposium,* and that public interest in homosexuality had been inflamed by sensational newspaper headlines detailing State Department purges."[2]

(above, left) **Anonymous. Adam and Two Eves.** *New York: Beacon, 1956.*

(above, right) **Tereska Torres. Women's Barracks.** *New York: Gold Medal, 1950.*

(right) **Joan Henry. Women in Prison.** *New York: Permabooks, 1953.*

Mainstream public interest in homosexuality—whether for titillation, information, or both—was quite different from the interests a lesbian reader might have brought to the books. The pulps traversed a particular spatial milieu, usually Greenwich Village, functioning as travelogues and guidebooks to "the gay life" at a time when there were few

others. Leading readers through the streets, bars, and coffeeshops of the city, the pulps mapped a previously uncharted terrain of lesbian customs, dress codes, terminology, and etiquette. And as the dog-eared books were passed from friend to friend, they forged informal networks and valuable links between women who may have otherwise thought themselves alone.

In some cases, readers even reached out to pulp authors, sometimes seeking advice, at other times going so far as to ask directions to Greenwich Village. In 1961 Ann Bannon, author of the pulp classic *Beebo Brinker* series, wrote that: "To judge from the huge correspondence I get from my readers, almost all of them are gay . . . They aren't all, or even mostly, big-city sophisticates. Some of them write to ask if Greenwich Village is a real place. It is quite a responsibility to think that I am their only link with what must seem to them like an exotic Shangri-La they will never have the chance to see."[3]

The novels were an imaginary link to a real gay world. Although these novelistic worlds were much whiter, as well as considerably more romantic than many real lesbian social worlds, the books did capture the landscape of large, gay meccas. Ann Bannon and others charted the gay pulp territory of Greenwich Village, and writers like Gale Wilhelm, in her classic novel *We Too Are Drifting,* depicted a certain "artistic" San Francisco. But a few of the pulps did something else quite extraordinary: Even more than guiding gay readers to a physical place, they offered them a new way of being. In *Beebo Brinker,* Beebo comes to see herself in an entirely new light: "For the first time in her life she was proud of her size, proud of her strength, even proud of her oddly boyish face. She could see interest, even admiration on the faces of many of the girls. She was not used to that kind of reaction in people, and it exhilarated her."[4] Nowhere else in postwar culture would a budding butch get this kind of affirmation, and gain the knowledge that not only might her "oddly boyish face" be all right, but some sultry femme might just swivel on her barstool to admire it.

Of course, the pulps were hardly paeans to lesbian culture, and neither were they uniformly of a type. Some publishing houses marketed the books in more sensational ways than did others, playing on lesbianism as either a sinful secret or a social menace. Consider the difference between the back blurb for Lilyan Brock's 1953 *Queer Patterns* and that of Ann Bannon's 1962 edition of *Beebo Brinker.*

(below, left) Ann Aldrich. **We Walk Alone.** *New York: Gold Medal, 1955.*

(below, right) Lilyan Brock. **Queer Patterns.** *New York: Eton Books, 1953.*

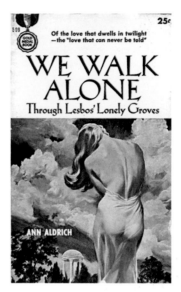

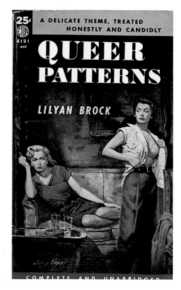

Queer Patterns

Here is a much-needed book which examines straight-forwardly the problem of women involved too intimately in one another's lives—a powerful novel of a little-known social menace. Read this book and gain an enlightened understanding of the lost women whose strange urges produce one of the great problems of modern society.

Beebo Brinker

Lost, lonely, boyishly appealing—this is Beebo Brinker—who never really knew what she wanted—until she came to Greenwich Village and found the love that smolders in the shadows of the twilight world.

(above, right) **Ann Bannon. Beebo Brinker.** *New York: Gold Medal, 1962.*

(above, left) **Vin Packer. Spring Fire.** *New York: Gold Medal, 1952.*

The decade that separates the two books has something to do with the difference in tone, but the difference can also be explained by the ways in which the two publishers (the authors did not have control over this process) chose to position the books. *Queer Patterns* is framed as a book about lesbianism as a "social problem," which the (presumably) straight reader can gain insight into while remaining fully unimplicated. *Beebo Brinker,* in contrast, is described as a novel of self-discovery, a book for a reader looking for similar answers.

Beebo Brinker's discovery of Greenwich Village as a gay mecca is paralleled in many of the novels. Almost all lesbian pulps have at least one scene where the heroine, unsure of what she wants, discovers other lesbians and in doing so realizes that she, too, is one. This scene from Artemis Smith's *The Third Sex* is archetypical of the genre:

> Jean looked about them. A group of girls had entered, most of them in pairs. They seemed to be tourists—but tourists with a difference. They were all women, and obviously Lesbians. Several of them were very attractive. . . . She felt, somehow, that she should be honest, that she shouldn't hide anymore, that she should somehow try to join the women who were to her so compellingly beautiful—the Lesbians.[5]

In many ways, lesbian pulps were 1950s "coming out" narratives. In them the heroine realizes that she is a lesbian because she sees others like herself and, finding this community, she "comes out" into gay society. As opposed to post-Stonewall coming-out stories in which coming out into heterosexual society is central to the narrative, coming out into mainstream society is never the point in these books. Ann Bannon's description of a character's coming out into Greenwich Village bar culture deftly inverted the dominant depiction of homosexuals as participants in a marginal and deviant underworld, subversively redefining the gay *demimonde* as civilization itself:

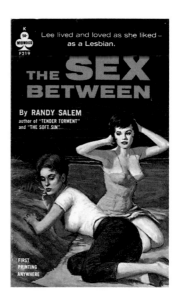

> And then she looked around the room again, and suddenly saw a girl with her arm around another girl at a table not far away. Her heart jumped. A pair of boys at the bar were whispering urgently to each other. *Gay,* Laura thought to herself. *Is that what they call it? Gay?* She was acutely uncomfortable now. It was as if she was a child of civilization, reared among the savages, who suddenly found herself among the civilized. She recognized them as her own.[6]

Lesbian pulps offered portrayals, not of lesbian "issues," but of tempestuous lesbian lives and bodies to match. On and between the covers, lean, dashing butches (almost always brunette) courted and caught charming, curvaceous femmes (almost always blond). And in a historical period when "women's novels" were about romance rather than sex, and the notion of female sexual agency was just a glimmer on a distant horizon, fifties pulp novel lesbians were unabashed in exploring sexual pleasure. The final scene:

> Nina, for once, was not laughing. She was spread beneath Beth like a carpet of warm silk. She moved with her, she murmured to her, she was as absorbed as Beth was in the fantastic luxury of sexual pleasure. When she tried to pull away a little Beth caught her from behind and kissed her bare neck and shoulders, her fingers pressed around Nina's lovely breasts and their legs entangled. Nina was surprised at the strength she felt in Beth's arms, and let herself be pushed back down on the bed with a sigh of ecstasy.[7]

(above, right) Randy Salem. The Sex Between. New York: Midwood Tower, 1962.

(above, left) Valerie Taylor. The Girls in 3-B. New York: Gold Medal, 1965.

PHYSIQUES

*We hope this book offends no one,
though we realize the mere portrayal of any part of the body
disturbs some whose minds have been pitifully warped by improper training . . .
It is hoped that all who take the trouble to study the book will get
a message of hope and inspiration from it, and will be
the better persons for the experience.*

—BOB MIZER,
"PURPOSE OF *PHYSIQUE PICTORIAL*," 1957

In 1948 amateur physique photographer Bob Mizer placed a small advertisement pitching his new photographic catalog of nearly naked young men in the back pages of a number of men's bodybuilding magazines. The ad read simply: "Invaluable for artists, inspirational for bodybuilders—For catalogue send fifteen cents in coins or stamps."[1] Mizer first imagined the catalog as a way to advertise the talent of local male models, but soon realized that his pics of beefy boys flexing for the camera were themselves a hot commodity. In fact, "art studies" of the male physique, like the bodybuilding magazines that featured similar poses, were enjoying a postwar boom. But Mizer's Athletic Model Guild and its photographic compendium, *Physique Pictorial,* would revolutionize the field of physique art and photography. Alongside the work of a few other artists, it would become synonymous with the burgeoning "physique movement."

Although ostensibly marketed to art appreciators or physical-fitness enthusiasts, these magazines were, for many men, homoerotic publications that were an important—for some, the only—way of experiencing their sexuality. Simply receiving these publications in the mail, let alone being involved in their production, were acts of defiance in the face of a society that stigmatized homosexuality.

This homoerotica provided images for isolated gay men to imagine themselves as (homo)sexual beings. One gay man remembered the delight and affirmation of being fifteen and finding Tom of Finland drawings among his friend's belongings. "That was the first time that I could see myself in a gay situation with men," he recalled, "because I could see myself in those pictures."[2] However unlikely it is that a skinny fifteen-year-old might have found someone who actually looked like himself among the beefy behemoths in Tom's fantasy scenes, the drawings may have provided a different kind of possibility: In the 1950s, physique art and photography were among the only places one could view overtly sexualized images of men together. These images flew in the face of both the classic stereotype of the homosexual as a limp-wristed pansy as well as 1950s propaganda that to be a homosexual was to be sick, miserable, and isolated. Through these depictions of strong, macho hunks, gay men could reimagine both who they could be and what they could desire.

In the late 1940s, there existed a small coterie of artists and photographers who produced physique art and photography. Most were concentrated in three major cities—London, New York, and Los Angeles—and all were acquainted with one another at least by reputation.[3] Often wearing only their first name and geographic location as moniker—Bruce of Los Angeles, Lon of New York, Tom of Finland—the artists, like many in their audience, were gay men.

The new wave of physique artists who began—however sur-

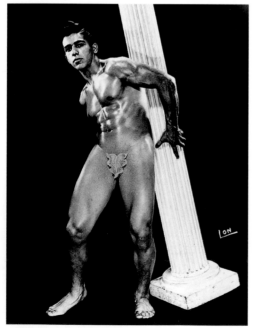

Lon. Male nude, New York, circa 1950. Lon of New York (born Alonzo Hanagan) built a flourishing studio business, which sprouted branches in Paris and London, and expanded into other areas, such as the sale of swim trunks and posing straps.

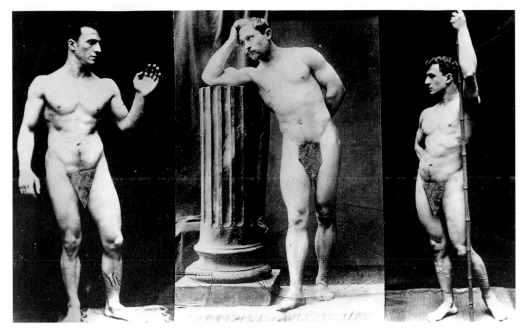

Three men in classic poses, early 1900s. This triptych from the early part of the century marks a tradition in homoerotica that takes its inspiration from classical antiquity. The models' poses are designed to invoke Greek and Roman statuary of the gods and the godlike.

reptitiously—to make the homoerotic content of their work explicit were a product of the post–World War II era. However, the physique movement and its publications have a much longer history. Beginning in the 1890s, at a time when middle-class white men were being thrust behind desks and further removed from work involving their hands and bodies, muscularity became increasingly central to a dominant ideal of manhood. As historian Gail Bederman has argued, "Middle-class men's new fascination with muscularity allowed strongmen like Eugene Sandow and Bernarr McFadden to make fortunes promoting themselves and marketing bodybuilding magazines like *Physical Culture.* By the 1890s, strenuous exercise and team sports had come to be seen as crucial to the development of powerful manhood."[4] Sandow, the Prussian bodybuilder, exhibited his feats of strength at the 1893 Columbian exhibition as a celebration of the highest accomplishments of muscular manliness. And tintypes featuring Sandow in nothing but sandals and a paste-on figleaf were all the rage in the 1890s.

This earliest male physique ideal, and one that has continued as an influence for decades, took classical antiquity as its inspiration. Sandow in his sandals, or any nameless beauty leaning against a Doric column, took from those props and conferred upon himself the glory that was ancient Greece and Rome. By invoking the putative birthplace of Western civilization, these images of male beauty at once reference, in cultural critic Richard Dyer's words, "classical antiquity as an unquestionable touchstone of the finest achievements of the human race" and, at the same time, position homosexuality at the center of that civilization. The classical ideal, thus, becomes a way of defending homosexuality in the present by calling up its heroic history in the distant past.[5] It also makes whiteness and Western culture central to depictions of homosexuality.

While a number of physique publications used Greece as a primary metaphor, another group came out of a tradition of physical culture, focusing on the body as a site of athletic prowess and physical fitness. Although there was considerable crossover between these two types of beefcake—bodybuilders adopted Greco-Roman poses and "Grecian" publications were filled with images of weightlifters—the physical culture genre emphasized building the body through exercise and sport rather than appreciating it as art object. Physical culture publications also directly engaged the reader, offering the average American man the chance to transform his own body and, presumably, model himself after the pictured ideals. Beginning in the 1920s, Charles Atlas featured advertisements for his regime of diet and exercise complete with photographic proof of how a "ninety-pound weakling" might re-create himself as the man of steel shown flexing for the camera. By the 1950s, the rise in muscle magazines reflected a boom in weightlifting and bodybuilding competitions across the country.[6]

Postwar physique publications were born out of this new muscle culture. Indeed, Bob Mizer tapped into the scene as a way to find models for his Athletic Model Guild, tracking down muscled hunks in their natural habitats. Mizer "did all his initial recruiting personally, visiting local gymnasiums and muscle beaches, setting up his tripod in the athletes' sporting hangouts. Flattered with the attention, men and boys were quite willing to flaunt their athletic prowess for the camera." These models were "dedicated bodybuilders . . . husky men muscled by hard labor, movie star hopefuls, drifters and an assortment of boy-next-door types."[7] Los Angeles was replete with these types, and if Bob could not make them all stars, he could at least put them in pictures.

The Athletic Model Guild began as an informal clearinghouse for the photographs of Mizer and his fellow artists. The Guild sent out bulk brochures crammed with photographs; typically more than a dozen shots filled one greeting card–size page. Because the brochures were to be dis-

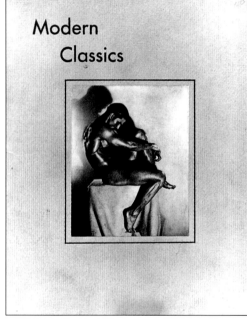

Tony Sansone. **Modern Classics.** *New York, 1932.* Dancer and artists' model Anthony J. "Tony" Sansone privately published this small volume of photographs of himself, taken by Edwin F. Townsend and Achille Volpe. Townsend is particularly renowned for his pictorialist treatment of the male figure, and had a profound influence on subsequent photographers of the male nude, including George Platt Lynes. Sansone proclaimed that this volume was "dedicated to artists, art lovers, body culturists."

tributed through the U.S. mail, the photographs needed to comply with U.S. postal regulations. At the time that meant—in practice, if not in clearly codified law—no full-frontal nudes could be shown; models' genitals needed to be covered by a "posing strap" (a loose-fitting jock strap); and no body hair could appear below the neck.

Complying with these strict postal regulations did not hurt business for AMG. Models wore the minimum U.S. postal requirement and, by 1950, Mizer decided that the artists' brochures, collected together with a cover by Los Angeles physique artist George Quaintance, could function as its own publication. In 1950 *Physique Pictorial* was born. Shortly thereafter, similar pictorials appeared as competition. *Tomorrow's Man,* which debuted in 1952, even outsold its "forerunner," though *Physique Pictorial* held a strong second place.[8] *Vim, Trim,* and *Grecian Guild Quarterly* added their titles to the physique pictorial genre. But *Physique Pictorial,* as well as being the originator, was unique to the genre for a number of reasons: Bob Mizer himself was more than just a purveyor of erotica. He was also a freethinker and antiestablishment civil libertarian who used his publication as a forum for his various battles. In tiny text below the images of boys in jock straps and sailor hats, Mizer urged his readers to join the American Civil Liberties Union, support homophile organizations, and fight censorship.

The publication also became a major venue for physique art, most

(top, left) **Physique Pictorial,** *October 1953.* COVER BY GEORGE QUAINTANCE

(below, left) **Physique Pictorial,** *September 1967.* COVER BY TOM OF FINLAND

Glenn Carrington. Amateur homoerotic photographs, New York, circa 1955. Men of color were seldom seen in the pages of physique magazines or among the glossy mail-order photographs. When images to one's particular liking were not readily available from commercial sources, resourceful connoisseurs manufactured their own erotica. Since these negatives had to be sent to a laboratory for processing, the use of posing straps was still considered prudent. The advent of Polaroid photography would change that aspect of homemade erotica for good.

significantly for the sketches of Tom of Finland. Born Touko Laaksonen in Helsinki, Tom of Finland was the name given him by Bob Mizer, who published the then-unknown artist's first sketches. Modeling his work on the physique art of George Quaintance, Tom substituted his own native characters (Finnish lumberjacks were his first offering) for Quaintance's very American archetypes. The first Tom of Finland cover debuted on the Spring 1957 issue of *Physique Pictorial,* which would go on to eventually commission and publish almost two hundred drawings by the artist over the next decade and a half.[9]

Tom of Finland is largely responsible for creating and disseminating new archetypes in the pantheon of homoerotica. Men in uniforms had a special place in Tom's *ouevre,* reflecting the artist's own experience of wartime Europe and finding an appreciative audience among American veterans of World War II.[10] This new physique art was resolutely modern. The classical gods of the earliest photographs were displaced by contemporary, working-class heroes: Sailors, athletes, cowboys, construction workers, and bikers edged out the men in sandals and gladiator helmets. This change was more than just a shift in style. To situate homosexuality, or at least homoerotica, in the present rather than the past was a new and radical move. As idealized and fantastic as Tom's world was, it was still closer to 1950s America than to either ancient Greece or Rome. His images conjured up Marlon Brando in *The Wild Ones* and James Dean in *Rebel Without a Cause.* They reflected and spoke to an emerging homosexual subculture in the United States, one that was just beginning to build its own public culture in print and in images.

Though postwar physique publications were drenched in homoerotic subtext and claimed a homosexual audience (as at least some segment of a larger audience), they never proclaimed themselves to be homoerotica as such. Indeed, the success of physique art and photography lay precisely in its ability to effectively "pass" and thus appeal to a broad public. By the mid-1950s, physique magazines claimed a wide circulation; according to one estimate, these publications counted a readership of between sixty thousand to seventy thousand.[11] In the 1950s and early '60s physique magazines were available by subscription and, in some parts of the country, could be purchased at local drugstores or picked up around bodybuilding gyms. Writing in the gay magazine *Body Politic,* Alan Miller reminisced about his "first encounter" with physique magazines, as a young boy in the early 1960s at a local barber shop: "The six barbers were—or so I vaguely remember—not the least bit embarrassed at having these things about, let alone that a young boy would be flipping through them." The physique pictorials of Miller's memory were very much a product of their time and, as he argues, "even when blatantly erotic, physique magazines were excused (one is not sure how successfully) as works for those interested in bodybuilding, art or nudism—anything to avoid labels being applied to the purchasers."[12]

But some did apply labels to the purchasers, and to physique publications in general, which were considered pornography in some quarters. Until 1965, mailable material was regulated and restricted by the 1873 Comstock Law, which forbade mailing or trading in "obscene, lewd, or lascivious" materials. The definition of obscenity was open to interpretation by the courts, but few small publishers could afford a lengthy or expensive court battle to test the matter. Beginning in the 1940s, the new postwar men's bodybuilding magazines were "warned to police their contents, even their ads" for homosexual content or face being barred from the U.S. mail.[13] Publishers of physique magazines tested the censors every time they used the U.S. mail.

The recipients of physique magazines—or of any kind of homoerotica—took great risks in receiving this material. Post office boxes, which could be held anonymously or under an assumed name, were one safeguard. Others employed more creative techniques of subterfuge. Because photographs with full-frontal nudity could not be sent through the mail, some ingenious inventor began painting fig leafs on the photographed nudes with washable ink. When the photographs arrived, the recipient merely needed to wash off the camouflage and enjoy.

The first major postal crackdown against physique pictorials occurred in 1960. Herman Womack, one of the largest distributors of

physique magazines, was selling forty thousand copies per month when the post office seized them in 1960. This occurred just six years after the postmaster of Los Angeles confiscated copies of the homophile magazine *One* and "refused to mail the magazine, on the grounds that it was 'obscene, lewd, lascivious and filthy.'" Homophile publications escaped further censure but the visual depiction of homosexuality remained a riskier matter.

In 1965 the Supreme Court heard Womack's case and in *Manual Enterprises* v. *Day* held that "even though the material appealed to the prurient tastes of male homosexuals and was 'dismally unpleasant, uncouth, and tawdry,' it lacked 'patent offensiveness' and therefore should not be considered obscene." The Court's decision created a climate in which physique magazines, and eventually a burgeoning market in gay pornography, could flourish. By 1965, total monthly sales of physique magazines topped 750,000. Circulation of new and more explicit gay porn magazines would eventually far outstrip those numbers.[14]

The patterns of making and distributing erotic materials changed dramatically in the late 1960s, when the far-reaching sexual revolution coincided with a series of court decisions that finally reversed many of the last vestiges of the nineteenth-century Comstock Law. In December of 1965, the first full-frontal male nude appeared in a publication: Philadel-

Bruce of Los Angeles. Envelope and physique photos, 1954. Bruce Bellas [Bruce of Los Angeles], publisher of *The Male Figure,* was another prolific photographer of the physique genre. Customers purchased these small prints by mail and might receive them, as this recipient did, as anonymous holders of post office boxes.

phia's *Drum* magazine, a homophile publication that combined "hard–hitting news, features, parodies, editorials and reviews" with campy comics and, after 1965, male nudes.[15] *Drum* heralded a new approach to gay male sexuality. As an advertisement for the magazine announced:

> *DRUM* stands for a realistic approach to sexuality in general and homosexuality in particular. *DRUM* stands for sex in perspective, sex with insight and, above all, sex with humor. *DRUM* presents news for "queers," and fiction for "perverts." Photo essays for "fairies," and laughs for "faggots."[16]

Following the lead of publications like *Drum*, it became increasingly clear to many in the gay community that homosexual liberation and a larger sexual liberation could never be separated.

Ralph Kelly. Two young men, Los Angeles, 1950s. Another technique used to skirt postal regulations that prohibited the mailing of photographs with frontal nudity was the use of washable ink. This rare pair of prints illustrates the "before and after" of this method.

Circa 1900.

FRIENDS AND LOVERS

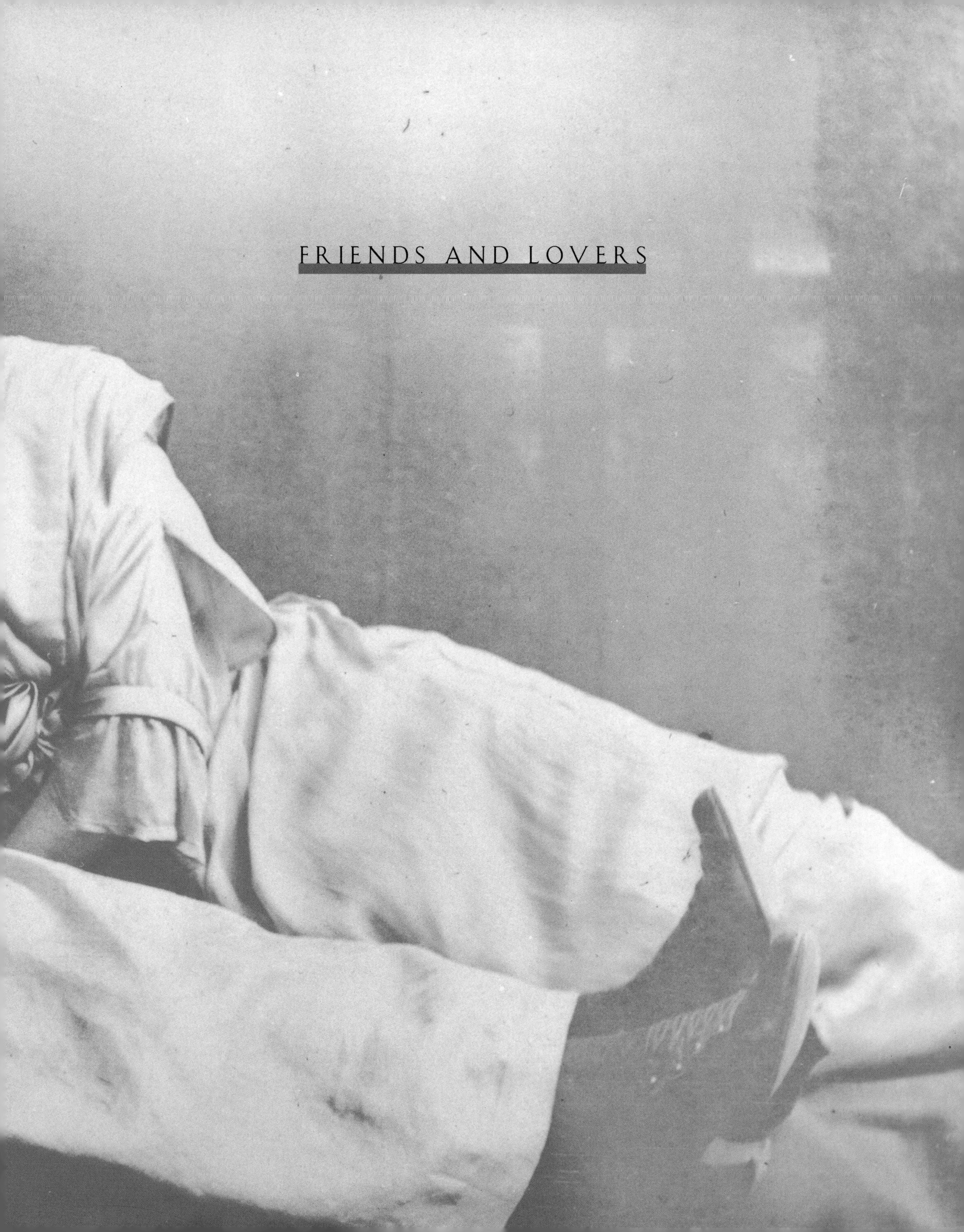

Circa the late nineteenth century.

Circa 1900.

Early twentieth century.

Early twentieth century.

Early twentieth century.

Early twentieth century.

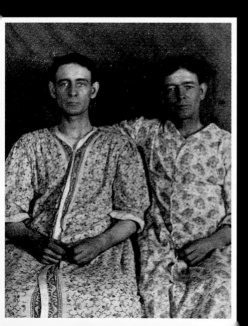

Early twentieth century.

Circa 1910.

Early twentieth century.

Early twentieth century.

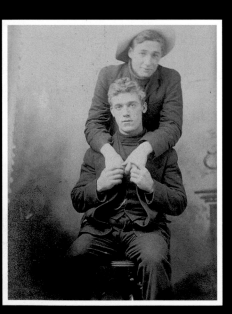

Coatesville, Pennsylvania, 1906.

Dorothee and friend,
Greenwich Village,
New York, 1929.

THE TREASURE BOX
GREENWICH VILLAGE
NEW YORK
23
©JESSIE TARBOX BEALS
OH HO! LETS GO TO THE TREASURE BO
AT 7 SHERIDAN SQUARE
WE'll SURELY FIND A MINE OF GIFIS
QUAINT AND RICH AND RARE_
MANDARIN COATS AND PERSIAN SCARVE
ODD RINGS AND CHINA NEW
WHICH TEDDY PECK AND BENJAMIN
WILL GLADLY SHOW TO YOU.
SO HO! YE HO THE TREASURE BOX
WITH PIRATES IN FULL VIEW.

Jessie Tarbox Beals. **The Treasure Box.** *Greenwich Village, New York, circa 1915.* COURTESY OF HOWARD GREENBERG GALLERY, NYC

Women in uniform, circa World War I.

Three men on a couch, New York, 1950s.

James Cummings and Glenn Carrington, Christmas card, Brooklyn, New York, circa 1960s.

A gay wedding, 1950s.

Helen and friend, Brooklyn, New York, circa 1936.

Priscilla and Regina, Brooklyn, New York, 1979.   © JEB (JOAN E. BIREN)

Gay Liberation Front activists Ronny and Jay, New York, 1969. © DIANA DAVIES

Please Join Us for Cocktails
to toast the
40th Anniversary of
Richmond Purington and Donald Vining
Sunday, May 4, 1986
4:30 to 7:00 P.M.
115 East 9th Street, Apt. 4C

Harry Gaeta, Tom Lenick, and Tom Wetmore

RSVP (212) 989-2047

Gifts Gratefully Declined.
(or, consider a donation to SAGE, if you wish.)

Longtime lovers
Richard Purinton
and Donald Vining,
1940s and 1980s.

Gay Pride March, New York, June 1981.
© BETTYE LANE

Embrace. Rob and John. *Gay Pride Rally, New York, 1992.* © BRUCE CRASTLEY

Domestic partners, March 1993. **Left to right:** *Gary Sechen, Wynn Miller, Fredda Rubin, and Katia Netto.*
© FRED W. McDARRAH

ORGANIZING

Homosexuals picketing in front of the White House, 1965.

AN EMERGING MINORITY

*Homosexuals constitute what can be termed
the unrecognized minority . . . Our minority status is similar,
in a variety of respects, to that of national, religious, and other ethnic groups:
in the denial of civil liberties; in the legal, extra-legal, and quasi-legal discrimination;
in the assignment of an inferior social position; in the exclusion
from the mainstreams of life and culture.*

—DONALD WEBSTER CORY,
THE HOMOSEXUAL IN AMERICA, 1951

World War II served as a national "coming out" for thousands of lesbians and gay men who met others like themselves and began to sense that they were part of a larger group.[1] Following the war, many decided to settle in the port cities with large gay subcultures. At the same time, a small number of lesbians and gay men began to see themselves as members of a minority group, drawing parallels between their struggle and those of African Americans

Frank Thompson with friend, New York, circa 1943. Frank Thompson befriended more than a few servicemen during World War II, when the city was overflowing with military personnel on leave.

and Jews. Though such ideas occasionally surfaced in gay novels and in the press in the late 1940s, the most important articulation of this argument appeared in Donald Webster Cory's groundbreaking book *The Homosexual in America,* published in 1951. Cory was particularly prescient in observing the specific challenge of organizing this newly defined minority. He observed that virtually all homosexuals at the time hid their sexuality because of shame and fear of "social punishment"; but it was only when gay people dared to be open about their homosexuality and came forward that others could do the same. Until society accepted homosexuals, few would so identify; but unless people spoke out about their homosexuality, societal attitudes would not change. Tellingly, "Donald Webster Cory" was itself a pseudonym.

By the time Cory's book was published, a few courageous lesbians and gay men had already taken up this challenge and began to found the first gay and lesbian organizations and publications. In the threatening climate of the McCarthy era these pioneers formed organizations that sponsored educational activities and social events, published newsletters and magazines, and cautiously worked to change attitudes as they tried to help the "deviant" or the "variant," as they called themselves, fit into American society.

One of the earliest efforts was launched by "Lisa Ben" (an anagram

HEADQUARTERS
97TH ENGINEER (GS) REGIMENT
CAMP SUTTON, NORTH CAROLINA

15 February 1944

Maggie dear girl-------,

        And how is my sweet one this A.M.? Just choking herself full of cock,
I bet. So much has happened since your last (and also your first) letter
to me that I felt I should pen you a few lines to give you a summary as to
what your daughterhas and is going through.

        To begin with, I was given a 6 day furlough.. Now don't start raving.
Darling that Giustizia woman monopolized all my time. Child she is getting
worse day by day. If I went to shit she had to come and smell my fart. I
dont know what I'm going to do with her.

        We went to the Onyx Club and saw Billie and Dizzy Gilespie and pitched
us a Bitch. You can get contact of her and geto some of those fine fine
buns. Drop her a line and make a date for Saturday night to go and see
Billie and suggest that he stay at your house. And Glenda my dear the rest
is up to you.

        This child I told you about in my other letter who was so fine. Well
Mary, I saw his meat at last. Lovely instrument. So round and full of life.
But I'm letting him rest for a while as I saw a boy with a bigger weapon and
he aint no slouch either!!!

        He came into my tent the other night and the lights were out and ofcourse
I was in bed and he sat on the side of my bed (andthere were two other fellows
in the tent) and we talked all of us and mother worked until she had the
whistle in her hand and Maizie we were kissing and carring on something awful
and still keeping up this heavy conversation... Oh Sister he is aw-Reet.....

        Also the Bugler swears he's gonna get some of my ass. And I think he's
right. Boy is he cute,... Do you think I can have all these children and
still be a lady???? Write and let me know your answer. I'm seriously
thinking of paying a visit to JOHN J. ANTHONY....

                        Your daughter,

                        THE ONE AND ONLY

(left) *Letter from "Shep" Salisbury to Glenn Carrington, February 15, 1944.* These boyfriends sustained a correspondence, often affectionately campy, throughout the war. Salisbury was one of the 700,000 African Americans who comprised 4 percent of the nation's military force during World War II.

(below) *Dorothee Gore and friend, probably Fort Oglethorpe, Georgia, circa 1943.* These women lived in New York's Greenwich Village in the early 1940s. When the United States entered World War II, they enlisted in the Women's Auxiliary Army Corps.

for lesbian), a young secretary in Los Angeles, who published nine issues of *Vice Versa,* the first lesbian "magazine" in the United States, in 1947–48. Unable to have it printed because of the subject matter, she typed the entire magazine twice with carbon paper, producing five copies each time, and distributed the ten copies among her "gay gal" friends, and their friends, in the Los Angeles area. Ben wrote most of the material herself—poems, book and movie reviews, humor, and occasional political commentary. Her own vision, radical for its time, infuses *Vice Versa:* "I for one consider myself neither an error of nature nor some sort of psychological freak. Friends

(above) **Vice Versa** *publisher "Lisa Ben,"* *1947.*

(right) **Vice Versa: America's Gayest Magazine.** *Los Angeles, February 1948.*

of similar tendencies . . . also refuse to regard themselves in this light . . . Is it not possible that we are just as natural and normal by our standards as so-called 'normals' are by theirs?"[2]

Ben had to stop publishing *Vice Versa* when she changed jobs and could no longer type the magazine at work. But her short-lived efforts were appreciated by her readers. One of them, writing to thank Ben for sending copies of the magazine, observed, "We have enjoyed reading them, and I, personally, felt that sought-after feeling of *belonging* to a group *somewhere* in 'society', while reading with you."[3]

Some of the first gay organizations also sprang up in the years immediately following the war.[4] In New York City, the Veterans' Benevolent Association, founded in 1945, had a membership of between seventy-five and one hundred and ran social functions for as many as four hundred or five hundred gay men. The group also informally helped those who were arrested, confronted employment problems, or encountered other difficulties because of their homosexuality. In Los Angeles, the Knights of the Clock, founded in 1950, was a social group for interracial gay couples. Most significantly, beginning in 1948, Harry Hay, a Los Angeles Communist Party activist and teacher, developed the idea for "a service and welfare organization devoted to the protection and improvement" of what he termed "Society's Androgynous Minority."[5] It took him over two years to find anyone who would join his enterprise. By late 1950, Hay had recruited four other men and they started what came to be called the Mattachine Society, named after the masked jesters who spoke out against authority in medieval times.

The founders of Mattachine believed that homosexuals were " 'largely unaware' that they in fact constituted 'a social minority imprisoned within a dominant culture.' "[6] Mattachine wanted to rouse this minority by focusing on homosexuals' differences from mainstream society, and by promoting the value of a distinctive gay culture, "paralleling the emerging cultures of our fellow-minorities—the Negro, Mexican, and Jewish Peoples." The group, as outlined in their mission statement, sought to unify homosexuals "isolated from their own kind" and give them a sense of "belonging," "to educate" homosexuals and heterosexuals, to "provide leadership to the whole mass of social deviants," and to organize political opposition to "discriminatory and oppressive legislation."[7]

The Mattachine founders were faced with an openly hostile society. Harry Hay recalls:

> The anti-Communist witch-hunts were very much in operation; the House Un-American Activities Committee had investigated Communist "subversion" in Hollywood. The purge of Homosexuals from the State Department took place. The country, it seemed to me, was beginning to move toward fascism and McCarthyism; the Jews wouldn't be used as a scapegoat this time— the painful example of Germany was still too clear to us. The Black organizations were already pretty successfully looking out for their interests. It was obvious McCarthy was setting up the pattern for a new scapegoat, and it was going to be us—Gays. We had to organize, we had to move, we had to get started.[8]

Mattachine Society Christmas party, Los Angeles, 1951 or 1952. *Left to right:* Dale Jennings (in profile), Harry Hay, Rudy Gernreich, Stan Witt, Bob Hull, Chuck Rowland, and Paul Bernard. © JIM GRUBER

Confronted with the difficulty of organizing homosexuals during the McCarthy era, Hay and two of his colleagues drew on their experience in Communist Party organizing. They created a secret cell-like structure for the group that offered members the privacy and safety they needed in a fearful and repressive political climate. Many participants used pseudonyms to protect their identities. As the organization grew, attracting mostly men but also some women, the Mattachine sponsored several discussion groups that dealt with various aspects of homosexual life.

In 1951, the Mattachine Society held its first semipublic dance in Los Angeles, attracting many people who were unaware of the discussion groups. Hay recalls that the dances, which drew upwards of three hundred men, were transformative. "One guy came up to me in the course of the evening and said, 'Man, you don't know what it means to be able to hold another man in your arms and dance and all of a sudden walk outside and stand under the stars and breathe.' "9

In 1952 the Mattachine Society organized its first political action around the issue of police entrapment when Dale Jennings, one of the founders, was arrested for "lewd and dissolute conduct" in a Los Angeles park. Forming an ad hoc committee to preserve Mattachine's secrecy, they raised money for Jennings's defense and publicized the case in the community. The flyers they distributed in Los Angeles's gay venues—beaches, bars, and cruisy parks and rest-

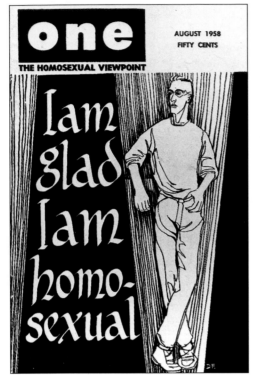

(above) **One.** *Los Angeles, August 1958.* *One*'s politics was so far ahead of some of its readers that when it published this issue, many subscribers responded to the head-line by canceling their subscriptions.

(right) **"How Can I Ever Face the World?"** *The Mattachine Society Inc. of New York, circa 1966.* This brochure characterized the man on its cover as a "doomed . . . outsider . . . cut off from his family, his country, and his God," who leads a life of "misery" and "loneliness."

This man presumably needed the Mattachine, which catered to "the better adjusted, less sensational, and more useful homosexual who not only makes valuable contributions to society, but is a decent law-abiding citizen."

rooms—were probably the first in the country to raise the issue of homosexual rights. Ultimately, the jury deadlocked and the charges were dropped, but the exposure generated by the case led to a significant increase in membership and the establishment of Mattachine discussion groups throughout southern California as well as in the San Francisco Bay area.10

This newer membership was more conservative and, in 1953, the founders were forced to resign because of their Communist ties. The group eliminated

the secret organizational structure, rejected the founders' radical vision of a distinctive gay culture, and adopted a more assimilationist approach: Homosexuals were the same as everyone else and simply needed help adjusting to mainstream society. The new philosophy is best summed up in the slogan for the Mattachine Society's 1954 convention, "Evolution, *Not* Revolution."[11]

With its more modest, primarily educational goals and a disavowal of political activity, the Mattachine Society and its publications grew through the 1950s. Its leaflets were printed in many languages and circulated globally. The group began publishing the *Mattachine Review,* which reached a

Homosexuals Are Different . . . *Mattachine Society Inc. of New York, 1966.* The New York chapter of the Mattachine Society, established in 1955, sponsored educational meetings, sought out the advice of professionals, tried to serve the needs of homosexuals, and operated a lending library of more than one thousand books on the subject of homosexuality.

national audience of approximately twenty-two hundred subscribers, and chapters were started in San Francisco, New York, Philadelphia, Chicago, Boston, Denver, and Detroit. Local groups also published newsletters and provided educational programs, as well as opportunities for socializing. But in spite of its modest success at sustaining an organization and creating a voice for homosexuals, Mattachine's total membership remained small— only 230 in 1960.

One of the Mattachine Society's discussion groups started an independent magazine called *One* in 1953. Within months it had a national circulation of two thousand, which grew to five thousand by the following year. The magazine promoted a positive and controversial view of homosexuality, less assimilationist than that of the Mattachine Society. *One* focused primarily on issues of concern to gay men, although occasional pieces addressed women's issues, and a number of lesbians—several of them original readers of *Vice Versa*—were on the staff. Eventually, the publishers of the magazine also founded the One Institute, which offered classes in homophile studies and published the *One Institute Quarterly,* the first scholarly journal on homosexuality in the United States.

One magazine led the way in fighting censorship, achieving one of the homophile movement's most important victories. When the October 1954 issue of *One* was seized by the postal authorities for being "obscene, lewd, lascivious and filthy," the magazine challenged the ruling. After losing cases at the federal district and appeals court levels, *One* was triumphant in 1958: in a landmark decision, the Supreme Court reversed the lower courts, in effect declaring that *One,* and by extension the discussion of homosexuality, was not per se pornographic.[12]

The Daughters of Bilitis (DOB), the first lesbian political organization in the United States, was started in San Francisco in 1955. Del Martin and Phyllis Lyon, who became the driving forces of DOB, were invited to the home of a friend who wanted to start a social group as an alternative to the lesbian bars. Four lesbian couples were in attendance. The women decided on an arcane name derived from the "Songs of Bilitis," a poem by the nineteenth-century French writer Pierre Louys, in which the songs are offered as the work of Bilitis, a poetess who supposedly lived on Lesbos in the time of Sappho. "We thought that 'Daughters of Bilitis' would sound like any other women's lodge—you know, like the Daughters of the Nile or DAR," recalled one of the founders. " 'Bilitis' would mean something to us, but not to any outsider. If anyone asked us, we could always say we belong to a poetry club."[13]

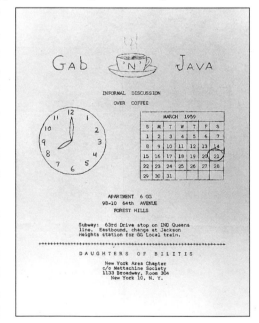

Though started as a social group, DOB quickly turned toward education and politics. The eight original members hammered out a constitution and by-laws and

Gab 'N' Java. *Daughters of Bilitis, New York Area Chapter, 1959.* Around thirty women would attend the DOB's meetings, which took place in women's homes. Discussion topics included issues of appearance ("Should Lesbians Wear Skirts?"), fitting in, legal problems, therapy experiences, and coming out to parents.

forged a mission statement for the new organization that included "education of the variant . . . to enable her to understand herself and make her adjustment to society"; "education of the public . . . leading to an eventual breakdown of erroneous taboos and prejudices"; and changing the laws regarding homosexuals.[14]

Barbara Gittings attended her first DOB meeting while visiting San Francisco. "I was in a room with twelve other lesbians for the first time in my life and, 'Oh! what a thrill that was!'"[15] Gittings went on to establish a DOB chapter in New York in 1958; others were founded in Los Angeles and Chicago, but membership remained small—110 in 1960. Though DOB's original eight members had been an even mix of middle-class and working-class women, the latter left to form a new social group when DOB became politically active. Thereafter the organization clung to notions of middle-class respectability, frowning on working-class bar culture and consequently failing to appeal to many of the most strongly lesbian-identified women in the 1950s—the butch-femme women who frequented the bars. DOB also faced the problem of organizing women who were fearful of the consequences of participating in a lesbian organization. In order to provide as much safety as possible, the group encouraged women not to use their own names.

The forces rallied against the founding of a lesbian political organization in the 1950s were formidable. Popular culture and the media demonized lesbians as sexual predators, as one typical article in *Jet* magazine, quoting a doctor, warned: "'The lesbian makes a point of seeking out widows, lonesome women, the victims of broken love affairs, and those who have suffered from nervous breakdowns and other mental ills.' . . . With one woman in four remaining unmarried in the U.S. today, spinsters more and more are becoming likely prey for lesbians."[16] Simply confronting such stereotypes, as DOB did, was a significant political challenge in a decade shadowed by McCarthyism.

Beginning in 1956 DOB published a magazine, the *Ladder,* which was distributed nationally. Reaching hundreds of readers, this publication fostered a lesbian community and gave voice to the concerns and interests of its readers. The *Ladder* addressed a host of important issues, though often in language that reflected the self-hating attitudes that went largely unquestioned at the time. For example, a piece about lesbians who had

The Ladder. *San Francisco, December 1956.* Published by the Daughters of Bilitis, *The Ladder* was distributed to a national audience, particularly "the lonely isolated lesbians away from the big cities."

children from previous marriages offered helpful information but was titled, "Raising Children in a Deviant Relationship."[17] Kay Lahusen, a New York DOB member, recalls the thinking of the time:

> The magazine was called *The Ladder* because you were supposed to climb up the ladder and into the human race on an OK basis. The little lesbian was beginning to climb the ladder, upgrading herself so that she would become an OK person instead of a "variant," who had a poor self-image, who didn't hold a regular job, who wasn't a participating member of society. As if there weren't thousands of lesbians who were great contributors to society.[18]

But the *Ladder* also provided a forum for some spirited exchanges, and occasional insightful observations. Playwright Lorraine Hansberry wrote in (anonymously) suggesting the "possible concept that homosexual persecution and condemnation has at its roots not only social ignorance, but a philosophically active anti-feminist dogma."[19]

Hansberry's participation, if only epistolary, was unusual as few people of color were active in the homophile movement. While two of DOB's original eight founders were a Filipina and a Chicana, they left early on and thereafter DOB was overwhelmingly white. The same was true of all the homophile groups. Los Angeles activist Jim Kepner recalls:

> There were usually one or two Blacks, two or three Latins and a very occasional Chinese, around ONE, DOB, Mattachine, and later groups such as Pride and SIR, but except for Tony Reyes who, as Don Slater's lover . . . was an incorporator of ONE, & long a silent vote on the Board of Trustees, they took no leadership positions.[20]

The Ladder: A Lesbian Review. *San Francisco, June 1966.* Ernestine Eckstein [pseud.], pictured on this cover, was the vice president of the New York chapter of the Daughters of Bilitis at the time. "Picketing I regard as almost a conservative activity now," observed Eckstein. "The homosexual has to call attention to the fact that he's been unjustly acted upon. This is what the Negro did."

DOB departed from this pattern in the mid-1960s when Ernestine Eckstein, an African-American woman, was elected vice president of the New York chapter.

Through the 1950s and 1960s, Mattachine Society, Daughters of Bilitis, and *One* worked together on what they called "homophile" issues. The choice of the term was central to their self-definition and suggests how these organizations positioned themselves in the political landscape of a repressive era. They pointedly presented themselves *not* as homosexual organizations, but rather as groups of concerned individuals (homosexual *and* heterosexual) that dealt with the problems of the homosexual. Seeking to educate themselves and the public, and to change social attitudes, the homophile movement drew on the expertise of liberal psychiatrists, doctors, lawyers, theologians, and others to make its case. Del Martin and Phyllis Lyon of DOB recall the ethos:

> It wasn't until [much later] that we realized we knew a whole lot more about homosexuality than Joe Psychiatrist and Joe Lawyer. Back then we didn't know . . . We needed support from the establishment, from heterosexuals. We were at a point where [we asked] how *we* could be the ones to deal with the public . . . You just can't begin to realize the fear that was involved and how scared we were. And we [the leadership] were just as scared as everybody else.[21]

While their membership remained small, the homophile organizations and their publications exerted a greater influence than their numbers might suggest. The very existence of these organizations helped isolated lesbians and gay men come to terms with their homosexuality. "They might still be isolated, geographically," reflects Barbara Gittings, "but as long as they knew that a thousand miles away there was a group, as long as they could occasionally get some kind of publication, it was so much better than simply living in their own little cocoon."[22]

As time went on, even the isolated lesbian or gay man who was unaware of the homophile groups and their publications could find out more about the gay world. In addition to the widespread availability of lesbian pulps (and a comparable male genre), the 1960s saw a boom in the publication of

Homo-scare pulps, 1962–67.

"homo-scare" paperbacks that raised the horrifying specter of homosexuality while simultaneously providing useful information about homophile organizations, gay neighborhoods, legal issues, and cruising venues.[23]

The decade also witnessed a barrage of mainstream media coverage of lesbians and gay men. In 1963 a front-page story in the *New York Times* disclosed "the city's most sensitive open secret—the presence of what is probably the greatest homosexual population in the world and its increasing openness."[24] Similar stories ran in newspapers around the country, as cities "discovered" the gay communities right under their noses. National magazines, including *Life, Look, Time,* and *Harper's,* also ran features. Though the coverage was mixed at best—and often deeply homophobic—it did give lesbians and gay men greater mainstream visibility.

In the early 1960s some members of homophile groups became increasingly militant: They challenged the conservatism of Mattachine and DOB leadership, questioned the groups' reliance on "experts," promoted media visibility, and adopted direct-action tactics like demonstrations. These activists looked to the civil rights movement for inspiration and lessons, concluding that a "vigorous civil liberties, social action approach" had been much more effective for African Americans than a "program of information and education." "We must DEMAND our rights, boldly," wrote Mattachine activist Frank Kameny, "not beg cringingly for mere privileges, and not be satisfied with crumbs tossed to us."[25]

On the East Coast, a handful of activists in New York's Mattachine and DOB, Philadelphia's Janus Society, and the Mattachine Society of Washington developed a more militant and confrontational vision for the homophile movement. In 1963 the four groups established East Coast Homophile Organizations (ECHO), a loose coalition whose monthly meetings and annual conferences became an important forum where the activists could exchange information, talk strategy, build alliances, and plan joint actions. As the activists made their views known and implemented some of their strategies, they attracted new members to the established homophile organizations, but their radical positions provoked fierce battles with an entrenched conservative leadership.

One of the most heated debates was over the issue of whether homosexuality was an illness, a view widely propagated by psychiatrists in the 1960s. Frank Kameny and Jack Nichols, the founders of the Mattachine Society of Washington, aggressively challenged the homophile activists to reject the medical model of homosexuality. Ultimately, Kameny and

Nichols's position prevailed when the Mattachine groups in Washington and New York adopted this resolution in 1965: "In the absence of valid evidence to the contrary, homosexuality is not a sickness, disturbance, or other pathology in any sense, but is merely a preference, orientation, or propensity, on par with, and different in kind from, heterosexuality."[26]

Demonstrations too were a source of controversy. For instance, many members of DOB believed that "demonstrations which define the homosexual as a unique minority defeat the very cause for which the homosexual strives—*to be an integral part of society*."[27] Nevertheless, in keeping with their more confrontational vision, the activists, including some DOB women, proceeded with demonstrations. The first homosexual rights demonstration in New York (and probably the first in the country) was held in 1964 to protest the army's treatment of homosexuals. In 1965 ECHO members picketed at the White House, the Pentagon, the State Department, the Civil Service Commission, and the United Nations. Also that year, activist Craig Rodwell dreamed up the idea of an annual

(left) **A button from the 1964 ECHO conference.** This is the earliest known homosexual rights button.

(below) **Group portrait, officers of homophile organizations (including Chicago and San Francisco groups), East Coast Homophile Organizations Conference (ECHO), Barbizon Hotel, New York, 1965.** The theme of ECHO's 1965 meeting was "The Homosexual Citizen in the Great Society."

(below, right) **The Homosexual League of New York and the League for Sexual Freedom picketing at the U.S. Army's Induction Center on Whitehall Street, New York, September 19, 1964.** Renée Vera Cafiero is at left.

(below, inset) **The original placard carried in the 1964 demonstration.**

New York's first homosexual rights demonstration had only ten participants, half of whom were heterosexual. Picketers protested the army's policy of dishonorably discharging lesbians and gay men and for not respecting the confidentiality of draft records.

demonstration at Independence Hall on July 4th, to remind people "that a group of Americans still don't have their basic rights to life, liberty and the pursuit of happiness."[28]

These early demonstrations for homosexual rights were relatively small affairs, with anywhere from ten to fifty people participating. "Dress and appearance" were to be "conservative and conventional," according to Mattachine rules. "Good order, good appearance, and dignity of bearing are essential." The women wore dresses, stockings, and heels and the men donned suits, white shirts, and ties. Beards were "discouraged." These early pickets had a profound effect on those who participated. Demonstrators in the First Annual Reminder at Independence Hall on July 4, 1965, reported the following reactions: "Today I lost the last bit of fear"; "Today it was as if a weight dropped off my soul"; and "This was the proudest day of my life."[29]

The homophile movement also worked on a number of other less-public fronts. Through letter-writing campaigns, meetings with officials, and court challenges, activists pressured both federal and local governments to end harassment and discrimination against lesbians and gay men. Washington Mattachine took on the Civil Service Commission; New York Mattachine successfully worked to end police entrapment, pressured the city to curtail antigay discrimination in municipal hiring, and challenged state regulations that effectively made gay bars illegal.

In one noteworthy action, four homophile activists decided to challenge the New York State Liquor Authority's regulation that prohibited

bars and restaurants from serving homosexuals. Accompanied by five reporters, the group visited a number of bars until they were denied service at Julius', a longtime Greenwich Village gay bar. The incident drew a denial from the SLA chairman that his agency told bars not to serve homosexuals and precipitated an investigation by the chairman of the city's Human Rights Commission.

Mattachine Society members at Julius' bar during the "sip-in," New York, April 21, 1966. Left to right: John Timmins (coat over shoulder), Dick Leitsch, Craig Rodwell, and Randy Wicker.
© FRED W. McDARRAH

On the West Coast, a number of progressive developments occurred in San Francisco in the early 1960s, most notably political organizing in gay bars. Drawing on his popularity among bar patrons, drag queen José Sarria drew six thousand votes when he ran for the Board of Supervisors as an open homosexual in 1961. New groups like the Tavern Guild and the Society for Individual Rights (SIR) also found many of their members in the bars, perceiving a potentially large constituency that the other homophile groups ignored. SIR was innovative in recognizing that in order to build a gay political movement it was necessary to foster a sense of community, and that social activities were central to that mission.[30] The organization bought its own building and started a community center, probably the first gay center in the country. San Francisco was also in the forefront when, in 1964, homophile activists and liberal Protestant clergy founded the Council on Religion and the Homosexual, an organization that proved critical in fostering support for homosexual rights among liberal heterosexuals.

The homophile developments of the 1960s took place in a decade that witnessed radical changes throughout American society. These changes affected not just homophile activists, but all homosexuals, and ultimately had a profound influence on the direction of lesbian and gay politics and culture. The civil rights movement became the model for the liberation struggles not only of gays and lesbians, but of women, Chicanos, and other minorities. The New Left formulated a radical critique of

American society, and people took to the streets to protest the escalation of the war in Southeast Asia. The student movement disrupted the nation's campuses, and riots erupted in Detroit, Newark, Cleveland, and Los Angeles's Watts. Social mores changed as the development of the birth control pill facilitated an explosive sexual revolution, and the counterculture took hold as sex, drugs, and rock and roll became widely popular. The establishment was challenged on all levels as "Question Authority" became the leitmotif of the decade. Many lesbians and gay men, although usually closeted to others, were present in every organization, movement, march, and protest, from Selma to Chicago, from the NAACP to the yippies. Many more, as noncombatant citizens of the global village, watched all of the decade's developments on television.

As participants and viewers, masses of lesbians and gay men became politicized and began to see the extent of their own oppression. Black les-

Demonstrators marching at Independence Hall during the "2nd Annual Reminder," Philadelphia, July 4, 1966. Initiated in 1965, the reminders occurred every year through 1969.

"NOW WE ARE MARCHING ON"

Mine eyes have seen the struggles of the Negroes and the Jews,
I have seen the countries trampled where the laws of men abuse,
But you crush the homosexual with anything you choose,
Now we are marching on.

[CHORUS]
Glory, glory, hallelujah,
Glory, glory, hallelujah,
Glory, glory, hallelujah,
Now we are marching on.

Your masquerading morals squad has twisted all we've said,
You've put peepholes in our bathrooms, and made laws to rule our bed,
We ask you to treat us fairly, but you always turn your head,
Now we are marching on. [Chorus]

In your so-called Great Society you've given us no place,
We bring to you our problems, and you stand and slap our face,
How can you boast of freedom and ignore this great disgrace,
Now we are marching on. [Chorus]

Now we've asked, and begged, and pleaded for the right to have a life,
Free to choose the one we love, and free from man-made strife,
But you turn around and stab us with your legislative knife,
Now we are marching on. [Chorus]

We've been drowned out by injustice till our whispers can't be heard,
You have shattered all our dreams and hopes and yet we never stirred,
But we're rising in a chorus and you'll soon hear every word,
Now we are marching on. [Chorus]

The civil rights you took from us we want them back again,
We will talk and write and picket, until we see you bend,
If you do not give them freely, we will take them, my friend,
Now we are marching on. [Chorus]

Sung to the tune of "The Battle Hymn of the Republic"; lyrics written for the "2nd Annual Reminder," Independence Hall, Philadelphia, July 4, 1966.[31]

Homosexual rights buttons, New York, circa 1965. These buttons were created by activist Randy Wicker. The lavender = sign was inspired by the civil rights movement's black = sign.

(left) **Counterdemonstrator at an anti-Vietnam War protest, Washington, D.C., 1965.** © DIANA DAVIES

(right) **Students for a Democratic Society (SDS) poster, 1968.**

bian activist Maua Adele Ajanaku reflects, "African Americans said 'No More!' [We] refused to hide behind the stereotypes we were supposed to have . . . And then everybody got to feeling whatever their oppression was, 'Well maybe I don't have to take this either.' "[32] By the late 1960s more and more lesbians and gay men got this message and the pace of developments accelerated. New homophile political organizations and alliances were formed. In 1966 fifteen groups founded the North American Conference of Homophile Organizations (NACHO), the first national gay and lesbian coalition. The groups' combined memberships totaled more than six thousand. NACHO established a national legal fund that supported court cases that challenged discriminatory immigration and military policies, published studies on homosexual law reform and employment discrimination, and helped start homophile groups in unorganized cities. In 1967 activists at Columbia University started the Student Homophile League, the first gay group on an American campus, and chapters followed at New York University, Cornell, and Stanford. Also that year, approximately two hundred gay men and lesbians in Los Angeles publicly protested police harassment and raids on gay bars in what was then the largest gay demonstration to date.

The late sixties also witnessed significant cultural developments. In

1967, activist Craig Rodwell opened the Oscar Wilde Memorial Bookshop in Greenwich Village, the first lesbian and gay bookstore in the world. That same year in Los Angeles, the *Advocate,* later to become a national gay magazine, started publishing, and the Reverend Troy Perry established the Metropolitan Community Church, a nondenominational church for lesbians and gay men. In 1968 Los Angeles's first gay-in took place in Griffith Park.

By the end of the decade, there were about fifty homophile organizations in more than twenty-five cities around the United States. Homophile groups were active in New York, Philadelphia, Washington, D.C., Boston, San Francisco, and Los Angeles. Lesbians and gay men in smaller cities were also organizing; there were groups in Bethlehem, Pennsylvania; Syracuse, Ithaca, and Albany, New York; Lincoln, Nebraska; Kansas City and Denver; Dallas and Houston; Sacramento and Seattle; and Ohio alone had *eight* Mattachine chapters. Many lesbian and gay activists were no longer looking toward the experts and society for understanding and acceptance. Instead, they had come to recognize and fight for their equal rights within American society.

Emblematic of this new attitude was a dramatic change in language. In 1968, NACHO, inspired by the "Black Is Beautiful" slogan, adopted "Gay Is Good" as its motto. In even more radical rhetoric, in the spring of 1969, West Coast activists began to agitate for "gay revolution" and "gay power" and called themselves Pink Panthers. On the East Coast too there was a new rebellious spirit. Only months before Stonewall, Philadelphia's Homophile Action League published these prescient words: "We are living in an age of revolution, and one of the bywords of revolution in this country is 'confrontation.'"[33]

(above) **Demonstrators protest police harassment and raids outside the Black Cat bar, Los Angeles, 1967.** This protest was part of a coordinated effort by minority groups to protest the brutal policies of the Los Angeles police. Following the Black Cat demonstration, gay organizations in Los Angeles became more militant and attracted more participants.

(below) **Buttons, circa 1968.**

Gay Liberation Front, New York, 1969.
© DIANA DAVIES

GAY LIBERATION

*Homosexuals took to the streets in New York City
last weekend and joined the revolution.*

—LEO E. LAURENCE,
BERKELEY BARB, JULY 4, 1969

The night when the Stonewall Riots came along," observed Craig Rodwell, "just everything came together at that one moment. People quite often ask, 'Well what was special about that night, Friday, June 27, 1969?' There was no one thing that was special about it, it was just everything coming together."[1] Stonewall was actually only the beginning of this "coming together." An explosion of activity followed the riots as gay men and lesbians

(right) **Buttons, *circa 1969.***

(below) ***First Christopher Street Liberation Day March, June 28, 1970.*** In the wake of Stonewall, activists decided that the Annual Reminder should be replaced by a march in New York the following June to commemorate the anniversary of the riots.
© FRED W. McDARRAH

organized into a mass movement for the first time in history. The name they gave to their struggle, "gay liberation," embodied their radical agenda. The new activists rejected the medical label "homosexual" and the euphemistic "homophile," and embraced the word "gay," a term popular among lesbians and gay men themselves. They saw society's "homophobia," a new term that described the irrational fear and hatred of homosexuals, as the problem and demanded "GAY POWER TO GAY PEOPLE!"[2]

Thousands of lesbians and gay men were drawn to the movement. While an earlier homophile demonstration might have attracted fifty people, in June 1970 several thousand participated in a march commemorating the first anniversary of the Stonewall Riots. These new activists created an extraordinary number of organizations in the wake of the riots. By the end of 1970, the roughly fifty homophile groups that existed at the time of Stonewall had mushroomed to two hundred, and by the end of 1973, more than one thousand lesbian and gay organizations had been founded nationwide—gay churches and synagogues, political caucuses and youth groups, counseling centers and consciousness-raising groups.

In its most radical formulation, the goal of gay liberationists was not simply to win acceptance for a lesbian and gay minority. Rather, they questioned the very categories "homosexual" and "heterosexual" and be-

lieved in the ultimate dissolution of this sexual bi-
nary: They wanted to liberate the homosexual in
everyone. Dennis Altman formulated this view in
his seminal 1971 book *Homosexual: Oppression and
Liberation*:

> The vision of liberation I hold is precisely one
> that would make the homo/hetero distinction
> irrelevant. For that to happen, however, we shall
> all have to recognize our bisexual
> potential . . . The liberal sees homosexuals as a
> minority to be assisted into a full place in soci-
> ety. The radical sees homosexuality as a compo-
> nent of all people including her/him-
> self . . . Gay liberation liberates straights as much
> as gays.[3]

Proud, open, and defiant about their sexuality, gay
liberationists made "coming out" the linchpin of a
strategy that emphasized gay visibility. "Out of the
Closets, Into the Streets!" became the rallying cry
of the new generation. "Coming out," which had
long meant making one's debut in gay society, was redefined as the act of
publicly acknowledging one's homosexuality to the straight world.

    Historian John D'Emilio has argued that coming out was a "tactical
stroke of great genius," since this act was something that any gay man or
lesbian could do to radically transform his or her own life and potentially
change societal attitudes. Once they had given up the protection of their
privacy, they then had a personal stake in building a gay liberation movement that would offer them a new kind of defense. Initiated by radicals
who were accustomed to challenging the status quo, coming out was
quickly adopted as a popular stategy by many gay people. Indeed, "Coming out became . . . the quintessential expression of sixties cultural radicalism. It was 'doing your own thing' with a vengeance; it embodied the
insight that 'The personal is political' as no other single act could."[4]

    The coming-out strategy gave the gay liberation movement a poten-
tially vast number of recruits. As one flyer stated, "Every gay person who
makes love, feels frustrated or oppressed, or is angered by discrimination

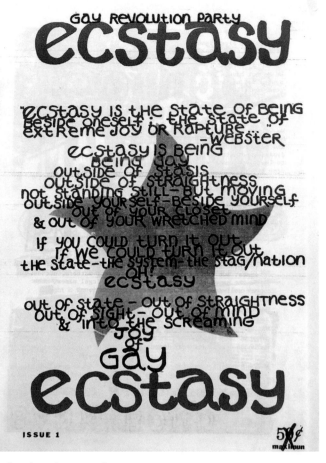

Ecstasy. New York, circa 1971.

Gay Is Angry. *New York, circa 1972.*
COLLAGE BY JUAN CARLOS

(opposite, top) **Gay Liberation Front meeting, Washington Square Methodist Church, New York, 1970.** © DIANA DAVIES

against gays is a political person." Even those who never participated in organizations or demonstrations were affected as openness and pride were widely embraced by lesbians and gay men. Perhaps most significantly, as D'Emilio has noted, "Gay liberation transformed homosexuality from a stigma that one kept carefully hidden into an identity that signified membership in a community organizing for freedom."[5]

"Before I joined Gay Lib I was ashamed of being a lesbian," commented activist Karla Jay in 1970. "I thought there was something wrong with me. The first time I told somebody I was a lesbian I had a real trauma. I couldn't get the word out of my mouth. But in Gay Lib I saw other people saying they were gay and proud. They were so beautiful and free—I was really touched by their contagious pride."[6]

The new gay liberation groups dismissed the work of their homophile forebears, disparagingly characterizing them as Uncle Toms or the gay NAACP. "The older groups," commented Michael Brown of Gay Liberation Front, "are oriented toward getting accepted by the Establishment but what the Establishment has to offer is not worth my time." Not surprisingly, many of the older homophile activists were critical of gay liberation, much as they had objected to the ideas and strategies of the more militant homophile activists in the 1960s. As Don Slater, active in Los Angeles homophile politics and publishing since the early 1950s, commented in 1970, "People should stop thinking of homosexuals as a class. They're not. We have spent 20 years convincing people that homosexuals are no different than anyone else, and here these kids come along and reinforce what society's thought all along—that homosexuals are different—that they're 'queer.' 'Gay' is good! To hell with that. Individuals are good."[7]

Some militant homophile activists, like Frank Kameny, were delighted with the new developments. Speaking of the first Christopher Street Liberation Day March, Kameny remembered, "I was moved to a feeling of pride, exhilaration, and accomplishment, a feeling that this crowd of five thousand was a direct lineal descendant of our ten frightened people in front of the White House five years ago! I thought it was wonderful!"[8] While Kameny and Barbara Gittings, among others, were comfortable working with the new organizations, most homophile activists clung to more moderate positions and the homophile groups became increasingly irrelevant in the new political climate.

Critical in this explosion of activity was the founding of Gay Liberation Front (GLF) in New York in July 1969. In short order, GLF groups sprang up in cities and on college campuses around the country. Drawing on Third World liberation struggles for inspiration, and basing their name on Vietnam's National Liberation Front, GLF activists were self-identified radicals. Many of them had been active in "the movement"—the era's umbrella term for the New Left, the anti–Vietnam War movement, the counterculture, the Black Panthers, and other liberation movements. Now these activists applied the movement's analysis and their political energies to their own oppression as gay people. Building alliances with other struggles, GLF challenged what they considered to be the sexist and racist capitalist system at the root of gay oppression. The group's first statement proclaimed, "Gay Liberation Front is a revolutionary group of homosexual women and men formed with the realization that complete sexual liberation for all people cannot come about unless existing social institutions are abolished." Historian Terence Kissack has argued that "by allying itself with the movement, the Front placed itself outside the boundaries of homophile activism and self-consciously joined in the radical ferment of the 1960s." However, GLF had nonetheless absorbed a fundamental homophile precept, though perhaps unwittingly; it, too, identified itself as a coalition "committed to fight the oppression of the homosexual as a minority group."[9]

New York's GLF organized into cells based on the interests of its dis-

***Carl Wittman.* The Gay Manifesto.** Carl Wittman, a member of SDS (Students for a Democratic Society) in the mid-1960s, wrote this influential analysis of gay oppression and liberation in 1969. Wittman noted, "Our first job is to free ourselves; that means clearing our heads of the garbage that's been poured into them . . . self-educating, fending off attacks, and building free territory. Thus basically we have to have a gay/straight vision of the world until the oppression of gays is ended."[10]

parate members. By late 1970, it had nineteen cells, twelve consciousness-raising groups, three communal households, a Marxist study group, and miscellaneous other caucuses that met on a regular basis. The various collectives produced a newspaper, *Come Out!;* published theoretical pamphlets; sponsored demonstrations and dances; and established a community center. Without formal leaders, members, or dues, the group, which operated by consensus, was radically democratic, sometimes chaotic, and often extremely divided as to political strategies.

GLFers attended Black Panther demonstrations and organized banner-carrying gay contingents for the antiwar moratoriums. The group's first specifically gay action in September 1969 was a noisy picket of the *Village Voice,* which refused to print the word *gay* in GLF's ads because the paper considered the word obscene. Similar actions followed at Time, Inc., and ABC Television, protesting their representation of gays. Among its other activities, GLF participated in marches and demonstrations to protest police harassment, challenged the homophile movement to accept radical strategies, and sponsored classes at a regular Friday evening "Gay Night" at New York's Alternate U., home to many of the city's radical political and cultural groups.

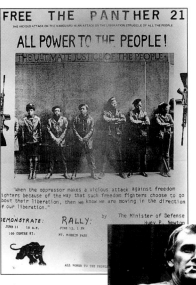

Gay liberationists, many already involved in the movement, found lesbian and gay recruits among their radical compatriots at antiwar demonstrations, women's liberation actions, and rallies held by the Black Panthers and the Puerto Rican liberation organization the Young Lords. But there were violent disagreements within GLF over what gay liberation's relationship to the movement should be. Some members believed that it was important to build common cause with other movement groups like the Panthers. Others believed that such efforts drained time and resources from the fight for lesbian and gay liberation. A vocal contingent within GLF opposed joining the movement because most of its activists had little sympathy for gay liberation and were unwilling to invest any time or energy on behalf of gay people.

The political disagreements within GLF were also fraught

(opposite) **Gay Liberation.** *New York, 1970.*

(below, left) **Free the Panther 21.** *New York, June 15, 1970.* GLF's support of the Black Panthers was a major source of contention within the organization, particularly as the Panthers were widely perceived to be violently male chauvinistic and homophobic.[11]

(below, right) **Gay Liberation Front members at a Black Panthers demonstration, New York, 1969.** Bob Kohler is at left. © ELLEN SHUMSKY/IMAGE WORKS

(right) **Gay Liberation Front Women, gay liberation march on the state capital, Albany, New York, 1971.** © DIANA DAVIES

(below) **Marsha P. Johnson, co-founder of STAR (Street Transvestite Action Revolutionaries), at a gay liberation march on the state capital, Albany, New York, 1971.**
© DIANA DAVIES

with tensions along gender and racial lines, and in 1970 several groups left to form separate organizations to address their own needs. Lesbians, feeling that they needed to address sexism as well as homophobia, formed their own caucus (Gay Liberation Front Women). Ultimately these women left GLF, some founding the independent Gay Women's Liberation Front and others forming Radicalesbians.

Alienated by racist attitudes within GLF, the small number of people of color in the group first started their own caucus and then left to form Third World Gay Revolution (TWGR) in 1970. The group stated its position:

> Third world gays suffer an oppression which is not shared by our white sisters and brothers, one which they could never really FEEL. Therefore, despite the many organizations emerging in the Gay Liberation movement, third world people haven't been able to relate to any of these. This is due to the inherent racism found in any white group with white leadership and white thinking.[12]

Drag queens and transgenderists, too, felt disenfranchised in gay liberation, and left GLF. Drag queens Sylvia Rivera, Marsha P. Johnson, and others founded STAR (Street Transvestite Action Revolutionaries) to take care of young street queens. They even established a short-lived home for them in New York's East Village. "The community was not going to help us," recalls Rivera.

> The community is always embarrassed by the drag queens because straight society says, "A faggot always dresses in drag, or he's effeminate." But you've got to be who you are. Passing for straight is like a light-skinned black woman or man passing for white. I refuse to pass. I couldn't have passed, not in this life-time."[13]

Other GLF activists, disenchanted with the group's radical agenda, affiliations with the Panthers, and lack of formal structure, left to form the Gay Activists Alliance (GAA), an organization that focused exclusively on gay concerns. Unlike GLF, GAA was a formal organization with a constitution, officers, and a system of committees; meetings were conducted according to *Robert's Rules of Order.* The members' goal was more reformist than radical: instead of destroying the system, they wanted to participate in it fully as gay people. Accordingly, the group—much like the earlier homophile activists—placed heavy emphasis on changing laws, getting involved in electoral politics, and targeting other bastions of power. But unlike the homophiles, the gay liberationists adopted confrontational tactics and rhetoric. The powers that be were placed on notice: "Today we know not only that gay is good, gay is angry," pronounced GAA co-founder Arthur Evans. "We are telling all the politicians and elected officials of New York State that they are going to become responsible to the people. We will make them responsible to us, or we will stop the conduct of the business of government."[14]

In promoting its agenda, Gay Activists Alliance employed "direct action" tactics known as "zaps." For example, GAA members would surprise New York City Mayor John V. Lindsay in the lobby of the Metropolitan Opera House, shouting "Gay Power!" and "End Police Harassment!" or

Gay Activists Alliance "zap" at the Board of Education to protest discrimination against homosexuals in the school system, New York, 1971. © RICHARD C. WANDEL

(opposite, top) **Gay Activists Alliance demonstrates at City Hall, in support of a bill granting gays equal employment protection, New York, June 25, 1971.** Arthur Evans is at right. © BETTYE LANE

(opposite, bottom left) **Gay Liberation Front poster, circa 1970.**

(opposite, bottom right) **Gay Activists Alliance Firehouse, 99 Wooster Street, New York, 1971.** © DIANA DAVIES

(below) **Police arresting gay activists at a demonstration in favor of a gay rights bill, New York, April 27, 1973.** © BETTYE LANE

shake Lindsay's hand on a receiving line at the Metropolitan Museum of Art while asking him, "What are you going to do about homosexual rights, Mr. Mayor?" Activists were committed to their struggle, sometimes risking arrest for their beliefs. A sit-in at the headquarters of the Republican State Committee resulted in the arrest of several activists who refused to leave. Dubbed the "Rockefeller Five," they became a cause célèbre and their trial an opportunity to publicize gay liberation. Zaps were a source of embarrassment to public officials, and, with a sense of theater and media savvy, GAA furthered its agenda by gaining media coverage for such actions. When they zapped the City Clerk's office to protest the marriage laws, they brought along a wedding cake with pairs of male and female same-sex lovers and a "Gay Power to Gay Lovers" sign. GAA activists were confrontational and "in your face." At one picket line, Vito Russo challenged a bystander, "We're not 'girls,' lady; we're men who fuck each other, and you'd better get used to it!"[15]

GAA also became involved in the political process. It got out the gay vote, ran gay candidates, and worked on behalf of gay-friendly candidates. In 1971 GAA initiated the fight for passage of a gay rights bill in New York City and held annual demonstrations when the bill came up for hearings and was repeatedly defeated. The group also sponsored marches on New York's state capital, Albany, demanding statewide protection from discrimination in housing and employment for gays, and participated in marches to protest ongoing police raids on gay bars and police harassment of lesbians and gay men. Additionally, GAA sponsored committees that researched and published booklets on topics such as the repeal of sodomy laws and antigay employment practices.

GAA also fostered the gay culture growing in the fertile soil of gay liberation. The Culture Committee—one of some nineteen GAA committees—consciously strove to create a gay culture that would be an alternative to the limited

world of the bars and sex clubs. To this end, they sponsored activities "which celebrated, analyzed, or propagated gay liberation."[16] In 1971 GAA established its headquarters in an old firehouse in New York's SoHo that became the hub of this politically inspired cultural reform. "The Firehouse," as it became popularly known, functioned as an early gay community center, drawing thousands to its dances, discussion groups, self-defense classes, and literary and theatrical events.

However, the culture that flourished in GAA was primarily that of middle-class, gay, white men. Like the lesbians of GLF, the small number of women in GAA grew frustrated with second-class status in the organization; in 1971 they formed their own Women's Subcommittee, which became the Lesbian Liberation Committee the following year. The women sponsored "Lesbian Sundays." "That was really amazing for me," recalls Joan Nestle. "To see lesbian women, not in a bar, not living with the fear of the police, talking to one another in this way . . . At any given [general GAA meeting] there could be anywhere from fifteen to twenty-five women, but when we formed our Sunday groups, there were hundreds of

women, so that really spoke to the need for separatism."[17] By 1973 the GAA women broke away to create an independent group, Lesbian Feminist Liberation (LFL).

As in GLF, the relatively few people of color in GAA also felt that the organization did not hear their concerns. They

(right) **New York Mattachine Times. July/August 1972.** Jeanne Manford, a Flushing schoolteacher, marched with her son, GAA activist Morty Manford, in the Christopher Street Liberation Day March in June 1972. As they marched, people screamed with joy and ran over to kiss Jeanne and ask her if she would talk to their parents. Jeanne and her husband, Jules, went on to found Parents of Gays, now called P-FLAG (Parents, Families and Friends of Lesbians and Gays), which currently boasts more than 340 chapters around the country.

(below, inset) **Original placard carried by Jeanne Manford in the Christopher Street Liberation Day March, June 1972.**

formed a Third World Caucus within GAA, as well as a black lesbian caucus, which met intermittently to address their liberation as gay women of color. "Black women didn't have the time for the Gay Activists Alliance . . . they didn't understand the depths of what we were experiencing," recalled activist Candice Boyce.

I'd look around and find almost no people of color . . . it wasn't comfortable there. They did good work, but they just didn't know how to be inclusive. To be a white male in America and to realize your gayness and find out that you're oppressed is a very different thing than being oppressed all your life as a woman of color.[18]

The tensions over race, gender, and political ideology played out in GAA and GLF were not unique to New York. A similar pattern of grouping and regrouping occurred around the country as gay men and lesbians defined and redefined their political movements in the early 1970s. In the wake of Stonewall, gay liberation had indeed become a national—and international—phenomenon. Shortly after the founding of GLF in New York in July 1969, a GLF was established in Berkeley; Chicago, Philadelphia, Los Angeles, Minneapolis, Detroit, and Madison followed shortly thereafter. Within a couple of years, GLFs—as well as Gay Activist Alliances, Radicalesbians, Third World Gay Liberations, and Gay Youth groups—raised hell in more than thirty-five states. The message had gone well beyond the major cities. GLFs could be found in Modesto, California; Sarasota, Florida; Tucson, Arizona; and Spokane, Washington; and on dozens of campuses—from the University of Iowa in Iowa City to Rocky Mountain College in Billings, Montana.[19] And gay liberation did not stop at the nation's borders. In 1970 GLFs started in Vancouver, London, and Sydney, and gay liberation–style organizations were founded in Paris, Berlin, and other European cities.

The emergence of a gay liberation press played a critical role in the rapid growth of this new movement; it kept activists informed of their comrades' actions around the country and helped recruit new members. Just months after Stonewall, three papers emerged in New York—GLF's *Come Out!*, *GAY*, and *Gay Power*—the latter two reaching astounding circulations of approximately twenty-five thousand within months. In the next couple of years, San Francisco's *Gay Sunshine*, Boston's *Fag Rag* and *Gay Community News*, Detroit's *Gay Liberator*, and Toronto's *Body Politic* became significant voices of gay liberation. And Los Angeles's *Advocate*, which had begun publishing in 1967, flourished in the year following Stonewall, as it reached an unprecedented circulation of more than forty thousand.

Gay liberationists also saw the mainstream media as crucial

Gay Power. *New York, September 1969.*

(right) **Gay men walking down the street, Hollywood, California, 1971.** Some gay liberationists donned gender-fuck drag in a stylish blending of fashion and politics.

PHOTO BY GREY VILLET, *LIFE* MAGAZINE

(below) **Gay. New York, December 1, 1969.**

to their efforts to change public attitudes. Consequently, they targeted publications and networks that promulgated antigay views. Among myriad actions around the country, gay liberationists picketed the *San Francisco Examiner* for running a piece that characterized homosexuals as "queers," "semi-males," "drag darlings," and "women who aren't exactly women"; demonstrated at the *Los Angeles Times* for the paper's refusal to use the word *homosexual;* held a sit-in at *Harper's* New York office to protest an article in which the author stated that homosexuals are "condemned to a state of permanent niggerdom among men," and that he "would wish homosexuality off the face of this earth"; and zapped *The Tonight Show* to protest Johnny Carson's "fag jokes."[20]

Gay liberationists also tried to introduce their own message into mainstream media, affecting local and national press coverage of gay issues with some success. Many mainstream newspapers and magazines ran stories about the "new homosexuals," and although journalists frequently voiced homophobic attitudes, gay liberationist views were often included as well. *Look*'s 1971 issue on the American family included " 'married' homosexuals" in the cover headline and featured an article about Jack Baker and Michael McConnell, a Minneapolis couple who had unsuccessfully applied for a marriage license. And *Life,* in its 1971 "Year in Pictures" issue, featured an eleven-page story titled "Homosexuals in Revolt," with big, glossy photographs of GAA demonstrations, a gay commune, and gay men in gender-fuck drag. In a tone of wide-eyed wonder, the story began:

It was the most shocking and, to many Americans, the most surprising liberation movement yet. Under the slogan "Out of the closets and into the streets," thousands of homosexuals, male and female, were proudly confessing what they had long hidden. They were, moreover, moving into direct confrontation with conventional society. Their battle was far from won. But in 1971 militant homosexuals showed that they were prepared to fight it.[21]

Gay liberationists were also occasionally able to reach a national television audience, appearing on talk shows like *The Dick Cavett Show* and *The David Susskind Show.*

(above) **Time. October 31, 1969.** This national news magazine first reported on the Stonewall Riots in the fall of 1969 when it ran a seven-page story on homosexuals. Gay Liberation Front organized a protest because the story included statements that homosexuals were mentally ill and immoral.

(left) **Gay Liberation Front picketing at the Time-Life Building, New York, 1969.** *Left to right:* Linda Rhodes holds the TIME INC. I AM A HUMAN BEING sign. To her left are Lois Hart, Ellen Broidy, and Jim Fouratt.
© DIANA DAVIES

Gay Contingent, Anti–Vietnam War march, New York, November 6, 1971. Gay liberation activists drew parallels between the policies of the U.S. government in Southeast Asia and practices at home. "The same government that is responsible for the oppression of Gays is carrying out a racist, sexist war of aggression in Southeast Asia," proclaimed the Student Mobilization Committee's Gay Task Force.[22]
© DIANA DAVIES

They spread their message in all sorts of other ways, too. In 1970 Louisville gays started a class in gay liberation at the University of Kentucky; Boston GLF leafleted the city's major shopping centers and subway stations; Denver GLF sponsored guerrilla theater; and Seattle GLF marched through the streets on Memorial Day, distributing oranges that were stamped GAY IS GOOD.

Society's definition of homosexuality as a mental illness, an important issue for the homophiles, became a critical target for gay liberationists as well. They attacked the annual meetings of the American Psychiatric Association (APA), the American Medical Association, and other professional organizations. And almost one hundred protesters stormed the 1972 convention of the Association for the Advancement of Behavioral Therapy, decrying the use of aversion therapy to cure homosexuals. Ultimately, the pressure of gay liberationists was instrumental in forcing the APA's momentous 1973 decision to remove homosexuality from its list of psychiatric disorders. The gay position was clear, as outlined by Chicago's GLF in this 1970 attack on the medical and mental health establishment: We refuse to adjust to our oppression, and believe that the key to our mental health . . . is a radical change in the structure and accompanying attitudes of the entire social system . . . OFF THE COUCHES, INTO THE STREETS! New York's GAA put it more succinctly, quipping, "One good zap is worth six months on a psychiatrist's couch."[23]

This irreverent attitude was typical of gay liberationists, who infused their politics with humor, outrageousness, and cultural radicalism. Los Angeles celebrated gay ins in Griffith Park, where people painted their bodies with slogans like "Super Fag" and "Fuck Forever." Chicago GLF mounted boycotts and leafleting campaigns to force gay bars to allow dancing. Houston GLF picketed a local gay bar that had a racist door policy. San Jose GLF held a public kiss-in. Approximately five hundred lesbian, gay, and straight students turned out for a gay dance at the University of Kansas at Lawrence. Gay antiwar demonstrators attended moratorium demonstrations bearing banners and posters that read, "Bring The Beautiful Boys Home," "Soldiers: Make Each Other, Not War," and "Suck Cock, Beat the Draft." One hundred gay people toted balloons through downtown Dallas proclaiming "Love Day." Two lesbians in Milwaukee went to Federal Court when their application for a marriage license was denied by the county clerk. Gay men and lesbians briefly embraced the notion of taking over Alpine County, California, so they could create "Stonewall Nation." And colorful, exuberant, campy—and political—gay pride marches occurred every June in an increasing number of cities. Demonstrators everywhere chanted, "Two-Four-Six-Eight, Gay Is Just As Good As Straight!" and "Say It Loud, Gay Is Proud!"

Everyday activities

Manonia Evans and Donna Burkett appearing at Federal Court to challenge the county clerk's refusal to issue them a marriage license, Milwaukee, Wisconsin, 1971.

(opposite) **Never Again! Fight Back!, San Francisco, 1978.**

(right) **Gay liberation buttons, 1969–1970s.**

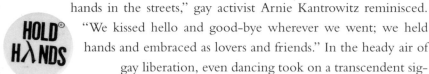

became acts of defiance and cause for celebration as the personal truly did become the political. "My favorite demonstration was simply holding hands in the streets," gay activist Arnie Kantrowitz reminisced. "We kissed hello and good-bye wherever we went; we held hands and embraced as lovers and friends." In the heady air of gay liberation, even dancing took on a transcendent significance. "We were feeling the high energy of the revolution based on love," wrote a gay reporter describing the first gay dance at Philadelphia's Temple University. "Dancing together is a sharing thing . . . We know that sisters dancing with sisters, brothers dancing with brothers, touching, kissing and balling people of the same sex is a far loving out expression of living."[24]

In the early 1970s, lesbians and gay men were imbued with a sense of mission, a radical vision of social transformation, and the belief that they would triumph. "This was a very idealistic era," recalled GAA activist Morty Manford, "when young people felt they could change the world. We truly felt we were being a part of history. We were doing something new. We were doing something righteous." Possibility was blowing in the wind. Freedom was just around the corner. "*Our* time had come," said one gay man in 1970. "We took to the streets . . . and we're not going back to the Closet, the back of the bus . . . Ready or not, baby, here we come! We're freakin' on in!"[25]

NEVER AGAIN!

FIGHT BACK!

The pink triangle was used to identify the thousands of gay people who died in concentration camps in Nazi Germany.

SEXUAL FREEDOM MEANS ALL OF US

LESBIAN =
WOMAN IDENTIFIED WOMAN =
DYKE = LAVENDER MENACE =
HUMAN BEING = WOMAN
LOVING WOMAN =
ME!

Lesbians marching in the Christopher Street Liberation Day March, June 25, 1978.
© BETTYE LANE-

LESBIAN FEMINISM

Feminism is the theory, lesbianism is the practice.

1970S SLOGAN

Separatism—working only with women, not with men, is the only real way I can create any alternatives that will give me support toward being a strong lesbian," wrote Morgan Muriel-child when she left the Gay Liberation Front. "Gay men for the most part are as sexist and woman hating as straight men . . . It is self-deluding to believe any man is nonsexist. Beyond all this, working with men only takes away valuable time that should be spent working with lesbians."[1]

Murielchild's experience in New York was typical of lesbians around the country in the early 1970s. Although initially many worked together with gay men in gay liberation, these women increasingly found gay male sexism and domination of the movement intolerable. In a pattern paralleling the other radical movements of the late 1960s and early 1970s, women were often denied decision-making roles and remained a minority in most gay liberation organizations. The situation became untenable for many lesbians who, influenced by the new wave of feminism, refused to be second-class citizens. These women decided to form their own caucuses and committees within the gay liberation groups, and significant numbers of them opted to establish their own separate organizations.

Sisterhood Is Blooming.
Chicago Women's Liberation Union, 1972.

Many lesbians who had cast their lot with their feminist sisters in women's liberation were also frustrated. While the movement addressed their common needs as women, they felt that their sexuality was neither acknowledged nor accepted among straight women. In the early 1970s, disaffected women from gay liberation and women's liberation joined together to create a new movement—lesbian feminism—that would address the dual oppressions of sexism and homophobia. Lesbian feminists radically redefined both lesbianism and feminism. They proclaimed that lesbianism was a political act, indeed the inevitable outcome of feminist thinking that women needed to be independent of men. They recast lesbianism as the ultimate expression of women's solidarity: "Feminism is the theory, lesbianism is the practice," became the slogan of the era.

Such a redefinition was no simple matter. In the late 1960s and early 1970s, the issue of lesbianism prompted an extremely divisive debate among feminists, despite the fact that many lesbians, often invisible, had been in the forefront of

Women's march down Fifth Avenue, New York, 1971. © BETTYE LANE

the movement. "The women's movement provided a safe haven for a lot of women who were struggling with their sexuality," recalled Ivy Bottini, former President of NY-NOW (National Organization for Women). "Many lesbians were the early beginners of NOW. And NOW was the women's movement then [1966]. I mean that was it, there was nothing else."[2] Betty Friedan, a founder of NOW, warned that a "lavender menace" would tarnish the movement's image and scare away straight women. Others at NOW also feared lesbianism. In 1969 when lesbian activist Rita Mae Brown and two of her NOW colleagues resigned over this homophobia, they wrote, "Lesbianism is the one word which gives the New York N.O.W. Executive Committee a collective heart attack."[3]

Lesbianism was less anathema to a few radical feminists, among them theorists like Kate Millett and Shulamith Firestone, who believed that feminism would usher in a world of sexual freedom of all types ("bisex, or the end of enforced perverse heterosexuality," as Millett put it). Nonetheless many radical feminists were still uncomfortable, even hostile, toward lesbians. "Most commonly," historian Alice Echols has pointed out, "they dismissed lesbianism as sexual rather than political," and saw it as a form of male-identified role-playing that reinforced a sexist system.[4]

In early 1970, some disaffected women from Gay Liberation Front joined with a number of lesbians who were disenchanted with feminist organizations to form consciousness-raising groups modeled on those of the radical feminist group Redstockings. These women decided to confront the "lesbian issue," as it came to be called, head on at the second Congress to Unite Women, which took place in New York in May 1970. Approximately forty of them, wearing "Lavender Menace" T-shirts, seized the stage, filled the aisles, and forced a discussion of lesbianism on

Lavender Menace incident at the second Congress to Unite Women, New York, May 1970. Rita Mae Brown is at right.

© DIANA DAVIES

the floor. They distributed the *Woman Identified Woman,* a statement that became the definitive radical manifesto for the new lesbian feminist movement. This groundbreaking paper, written by the women in one of the consciousness-raising groups, appealed to heterosexual feminists by fundamentally reconceptualizing lesbianism, defining it as primarily a political choice, and casting lesbians as the vanguard among feminists:

> What is a lesbian? A lesbian is the rage of all women condensed to the point of explosion . . . Lesbian is the word, the label, the condition that holds women in line . . . Lesbian is a label invented by the Man to throw at any woman who dares to be his equal, who dares to challenge his prerogatives . . . who dares to assert the primacy of her own needs . . . It is the primacy of women relating to women, of women creating a new consciousness of and with each other, which is at the heart of women's liberation, and the basis for the cultural revolution.[5]

After two days of heated debate, the Lavender Menace presented the Congress with a series of resolutions, declaring that "Women's Liberation is a·lesbian plot," that "whenever the label lesbian is used against the movement collectively or against women individually, it is to be affirmed, not denied," that homosexuality be discussed as a valid method of contraception, and that lesbianism be included in sex education curricula "as a valid, legitimate form of sexual expression and love."[6]

In the wake of the Congress to Unite Women, feminists and women's liberation organizations were forced to confront their own attitudes and policies regarding lesbianism. Fifty women responded to the Lavender Menace's call to join consciousness-raising groups. The women of Lavender Menace officially took the name Radicalesbians and, in addition to organizing the groups, they continued to generate theory, studied women's issues like health care, sponsored dances, widely distributed their manifesto, and tried to imagine the new lesbian future. Through this work the Radicalesbians helped make lesbianism more acceptable to straight radical feminists. Many came to accept the redefinition of lesbianism as a political choice, saw that the pejorative "dyke" was used to oppress all women, and recognized that the freedom to control one's own body was at the root of both the women's and gay liberation movements. In fact, many women who were ideologically—but

Radicalesbians committee meeting, New York, 1970. © ELLEN SHUMSKY/IMAGE WORKS

generally, not sexually—lesbians, came to identify themselves as "political lesbians."[7]

The sympathies of straight feminists were put to the test in December 1970 when *Time* magazine reported Kate Millett's acknowledgment that she was bisexual and suggested that her disclosure would discredit her as a spokeswoman for women's liberation. Leading feminists quickly responded with a press conference in which they challenged *Time*'s attempt to use lesbianism to malign the women's movement and declared that "Women's Liberation and Homosexual Liberation are both struggling towards a common goal: a society free from defining and categorizing people by virtue of gender and/or sexual preference."[8]

Although individuals from NOW supported this statement, the organization itself continued to struggle with the lesbian issue and the existence of lesbians in its ranks. Furious internal battles racked the organization as leaders in New York, like Friedan, argued that lesbianism was a "bedroom issue" that distracted from women's liberation. Rumors about various women's sexual preferences were spread, lesbians were purged from elected positions in the NY-NOW office, and charges and recriminations flew as closeted lesbians were accused of working against their sisters because they feared exposure. Other NOW chapters, especially those on the West Coast, took up the question, often in a more open-minded fashion than in New York. When the topic was raised for

New York delegates at International Women's Year National Women's Conference, Houston, Texas, November 1977. The lesbian issue reached a critical moment when the delegates to the International Women's Year conference passed a historic resolution supporting the right of sexual preference.
© BETTYE LANE

the first time at NOW's national convention in the fall of 1971, in a move that surprised many, a resolution supporting lesbianism was passed. This resolution recognized "the double oppression of women who are lesbians," affirmed "that a woman's right to her own person includes the right to define and express her own sexuality and to choose her own life-style," and acknowledged "the oppression of lesbians as a legitimate concern of feminism." A further resolution adopted in 1975 made the lesbian issue a "national priority."[9]

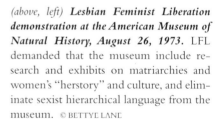

(above, left) **Lesbian Feminist Liberation demonstration at the American Museum of Natural History, August 26, 1973.** LFL demanded that the museum include research and exhibits on matriarchies and women's "herstory" and culture, and eliminate sexist hierarchical language from the museum. © BETTYE LANE

(above, right) **Women at a rally in support of the gay rights bill, New York, 1974.**
© BETTYE LANE

Lesbian feminism drew many adherents, but other lesbians who saw gay oppression as their top priority continued to work with mixed organizations like Gay Liberation Front and Gay Activists Alliance. The GLF Women proclaimed:

> Our strongest common denominator and greatest oppression lie with society's injustice against us as homosexuals. We are discriminated against as women, but lesbians who live openly are fired from jobs, expelled from schools, banished from their homes, and even beaten. Lesbians who hide and escape open hostility, suffer equal oppression through psychic damage caused by their fear and guilt. With this understanding, we focus on Gay Liberation, giving priority to gay issues and gay problems. We are part of the revolution of all oppressed people, but we cannot allow the lesbian issue to be an afterthought.[10]

However, many of these women also became increasingly fed up with the sexism of the men in the gay liberation groups and their denial of the specific concerns of women and lesbians. GLF women ultimately broke away and formed Gay Women's Liberation Front, while GAA women left to create the independent Lesbian Feminist Liberation in 1973. "We ended up splitting from the men by forming Lesbian Feminist Liberation, LFL," recalled Jean O'Leary.

> We were trying to establish our identity and, wherever we could, gain visibility. Just as gay people have had to become visible in society, lesbians had to become visible within the gay community, as well as in the larger society. Up until that time, whenever people thought about gays, they thought only about gay men.[11]

Christopher Street Liberation Day March, New York, 1971. © DIANA DAVIES

LFL pursued a reform agenda in politics, initiating demonstrations to protest media treatment of lesbians, calling for passage of the New York City gay rights bill, and working with other women's organizations. LFL also developed a strong program of activities—discussion groups, social programs, dances, and cultural events.

Lesbian feminists ceased to call themselves gay and embraced the word *lesbian*. "We are angry, not gay!" they proclaimed. "Gay doesn't include lesbians any more than 'mankind' includes love and sisterhood."[12] The pejorative *dyke* was similarly adopted as a term of proud defiance. Some women created new spellings of woman and women—womyn, womon, and wimmin—purging "man" from the word. And in an act of historical reclamation, lesbians adopted the Amazons, a mythical tribe of women warriors, as foremothers, taking up the labyris, the double-bladed axe said to have been used by the Amazons, as a lesbian feminist symbol.

Lesbian feminist organizations, like the gay liberation groups, attracted mostly middle-class white women. Lesbians of color often felt alienated from existing lesbian and gay organizations because of racial and class differences, and the way such differences commonly went unacknowledged. In the mid-1970s, they began to artic-

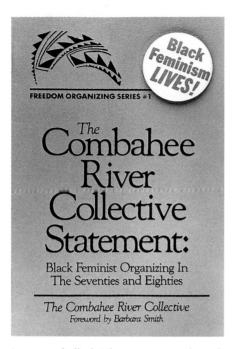

ulate their own agendas, found their own groups, and synthesized a lesbian and feminist project based on their own experiences rather than those of white women. In 1974 a group of black and Latina New Yorkers founded Salsa Soul Sisters as an alternative to the bars, which had "historically exploited and discriminated against" lesbians of color.[13] Activist Candice Boyce recalled finding her way to Salsa Soul. "Right away I knew this was what I was looking for and it just snowballed. There was no other place for women of color to go and sit down and talk about what it meant to be a black lesbian in America."[14] Salsa Soul offered women of color a space where they could safely address issues of racism and lesbianism, including "survival issues" such as employment, housing, and single lesbian parenting. The group offered lesbians of color the possibility of—and support for—pride in their racial and ethnic heritages, sexuality, and gender.

A distinctive aspect of lesbian feminism was the project of building an alternative community: creating separate organizations, institutions, and social spaces. Typically identified as "women's spaces," they were often run by and for lesbians. Women's bookstores, restaurants, publishing collectives, and softball leagues fostered a flourishing lesbian culture. As the 1970s progressed, the emphasis of lesbian feminist politics shifted more and more toward building "Amazon Nation" or "Lesbian Nation," a network of autonomous, sometimes separatist, communities.

In contrast to gay men who flocked to the "liberated zones" of big cities, significant numbers of lesbian feminists moved to rural communes, which proliferated around the country. College towns, such as Ann Arbor, Michigan; Northampton, Massachusetts; Ithaca, New York; and Boulder, Colorado became lesbian havens. Vibrant lesbian communities also grew in a number of major cities. Brooklyn's Park Slope was home to one of the most highly visible concentrations of lesbians, and came to be called "Dyke Slope" by those in the know. Other cities too became centers for

(left) **The Combahee River Collective Statement.** *Kitchen Table: Women of Color Press, 1986.* This groundbreaking manifesto on black feminism, written in 1977 by Lesbians Demita Frazier, Barbara Smith, and Beverly Smith, has served as a foundation for organizing by feminists of color in the 1980s and 1990s.

(below) **Salsa Soul Sisters.** *Third World Women, Inc., New York, 1976.*

Black Lesbian Caucus, Christopher Street Liberation Day March, New York, 1973. © BETTYE LANE

strong "women's communities," notably Noe Valley and the Mission in San Francisco, Berkeley, and North Oakland in the Bay area; and Jamaica Plain and Somerville in the Boston area.

Some lesbian feminists espoused separatism, a philosophy and a lifestyle that encouraged lesbians to live their lives apart from the patriarchal, heterosexist mainstream society. Separatists chose not to organize with straight women or gay men and developed lesbian-only organizations and institutions. While for some women separatism meant that their social and political lives were lesbian-only, others envisioned a more complete separatism and created lesbian-only rural—and urban—communes. Prominent in this movement were the Furies, a Washington, D.C.–based collective founded in 1971. Many of its dozen members were leading theorists of lesbian feminism and, though the group only lasted a year, the group's eponymously titled magazine had an extraordinary influence.

The Furies believed that lesbians had to build their own political movement. "Straight women are confused by men, don't put women first," wrote Rita Mae Brown who helped found the collective. "They betray lesbians and in its deepest form, they betray their own selves. You can't build a strong movement if your sisters are out there fucking with the oppressor." Furthermore, the Furies rejected working with "men, straight or gay, because men are not working to end male supremacy."[15] In the first issue of the *Furies,* Charlotte Bunch elaborated:

> Lesbianism threatens male supremacy at its core. When politically conscious and organized, it is central to destroying our sexist, racist, capitalist, imperialist system . . . Lesbians must become feminists and fight against woman oppression, just as feminists must become Lesbians if they hope to end male supremacy . . . Lesbians must form our own political movement in order to grow.[16]

While the lesbian-separatist ideal permeated much of what became known as "women's culture," "women-only" rather than "lesbian-only" spaces and events were more common in practice. Significantly, complete separatism was not an attractive option for many lesbians whose lives and political commitments were inextricably bound to other communities.

(opposite) **Lesbian sticker and buttons, 1970–90s.**

(left) **Lesbian Pride Week 80.** *Lesbian Feminist Liberation, New York, 1980.*

This was the case for lesbians who continued to work in the women's and gay rights movements as well as for lesbians of color. "My survival has always been intertwined with all the members of my ethnic group—contemporary and historical," wrote writer and activist Jewelle Gomez. "Even when black men have been rude, abusive, or willfully ignorant, our historic bond and our resistance to white supremacy stood firm. To break away from those who've been part of our survival is a leap many women of color could never make."[17] Separatism was also infeasible for the many women who, inspired by their lesbian feminist politics, did significant work as open lesbians in other progressive movements for social change, among them the battered women's, rape crisis, peace, disarmament, antiracist, antiapartheid, and prisoners' rights movements.

(*right*) **DYKE.** ***New York, Spring 1976.*** This separatist magazine was published by women who believed in a "Lesbian Only" community and culture.

(*below*) **Come Shop/Lesbian Food Conspiracy.** ***New York, 1973.***

Furthermore, separatism was alien to the vast majority of lesbians who did not totally define their lives in terms of their sexuality and politics. "Where are you—you middle-of-the-roaders?" wrote one woman to *Lesbian Connection* in 1976. "From what I've read in LC (and maybe I haven't read enough yet), most of you are either politicos or separatists. Aren't there any of you out there who are just plain ordinary, everyday lesbians who enjoy living in a peaceful existence?"[18]

Critical to the project of building a lesbian community, lesbian feminists in the 1970s created a wide network of publications and presses that spread their message to women around the country. Magazines proliferated—*Lesbian Tide* (Los Angeles); *Lavender Woman* (Chicago); *The Furies* (Washington,

(above) **Radicalesbians commune, Andes, New York, 1970.** © ELLEN SHUMSKY/IMAGE WORKS

(left) **Kady reading at Womanbooks, New York, 1976.** Womanbooks was one of several women's bookstores that flourished in New York in the 1970s, during the height of the women's and lesbian feminist movements. © DIANA DAVIES

D.C.); *The Lesbian Feminist* (New York); *Amazon Quarterly* (Oakland); and *Lesbian Connection* (East Lansing, Michigan). By 1975 there were some fifty lesbian publications with a total circulation of approximately fifty thousand. Assessing the enormous impact of the lesbian press, Joan Nestle observed:

A woman would read just one article that touched a certain sensibility in her—and suddenly her life was turned upside down. She embraced the lesbian culture as the center of her very existence. When that process is repeated for women in tiny, isolated communities from coast to coast—women who previously trembled in fear but then began asserting their own self-worth—the impact cannot be measured in mere numbers.[19]

The seventies and early eighties also saw the development of a network of women's presses—Diana Press; Naiad; Daughters, Inc.; and Kitchen Table: Women of Color Press among others—and bookstores that created a whole new forum for lesbian concerns and the stories of lesbian lives. Barbara Grier, founder of Naiad in the early 1970s, recollected, "I wanted a woman to be able to walk into any bookstore and find the material she needed to make her feel good about herself."[20]

Music too played a central role in the lesbian feminist movement as the decade saw the emergence of a concert circuit and production companies for "women's music." Holly Near, Chris Williamson, and Meg Christian became (lesbian) household names. Their songs embodied the politics, the lifestyles, and the passions of many lesbian feminists. The Michigan Womyn's Music Festival, started in 1976, developed into an annual ritual drawing thousands of women from around the country, and many smaller regional festivals filled the calendar.

Women's culture in the 1970s also witnessed the development of a lesbian feminist ethos of sexuality that devalued genital and orgasm-centered forms of sexual expression—which were seen as male-identified—in favor of a more total body sensuality. "For me, coming out meant an end to sex," wrote Radicalesbian Sue Katz in her essay "Smash Phallic Imperialism."

Sex means oppression, it means exploitation . . . Physical contact and feelings have taken a new liberatory form. And we call that SENSUALITY . . . It is touching and rubbing and cuddling and fondness. It is holding and rocking and kissing and licking. Its only goal is closeness and pleasure. It does not exist for the Big Orgasm . . . The sensuality I feel has transformed my politics . . . because the energies for our feminist revolution are the same as the energies of our love for women.[21]

Azalea: A Magazine by Third World Lesbians. *Brooklyn, New York, Fall 1978.*

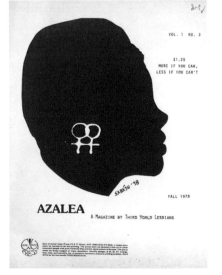

Coupled with this emphasis on sensuality was a rejection of monogamy as a constraint rooted in a patriarchal system in which men owned and controlled women's bodies.

By the late 1970s and early 1980s explosive debates about sexuality—or the "Sex Wars," as they came to be called—divided much of the lesbian and women's movements. Pornography, sadomasochism, and butch-femme became the targets of antiporn feminists. Arguments raged over whether pornography was antiwoman and whether certain sexual practices and fantasies were antifeminist. Some lesbian feminists and sex radicals fought back, questioning the lesbian feminist ethos of sexuality. "It set up a 'perfect' vision of egalitarian sexuality, where we could magically leap over our heterosexist conditioning into a mutually orgasmic, struggle-free, trouble-free sex," wrote lesbian sex radicals Amber Hollibaugh and Cherrie Moraga. "We feel this vision has become both misleading and damaging to many feminists, but in particular to lesbians. Who created this sexual model as a goal in the first place? Who can really live up to such an ideal?"[22]

Sadomasochism and leather provoked particular controversy in the lesbian community and the letters columns raged in women's publications. "S&M needs no justification," wrote one lesbian from Eugene, Oregon, in *Lesbian Connection*. She continued:

> Any consensual sharing between lesbians is alright, and any lesbian should know that . . . For you to say 'I am trying to see clearly the issue of sex and violence—my gut feeling is that S&M merges the two, and I think this is imitative of male concepts of sexuality, is womon hating, and is dangerous' just infuriates me. Get your gut feelings off my body and out of my life.[23]

These arguments came to a head during the Scholar and the Feminist Conference IX ("Towards a Politics of Sexuality") held at Barnard College

In Concert. *New York, 1975.*

(right) **Lesbian Herstory Archives, New York, 1979.** Co-founders Joan Nestle (*left*) and Deborah Edel (*seated*); Valerie Itnyre is at right. The archives was started in 1974 by a small group of lesbians to preserve and document lesbian history and culture. The archives is the oldest and largest lesbian collection in the world. © BETTYE LANE

in 1982. The conference organizers were concerned that a "premature orthodoxy . had come to dominate feminist discussion" and that feminists had focused on sexual violence and sexual danger rather than on exploring sexual pleasure.[24] Members of Women Against Pornography, Women Against Violence Against Women, and New York Radical Feminists denounced the conference as "antifeminist." After Barnard seized the conference-planning diary and a major funder rescinded support for the conference, hundreds of people signed a petition protesting this censorship, and a "sexual speak-out" followed.

The battles over separatism, the sex wars, and the faults along racial and class lines, suggested the limitations of the lesbian feminism that had developed in the 1970s. Over the course of the decade the politics of lesbian feminism had evolved into a cultural feminism in which the development of a sometimes insular women's community often took precedence over the formation of a political movement.[25] In fact, this tendency had been recognized relatively early. In 1974 one radical lesbian observed that "somewhere along the way we stopped calling ourselves a movement and now call ourselves a community . . . Communities may be groovy things to belong to . . . but communities don't make a revolution."[26]

But despite all the divisions that emerged among lesbian feminists, and the waning of lesbian-feminism's hegemonic influence in the 1980s, the movement was profoundly significant. In all its manifestations—political as well as cultural—lesbian feminism offered a new generation a radically different, positive, and empowering way of being lesbian. These women built long-standing communities, institutions, and ideas that continue to play a vital role in the lives of lesbians today.

(opposite, top, left) **What Color Is Your Handkerchief. Samois, 1979.** A firestorm of controversy broke out when this 1979 anthology was published by Samois, a group of S&M feminist lesbians in the Bay Area. Heretofore, such issues had rarely, if ever, been addressed in print among lesbians.

(opposite, bottom, left) **Sex Issue. Heresies, 1981.** This "pro-sex" publication by a feminist collective showcased the diversity of opinions and experiences in the areas of women's, and especially lesbian, sexuality. Sadomasochism, butch-femme, pornography, and fantasy were a few of the subjects addressed by the writers and artists who contributed their work.

(above, top) *Las Buenas Amigas, a group of Latina lesbians, marching in the Lesbian and Gay Pride March, New York, 1991.* © FRED W. McDARRAH

(above) *Lesbian Herstory Archives marching in New York's Lesbian and Gay Pride March, 1980.* © MORGAN GWENWALD

(right) *March, New York, circa 1982.*

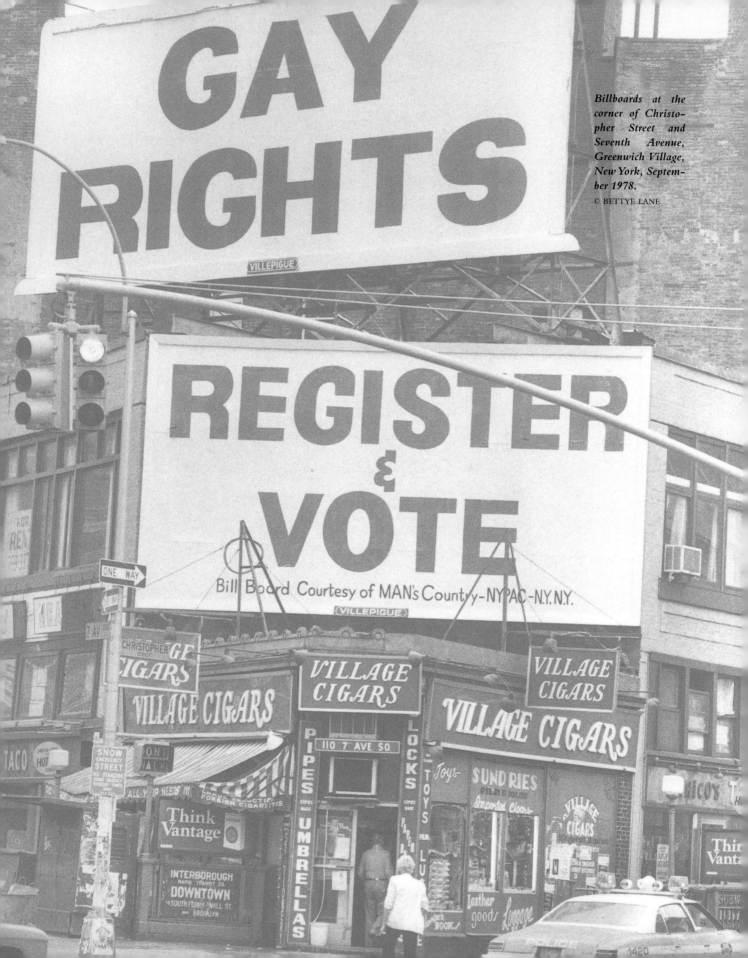

Billboards at the corner of Christopher Street and Seventh Avenue, Greenwich Village, New York, September 1978.
© BETTYE LANE

GAY RIGHTS

Perhaps it is a welcome sign of the times
that the straight world is no longer shocked by a parade of gay people . . .
It is now time to move out of our ghettos, to challenge and confront society and
its fundamental values . . . which oppress gay people. It is time for us
to get on down . . . to the Courts, to the Federal Building, to the State capital,
to the Police stations, to the politician's doors.

—Jeanne Córdova,
Lesbian Tide, July 1972

While radical gay liberation still had its adherents, and lesbian feminism continued to attract a significant number of women who wanted to organize autonomously, after the early 1970s the reform-oriented strain of gay liberation—typified by Gay Activists Alliance—increasingly came to dominate the movement. Following a progression typical of other groups in American society, this shift in strategy also mirrored larger political developments,

NGTF brochure, New York, circa 1976.
The National Gay Task Force, founded to
be a kind of gay NAACP, has grown over
the years to become one of the few major
voices for lesbian and gay Americans at the
national level.

as the radical movements of the 1960s waned and the country became
more conservative. Many gay men and lesbians increasingly focused their
attention on securing civil rights as they moved away from an emphasis on
liberating human sexuality. People spoke less of smashing the system than
of demanding lesbian and gay participation within it. Gay candidates ran
for elective office and, as a gay voting bloc coalesced, mainstream politicians increasingly courted the lesbian and gay community. Gay men and
lesbians founded national organizations and political action committees
and worked for change through the judicial system; simultaneously, they
created a multitude of organizations to meet the cultural, social, spiritual,
and medical needs of their communities.

Historian John D'Emilio has noted that the movement "returned to
the reform-oriented perspective of the pre-Stonewall homophile movement. Rather than a struggle for liberation, the movement had become,
once again, a quest for 'rights.' " But the politics of gay rights activists was
distinctly different from that of the homophiles, for they had absorbed
"the legacy of lesbian and gay liberation."

> Certain key changes effected by gay liberation were enthusiasti-
> cally incorporated into the outlook, the style, and the program of
> these newer groups. Among these, the imperative to come out
> publicly, with all that implied about pride, self-affirmation, and
> the rejection of mainstream cultural views of homosexuality,
> stands out. Many gay activists remained as bold and brazen as their
> GLF predecessors had been. They expected and demanded accep-
> tance for who they were, without apology.[1]

Among these new groups were reform-minded organizations working for
gay issues on the national level. Most notably, the National Gay Task Force
(NGTF) was established in New York in 1973 by one-time members of
Gay Activists Alliance who had become fed up with the infighting and
paralysis of GAA. NGTF's founders wanted to create a more effective,
structured organization with a board of directors, a paid staff, and a membership; in an effort to win a measure of mainstream respectability, they
recruited a number of prominent openly lesbian and gay professionals to
their board. While NGTF was criticized by some for "going establishment," others viewed its professionalism as a sign that the movement had
reached a new level of maturity. Over the years, NGTF was joined in the

Liberty for All. New York, 1989. Lambda Legal Defense and Education Fund has been an advocate in many of the major legal battles faced by lesbians and gays in the last two decades. It has fought for the rights of lesbian mothers, gays in the military, and People With AIDS; challenged immigration policies that bar homosexuals; confronted antigay discrimination and legislation; and championed same-sex marriage.

national political arena by Lambda Legal Defense and Education Fund (also founded in 1973), Gay Rights National Lobby (founded in 1976), and Human Rights Campaign Fund (founded in 1980).

Foremost on gay rights activists' agendas was working for change in the legal arena. Capitalizing on the fact that many states were modernizing their legal codes, activists challenged state sodomy laws. While all but one state—Illinois—still had sodomy statutes on the books at the beginning of

SODOMY and JUSTICE FOR ALL

NO BIG BROTHER IN OUR BEDROOMS.

GPU-NYU.

DEFY THE SUPREME COURT:

FUCK IN THE PARK!

JULY 11th – JULY 16th

THE RAMBLES

CENTRAL PARK!
TREES, FLOWERS, SUNSHINE AND NAKED BODIES;
CELEBRATE GAY PRIDE AND GAY LOVE!

RUMOR HAS IT THAT THERE WILL BE AN ORGY ON
SUNDAY NIGHT, JULY 11TH. SODOMITES UNITE!

(AN UNSPONSORED EVENT WITH SPONTANEOUS SEX.)

(far left) **Demonstrators protesting an appearance by Chief Justice Warren E. Burger following a ruling by the Supreme Court upholding Virginia's sodomy law, New York, April 30, 1976.** Jim Owles is at left; Arnie Kantrowitz is at right.

© BETTYE LANE

(left) **Flyer, New York, 1986.** The Supreme Court's *Bowers* v. *Hardwick* ruling caused great outrage (and at least in the case of the flyer shown here, a burst of sardonic humor) in the gay and lesbian community.

(below) **Gay Activists Alliance flyer, New York, 1974.**

the 1970s, by the end of the decade half the states no longer considered sodomy a crime. New York joined this national trend when the state's highest court overturned the sodomy statute in 1980. But progress in sodomy law reform was met by a countertrend: Between 1973 and 1977, six states amended their sodomy laws to apply only to same-sex acts. (Two more states followed suit in the 1980s.) Most significantly, the gay movement lost two crucial Supreme Court cases. In 1976 the Court affirmed Virginia's sodomy statute and in 1986, in the precedent-setting *Bowers* v. *Hardwick* case, the court ruled that the Georgia sodomy law was constitutional.

Gay and lesbian activists did win significant advances in the mid-1970s with the passage of antidiscrimination legislation at the local level. Within the space of a few short years gay rights bills and policies were enacted around the country; by the end of 1977 more than forty cities and counties had adopted some form of gay rights protection. Some locales offered nondiscrimination protection only in municipal employment—among them Atlanta, Detroit, Santa Barbara, Los Angeles, Ithaca, Portland, and Chapel Hill. But other cities—Ann Arbor, Minneapolis, St. Paul, Wichita, Tucson, Columbus, Madison, Champaign, and Eugene, among others—enacted fuller protection that extended to private employment, housing, and public accommodations. Though hampered by fierce opposition in some quarters and challenged by repeal drives through the years, by the late 1990s, more than one hundred municipalities

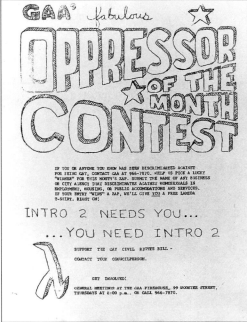

GAA's fabulous

OPPRESSOR OF THE MONTH CONTEST

IF YOU OR ANYONE YOU KNOW HAS BEEN DISCRIMINATED AGAINST
FOR BEING GAY, CONTACT GAA AT 966-7870. HELP US PICK A LUCKY
"WINNER" FOR THIS MONTH'S ZAP. SUBMIT THE NAME OF ANY BUSINESS
OR CITY AGENCY THAT DISCRIMINATES AGAINST HOMOSEXUALS IN
EMPLOYMENT, HOUSING, OR PUBLIC ACCOMODATIONS AND SERVICES.
IF YOUR ENTRY "WINS" A ZAP, WE'LL GIVE YOU A FREE LAMBDA
T-SHIRT. RIGHT ON!

INTRO 2 NEEDS YOU...
...YOU NEED INTRO 2

SUPPORT THE GAY CIVIL RIGHTS BILL -
CONTACT YOUR COUNCILPERSON.

GET INVOLVED!
GENERAL MEETINGS AT THE GAA FIREHOUSE, 99 WOOSTER STREET,
THURSDAYS AT 8:00 p.m.. OR CALL 966-7870.

GAA-sponsored candlelight march to City Hall in support of a bill that would have added "sexual orientation" to New York City's Human Rights Law, New York, June 24, 1971. © RICHARD C. WANDEL

have enacted antidiscrimination laws to protect lesbians and gay men.

While other cities around the country passed gay rights ordinances, New York, arguably the city with the nation's largest gay and lesbian population, was unable to enact such legislation. Efforts to pass a bill that would prohibit discrimination based on sexual orientation in employment, housing, and public accommodations began in 1971, but were immediately stymied. Gay Activists Alliance and other groups persisted in their fight, for as GAA activist Marty Robinson observed in 1972:

> When GAA undertook Intro 475 [New York City's gay rights bill], it was not advocated as the goal for the movement but as a tactic, a tool toward liberation. It was called anti-closet legislation,

to underline how the threat of loss of employment had been used to keep Gays in silent submission . . . Many Gays came out of the closet for the struggle and many more will join them as that struggle continues.[2]

The battle for a gay rights bill became a major focus for New York City's lesbian and gay activists. The annual hearings before the City Council, which pitted gays against their staunch opponents, became a fixture in New York political life. Year after year the bill was defeated in committee, only to be reintroduced again the following year. Though parts of Manhattan had a large gay population and at least a veneer of liberal sophistication regarding gay issues, the other boroughs were considerably more conservative and provided the necessary votes to veto the legislation. After almost fifteen years of struggle, New York City finally passed gay rights legislation in 1986.

Activists also fought for antidiscrimination protections at the state level, but in general these were slower in coming than those at the local level. In 1976 Pennsylvania governor Milton Shapp issued an executive order making that state the first to prohibit discrimination based on sexual orientation in state employment. It was not until 1982, however, that Wisconsin became the first state to pass a bill that offered comprehensive protections to its lesbian and gay citizens. Massachusetts enacted a statewide gay rights bill in 1989 and since then eight other states—California, Connecticut, Hawaii, Minnesota, New Hampshire, New Jersey, Rhode Island, and Vermont—have banned discrimination against lesbians and gay men.[3]

On the national level, the National Gay Task Force and other activists organized support for a federal gay rights bill that was first introduced in Congress in 1974. Though the bill (and its descendants) have been debated in Congress for over twenty years, it has never been passed. Nonetheless, there were several triumphs at the federal level in the 1970s; the United States Civil Service Commission eliminated its ban on hiring lesbians and gay men in 1975 and the State Department followed suit in 1977. Notably, the new civil service guidelines exempted the

New York Daily News, *March 21, 1986.* This catchy headline referred to two votes: The New York City Council finally passed a gay rights bill on the same day that Congress defeated support for the Contras, the U.S.–backed guerrilla forces who were, at the time, fighting to overthrow Nicaragua's Sandinista government.
© BETTYE LANE

Federal Bureau of Investigation and the Central Intelligence Agency, providing the reasoning that lesbians and gay men were still considered more easily subject to blackmail.

In the 1970s, lesbians and gay men also became a force in electoral politics. A concerted effort was begun to elect openly gay people to public office. In 1974 Elaine Noble captured national media attention when she won a seat in the Massachusetts state legislature, becoming the first openly gay state representative.[4] Spurred by Noble's win, Minnesota state senator Allan Spear came out publicly and easily won reelection two years later. Lesbians and gay men also campaigned on behalf of mainstream candidates and worked to build and publicize the so-called gay vote. In certain cities around the country, particularly those in which there was a concentrated gay presence, gay men and lesbians achieved a certain measure of political power and became a constituency to be reckoned with. By the 1990s there would be hundreds of openly gay and lesbian elected officials, prominent among them Representative Barney Frank, a vocal supporter of gay rights in the Congress.

Lesbians and gay men became especially active in the Democratic Party. Recalls lesbian activist Virginia Apuzzo, "We were a new breed and we were going to come into the Democratic Party and we were going to make changes. They may not like us and they may not want to be bosom buddies with us. But lesbians and gays were going to be part of the new coalition and they had to get it."[5]

Beginning with five openly lesbian and gay delegates and alternates in 1972, gay men and lesbians became quite visible as delegates to the Democratic National Convention. In 1972 Jim Foster, a delegate from San Francisco, delivered these ringing words to the convention (though admittedly few heard since he spoke in the early morning hours):

> We do not come to you pleading for your "understanding" or begging your "tolerance." We come to you affirming our pride in our lifestyle, affirming the validity of our right to seek and to

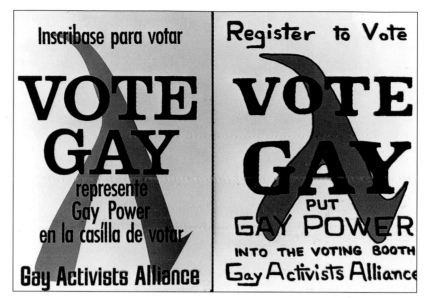

(above) ***Stickers, New York, 1970s.*** While gay candidates first ran for office in New York in the early 1970s, it would be another two decades before they attained office. In 1990, Deborah J. Glick became the first open lesbian elected to the New York State Assembly; and in 1991 Tom Duane became New York's first openly gay—and HIV-positive—member of City Council.

(opposite) ***Lesbian and gay march on Albany, 1971.*** In 1970 and 1971, lesbian and gay activists marched on the New York State capital in support of statewide legislation banning discrimination against homosexuals. © DIANA DAVIES

maintain meaningful emotional relationships, and affirming our rights to participate in the life of this country on an equal basis with every other citizen.[6]

As delegates and as members of the Platform Committee, gay men and lesbians fought to have their issues included in the Democratic Party's platform. Though they failed in 1972 and 1976, a gay rights plank was added for the first time in 1980, at a convention that boasted seventy-seven openly lesbian and gay delegates. That year, in a strongly worded speech to the convention, delegate Melvin Boozer, an African-American gay activist from Washington, D.C., queried,

> Would you ask me how I dare to compare the civil rights struggle with the struggle for lesbian and gay rights? I know what it means to be called a nigger and I know what it means to be called a faggot, and I understand the difference, in the marrow of my bones. And I can sum up that difference in one word: nothing. Bigotry is bigotry.[7]

Delegate Gwenn Craig at the Democratic National Convention, New York, August 14, 1980.

But the inroads made by lesbians and gay men also engendered a backlash as this new gay and lesbian visibility was met with an upsurge in antigay violence. In 1973 a series of fires rocked communities around the country: Metropolitan Community Churches in Los Angeles and San Francisco were attacked by arsonists, a gay bar in New Orleans was torched, killing thirty-two, and gay bars in San Francisco and Springfield, Massachusetts, were attacked with fire or bombs. The following year, the Gay Activists Alliance's headquarters in New York was the target of arson. Through the seventies and beyond, gay businesses, bars, and bathhouses continued to be the targets of arson and police harassment. The incidence of antigay harassment, assaults, and murders also escalated in cities around the country.

The significant advances made by lesbians and gay men in the legislative, judicial, and electoral arenas brought a vigorous attack from the ascendant New Right as the national political climate took a conservative turn in the late 1970s. Lesbians and gay men were targeted as part of a broader at-

(left) **Marchers protesting Anita Bryant's antigay campaign, Christopher Street Liberation Day March, June 26, 1977.** In 1977 record numbers turned out for lesbian and gay pride marches around the country to oppose Anita Bryant's campaign to overturn gay rights ordinances. An estimated seventy-five thousand marched in New York, five times the number who had marched the year before.

(below) **Anti-Anita Bryant ephemera, 1977.**

ANITA IS A LEMON

WANTED: FOR CRIMES AGAINST HUMANITY

Will History Repeat Itself? HITLER, McCARTHY, ANITA

© COPYRIGHT 1977 (GK)2

Squeeze Anita (BUY APPLES)

Dear Anita,

We Are Switching To Prune Juice And We Will Send You The Results.

tack on women, people of color, and poor and working-class people. Some of the objectives that topped the Right's agenda were the repeal of gay rights, defeat of the Equal Rights Amendment (ERA), and the rollback of affirmative action and abortion rights. The New Right mounted its first major challenge to gay rights in 1977 when singer Anita Bryant, spokeswoman for the Florida Citrus Commission, led the drive to overturn a recently passed gay rights ordinance in Dade County, Florida. The effort drew na-

Dykes and Tykes at a demonstration in support of Intro 384, the gay rights bill, New York, 1978. © BETTYE LANE

tional media attention to the struggle for gay rights. Bryant's campaign, led by her group, Save Our Children, appealed to people's stereotypical fears of homosexuals as child molesters. Typical of her fearmongering was a flyer that vilified homosexuals and cautioned parents about "a hair-raising pattern of recruitment and outright seduction and molestation—a growing pattern that predictably will intensify if society approves laws granting legitimacy to sexual perverts."[8]

Bryant assembled a broad base of both national and local supporters, including the Reverend Jerry Falwell, the National Association of Evangelicals, the Roman Catholic archbishop of Miami, the president of the Miami Beach B'nai B'rith, the Florida senators and governor, and anti-ERA and antiabortion activists, among others. Playing on Bryant's advertisements for orange juice, her opponents adopted the slogan "A Day Without Human Rights Is A Day Without Sunshine," and gay and lesbian activists around the country raised funds to help out their brothers and sisters in Miami. However, they were overpowered by Bryant and the opponents of gay rights: In a stunning victory for the Right, Dade County's voters repealed the gay rights ordinance by more than a two-to-one margin.

The defeat in Miami was a wake-up call to the lesbian and gay masses who had been lulled into passivity by the relatively steady gains of the early to mid-1970s. Following the repeal of Dade County's ordinance in early June 1977, lesbians and gay men turned out in record numbers to show their anger and affirm their strength at that year's gay pride celebrations nationwide. In New York, around seventy-five thousand attended, and in San Francisco an estimated three hundred thousand marchers thronged the streets. "Through Anita Bryant, the gay movement has been 'born again' in greater numbers and with greater determination than ever before," wrote

Robert I. McQueen and Randy Shilts in the *Advocate* the month following the setback in Miami. "The success of her hysterical 'Save Our Children' campaign in Dade County resurrected a slumbering activism and converted apathy to anger and action." An editorial in the *Nation* put it even more bluntly: "Anita Bryant is the best thing ever to happen to American homosexuals."[9]

Bryant's Florida campaign was only the first salvo in the New Right's growing crusade to overturn the gains of the gay rights movement. In the following months, Bryant traveled to cities around the country trying to replicate her Dade County victory. Gays and lesbians, along with their straight allies, mounted a nationwide campaign against Bryant, including a boycott of Florida orange juice, in an ultimately successful effort to force the Florida Citrus Commission to drop her as their spokeswoman. "We essentially trailed her and used the threat of Anita Bryant to try to wake up the sleeping giant of lesbians and gays in the middle of the country," recalls Virginia Apuzzo, co-chair of the Gay Rights National Lobby at the time.[10]

Still, with Bryant's help, in the spring of 1978 gay rights ordinances were repealed in St. Paul, Minnesota; Wichita, Kansas; and Eugene, Oregon. Disheartened as many lesbians and gay men were at this retrenchment, things looked even worse when California State Senator John Briggs sponsored a state initiative, Proposition 6, to ban lesbian and gay teachers from the public school system and prohibit any teacher or school employee (gay or straight) from saying anything positive about homosexuals. Openly gay San Francisco Supervisor Harvey Milk became a leading figure in the battle against the Briggs Initiative. Speaking at San Francisco's Gay and Lesbian Freedom Day rally in June 1978, he appealed:

> I want to recruit you. I want to recruit you for the fight to preserve your democracy from the John Briggs and the Anita Bryants who are trying to constitutionalize bigotry. We are not going to allow that to happen. We are not going to sit back in silence as three hundred thousand of our gay brothers and sisters did in Nazi Germany. We are not going to allow our rights to be taken away and then march with bowed heads into the gas chambers. On this anniversary of Stonewall, I ask my gay sisters and broth-

Morty Manford and his niece Avril Swan at the Christopher Street Liberation Day March, New York, 1976. © BETTYE LANE

ers to make the commitment to fight. For themselves. For their freedom. For their country.[11]

The battle over Proposition 6 received a great deal of national attention. Working together in more than thirty organizations, lesbians and gay men initiated a massive grass-roots mobilization of both straight and gay voters, and enlisted the support of prominent politicians and celebrities. Even President Jimmy Carter and former California Governor Ronald Reagan issued statements against the Briggs Initiative. In November, the initiative was defeated 59 percent to 41 percent. The victory in California was of critical importance to the gay rights movement, because it was a win at the statewide, rather than simply municipal, level. Furthermore, it momentarily halted a nationwide trend to roll back gay rights. Lesbians and gay men

White Night Riots, San Francisco, May 21, 1979.

received another lift that November from the election results in Seattle, where voters, by a two-to-one margin, voted against repeal of that city's gay rights ordinance.

The momentary celebration at rebuffing the right-wing opposition was shattered on November 27, 1978, when openly gay San Francisco Supervisor Harvey Milk and Mayor George Moscone were assassinated by homophobic right-wing Supervisor Dan White, just weeks after Milk's prominent role in defeating the Briggs Initiative. The murder shocked the city and the nation; it brought into sharp relief the depths of antigay prejudice and the potential for violence. Gay and lesbian communities around the country organized memorials and candlelight vigils.

While White could have received the death penalty for the murders of two public officials, he was only convicted of manslaughter and sentenced to seven years and eight months. In response to the verdict, gay men and lesbians in San Francisco rioted. In what came to be called the White Night Riots, hundreds of demonstrators marched from the Castro district and descended on City Hall—smashing windows, storming the doors, setting police cars on fire, and inflicting property damage in excess of one million dollars. Many members of the lesbian and gay community worried that the violent image of the riots would undercut the significant gains that they had won in becoming part of the American mainstream. Yet others felt empowered by this resurgence of radical energy and were less interested in fitting in than in fighting back. They drew parallels between this militant response and the violent birth of gay liberation at Stonewall.

The divergent responses to the White Night Riots reflected a schism in the lesbian and gay community that had widened throughout the seventies. Conservative gays, such as David B. Goodstein, the publisher of the *Advocate,* emphasized the need for respectability and were pleased with the strides that had been made toward this end. Goodstein railed against "the gay 'radical left' and 'obstructionists' who could derail the movement's push into the mainstream."[12] He heartily editorialized in favor of the closet and believed that the gay movement's successes had been achieved by "moderates," often closeted and working behind the scenes, rather than by "left-wing radicals."

On the other hand, although they appreciated legislative and elec-

Tribute to Harvey Milk, *circa 1979.* This poster memorialized openly gay San Francisco Supervisor Harvey Milk who was a much-loved hero to many gay men and lesbians. Before his assassination, Milk had been an outspoken advocate for a national lesbian and gay march on Washington.

Demonstrators protest the appearance of Moral Majority leader Jerry Falwell, Town Hall, New York, December 1984.

© DONNA BINDER/IMPACT VISUALS

toral gains, radical gays criticized the reformist civil rights strategy and perceived the limits of this approach. For example, when the Supreme Court upheld Virginia's sodomy statute in 1976, John D'Emilio criticized the gay movement for its increasing reliance on "court cases and legislative lobbying efforts":

> As a whole the movement has been defining its goals and developing its tactics in a narrower and narrower way . . . Reform-oriented tactics won't take us all the way to liberation . . . In the long run we cannot end gay oppression without political activity that aims at the roots of our social organization. If we rely solely on the courts, we allow those in power to deny us our freedom. [13]

As the 1980s dawned, the lesbian and gay community faced a New Right emboldened by President Ronald Reagan's election and the advent of AIDS—which religious leaders on the right characterized as divine punishment of homosexuals. Jerry Falwell founded the Moral Majority in 1979 and, along with other religious right leaders like Pat Robertson and the Reverend Donald Wildmon, fomented stridently antigay attitudes among his fundamentalist supporters. Through televangelism and highly sophisticated direct-mail techniques, these leaders tapped into, and incited, fear and moral indignation among their followers, creating a formidable opposition to the lesbian and gay movement. Demonstrating their growing power, in 1980 approximately two hundred thousand fundamen-

From the outset of the gay movement, lesbians and gay men have felt the need to organize independently around their own racial and cultural identities. Typically these groups worked both within the larger gay community as well as within their own communities of color. As early as 1970, Third World Gay Revolution groups were started in New York and Chicago, and Unidos, a gay Chicano/Chicana group, was founded in Los Angeles. The founding of the National Coalition of Black Gays in 1978 signaled a new level of political organization. NCBG sponsored the landmark "3rd World Lesbian and Gay Conference," held in conjunction with the first National March for Lesbian and Gay Rights in 1979. Activists from around the country went home to organize and the 1980s and 1990s have seen an extraordinary proliferation of gay and lesbian organizations for African Americans, Latinos, Asian Americans, and Native Americans.

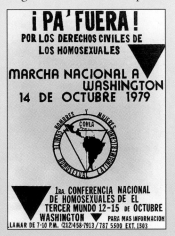

(top, left) **Poster for 3rd World Conference, Washington, D.C., 1979.**

(below, right) **¡Pa' Fuera! 1979.** "Come out! For the civil rights of homosexuals" announces this poster from the Comite Homosexual Latinoamericano (Latin American Homosexual Committee) promoting the upcoming conference of third world gays.

talists participated in the Washington for Jesus march in the nation's capital. Antigay rhetoric reached new extremes with the religious right. At one point Dean Wycoff, chairperson of the Santa Clara, California, Moral Majority, indicated that his group would seek the death penalty for homosexuals: "I agree with capital punishment, and I believe homosexuality is one of those [crimes] that could be coupled with murder and other sins."[14]

Lesbians and gay men faced further threats when fundamentalist lawmakers introduced antigay legislation in Congress. In 1981 the New Right began promoting the Family Protection Act, which as part of a broad "pro-family" agenda, would have denied lesbians and gay men their civil rights, their freedom of association, and their right to collect govern-

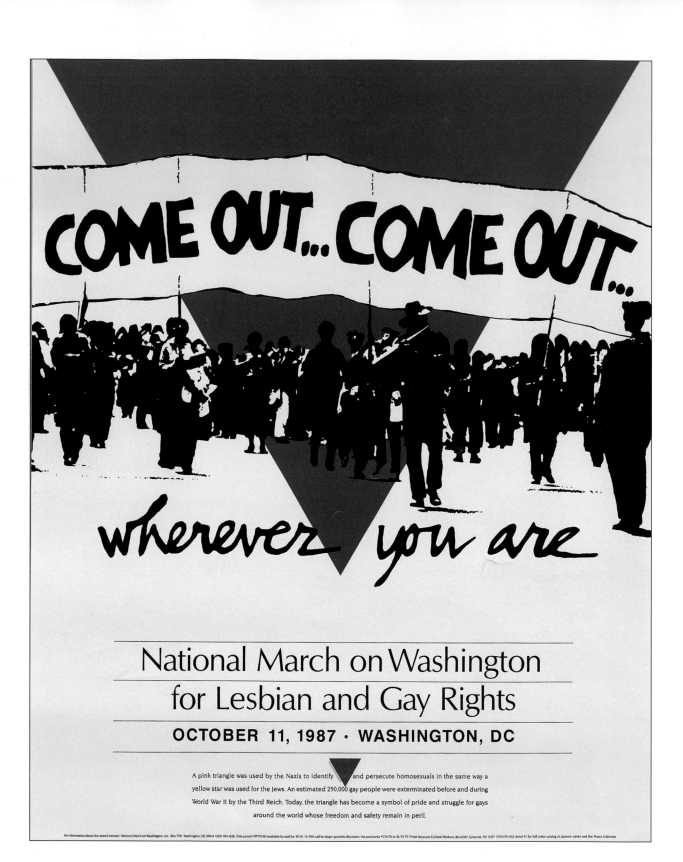

COME OUT... COME OUT...

wherever you are

National March on Washington
for Lesbian and Gay Rights
OCTOBER 11, 1987 · WASHINGTON, DC

A pink triangle was used by the Nazis to identify and persecute homosexuals in the same way a yellow star was used for the Jews. An estimated 250,000 gay people were exterminated before and during World War II by the Third Reich. Today, the triangle has become a symbol of pride and struggle for gays around the world whose freedom and safety remain in peril.

For information about the march contact: National March on Washington, Inc., Box 7781, Washington, DC 20044 (202) 783-1828. This poster (#P79CW) available by mail for $8.50, 10/$39; call for larger quantity discounts. (As postcards #C91CW at 30/$5.75.) From Syracuse Cultural Workers, Box 6367, Syracuse, NY 13217 (315) 474-1132. Send $1 for full color catalog of posters, cards and the Peace Calendar.

(opposite) *Poster for the National March on Washington for Lesbian and Gay Rights, 1987.*

(left) *Black and White Men Together, in the Lesbian and Gay Pride March, New York, 1982.* © BETTYE LANE

(below) *Senior Action in a Gay Environment (SAGE), in the Lesbian and Gay Pride March, New York, 1985*

© BETTYE LANE

ment benefits such as social security, welfare, student aid, and veterans' benefits. In fund-raising, right-wing supporters of the bill emphasized the gay threat within a wider context of evils:

> Immorality . . . homosexuality . . . abortion . . . child pornography . . . drug addiction . . . parental harassment . . . are all signs of a cancer eating away at our moral fiber . . . Now there is an answer to all the organized abortionists, homosexuals, atheists and radicals. It's the Family Protection Act . . . Your tax dollars will be totally prohibited from going to any group that presents homosexuality as acceptable . . . Don't you think it's time to stand up to the militant homosexuals?[15]

Although the Family Protection Act was introduced a number of times in the early eighties, lesbians and gay men worked in concert with other progressive forces and the bill never passed.

Much as gay people were under siege in this increasingly conservative—often reactionary—political climate, they had nevertheless become an organized community in the decade since Stonewall. Aside from leg-

(opposite) *Lesbians and gay men on the Mall, March on Washington for Lesbian and Gay Rights, October 11, 1987.*

(right) *Sergio Cordova and Jim Quinlan kiss on the Mall, March on Washington for Lesbian, Gay and Bi Equal Rights and Liberation, April 25, 1993.*

There have been three national Marches on Washington as part of the contemporary gay rights movement—in 1979, 1987, and 1993. Reflecting the growing strength of the movement, the number of marchers rose (according to the organizers) from around one hundred thousand marchers in 1979 to approximately eight hundred thousand in 1993.

islative, judicial, and electoral achievements, they had created thousands of organizations nationwide to meet the needs of what was in fact many lesbian and gay communities. In addition to the political organizations that fought for gay rights, gay and lesbian religious groups of all denominations were flourishing. The Metropolitan Community Church established dozens of congregations nationwide. Dignity was founded by gay Catholics, Integrity by gay Episcopalians, and lesbian and gay Jews founded a host of synagogues. Social and recreational groups also boomed: gay and lesbian outdoor groups, running clubs, bridge and Scrabble clubs, bowling leagues, swim teams, square dancing groups, and organizations for every type of fetish and sexual taste. Organizations were created for gay youth, lesbian mothers, and gay fathers, not to mention professional organizations for librarians, doctors, lawyers, academics, and nurses, among others. Groups for lesbians and gay men of color were formed by African Americans, Latinos, Asian Americans, and Native Americans. Cultural expression was fostered by gay theater companies such as the Glines in New York and Theater Rhinoceros in San Francisco. Archives and history projects retrieved the gay and lesbian past while documenting the 1970s as they happened. And cities around the country supported lesbian and gay switchboards and community centers. In little over a decade, lesbians and gay men transformed "gay power" into "gay community."

Graffiti, Greenwich Village, New York, 1985.
© BETTYE LANE

CONFRONTING AIDS

The fact is, no one knows where to start with AIDS.
Now, in the seventh year of the calamity, my friends . . . can hardly recall
what it felt like any longer, the time before the sickness . . .
It comes like a slowly dawning horror. At first you are equipped with a hundred
different amulets to keep it far away. Then someone you know goes into the
hospital, and suddenly you are at high noon in full battle gear. . .
You fight tough, you fight dirty, but you cannot fight dirtier than it.

—PAUL MONETTE,
BORROWED TIME, 1988

In the 1980s, the gay and lesbian community came under siege as it confronted an entirely new enemy—a lethal virus. The gay community was decimated by fear and illness and death as thousands—and then tens of thousands—of lives were lost. However, relying on the solid institutions built in the 1970s, the community mounted an extraordinary response to the health crisis. Using organization-

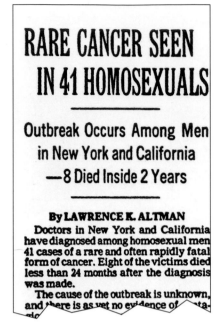

RARE CANCER SEEN IN 41 HOMOSEXUALS

Outbreak Occurs Among Men in New York and California —8 Died Inside 2 Years

By LAWRENCE K. ALTMAN

Doctors in New York and California have diagnosed among homosexual men 41 cases of a rare and often rapidly fatal form of cancer. Eight of the victims died less than 24 months after the diagnosis was made.

The cause of the outbreak is unknown, and there is as yet no evidence of conta...

The New York Times, *July 3, 1981.* This was the first major news report on what would come to be called AIDS. Buried on page A20: "The cause of the outbreak is unknown, and there is as yet no evidence of contagion."

building skills and knowledge acquired in the struggle for gay rights, gay people created a network of social service agencies and advocacy organizations, challenged the medical and scientific establishments, invented "safe sex," developed innovative educational initiatives, and achieved an unprecedented participation in public policy-making.

The first reports of cases of an unusual pneumonia and a "rare cancer" among gay men in Los Angeles, San Francisco, and New York that appeared in 1981 sent shock waves through the gay world. Confusion, fear, denial, and conflict engulfed gay men, as the number of cases grew amidst uncertainty over what was causing the diseases and how they could be transmitted. Every new discovery of a slight skin discoloration became cause for alarm and prompted terrified trips to the doctor. The community rejected the idea that the disease was contagious. It seemed to defy logic that a disease could pick out gays to prey upon; and if the disease did prove to be contagious, it would turn gay men into sexual lepers. " 'How can a disease pick out gays?' they asked; it had to be 'medical homophobia.' "[1] Nonetheless, since the illnesses were first noticed among gay men, some scientists dubbed the outbreak Gay-Related Immunodeficiency (GRID). By late 1982, however, it became clear that the disease also struck other groups, particularly intravenous drug users, hemophiliacs, and recipients of blood transfusions. It was renamed Acquired Immune Deficiency Syndrome, or AIDS.

In looking for the etiology of the disease, attention turned to "lifestyle factors" that might be implicated, such as multiple sex partners and recreational drugs. Gay men's sexual behavior became the focus of fierce battles and denunciations, both within the community and in society at large. Some denounced "promiscuity" while others dismissed these criticisms as moralizing attempts to turn back the sexual advances of gay liberation. And as Robert A. Padgug and Gerald M. Oppenheimer have argued, "The persistence of the identification of the entire gay community as a risk group because of its sexual practices meant that gay sexuality itself, was, in effect, identified as the 'risky' factor."[2]

Sexual establishments came under attack as some gay men and public health officials blamed bathhouses and sex clubs for the spread of the disease and called for their closings. On the other side were gay men who argued that this strategy would simply send gay sex underground and that sexual venues were the ideal places to distribute information on safe-sex practices. Commenting on the tensions within the gay community, author John Rechy wrote in 1983, "AIDS commands our lives. Every homosexual has contracted a form of it, in fear, suspicion . . . and accusation."[3]

At the beginning of the epidemic the mainstream media largely ignored it. When they did run stories, the press sensationalistically characterized AIDS as the "gay plague," and further stigmatized gay men by referring to members of other risk groups—hemophiliacs, blood-transfusion recipients, or children of mothers with AIDS—as "innocent victims," implying that gay men and intravenous drug users with AIDS were guilty. The media only became interested in the epidemic when it appeared that the implicitly heterosexual "general population" might be at risk. Many critics saw the media's response to the epidemic as unabashedly homophobic. Journalist Randy Shilts, discussing the early AIDS years, wrote: "There was only one reason for the lack of media interest . . . : the victims were homosexuals. Editors were killing pieces, reporters told Curran [head of the Centers for Disease Control's AIDS task force], because they didn't want stories about gays and all those distasteful sexual habits littering their newspapers."[4] When the press did cover AIDS, it often appealed to fear and printed incendiary headlines to attract the public. For example, the July 1985 cover of *Life* magazine boomed in bright red letters, "Now, No One Is Safe From AIDS." Finally, the disclosure that same month that actor Rock Hudson had AIDS was a critical turning point in the coverage, as the country finally had a "victim" with whom it could truly sympathize.

In the face of mainstream media silence, the gay press, particularly the *New York Native,* assumed the responsibility for publicizing the burgeoning health crisis. The *Native* printed the numbers of AIDS cases and deaths in each issue, sometimes displaying them in stark headlines on the front cover. The paper became an indispensable source of medical information on the epidemic for gay men around the country. It provided a forum for discussion of the health crisis in a time of great confusion and uncertainty, when the gay community was still trying to figure out how to respond to the epidemic. The *Native* published a series of articles by writer Larry Kramer, one of the founders of Gay Men's Health Crisis, who crit-

(inset) **Barry Leach and Spencer Beach, New York, 1972.**

(bottom) **Letter to friends from Barry L[each] and Spencer B[each], New York, June 29, 1981.**

When Spencer Beach was diagnosed with Kaposi's sarcoma (KS) and lobar pneumonia in 1981, neither he nor Barry Leach, his lover of twenty-five years, nor their friends and families, understood what was happening. Beach, who died in 1982 of what would become known as AIDS, was one of the first men in New York to be diagnosed with this rare "gay cancer."

(right) **Showers, *1982*.** Gay Men's Health Crisis's first benefit was held in early 1982 before the term *AIDS* was coined. At the time, Kaposi's sarcoma, a skin cancer with purple lesions, and *Pneumocystis carinii* pneumonia (PCP) were the two opportunistic infections that were symptomatic of this mysterious illness, which had inaccurately been dubbed gay-related immunodeficiency (GRID). By the end of the year the disease was renamed AIDS.

(far right) **Fighting for Our Lives, *1983*.** In the first major expression of communal grief and demand for government action, cities around the nation held AIDS marches on May 2, 1983.

icized gay men for their muted response to the epidemic and for not modifying their sexual behavior. Typical of Kramer's incendiary style was his famous wake-up call, "1,112 and Counting," published in 1983, which was widely reprinted in gay newspapers around the country:

> If this article doesn't scare the shit out of you, we're in real trouble. If this article doesn't rouse you to anger, fury, rage, and action, gay men may have no future on this earth. Our continued existence depends on just how angry you can get . . . Unless we fight for our lives we shall die. In all the history of homosexuality we have never before been so close to death and extinction. Many of us are dying or already dead.[5]

Kramer and others also criticized the government for its slow response to the epidemic. They believed that decisions were being based on a politics of morality rather than on reasoned public health concerns, and typically contrasted this response to the government's (as well as the media's) reaction to other recent public health emergencies such as Legionnaire's disease and toxic shock syndrome, which had both attracted extensive attention and funding. While most politicians shied away from the subject, activists were supported in their critique by a few select politicians. For example, in April 1982 Democratic Congressman Henry Waxman arranged the first congressional hearings on GRID at Los Angeles's Gay and Lesbian Community Services Center in his district. In his opening remarks, Waxman observed:

> I want to be especially blunt about the political aspects of Kaposi's sarcoma. This horrible disease afflicts members of one of the nation's most stigmatized and discriminated against minorities . . . There is no doubt in my mind that, if the same disease had appeared among Americans of Norwegian descent, or among tennis players, rather than gay males, the responses of both the government and the medical community would have been different.[6]

The Reagan administration ignored the epidemic and budgeted no money for AIDS research in 1982 or 1983, though Congress did allocate a meager $33 million. The National Institutes of Health only began a concerted research effort in 1983. The federal government's attempts to inform the public were also half measures; a hotline set up by the U.S. Department of Health and Human Services in 1983 had only six operators to answer more than ten thousand calls a day, and in the course of just one month, July 1983, they left ninety thousand calls unanswered. But Secretary of Health and Human Services Margaret Heckler assured the country in 1984, when announcing the discovery of the HIV virus, that AIDS would be stopped before it reached the "general population" (which by definition did not include homosexuals).

Despite this assurance, through the 1980s the Reagan administration requested less money for AIDS than did Congress and proposed cuts to congressional allocations, even as the number of AIDS cases mushroomed and the disease struck a wider range of the population. Concerns about "promoting" homosexuality hindered the federal government from issuing explicit "safe sex" educational

AIDSGATE. *Silence = Death Project, New York, 1987.* President Ronald Reagan ignored the urgency of the health crisis, withheld crucially needed federal money for research and education, and failed to provide moral leadership when the American public was in the midst of hysteria over AIDS. Although the epidemic first became known in 1981, President Reagan waited until 1987, six years into the epidemic, before giving his first speech on AIDS. By then, there were thirty-six thousand reported AIDS cases in the United States and almost twenty-one thousand Americans had died of the disease.

This Political Scandal Must Be Investigated!
54% of people with AIDS in NYC are Black or Hispanic. . . AIDS is the No. 1 killer of women between the ages of 24 and 29 in NYC
By 1991, more people will have died of AIDS than in the *entire* Vietnam War. . . What is Reagan's *real* policy on AIDS!
Genocide of all Non-whites, Non-males, and Non-heterosexuals? . . .
SILENCE = DEATH

information, despite Surgeon General C. Everett Koop's strong support for a sex-education curriculum that addressed AIDS and homosexuality. Since education was undeniably the one sure way of slowing the spread of the epidemic, the government's capitulation to conservatives proved lethal as large portions of the American public remained ignorant of how they could prevent exposure to the virus. To a large extent, state and local governments followed the federal example of underfunding AIDS, though there were notable exceptions such as San Francisco, where a unique partnership between the city and community organizations created an extremely effective response to the epidemic.

Many AIDS activists experienced the government's response as blatant homophobia. Gay liberationist Vito Russo, who became an outspoken AIDS activist, articulated this view:

> It was sort of a sickening revelation that my government so hated gay people that they didn't want to spend money on AIDS. It took Reagan six years to even say the name. We've learned that no matter how much medical care you can afford, it's not enough. Even if you're white and you're wealthy, the truth is, when it comes to AIDS, you're nothing but a homosexual.[7]

Another AIDS activist, Diego Rivera, put it more bluntly when he said, "I may eventually die as a result of this disease, but I would consider my death an act of murder for the lack of government funding. I would consider it murder by my own government."[8]

Padgug and Oppenheimer have observed that in the absence of a timely and effective response from the government and public health officials, the gay and lesbian community took control of the epidemic and became "the

Gay Men's Health Crisis information table in Sheridan Square, New York, October 1983. Early in the epidemic, GMHC was out on the streets of Greenwich Village every weekend, raising public awareness about the AIDS epidemic. © BETTYE LANE

People With AIDS Coalition marching in the Lesbian and Gay Pride March, New York, 1985. Among the men in this photograph are a number of well-known fighters in the battle against AIDS, including Sal Licata, David Summers, and Michael Callen, all of whom have since died. © ELLEN NEIPRIS

single most powerful force in the struggle against AIDS." The community "insisted that there be a gay voice—a public presence—in all aspects of the epidemic and its management."[9] Building on the institutions that had grown in the 1970s, the community created a network of hundreds of new organizations to meet the needs of those living with HIV and AIDS. New York's Gay Men's Health Crisis (GMHC), the first and largest, was founded in Larry Kramer's living room in 1982 by six gay men who had watched many of their friends die from the new, as yet unidentified disease. That first year, GMHC established the world's first AIDS hotline and distributed 250,000 copies of the group's Health Recommendation Brochure to gay bars in New York. The organization went on to provide support groups, a buddy program, legal and financial counseling, hot meals, and recreational activities for people with HIV and AIDS. They also distributed educational and safe-sex materials. GMHC became a model for volunteer-based AIDS service organizations throughout the United States and Europe. Similar community-based organizations were established in other cities hit hard by the epidemic: AIDS Project Los Angeles began in 1982, and San Francisco's Shanti Project also started to focus on AIDS in the same year, making AIDS its sole mission in 1984.

Aside from the AIDS service organizations, individuals who were developing AIDS took the offensive in organizing themselves. Early in the epidemic, they began to speak out against such terms as "AIDS victims" or "AIDS patients," and meeting in Denver in 1983, they adamantly stated: "We condemn attempts to label us as 'victims,' which implies defeat, and we are only occasionally 'patients,' which implies passivity, helplessness, and dependence upon the care of others. We are 'people with AIDS.' "[10] People With AIDS—PWAs, as they came to be known—trailblazed a new kind of advocacy in which they not only defined the terms of their illness, but also managed the course of their own care. The People With AIDS Coalition was founded in New York in 1985 and similar groups sprang up in San Francisco, Los Angeles, and other cities. Responding to the lack of available information for PWAs, these groups circulated newsletters and aggressively sought out alternative treatments, often through buyers' clubs that obtained drugs unavailable in the United States. A leader in the effort to help PWAs become the most informed group of patients in the country was Project Inform, founded in San Francisco in 1985. As it became clear that HIV-positive people could live healthy and productive lives for many years, activists established organizations like New York's Body Positive to provide services tailored to this group.

Safe-sex posters, 1992.
© STEVE MEISEL, PHOTOGRAPHS, 1992;
© RED, HOT AND DANCE LTD, 1992

Early on the gay community took the lead in addressing the crucial issue of what to do about sexual behavior during a sexually transmitted epidemic. In an extraordinarily novel approach to public health, gay men themselves developed the idea of "safe sex," or more precisely "safer sex," in an effort to maintain satisfying erotic lives while coping with the threat of AIDS. Safe sex was initially seen not only as a lifesaving technique but as a politically empowering activity. As Cindy Patton has noted:

> Safe sex organizing efforts before 1985 grew out of the gay community's understanding of the social organization of our own sexuality . . . Informed by a self-help model taken from the women's health movement and by the gay liberation discussion of sexuality, safe sex was viewed by early AIDS activists, not merely as a practice to be imposed on the reluctant, but as a form of political resistance and community building that achieved both sexual liberation and sexual health.[11]

Safe-sex parties and educational workshops became popular events in the gay community. AIDS service organizations produced explicit educational materials in an attempt to reach people by eroticizing safe sex and using everyday language, rather than medical terminology. Such community-generated information was crucial, since many government-funded efforts at education were stymied by conservatives, particularly Senator Jesse Helms, who opposed candid discussions of homosexuality, let alone of gay sexual practices.

Helms and other right-wing zealots, on the ascendance in the early 1980s, seized on AIDS to further the antigay agenda they had been promoting since the mid-1970s. In 1983 Patrick Buchanan wrote, "The sexual revolution has begun to devour its children. And among the revolutionary vanguard, the Gay Rights activists, the mortality rate is highest and climbing . . . The poor homosexuals—they have declared war upon nature, and now nature is exacting an awful retribution." And Jerry Falwell proclaimed that "AIDS is God's judgment on a society that does not live by His rules." Gays quipped that if AIDS was God's punishment on gay men for their homosexual acts, then lesbians, who had exceedingly low rates of HIV infection, must be God's chosen.[12]

Media silence and sensationalism, government neglect, right-wing prognostications, and public distrust of both the government and scientific

Antigay demonstrators protesting outside City Hall during City Council hearing on the proposed gay rights bill, New York, March 20, 1986. © BETTYE LANE

"experts," created an atmosphere of panic, hysteria, and widespread misinformation. Frequent calls for mandatory testing and quarantine were heard, and William F. Buckley called for the tattooing of everyone with AIDS. In some cities, efforts were undertaken to criminalize the sexual behavior of people with HIV and AIDS. In one extreme case, San Antonio sent people with AIDS a letter informing them that having sex with a partner who wasn't similarly infected was a third-degree felony, subject to a two- to ten-year sentence. Some funeral homes refused to handle the bodies of people who had died of AIDS and numerous physicians and health-care workers, fearing contagion from casual contact, refused to treat patients with AIDS or enter their hospital rooms. Given this response by medical professionals, it is not surprising that, in spite of scientific evidence that HIV could not be spread through casual contact, a *New York Times*/CBS poll in 1985 showed that 47 percent of Americans believed that they could catch AIDS from a drinking glass while 28 percent thought the disease transmissable on toilet seats. Thirty-four percent in another survey considered it dangerous to "associate" with someone with AIDS even if there was no direct physical contact. Once the first test for antibodies to the HIV virus became available in 1985, polls indicated that 72 percent of Americans favored mandatory testing, 51 percent supported quarantine, and 15 percent thought people with HIV should be tattooed.

In this climate, people with AIDS became pariahs. They were stigmatized and subjected to discrimination; some were fired from jobs, evicted from apartments, and generally shunned. The discrimination extended to members of groups perceived to be at risk for AIDS—gay men and intravenous drug users. Firemen would sometimes refuse to resuscitate men perceived to be gay, and police routinely wore rubber gloves when arresting demonstrators at gay rights or AIDS activist demonstrations. The public's reaction was inevitably effected by the construction of AIDS as a "gay disease." Historian Allan M. Brandt has observed:

> Underlying the fears of transmission were deeper concerns about homosexuality . . . AIDS threatened heterosexuals with homosexual contamination. In this context, homosexuality—not a virus—causes AIDS. Therefore, homosexuality itself is feared as if it were a communicable, lethal disease. After a generation of work to strike homosexuality from the psychiatric diagnostic manuals, it had suddenly reappeared as an infectious, terminal disease.[13]

Bearing out Brandt's analysis, homophobia escalated in the wake of the epidemic. "Instead of calling us queer," commented Roberta Achtenberg of San Francisco's Lesbian Rights Project in 1986, "now they have something that's more legitimate-appearing to hide behind. AIDS provides a veil for basic homophobia."[14] The threats went beyond words, as the incidence of antigay violence rose in cities around the country.

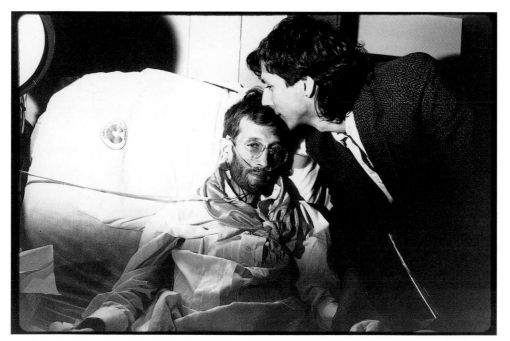

Michael Callen gives Bob Herman a birthday kiss, New York, 1986. Hospital visits became an all-too-common activity for many New Yorkers in the 1980s and '90s.
© JANE ROSETT

Silence = Death *Project, New York, 1986.*
The "Silence = Death" logo, widely disseminated by ACT UP, has become emblematic of AIDS activism.

In reaction to these attitudes in the early years of the epidemic, AIDS activists and their supporters found themselves in the curious position of having to deemphasize the gay aspects of AIDS in order to attract media attention and government funding; only the fear that the "general population" would be affected seemed to rouse concern. By 1985 the standard line of AIDS activists became, "AIDS is not a gay disease." But this strategy was problematic because it denied the devastation in the gay community and the reality that most PWAs were indeed gay.

In 1987, angered by the limited government and media response to the health crisis, and frustrated by what they saw as the accommodationist tactics of AIDS service organizations like GMHC, some New York activists formed ACT UP (AIDS Coalition to Unleash Power). The new

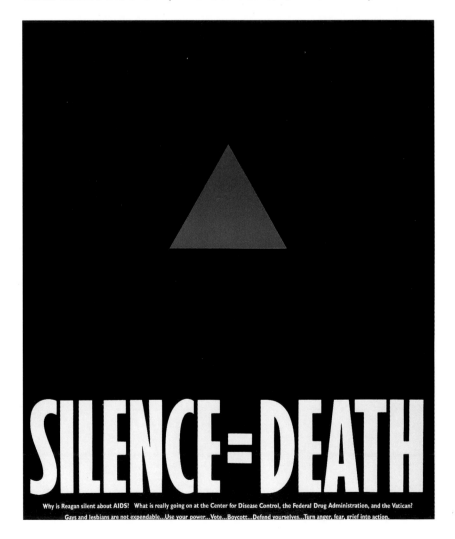

SILENCE=DEATH

Why is Reagan silent about AIDS? What is really going on at the Center for Disease Control, the Federal Drug Administration, and the Vatican? Gays and lesbians are not expendable...Use your power...Vote...Boycott...Defend yourselves...Turn anger, fear, grief into action.

Three-thousand-strong ACT UP demonstration demanding that the Koch administration commit more money for AIDS services, housing for homeless PWAs, and expanding overcrowded hospitals, City Hall, New York, March 28, 1989. © FRED W. McDARRAH

group employed "direct action" tactics reminiscent of the gay liberationists, holding demonstrations, engaging in civil disobedience, and attracting media attention. Integral to ACT UP's strategy was the
sophisticated use of bold graphics to convey its message in widely displayed
posters, stickers, flyers, T-shirts, and buttons. ACT UP's approach took off
as other cities followed New York's lead and started more than seventy autonomous ACT UPs around the country, as well as in Paris, London, and
Berlin.

Media-savvy ACT UP activists used confrontational strategies to focus
public attention on AIDS issues. "It's about time we upped the stakes during
the epidemic," said ACT UP activist Peter Staley in 1990. "We're fighting
criminal negligence on the part of the government. They're literally killing
us."[15] ACT UP demonstrated at the National Institutes of Health (NIH) and
the Food and Drug Administration (FDA), infiltrated the New York Stock
Exchange to attack Burroughs-Wellcome for the high price of AZT (the
first FDA-approved drug to treat AIDS cost $10,000 a year per patient, the
most expensive prescription drug in history), chained themselves to fences
and vehicles at pharmaceutical companies, and protested the church's opposition to safe-sex education.

Complementing their street activism, some ACT UP members became experts on AIDS treatment and drug issues, housing problems, and
needle-exchange programs, and worked on the outside—and sometimes
on the inside—to change the government's handling of the health crisis.
Activists' intervention into the public health and scientific bureaucracy was

The Names Project AIDS Memorial Quilt in Central Park, New York, June 1988. The San Francisco–based Names Project's AIDS memorial quilt was begun in 1986 as a communal effort to remember those lost to AIDS and to visually suggest the magnitude of the epidemic. Rooted in the historical quilting tradition, but with a gay twist, by 1990 the quilt had grown to more than forty-three thousand panels. Portions of the quilt have traveled to hundreds of cities around the country and the world, and the entire quilt has been exhibited several times on the Mall in Washington, D.C. © Y. NAGASAKI

a development of historic note. Sociologist Steven Epstein has suggested that "the AIDS movement [was] the first in the United States to accomplish the mass conversion of disease 'victims' into activist-experts."[16] Scientists and doctors were forced to acknowledge the value of activists' opinions and the critical role that they could play in scientific research and policy, and by 1990 almost two dozen activists had been appointed to sit on government panels overseeing clinical drug trials.

The success of AIDS activists in challenging and changing the medical and scientific establishment has had broad ramifications as it has inspired other health-care advocates, including women fighting breast cancer and those addressing "environmental illness," among others, to adopt a more aggressive style of activism in fighting for more funding and media attention and in raising public awareness.

(above) **Gay/AIDS contingent in the Puerto Rican Day Parade, New York, June 1990.** For the first time, in 1990 a contingent of gay Latino AIDS activists marched in the Puerto Rican Day Parade, protesting AIDS policies on the island.
© MICHAEL ROHRER

(right) **Vito Russo's diary, San Francisco, 1990.** Writer and activist Vito Russo detailed his battle with AIDS in his personal journals. On November 4, 1990, he wrote his last entry in a barely legible hand:

> I've been having those weaknesses in my leg again. As it stands now I can still get out of here but for only a limited time. The PCP [*Pneumocystis carinii* pneumonia] and CM [cytomegalovirus] are treatable but the internal KS [Kaposi's sarcoma] is not and that's certainly what they think I'm getting. So now it's a matter of time and how to use it.

He died three days later of AIDS-related causes, at age forty-four.

By the late 1980s, New York had almost one quarter of all AIDS cases and deaths in the country, and AIDS had become the leading cause of death for New York men and women aged twenty-five to forty-four. The demographics of the disease had also dramatically shifted. In cities like New York, AIDS had become a major epidemic among the poor, people of color, intravenous drug users, and women. By the end of the decade, approximately 40 percent of gay and bisexual men with AIDS in New York were African American or Latino, and more than two thirds of all people with AIDS in New York were people of color. In response to the growing magnitude of the epidemic, as well as the specific needs of this changing population, existing organizations expanded their services. New Yorkers created dozens of other organizations—some largely gay, others not—including, among others, the Minority Task Force on AIDS, the Women and AIDS Resource Network, the Hispanic AIDS Forum, and GMHC's Lesbian Aid Project.

By the late eighties and early nineties, the extent and quality of media coverage on AIDS had improved. Government-funding levels had grown significantly, though never enough to keep up with the demands of activists and the needs of AIDS service organizations. In 1990 Congress passed the Ryan White Comprehensive AIDS Resources Emergency Act, authorizing $2.9 billion dollars over five years for planning and services in the cities and states hardest hit by AIDS, although it was not actually funded at that level. That same year, Congress passed the Americans with Disabilities Act, which extended antidiscrimination protection to the disabled, including people with HIV/AIDS. By then, public hysteria had diminished as a broad segment of the American public—or at least liberals and Hollywood celebrities—regularly turned out for AIDS benefits, observed World AIDS Day (an annual event initiated in 1988), participated in AIDS Walks around the country to raise money for AIDS service organizations, and donned red ribbons to show their support for people with HIV and AIDS. In December 1990, deaths from AIDS in the United States passed the 100,000 mark out of a total 161,000 reported cases.

When AIDS struck in 1981, the gay rights movement was already reeling from right-wing efforts to roll back the gains of the 1970s. The additional stigma of AIDS threatened these advances and prompted some reversals of hard-won gains. As *Time* magazine seemed to gloat in 1983: "The flag of gay liberation has been lowered . . . and many do not regret it."[17] Under siege, gay people struggled to cope

Postcard issued by **DPN** *[Diseased Pariah News], San Francisco, 1991.* DPN, first published in 1990, specializes in a type of black humor that people with HIV/AIDS have developed as a coping strategy.

(right) ***Red ribbon, 1993.*** The red ribbon, originally created by Visual AIDS, has taken on a life of its own and been adapted as a fashion accessory, designer pattern, and even a U.S. postage stamp. Its ubiquity has also engendered a backlash by some who consider it a weak and empty gesture.

(below) ***AIDS memorial candlelight vigil on Christopher Street, New York, 1992.***
© Y. NAGASAKI

with the epidemic while vigilantly guarding their civil rights, historically a difficult challenge during public-health emergencies. The gay community frequently found itself at odds with government and public-health officials, though views were far from monolithic in any of the camps. Gay people argued for the screening of blood rather than the exclusion of gay men as blood donors, generally opposed tracing of sexual partners, and fought among themselves over bathhouse closure.

The HIV antibody test, licensed in 1985, was particularly contentious. For the first few years after it was introduced, gay doctors and AIDS advocacy groups strongly advised gay men not to take the test, since stigma, loss of health insurance, and the possibility of losing a job or an

apartment were real possibilities if confidentiality were broken. There were also concerns that voluntary testing could potentially lead to mandatory testing with the ultimate possibility of quarantine. The community's attitude toward voluntary testing began to change in the late 1980s when preemptive treatments started to become available. While voluntary testing has come to be seen by many as a medically advisable choice, opposition to any kind of mandatory testing has remained strong.

Through the 1980s, AIDS seemed to consume much of the energy and resources of the gay and lesbian community. Matters of life and death inevitably took precedence over other concerns. Yet AIDS reenergized the gay rights movement in a number of significant ways. Historian John

D'Emilio has noted that "through the imperative of mounting an effective response to the epidemic, the movement has achieved a level of sophistication, influence, and permanence that activists of the 1970s could only dream about."[18] Government inaction and media indifference, as well as the public hysteria around AIDS, politicized many gay men who had never thought of becoming activists until they saw their friends and lovers dying, or they themselves were diagnosed with HIV or AIDS. Volunteering for AIDS service organizations became a regular feature of gay life in the 1980s, creating a degree of organized participation in the community far greater than in the 1970s.

The rise of AIDS in the 1980s also prompted dramatic changes in relations between lesbians and gay men. On the one hand, the old tensions continued. As Dennis Altman noted in 1986: "Many lesbians feel resentment that gay men, who never showed any interest in questions of women's health, now seem to expect total commitment to AIDS activity from them."[19] But on the other hand, many lesbians, already veterans of the women's, pro-choice, and gay rights movements, joined gay men to fight AIDS and a new sense of solidarity developed. As writer and activist Sarah Schulman observed in 1985, "We're in this together now. Not only are lesbians losing friends and relatives to AIDS, but they are feeling the effects of the new homophobia accompanying AIDS hysteria."[20]

D'Emilio has observed other profound effects on lesbian and gay politics. There has been a "dramatic increase in the level of organization and visibility of gays of color" as significant numbers of them have taken on leadership roles in AIDS service

(left) **Ronald I. Jacobowitz's diary, New York, 1994–95.** Activist, political organizer, and chef Ron Jacobowitz founded Gay Men of the Bronx. Jacobowitz's diary reflects his struggle with AIDS. As he wrote elsewhere in the diary: "This disease is so insidious, not only physically, certainly emotionally, but in terms of identity. Fighting myself to be more than my illness." Jacobowitz died on November 10, 1995, at the age of thirty-six. The City of New York honored him for his activism by naming the street he lived on in the Bronx in his memory.

(below) **Memorial plaque created by Ramon Santos for Luisito, Brooklyn, New York, 1990.**

In Memory of Luisito
For our friendship
and for how much
you loved nature.
Those who loved you
will never forget you
—Ramon

organizations. AIDS has also prompted the resurgence of the direct-action and civil-disobedience tactics of the early gay liberationists, while at the same time activists have developed an often complex—and successful—combination of insider and outsider strategies. Finally, AIDS has tapped into tremendous financial resources within the gay and lesbian community and created a tradition of giving that has spilled over into gay rights issues.[21]

In large measure the gay liberation movement of the 1970s had been predicated on coming out and a politics of visibility. In the 1980s, AIDS created a whole new level of visibility for gay people in American society as discussions of homosexuality necessarily became much more widespread in the media, the classroom, and the home. Middle America finally had to acknowledge AIDS and homosexuality as its gay sons came home to die. While the epidemic and this new visibility engendered a backlash in some quarters, the gay and lesbian community's extraordinary response to the health emergency and the courage of people with AIDS prompted a greater acceptance of and respect for gay people. And as they have worked with public-health officials, scientists, and politicians in managing the epidemic, gay men and lesbians have become less marginalized in American society.

The AIDS epidemic has been a part of the gay and lesbian community—and the world—for more than fifteen years and has taken its toll in lives lost, resources sacrificed, and the fear and grief with which so many people live. As of early 1998, more than 100,000 people in New York City had been diagnosed with AIDS and more than 66,000 had died, and it is estimated that about 200,000 more New

Public service announcement, GMHC, 1993.

Yorkers are currently infected with HIV. Through mid-1997, more than 612,000 had been diagnosed with AIDS nationally and 380,000 had died. The Centers for Disease Control and Prevention currently estimates that between 650,000 and 900,000 Americans are HIV-infected.

In the late 1990s there seems to be cause for both serious concern and cautious optimism. Almost 50,000 new AIDS cases are reported each year in the United States, as AIDS is increasingly a disease not only of gay men, but of women, the poor, and people of color. But while the vaccines and cures that were optimistically promised in the 1980s have not materialized, in the last few years scientists and doctors have developed new drugs and treatment strategies that have prolonged lives and increased the quality of life for people living with AIDS. Experts believe that within the next decade AIDS will become a "manageable" chronic illness, and some people with AIDS are now looking forward to the possibility of living long and rich lives. Unfortunately, the cost of the lifesaving drugs is so prohibitive that they are unlikely to be available to most PWAs.

Notably, in 1996, for the first time in the history of the epidemic, AIDS deaths nationally decreased by 23 percent (in New York the drop was 30 percent). The trend has continued: In the first six months of 1997, AIDS deaths nationally declined by 44 percent (in New York the drop was 48 percent for all of 1997). Infection rates among gay men have declined, but as the AIDS epidemic approaches the end of its second decade, some men are having a difficult time sustaining safe-sex practices for years on end and there are concerns about a second wave of AIDS among young gay men who, some studies indicate, are having unprotected sex at alarming rates. So while recent medical developments are encouraging, the gay community and the nation face an uncertain future.

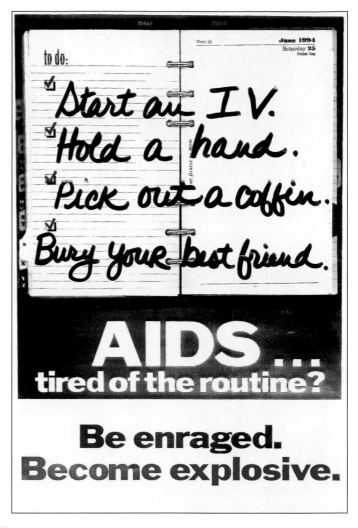

Poster, Fierce Pussy, New York, 1994. Well into the second decade of the AIDS epidemic, a New York-based lesbian artist/activist public art collective expressed the frustration of many at the "normalization" of AIDS.

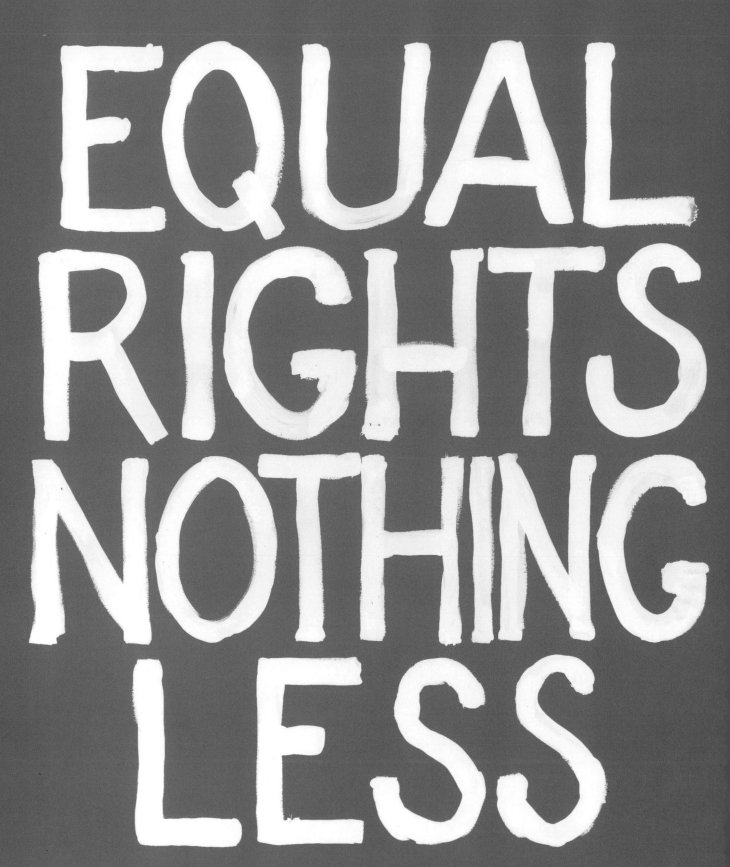

Placard carried at the March on Washington for Lesbian, Gay and Bi Equal Rights and Liberation, April 25, 1993.

THE QUEER NINETIES

We're here! We're queer!
We're fabulous! Get used to it!

—QUEER NATION CHANT

In the 1990s, many lesbians and gay men who had learned their politics through AIDS activism used these same bold tactics to confront other gay and lesbian issues. "We would not be able to have the Year of the Queer, the decade of the nineties, if it were not for the last decade of the AIDS epidemic," wrote Torie Osborn, former director of the National Gay and Lesbian Task Force in

1993. "It has created such unstoppable, ferocious determination in all of us. It has telescoped what would have been decades of change."[1] Indeed, lesbian and gay activism has flourished in the 1990s, as the movement has been reinvigorated by a new generation, many of whom have rejected the terms *gay* and *lesbian* as too limiting and mainstream, and proudly adopted the self-designation, *queer.* Many in this generation were not even born until *after* Stonewall and consider being "out and proud" as a birthright.

Indeed, visibility and controversy have been emblematic of a decade in which lesbians and gay men have made it onto the national political agenda and national television. This growing visibility has been challenged by conservative Republicans and the religious right, who have tried to roll back the gains of the preceding decades. They have used fear of queers as a hot-button issue to raise money and increase their memberships. While in earlier drives the right had fought for repeal of existing gay rights laws, in the early 1990s they developed a new, more aggressive strategy of putting antigay initiatives before the electorate. These hate campaigns have fomented increased violence against lesbians and gay men.

In 1992 Oregon and Colorado became battlegrounds. The Oregon measure, which characterized gay people as "abnormal" and "perverse," was defeated by a 57 to 43 percent vote, but the following year antigay activists, having lost the statewide fight, regrouped to pass more than a dozen local antigay initiatives. In Colorado, voters, by a 53 to 47 percent margin, approved Amendment 2, a constitutional provision that nullified existing gay rights protections in Denver, Boulder, and Aspen, and banned any new antidiscrimination protections for homosexuals in the state. The success of Amendment 2 emboldened

(above and right) **Public service announcement, New York City Gay & Lesbian Anti-Violence Project, 1993.** Violence against lesbians and gay men has been a longstanding problem. In one positive development, after a decade of prodding by gay activists, in 1990 Congress passed a bill that mandated that the federal government compile statistics on hate crimes, including those based on sexual orientation.

Demonstrators protesting antigay initiatives passed in Colorado and threatened in other states, Lesbian and Gay Pride March, New York, June 27, 1993.

the right wing to pursue the strategy of antigay initiatives elsewhere. In response, lesbians and gay men challenged the amendment in the courts and organized a national boycott of Colorado in an effort to use gay economic clout to dissuade other states and cities from enacting similar legislation. Gay activists fought to defeat these initiatives, and most never reached the ballot. Those that did, like Cincinnati's, were challenged in the courts.

A major thrust of the right wing's campaign was the characterization of gay rights laws as granting "special rights" to homosexuals. However, in 1996 the Supreme Court, in the landmark *Romer* v. *Evans* decision, struck down Colorado's Amendment 2 for violating the Constitution's Equal Protection Clause, forcefully stating that civil rights protections for homosexuals were not "special rights," but rather the same protections enjoyed by all other Americans. In a ringing denunciation of the amendment, Justice Anthony M. Kennedy wrote that "Amendment 2 classifies homosexuals not to further a proper legislative end but to make them unequal to everyone else. This Colorado cannot do. A state cannot so deem a class of persons a stranger to its laws."[2] The decision positively impacted a number of other cases in which antigay initiatives had been challenged, and effectively halted the use of this strategy by the religious right. Furthermore, "Romer . . . is so strong and respectful in vindicating the gay plaintiffs that its impact extends well beyond the case's direct result," observed Ruth Harlow, managing attorney at Lambda Legal Defense and Education Fund. "The Romer decision has opened judges' minds to our rightful invocation of all the legal protections that non-gay people take for granted."[3]

It was not just the religious right that attacked lesbians and gay men in the nineties. Mainstream politicians also jumped on the bandwagon. At their national convention in 1992, the Republicans, embracing a broad social agenda that they labeled "family values," repeatedly attacked gay men and

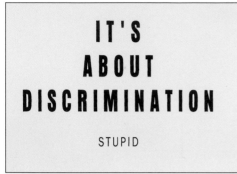

IT'S ABOUT DISCRIMINATION
STUPID

(above) **Placard carried in a march protesting the ban on gays in the military, New York, January 30, 1993.** In their effort to get President Bill Clinton to keep his pledge to eliminate the ban on gays in the military, activists echoed the Clinton campaign slogan "It's the economy, stupid" to drive home the point that the ban was a simple matter of discrimination.

(below) **Buchanan delegate at the Republican National Convention, Houston, August 19, 1992.** JENNIFER WARBURG/IMPACT VISUALS

Keep American Values Strong:
Family Rights Forever "Gay" Rights Never!
Public Advocate of the U.S.

lesbians. Leading the charge, Patrick Buchanan called for a "cultural war" against queers. In the course of the campaign, in somewhat less bellicose tones, President George Bush, Vice President Dan Quayle, Representative Newt Gingrich, and other leading Republicans denounced the "immorality" and "deviance" of homosexuality. They also condemned Democratic candidate Bill Clinton for courting the gay and lesbian community. The 1992 Republican Party's platform denounced civil rights protections for gays at the federal, state, and local levels, and supported the continued ban on lesbians and gays in the military.

During his 1992 presidential campaign, Clinton promised that he would overturn the long-standing ban against lesbians and gay men in the armed forces. Once elected, the issue provoked enormous controversy and became the gay community's first real fight in the national arena. Though the military's treatment of homosexuals was hardly at the top of the gay rights agenda, and many progressives felt ambivalent about fighting for the right to serve, the community had no choice but to confront the issue. But the gay community lost the battle. In the face of military, congressional, and public resistance, Clinton capitulated and the compromise "Don't Ask, Don't Tell" policy was adopted. The new policy turned out to be worse than the status quo, making it a particularly bad defeat for lesbian and gay service members.

Lesbian and gay domestic issues have also taken center stage in the nineties as queers have created their own "family values," and demanded public recognition for their relationships and the same benefits and safeguards enjoyed by other Americans. The aging of the Stonewall generation, the impacts of AIDS, and the lesbian baby boom all contributed to the push for legal sanctioning of gay relationships. Beginning in the late 1980s and into the 1990s, the fight for domestic-partnership benefits

Gay and lesbian couples writing their names on the ground in front of the Internal Revenue Service before "The Wedding," Washington, D.C., April 1993. Large mass-wedding ceremonies have been performed at the national gay and lesbian marches on Washington in 1987 and 1993. The ceremonies protested government policies prohibiting same-sex marriage and celebrated lesbian and gay relationships.

(right) **Make Lesbian and Gay History.**
*Gay and Lesbian Alliance Against
Defamation, New York, 1993.*

(below) **DYKE: The Final Frontier.** *fierce
pussy, New York, 1994.*

MAKE Lesbian and gay **HISTORY.**

REGISTER FOR DOMESTIC PARTNERSHIP ON MARCH 1ST, 1993.

On *March 1st, 1993*, Domestic Partnership Registration will go into effect.
For the first time in New York City, lesbian and gay couples will be formally recognized.
For information on how you can be part of this historic mass registration –
Call GLAAD/NY today at 212-807-1700. Be a part of history!

DYKE
THE FINAL FRONTIER

To Explore Strange New Worlds
To Seek Out New Life & New Civilizations
TO BOLDLY GO WHERE NO MAN HAS GONE BEFORE

fierce pussy ©

became the focus of many gay rights activists. By 1997, more than two dozen cities had established domestic-partnership registries, and over fifty cities now offer domestic-partnership benefits to municipal employees. Additionally, the private sector has responded, and a growing number of colleges and universities, labor unions, and corporations—IBM, Disney, and Levi-Strauss among them—have granted domestic-partnership benefits. By 1997 half of the Fortune 1000 companies offered domestic partnership health benefits.

The fight for legal sanction of lesbian and gay relationships took a new turn with the debate over "gay marriage," as lesbians and gay men sought to enjoy the same freedom to marry that heterosexuals do. The issue exploded into national debate in 1996 when it appeared that Hawaii would become the first state to legalize same-sex marriage. State after state reacted to the prospect that they would have to recognize such unions by trying to pass preemptive legislation denying gay people the right to marry. By early 1998, twenty-six states had passed legislation that perpetuated discriminatory marriage laws, though activists had defeated attempts in twenty-two other states. The issue was also taken up at the national level as gay and lesbian lives were once more debated in Congress. In 1996 lawmakers passed the Defense of Marriage Act, which President Clinton signed into law. The act defined marriage as a union between a man and a woman, thereby denying federal recognition (and associated benefits) to marriages between same-sex partners. While many lesbian and gay rights leaders had not seen the freedom to marry as a high priority, it resonated strongly with many in the community who wanted recognition for their relationships and their chosen families.

Queer visibility in popular culture, the arts, and the media have also marked the nineties. The "culture wars" heated up in 1989 when Senator Jesse Helms and the religious right attacked the National Endowment for the Arts for funding an exhibit of Robert Mapplethorpe's homoerotically explicit photographs, as well as works by other artists that addressed social issues, including sexuality, AIDS, and religion. A battle ensued over the NEA's funding, and the authorization included a provision that required the NEA to implement restrictions on obscenity in all grants. "Outing" became a hot debate as some gay journalists, notably Michelangelo Signorile of New York's *Outweek,* revealed the sexuality of public figures. A debate raged in the community over the circumstances under which it was acceptable to "out" celebrities and politicians, particularly closeted ones who worked against the interests of the gay community. "Lesbian chic," the media's sudden, and fleeting, interest in lesbians had its moment in the early nineties. Celebrities, notably musicians Melissa Etheridge, k.d. lang, and comedian Ellen Degeneres, came out publicly. Finally, in a turn of events that entertained and amazed many, gay people arrived on prime-time television; at one point in 1997 some two dozen lesbian and gay characters could be seen in American living rooms.

Gay organizations, too, found a wider audience. Established organizations, with roots in the 1970s and '80s, have met the challenges of the nineties: The Human Rights Campaign has raised millions to support and elect progay candidates; the National Gay and Lesbian Task Force has fostered grass-roots organizing in response to antigay initiatives; the

Daddy's Roommate. *Alyson Publications, 1990.* This children's book about a gay man, his lover, and his son was the book most frequently challenged by censors who wanted to ban it from libraries in 1993. Despite the wide variety of gay domestic arrangements, and the lesbian baby boom of the eighties and nineties, there has been strong resistance to acknowledging gay and lesbian families.

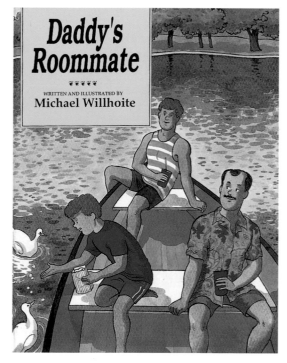

(above) **Placard carried at an ACT UP demonstration during the weekend of the March on Washington for Lesbian, Gay and Bi Equal Rights and Liberation, 1993.**

(opposite) **Stickers, 1990s.**

Lambda Legal Defense and Education Fund has championed gay rights in the courts; the Gay and Lesbian Alliance Against Defamation has combatted homophobic misrepresentation in the press; and hundreds of AIDS organizations have continued their work as the epidemic continued unabated.

These organizations were joined in the fray by a new generation of confrontational queer activists. In the lead was Queer Nation, founded in New York in 1990 when a number of ACT UP members decided it was time to employ militant AIDS-activist tactics to other gay and lesbian issues. The organization, which spawned branches around the country, brought men and women together and embraced the pejorative "queer" as an all-inclusive one-word umbrella for lesbians, gay men, bisexuals, and transgender people. Queer Nation held kiss-ins, sponsored shop-ins at suburban malls, and generally promoted in-your-face queer visibility.

Lesbian Avengers, founded in New York in 1992, employed similar direct-action tactics to promote "lesbian survival and visibility." The group courted controversy; at its very first action the women marched at an elementary school in a conservative Queens, New York, neighborhood, wearing I WAS A LESBIAN CHILD T-shirts and distributing lavender balloons that proclaimed, ASK ABOUT LESBIAN LIVES. The Avengers went on to organize the Dyke March on the White House during the 1993 March on Washington as well as the annual Dyke Marches in New York. The group has spawned many branches around the country and spread their message in their *Lesbian Avenger Handbook,* subtitled *A Handy Guide to Homemade Revolution.*

The lesbian and gay community has grown increasingly diverse in the nineties as more voices have come to be heard in a decade that has given rise to both queer nationals and gay conservatives, with a vast range of perspectives in the middle. Organizing among lesbians and gay men of color has accelerated, creating groups for ever-more specific identities, while also trying to define a common agenda for a united gay community of color. Bisexuals too have achieved a greater level of organization and sought a place for themselves in the gay and lesbian movement. And transgenderists—transsexuals, cross-dressers, drag queens and drag kings, and other "gender outlaws"—have organized as a new force against oppressive gender norms.

Diversity has been a source of strength for the movement in its bid to gain power and draw troops. But in a movement that now embraces a broader range of political perspectives than it did in the 1970s, the diversity of people, politics, and tactics has inevitably created tensions. Activist Urvashi Vaid neatly summed up the situation when she commented that "trying to organize the lesbian and gay community is like trying to organize the Milky Way galaxy."[4]

(opposite) **Dyke Manifesto.** *Lesbian Avengers, New York, 1993.* Distributed during the weekend of the March on Washington for Lesbian, Gay and Bi Equal Rights and Liberation, April 1993.

(right) **Queers Take Back the Night** *march to protest antigay violence, sponsored by Queer Nation, New York, June 16, 1990.*
© ELLEN NEIPRIS

(below) *Two Sirens, New York City, 1990.*
© KATHRYN KIRK

But lesbians and gay men have exhibited extraordinary vitality and endurance. Growing from a small band of homophiles in the fifties, to an army of queers in the nineties, they have built a mass movement for political and social change. And while the other progressive movements of the 1960s and 1970s have waned, the gay rights movement has flourished. In the three decades since Stonewall, queers have become an increasingly visible—and vocal—force to be reckoned with, challenging and changing America.

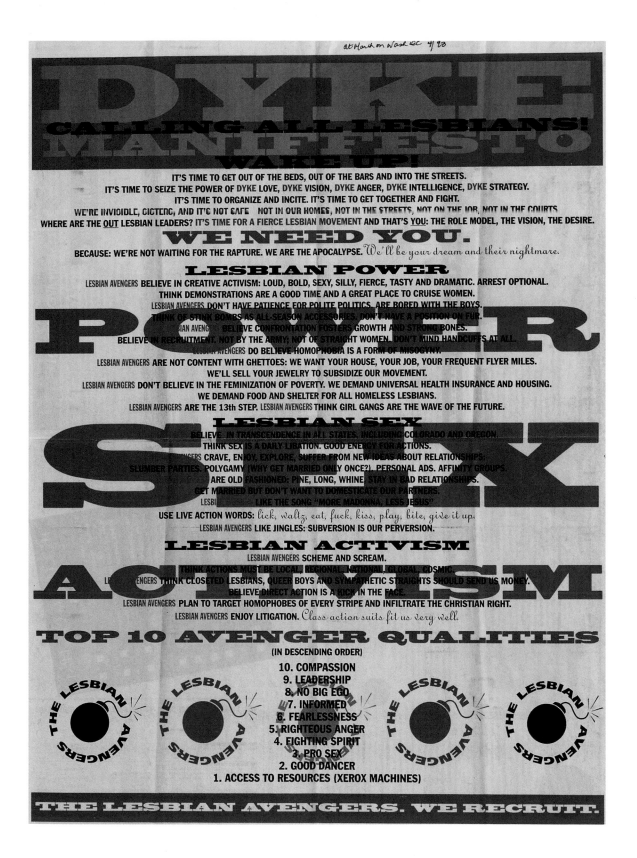

FURTHER READING

Abelove, Henry, Michele Aina Barale, and David M. Halperin, eds. *Lesbian and Gay Studies Reader.* New York: Routledge, 1993.

Beam, Joseph, ed. *In the Life: A Black Gay Anthology.* Boston: Alyson Publications, 1986.

Beemyn, Brett, ed. *Creating a Place for Ourselves: Lesbian, Gay, and Bisexual Community Histories.* New York: Routledge, 1997.

Bérubé, Allan. *Coming Out Under Fire: The History of Gay Men and Women in World War Two.* New York: The Free Press, 1990.

Blasius, Mark and Shane Phelan, eds. *We Are Everywhere: A Historical Sourcebook of Gay and Lesbian Politics.* New York: Routledge, 1997.

Boswell, John. *Christianity, Social Tolerance, and Homosexuality.* Chicago: University of Chicago Press, 1980.

Chauncey, George. *Gay New York: Gender, Urban Culture and the Making of the Gay Male World, 1890–1940.* New York: Basic Books, 1994.

Crimp, Douglas with Adam Rolston. *AIDS Demographics.* Seattle: Bay Press, 1990.

Deitcher, David, ed. *The Question of Equality: Lesbian and Gay Politics in America Since Stonewall.* New York: Scribner, 1995.

D'Emilio, John. *Making Trouble: Essays on Gay History, Politics, and the University.* New York: Routledge, 1992.

———. *Sexual Politics, Sexual Communities: The Making of a Homosexual Minority in the United States, 1940–1970.* Chicago: University of Chicago Press, 1983.

——— and Estelle B. Freedman. *Intimate Matters: A History of Sexuality in America.* New York: Harper & Row, 1988.

Duggan, Lisa and Nan D. Hunter. *Sex Wars: Sexual Dissent and Political Culture.* New York: Routledge, 1995.

Duberman, Martin. *Stonewall.* New York: Dutton, 1993.

———, Martha Vicinus, and George Chauncey, Jr., eds. *Hidden from History: Reclaiming the Gay & Lesbian Past.* New York: New American Library, 1989.

Echols, Alice. *Daring to Be Bad: Radical Feminism in America 1967–1975.* Minneapolis: University of Minnesota Press, 1989.

Escoffier, Jeffrey, Regina Kunzel, and Molly McGarry, eds. "The Queer Issue: New Visions of America's Lesbian and Gay Past," *Radical History Review,* no. 62 (Spring 1995).

Faderman, Lillian. *Odd Girls and Twilight Lovers: A History of Lesbian Life in Twentieth-Century America.* New York: Columbia University Press, 1991.

———. *Surpassing the Love of Men: Romantic Friendship and Love Between Women from the Renaissance to Present.* New York: Morrow, 1981.

Fee, Elizabeth and Daniel M. Fox, eds. *AIDS: The Burdens of History.* Berkeley: University of California Press, 1988.

———. *AIDS: The Making of a Chronic Disease.* Berkeley: University of California Press, 1992.

Foucault, Michel. *The History of Sexuality: An Introduction, Volume I.* Trans. Robert Hurley. New York: Vintage Books, 1978.

Goldberg, Jonathan, ed. *Reclaiming Sodom.* New York: Routledge, 1994.

Jay, Karla and Allen Young, eds. *Out of the Closets: Voices of Gay Liberation.* New York: A Douglas Book, 1972.

Kaiser, Charles. *The Gay Metropolis: 1940–1996.* Boston: Houghton Mifflin, 1997.

Katz, Jonathan. *Gay American History: Lesbians and Gay Men in the U.S.A.* New York: Thomas Y. Crowell Company, 1976.

———. *Gay/Lesbian Almanac: A New Documentary.* New York: Harper & Row, 1983.

———. *The Invention of Heterosexuality.* New York: Dutton, 1995.

Kennedy, Elizabeth Lapovsky and Madeline Davis. *Boots of Leather, Slippers of Gold: The History of a Lesbian Community.* New York: Routledge, 1993.

McDarrah, Fred W. and Timothy S. McDarrah. *Gay Pride: Photographs from Stonewall to Today.* Chicago: A Cappella books, 1994.

Marcus, Eric. *Making History: The Struggle for Gay and Lesbian Equal Rights 1945–1990.* New York: HarperCollins, 1992.

Marotta, Toby. *The Politics of Homosexuality.* Boston: Houghton Mifflin, 1981.

Moraga, Cherrie and Gloria Anzaldua, eds. *This Bridge Called My Back: Writings by Radical Women of Color.* 2nd ed. New York: Kitchen Table: Women of Color Press, 1983.

Nestle. Joan, ed. *The Persistent Desire: A Femme-Butch Reader.* Boston: Alyson Publications, 1992.

———. *A Restricted Country.* Ithaca, NY: Firebrand Books, 1987.

Newton, Esther. *Cherry Grove, Fire Island: Sixty Years in America's First Gay and Lesbian Town.* Boston: Beacon Press, 1993.

Patton, Cindy. *Inventing AIDS.* New York: Routledge, 1990.

Peiss, Kathy and Christina Simmons with Robert A. Padgug, eds. *Passion and Power: Sexuality in History.* Philadelphia: Temple University Press, 1989.

Ramos, Juanita, ed. *Compañeras: Latina Lesbians.* New York: Routledge, 1994.

Rosario, Vernon A., ed. *Science and Homosexualities.* New York: Routledge, 1997.

Rubenstein, William B., ed. *Lesbians, Gay Men, and the Law.* New York: The New Press, 1993.

Russo, Vito. *The Celluliod Closet: Homosexuality in the Movies.* New York: Harper & Row, 1987.

Schwarz, Judith. *Radical Feminists of Heterodoxy: Greenwich Village, 1912–1940.* Norwich, VT: New Victoria Publishers, Inc., 1986.

Sedgwick, Eve Kosofsky. *Epistemology of the Closet.* Berkeley: University of California Press, 1990.

Shilts, Randy. *And the Band Played On: Politics, People and the AIDS Epidemic.* New York: St. Martin's Press, 1987.

———. *Conduct Unbecoming: Lesbians and Gays in the Military, Vietnam to the Persian Gulf.* New York: St. Martin's Press, 1993.

Smith, Barbara, ed. *Home Girls: A Black Feminist Anthology.* New York: Kitchen Table: Women of Color Press, 1983.

Snitow, Ann, Christine Stansell, and Sharon Thompson, eds. *Powers of Desire: The Politics of Sexuality.* New York: Monthly Review Press, 1983.

Streitmatter, Rodger. *Unspeakable: The Rise of the Gay and Lesbian Press in America.* Boston: Faber and Faber, 1995.

Teal, Donn. *The Gay Militants.* New York: Stein and Day, 1971.

Terry, Jennifer and Jacqueline Urla. *Deviant Bodies: Critical Perspectives on Difference in Science and Popular Culture.* New York: Routledge, 1995.

Thompson, Mark, ed. *Long Road to Freedom: The Advocate History of the Gay and Lesbian Movement.* New York: St. Martin's Press, 1994.

Vance, Carole, ed. *Pleasure and Danger: Exploring Female Sexuality.* New York: Routledge, 1984.

Warner, Michael, ed. *Fear of a Queer Planet: Queer Politics and Social Theory.* Minneapolis: University of Minnesota Press, 1993.

Waugh, Thomas. *Hard to Imagine: Gay Male Eroticism in Photography and Film from Their Beginnings to Stonewall.* New York: Columbia University Press, 1996.

Weeks, Jeffrey. *Sex, Politics, and Society: The Regulation of Sexuality Since 1800.* London: Longman, 1981.

NOTES

Abbreviations:

IGIC   International Gay Information Center Archives, Manuscripts and Archives Division, The New York Public Library

LHA   Lesbian Herstory Archives/Lesbian Herstory Educational Foundation, Inc.

MSS   Manuscripts and Archives Division, The New York Public Library

NYPL   The New York Public Library, Astor, Lenox and Tilden Foundations

STONEWALL

"THERE'S A RIOT GOIN' ON"

1. For gay nightlife, see "The Gay Scene," flyer, March 1968, IGIC, Mattachine Society, Inc. of New York, box 11, f. 2; *New York City Gay Scene Guide Quarterly* (Mattachine Book Service: Spring 1968), MSS, Martin Michel Collection; and *Gay-Ways New York,* December 1969, p. 5, IGIC Periodicals.

2. Thomas Lanigan-Schmidt, "1969: Mother Stonewall and the Golden Rats," 1989, copy of handwritten manuscript provided to authors; and Jeremiah Newton, "Remembering the Stonewall," *New York Native,* 12 June 1989, p. 19.

3. Jay Levin, "The Gay Anger Behind the Riots," *New York Post,* 8 July 1969, p. 36.

4. Vito Russo, "I Remember Stonewall," *Soho Weekly News,* 21 June 1979, p. 12.

5. Supplement to *New York Mattachine Newsletter,* July 1969, 24, IGIC, Mattachine Society, Inc. of New York, box 11, f. 1.

6. For bar raids, see *New York Mattachine Newsletter,* August 1969, quoted in Donn Teal, *The Gay Militants* (New York: Stein and Day, 1971), p. 20.

7. For police nicknames, see Lanigan-Schmidt, "1969: Mother Stonewall and the Golden Rats." According to Section 887 (7) of the Criminal Code of New York State, people were required to wear a minimum of three pieces of clothing "appropriate to one's gender" (see Martin Duberman, *Stonewall* [New York: Dutton, 1993], p. 196 and n. 39, p. 299).

8. Sylvia Rivera quoted in Duberman, *Stonewall,* p. 196; Seymour Pine and Robert "Birdie" Rivera interviewed in "Remembering Stonewall," David Isay, producer, Pacifica Radio, 1989, MSS, Rudy Grillo Collection; and Craig Rodwell quoted in Thom Willenbecher, "Stonewall: Where It All Began," *Esplanade,* 1 July 1977, p. 24.

9. Lucian Truscott IV, "Gay Power Comes to Sheridan Square," *Village Voice,* 3 July 1969, pp. 1 and 18; "Present at the Creation: Talks to Jim Fouratt About the 'S' word," Jim Fouratt interviewed by Gabriel Rotello, *Outweek,* 26 June 1989, 44; and Craig Rodwell quoted in Duberman, *Stonewall,* p. 197.

10. Jerry Lisker, "Homo Nest Raided, Queen Bees Are Stinging Mad," *Daily News,* 6 July 1969, p. M1.

11. Howard Smith, "Full Moon Over the Stonewall," *Village Voice,* 3 July 1969, p. 25. Seymour Pine interviewed in "Remembering Stonewall."

12. Candice Boyce quoted in David Deitcher, ed., *The Question of Equality: Lesbian and Gay Politics in America Since Stonewall* (New York: Scribner, 1995), p. 77; and Sylvia Rivera interviewed in "Remembering Stonewall."

13. Mama Jean Devente interviewed in "Remembering Stonewall."

14. Horoscope, *Daily News,* 28 June 1969, p. 16.

15. Candice Boyce quoted in Deitcher, *The Question of Equality,* pp. 77–78.

16. Truscott, "Gay Power Comes to Sheridan Square," p. 18.

17. Ibid.

18. Randy Wicker quoted in Duberman, *Stonewall,* p. 207.

19. Homophile Youth Movement—HYMN, "Get the Mafia and the Cops Out of Gay Bars," flyer, 29 June 1969, MSS, Craig Rodwell Papers.

20. The *News* morgue cannot find a print or negative of this image. Jonathan Ned Katz told the authors that the photogra-

pher's nephew told him that his uncle had thrown out all of his photographs.

21. Truscott, "Gay Power Comes to Sheridan Square," p. 18.

22. "Gay Riots in the Village," *New York Mattachine Newsletter,* August 1969, quoted in Teal, *The Gay Militants,* p. 28.

23. "The Hairpin Drop Heard Around the World" and "Gay Riots" in Supplement to *New York Mattachine Newsletter,* July 1969, 21 and 24. IGIC, Mattachine Society, Inc. of New York, box 11, f. 1; Ronnie DiBrienza, "Stonewall Incident," *East Village Other,* 9 July 1969, p. 2. Lige [Clarke] and Jack [Nichols], "Pampered Perverts," *Screw,* 25 July 1969, p. 16.

24. Levin, "The Gay Anger Behind the Riots," p. 36.

25. Arnie Kantrowitz, *Under the Rainbow* (New York: William Morrow and Company, 1977), p. 138.

26. *Mattachine Midwest Newsletter,* June 1970, 1, IGIC Periodicals.

27. For example, Leo E. Laurence, "Gay Revolution," *Vector,* April 1969, 11.

28. "Policing the Third Sex," *Newsweek,* 27 October 1969, 76.

29. "Present at the Creation: Gabriello Rotello Talks to Jim Fouratt About the 'S' Word," *Outweek,* 26 June 1989, 44.

30. Donald Vining, *How Can You Come Out if You've Never Been In?: Essays on Gay Life and Relationships* (Trumansburg, N.Y.: Crossing Press, 1986), p. 51.

31. The Chinese Rainbow, "Message from Beijing," *Harvard Gay & Lesbian Review,* Fall 1995, 1; 58.

32. "The Stonewall Riots: The Gay View," *New York Mattachine Newsletter,* August 1969, quoted in Donn Teal, *The Gay Militants,* p. 29; Bob Kohler, "Where Have All the Flowers Gone," *Come Out!,* 10 January 1970, p. 14; Martha Shelley quoted in Eric Marcus, *Making History: The Struggle for Gay and Lesbian Equal Rights, 1945–1990* (New York: HarperCollins, 1992), p. 180; Thomas Lanigan-Schmidt, "1969: Mother Stonewall and the Golden Rats"; Virginia Apuzzo, interviewed by Fred Wasserman for the Brooklyn Lesbian and Gay History Exhibition Project, 6 April 1994, courtesy Brooklyn Historical Society; Stuart Timmons, *The Trouble with Harry Hay* (Boston: Alyson Publications, 1990), p. 229; Henry Baird and Seymour Pine in "Remembering Stonewall"; Renée Vera Cafiero, interviewed by Fred Wasserman for the Brooklyn Lesbian and Gay History Exhibition Project, 9 March 1994 courtesy Brooklyn Historical Society; Michael Bronski, "Sex and Stonewall," in Lynn Witt, Sherry Thomas, and Eric Marcus, *Out in All Directions: The Almanac of Gay and Lesbian America* (New York: Warner Books, 1995), p. 420; and Jewelle Gomez, "Stonewall: The Romance and the Politics," lecture at the New York Public Library, 7 March 1994.

SODOMITES, PERVERTS, AND QUEERS

LABELING AND POLICING

1. Story as told by Michael Hardwick in an interview with Peter Irons, reprinted in *Lesbians, Gay Men, and the Law,* William B. Rubenstein, ed. (New York: New Press, 1993), pp. 125–31.

2. *Bowers* v. *Hardwick,* 478 U.S. 186 (1986) (Burger, C.J., concurring; Blackmun, J., dissenting).

3. Michel Foucault, *The History of Sexuality: An Introduction, Volume I.* Trans. Robert Hurley (New York: Vintage Books, 1980), p. 101. See also the introduction to Jonathan Goldberg, *Reclaiming Sodom* (New York: Routledge, 1994).

4. "The crime not fit to be named" was how eighteenth-century English legal scholar Sir William Blackstone referred to sodomy. Chief Justice Warren Burger quoted Blackstone approvingly in his *Bowers* opinion, including Blackstone's description of sodomy as " 'the infamous crime against nature' as an offense of 'deeper malignancy' than rape, an heinous act 'the very mention of which is a disgrace to human nature.' " 478 U.S. 186 (1986) (Burger, C.J., concurring).

5. Justice Blackmun notes this discrepancy in his dissent, arguing: "Michael Hardwick's standing may rest in significant part on Georgia's apparent willingness to enforce against homosexuals a law it seems not to have any desire to enforce against heterosexuals." 478 U.S. 186 (1986) (Blackmun, J., dissenting).

6. Goldberg, *Reclaiming Sodom,* p. 8.

7. All translations are from the *King James Bible,* Modern Phrased Version (New York: Oxford University Press, 1980).

8. The canon of the Bible was officially established at the Council of Trent in 1546, although there had been general agreement among scholars as to the contents of the New Testament since at least the eighth century.

9. Louis Crompton, "The Myth of Lesbian Impunity: Capital Laws from 1270 to 1791," *Journal of Homosexuality* 6 (1980/81): 11–26.

10. See Alan Bray, *Homosexuality in Renaissance England* (London: Gay Men's Press, 1982).

11. However, the nature of those laws differed a great deal. When the Bill of Rights was adopted in 1791, three states (Connecticut, Massachusetts, and New Hampshire) had sodomy statutes that specifically condemned sex between men; eight state statutes (Delaware, New York, North Carolina, Pennsylvania, Rhode Island, South Carolina, New Jersey, and Virginia) proscribed "buggery" or "sodomy" without reference to the gender of the participants; one state (Maryland) may have had no law; and in one state (Georgia), the evidence is unclear. Anne B. Goldstein, "History, Homosexuality, and Political Values: Searching for the Hidden Determinants of *Bowers* v. *Hardwick,*" *Yale Law Review,* vol. 97, 1988: 1083–84.

12. Nan D. Hunter, "Life After Hardwick," in Lisa Duggan and Nan D. Hunter, *Sex Wars: Sexual Dissent and Political Culture* (New York: Routledge, 1995), p. 90.

13. The role of State Liquor Authorities in determining bar policy differed from state to state. Various other laws and their applications also differed, in language as well as in enforcement. Some cities, notably San Francisco, do not have a history of organized crime control of lesbian and gay bars. See the following chapter, "Out on the Town," for a more detailed history.

14. On the history of gay men and lesbians in the military during World War II, see Allan Bérubé, *Coming Out Under Fire: The History of Gay Men and Women in World War Two* (New York: Free Press, 1990).

15. "Homosexuals in Uniform, *Newsweek,* 9 June 1947, 54, quoted in Jonathan Ned Katz, *Gay/Lesbian Almanac* (New York: Harper and Row, 1983), p. 617.

16. Quoted in John D'Emilio, *Sexual Politics, Sexual Communities: The Making of a Homosexual Minority in the United States, 1940–1970* (Chicago: University of Chicago Press, 1983), p. 25.

17. Randy Shilts, *Conduct Unbecoming: Lesbians and Gays in the Military, Vietnam to the Persian Gulf* (New York: St. Martin's Press, 1993), pp. 16–17 and Bérubé, *Coming Out Under Fire.*

18. Numbers of women in the armed forces from Bérubé, *Coming Out Under Fire,* p. 3. WAC historian Mattie Treadwell writes that there was a "public impression that a women's corps would be the ideal breeding ground for [homosexuality]." Treadwell, *The United States Army in World War II: The Women's Army Corps* (Washington, D.C.: U.S. Army Office of the Chief of Military History, 1953), p. 625.

19. Bond quoted in *Long Time Passing: Lives of Older Lesbians,* Mary Adelman, ed. (Boston: Alyson, 1986), p. 166.

20. Shilts, *Conduct Unbecoming,* p. 5.

21. Numbers discharged under "Don't Ask, Don't Tell" continue to climb. A total of 850 soldiers were dismissed in 1996—the highest rate since 1987. See *Annual Report,* Servicemembers Legal Defense Network, February 1997. Thanks to Kirk Childress of SLDN for providing these figures.

22. "Perverts Called Government Peril," *New York Times,* 19 April 1950, p. 25.

23. D'Emilio, *Sexual Politics, Sexual Communities,* pp. 44–47.

24. FBI surveillance of ACT UP on both the East and West Coasts is well documented. See: Donna Minkowitz, "Police Probe ACT UP," *Village Voice,* 18 October 1988, p. 25; Guy Trebay, "Target Practice," *Voice,* 11 April 1989, p. 11; Robert W. Peterson, "Hitting the Graffiti-Scrawled Wall," *Advocate,* 4 July 1989, 9–12; Esther Kaplan, "ACT UP Under Siege," *Voice,* 16 July 1991, pp. 35–36; and Duncan Osborne, "ACT UP and the FBI," *Advocate,* 29 June 1993, 60–61.

25. Jonathan Ned Katz, *The Invention of Heterosexuality* (New York: Dutton, 1995), pp. 53–54.

26. Michel Foucault, *The History of Sexuality, Vol. I.,* p. 43.

27. Havelock Ellis, *Sexual Inversion,* vol. 2., *Studies in the Psychology of Sex,* 2nd ed. (Philadelphia: F. A. Davis Co., 1915), p. 250.

28. Magnus Hirschfeld, *Die Homosexualitat des Mannes und des Weibes [Homosexuality in Men and Women]* (Berlin: Louis Marcus, 1914).

29. "A Letter from Freud," *American Journal of Psychiatry,* April 1951: 786.

30. Freud, quoted in Ronald Bayer, *Homosexuality and American Psychiatry: The Politics of Diagnosis* (New York: Basic Books, 1987), p. 26.

31. Jonathan Katz, *Gay American History: Lesbians and Gay Men in the U.S.A.* (New York: Avon Books, 1976), p. 197.

32. Martin Duberman, *Cures: A Gay Man's Odyssey* (New York: Plume, 1991), pp. 3 and 262.

33. On phrenology and homosexuality, see Michael Lynch, "Here Is Adhesiveness: From Friendship to Homosexuality," *Victorian Studies 29* (Autumn 1985): 67–96. Recent examples of scientific research linking sexual orientation to biology include Simon LeVay, "Evidence for Anatomical Differences in the Brains of Homosexual Men," *Science* 253 (1991): 1034–37 and *The Sexual Brain* (Cambridge, MA: MIT Press, 1993); Dean H. Hamer and Peter Copeland, *The Science of Desire: A Search for the Gay Gene and the Biology of Behavior* (New York: Simon and Schuster, 1994).

SOCIAL WORLDS

EARLY WOMEN'S COMMUNITIES

1. Judith Schwarz, *The Radical Feminists of Heterodoxy: Greenwich Village, 1912–1940* (Norwich, VT: New Victoria Publishers, 1986,) p. i.

2. Roland Barthes, *Camera Lucida,* trans. Richard Howard (New York: Hill and Wang, 1990), p. 87.

3. John D'Emilio, "Capitalism and Gay Identity," in *Powers of Desire,* Ann Snitow, Christine Stansell, and Sharon Thompson, eds. (New York: Monthly Review Press, 1983), p. 103.

4. John D'Emilio and Estelle B. Freedman, *Intimate Matters: A History of Sexuality in America* (New York: Harper and Row, 1988), pp. 26–27, 189; and Barbara Epstein, "Family, Sexual Morality, and Popular Movements in Turn-of-the-Century America," in *Powers of Desire,* Snitow et al., eds., pp. 119–20.

5. D'Emilio, "Capitalism and Gay Identity," pp. 104–105.

6. Kathy Peiss, *Cheap Amusements: Working Women and Leisure in Turn-of-the-Century New York* (Philadelphia: Temple University Press, 1985), p. 67.

7. D'Emilio and Freedman, *Intimate Matters,* p. 190.

8. Nancy Sahli, "Smashing: Women's Relationships Before the Fall," *Chrysalis 8* (1979): 21.

9. D'Emilio and Freedman, *Intimate Matters,* p. 191.

10. Estelle Freedman, "Separatism as Strategy: Female Institution Building and American Feminism, 1870–1930," *Feminist Studies* 5 (1979): 517.

11. Lillian Faderman, *Surpassing the Love of Men: Romantic Friendship and Love Between Women in the Renaissance to the Present* (New York: William Morrow, 1981), p. 20.

12. Lisa Moore, " 'Something More Tender Still Than Friendship': Romantic Friendship in Early-Nineteenth-Century England," *Feminist Studies,* Fall 1992: 499.

13. Arthur Schlesinger Jr., "Interesting Women," *New York Times Book Review,* 17 February 1980, p. 31, quoted in Leila J. Rupp, " 'Imagine My Surprise': Women's Relationships in Mid-Twentieth-Century America" in Martin Duberman, Martha Vicinus, and George Chauncey Jr., eds., *Hidden from History* (New York: New American Library, 1989), p. 398.

14. Carroll Smith-Rosenberg, "The New Woman as Androgyne: Social Disorder and Gender Crisis, 1870–1936," in *Disorderly Conduct: Visions of Gender in Victorian America* (New York: Oxford University Press, 1985), p. 265.

15. Havelock Ellis, "Sexual Inversion in Women," quoted in Smith-Rosenberg, "The New Woman as Androgyne," p. 279.

16. Quoted in George Chauncey, *Gay New York: Gender, Urban Culture and the Making of the Gay Male World, 1890–1940* (New York: Basic Books, 1994), p. 234.

17. Florence Guy Woolston, "Marriage Customs and Taboo Among the Early Heterodites," 1919, reprinted in Schwarz, *The Radical Feminists of Heterodoxy,* p. 108.

18. Schwarz, *The Radical Feminists of Heterodoxy,* p. 36.

19. *Heterodoxy to Marie,* photograph album, 1920. Schlesinger Library on the History of Women in America, Radcliffe College: Inez Haynes Irwin Papers.

OUT ON THE TOWN

1. Ralph Werther, *The Female-Impersonators* (New York: Medico-Legal Journal, 1922), quoted in George Chauncey, *Gay New York: Gender, Urban Culture and the Making of the Gay Male World, 1890–1940* (New York: Basic Books, 1994), p. 131.

2. Quoted in Chauncey, *Gay New York,* p. 52.

3. Though, as Chauncey has noted, these were in fact multiple gay social worlds, structured and organized by the differences in gender, race, class, ethnicity, and sexual style of participants. Some of these worlds overlapped and intersected; others remained closed to outsiders. *Gay New York,* p. 3.

4. The term *gay ladies,* used in reference to female prostitutes, appears in the classic Victorian porn novel *A Secret Life,* by "Anonymous," published in 1894. Thanks to Jeffrey Escoffier for drawing our attention to this early written usage.

5. From the records of the Society for the Suppression of Vice, quoted in *Gay New York,* p. 148.

6. Dr. Allan McLane Hamilton, "Insanity in Its Medico-Legal Bearings," *A System of Legal Medicine,* 1894; quoted in Jonathan Ned Katz, *Gay/Lesbian Almanac* (New York: Harper and Row, 1983), p. 258.

7. Charles H. Hughes, "An Organization of Colored Erotopaths," 1893, quoted in Jonathan Ned Katz, *Gay American History: Lesbians and Gay Men in the U.S.A.* (New York: Avon Books, 1976), p. 66.

8. From *Report of the Special [Mazet] Committee of the Assembly* (Albany: J. B. Lyon, 1900), p. 1429. NYPL/General Research Division.

9. Quoted in Chauncey, *Gay New York,* p. 41.

10. Lewis Erenberg, "Village Nightlife," *Greenwich Village: Culture and Counterculture,* Rick Beard and Leslie Cohen Berlowitz, eds. (New Brunswick, NJ: Rutgers University Press, 1993), p. 364.

11. Quoted in Phillip Herring, *Djuna: The Life and Work of Djuna Barnes* (New York: Viking, 1995), p. 120.

12. "Village 'Joints' Out or Tame," *Variety,* 6 May 1926, p. 19, quoted in Chauncey, *Gay New York,* p. 237.

13. Quoted in Chauncey, *Gay New York,* p. 240.

14. Rian James, *Dining in New York: An Intimate Guide* (New York: John Day Company, 1930), p. 236.

15. Quoted in George Chauncey, "The Way We Were," *Village Voice,* 1 July 1986, p. 31.

16. Quoted in Chauncey, *Gay New York,* p. 252.

17. *Report,* 24 February 1928, NYPL/MSS, Committee of Fourteen Records.

18. *Variety,* 16 October 1929, quoted in Chauncey, *Gay New York,* p. 246.

19. Blair Niles, *Strange Brother* (New York: Liveright, 1931), p. 152.

20. Langston Hughes, *The Big Sea: An Autobiography* (New York: Knopf, 1940), p. 225.

21. Eric Garber, "A Spectacle in Color: The Lesbian and Gay Subculture of Jazz Age Harlem," in Martin Duberman, Martha Vicinus, and George Chauncey Jr., eds., *Hidden from History: Reclaiming the Gay and Lesbian Past* (New York: New American Library, 1989), p. 322.

22. Ibid., p. 323.

23. Richard Bruce, "Smoke, Lilies, and Jade," *FIRE!* November 1926, p. 36.

24. Quoted in Chauncey, *Gay New York,* p. 311.

25. Ibid., pp. 315–21.

26. Ibid., p. 166.

27. On the history of the Hays Office and the Hollywood Production Code, and analyses of homosexuality on stage and screen, see Robert Sklar, *Movie-Made America: A Cultural History of American Movies* (New York: Random House, 1975); Kaier Curtin, *"We Can Always Call Them Bulgarians": The Emergence of Lesbians and Gay Men on the American Stage* (Boston: Alyson,

1987); and Vito Russo, *The Celluloid Closet: Homosexuality in the Movies* (New York: Harper & Row, 1987).

28. Chauncey, *Gay New York*, p. 356.

29. Elizabeth Lapovsky Kennedy and Madeline D. Davis, *Boots of Leather, Slippers of Gold: The History of a Lesbian Community* (New York: Routledge, 1993), p. 30.

30. Lisa E. Davis, "The Butch as Drag Artiste," in Joan Nestle, ed., *The Persistent Desire: A Femme-Butch Reader* (Boston: Alyson, 1992), p. 48.

31. Ibid.

32. Anthony James, "Remembering the Thirties," *The Yellow Book: The Gay Monthly*, 1973; LHA, History/Files, 1930s.

33. George Chauncey, "The Policed: Gay Men's Strategies of Everyday Resistance," *Inventing Times Square: Commerce and Culture at the Crossroads of the World*, William R. Taylor, ed. (New York: Russell Sage, 1991), p. 326.

34. Allan Bérubé, *Coming Out Under Fire: The History of Gay Men and Women in World War Two* (New York: Free Press, 1990), p. 114.

35. Jeanne Flash Gray, "Memories," in *The Other Black Woman*, New York, vol. 1, no. 1, reprinted on *Tipin' Out in the Life*, 1980; LHA, Flat drawer 9.

36. Leo Adams, interviewed by Fred Wasserman, 10 June 1993. MSS, Leo Adams Papers.

37. Elizabeth Lapovsky Kennedy and Madeline D. Davis, *Boots of Leather, Slippers of Gold: The History of a Lesbian Community* (New York: Routledge, 1993), p. 4.

38. Quoted in Janet Kahn and Patricia A. Gozemba, "In and Around the Lighthouse: Working-Class Lesbian Bar Culture in the 1950s and 1960s," in *Gendered Domains*, Dorothy O. Helly and Susan M. Reverby, eds. (Ithaca: Cornell University Press, 1992), p. 93.

39. Joan Nestle, "Butch-Femme Relationships: Sexual Courage in the 1950s," in *A Restricted Country* (Ithaca: Firebrand Books, 1987), pp. 100–101.

40. Quoted in Kennedy and Davis, *Boots of Leather*, p. 39.

41. John D'Emilio, *Sexual Politics, Sexual Communities: The Making of a Homosexual Minority in the United States, 1940–1970* (Chicago: University of Chicago Press, 1983), p. 30.

42. Interviewed in *Before Stonewall: The Making of a Gay and Lesbian Community* (New York: Before Stonewall Incorporated, 1984). Produced by Robert Rosenberg, John Scagliotti, and Greta Schiller.

43. "Harlem's Strangest Nightclub," *Ebony*, December 1951, p. 80.

44. Audre Lorde, interviewed in *Before Stonewall*.

45. Allen Ginsberg, interviewed in *Before Stonewall*.

46. D'Emilio, *Sexual Politics, Sexual Communities*, p. 49.

47. Lyn Pedersen, "An Open Letter," *One*, January 1956, pp. 9–10; and D'Emilio, *Sexual Politics, Sexual Communities*, pp. 49–51.

48. James F. Kearful, "The New Nazism," *One*, May 1963, p. 7.

49. Leslie Feinberg, "Letter to Fifties Femme from a Stone Butch," in *The Persistent Desire*, p. 104.

50. Donald Vining, "Stonewall: A Good Symbol But Not the Birth of Gay Liberation," *Advocate*, 11 June 1985, p. 5.

"I LOVE THE NIGHTLIFE"

1. "The Bored, the Bearded, and the Beat," *Look*, 19 August 1958, 64. And see Nan Alamilla Boyd, "Homos Invade S.F!: San Francisco's History as a Wide-Open Town," in Brett Beemyn, ed., *Creating a Place for Ourselves* (New York: Routledge, 1997).

2. Quoted in John D'Emilio, *Sexual Politics, Sexual Communities: The Making of a Homosexual Minority in the United States, 1940–1970* (Chicago: Chicago University Press, 1983), p. 187.

3. *Stoumen v. Reilly* quoted in Nan Alamilla Boyd, "Activism, Leadership, and the Politics of Community Representation: San Francisco's Gay Bar Life, 1955–65," unpublished paper, p. 8.

4. Quoted in D'Emilio, *Sexual Politics, Sexual Communities*, p. 188.

5. "Homosexuality in America, *Life*, 26 June 1964.

6. *One Eleven Wines & Liquors, Inc.* v. *Division of Alcoholic Beverage Control* (N.J. 1967), in William B. Rubenstein, ed. *Lesbians, Gay Men, and the Law* (New York: New Press, 1992), p. 208.

7. On fag-baiting in the New Left, see Terence Kissack, "Freaking Fag Revolutionaries: New York's Gay Liberation Front, 1969–1971," *Radical History Review* 62 (Spring 1995): 111–13.

8. Quoted in George Katsiaficas, *The Imagination of the New Left: A Global Analysis of 1968* (Boston: South End Press, 1987), p. 146.

9. Interviewed in *Before Stonewall*, produced by Robert Rosenberg, John Scagliotti, and Greta Schiller.

10. Jack Star, "The Sad Gay Life," *Look*, 10 January 1967.

11. *New York City Gay Scene Guide Quarterly*, Spring 1968 (New York: Mattachine Book Service, 1968), MSS, Martin Michel Collection.

12. Frances FitzGerald, *Cities on a Hill: A Journey Through Contemporary American Cultures* (New York: Simon and Schuster, 1981), p. 42.

13. Randolphe Wicker, "A Businessman Sounds Off!" *GAY*, 15 December 1969.

14. Allen Young, "Out of the Closets, Into the Streets, *Out of the Closets: Voices of Gay Liberation*, Karla Jay and Allen Young, eds. (New York: A Douglas Book, 1972), p. 11.

15. Steven V. Roberts, "Homosexuals in Revolt," *New York Times*, 24 August 1970.

16. Ibid.

17. Jonathan Black, "The Boys in the Snake Pit: Games 'Straights' Play," *Village Voice*, 19 March 1970, p. 61.

18. Arthur Bell, *Dancing the Gay Lib Blues: A Year in the Homosexual Liberation Movement* (New York: Simon and Shuster, 1971), p. 46.

19. GAA flyer, reprinted in Donn Teal, *The Gay Militants* (New York: Stein and Day, 1971), p. 118.

20. Kooky's was one of only two bars catering primarily to lesbians in downtown Manhattan in the year after Stonewall.

21. Gay Women's Liberation Front, Daughters of Bilitis, Gay Activists Alliance, "Why Does Kooky's . . . ? flyer, 1970. NYPL/MSS Manford Papers.

22. See People's Coffee Grounds, *Come Out!* (Spring-Summer 1971) and Teal, *The Gay Militants,* p. 156.

23. Quoted in Kissack, "Freaking Fag Revolutionaries," p. 118.

24. Radicalesbians, "Leaving the Men Behind," first published in *Come Out!* (Dec. 1970–Jan. 1971), reprinted in *Out of the Closets,* pp. 290–91.

25. Radicalesbians, "Leaving the Men Behind," p. 291.

26. "New York All-Women's Dance," Radicalesbians flyer, LHA, Organization Files/GLF.

27. Radicalesbians, "Leaving the Men Behind," p. 291.

28. "New York All-Women's Dance," flyer, LHA, Organization Files/GLF. The anonymous author was writing as a member of the "Class Workshop," initiated by members of The Feminists, Chips & Scraps, Redstockings, a secretaries' group, and WITCH.

29. See Danae Clark, "Commodity Lesbianism," in Henry Abelove, Michele Aina Barale, David M. Halperin, eds., *The Lesbian and Gay Studies Reader* (New York: Routledge, 1993), p. 187.

30. It should be noted that for many lesbian feminists, Stonewall would be considered a less important milestone marking the creation of their movement than would be the birth of the women's liberation movement.

31. Arlene Stein quoted in Clark, "Commodity Lesbianism," p. 189.

32. Andrew Holleran, "Fast-Food Sex," *The Christopher Street Reader* (New York: Perigee Books, 1983), p. 71.

33. Michael Callen, from oral history conducted by filmmaker Robert Rosenberg.

34. Michael Denneny, *The Christopher Street Reader,* p. 14.

35. *Generations of Leather Pride, 1950–1995 / A Timeline / Selected Landmarks in the History of the Levi / Leather / SM / Fetish Community.* Compiled, edited, and selected by Robert L. Guenther, June 1995, NYPL/IGIC/Ephemera; Gayle Rubin, "The Catacombs: A Temple of the Butthole," in *Leatherfolk: Radical Sex, People, Politics, and Practice,* Mark Thompson, ed. (Boston: Alyson, 1991), p. 119.

36. *New York Gay Scene Guide Quarterly,* Spring, 1968, pp. 7–15.

37. Mineshaft Club Membership, ca. 1980. IGIC Ephemera/Bars.

38. Brandon Judell, "Sexual Anarchy," *Lavender Culture,* Karla Jay and Allen Young, eds. (New York: Harcourt Brace Jovanovich, 1978), p. 135. Originally printed in *Blueboy,* Aug.–Sept., 1977.

39. Ibid, p. 136.

40. Mel Cheren, "Club History 101," *HX Magazine,* June 1994.

41. Leigh W. Rutledge, *The Gay Decades* (New York: Plume, 1992), p. 81.

42. Ibid.

43. Andrew Holleran, *Dancer from the Dance* (New York: William Morrow, 1978), p. 38.

44. Gayle Rubin, "The Catacombs," p. 140.

CRUISING

1. Martin Goodkin quoted in George Chauncey *Gay New York* (New York: Basic Books, 1994), p. 201.

2. Quoted in Laud Humphreys, *Tearoom Trade: Impersonal Sex in Public Places* (Chicago: Aldine Publishing Company, 1970), p. 59.

3. Stephen Greco, "Manhattan Hunting Grounds," [1982] in *The Long Road to Freedom: The Advocate History of the Gay and Lesbian Movement,* Mark Thompson, ed. (New York: St. Martin's Press, 1994), p. 236.

4. Humphreys, *Tearoom Trade,* p. 2.

5. Ibid., p. 6.

6. Letter concerning tearoom incident to New York Public Library, New York, 28 March 1899. NYPL, Archives.

7. Humphreys, *Tearoom Trade,* p. 6.

8. Interviewed by Fred Wasserman for *Gay and Lesbian Life in Brooklyn,* report prepared for Brooklyn Historical Society and Lesbian Herstory Archives, 12 March 1994, p. 48.

9. Chauncey, *Gay New York,* p. 198.

10. John Howard, "The Library, the Park, and the Pervert: Public Space and Homosexual Encounter in Post–World War II Atlanta," *Radical History Review* 62 (Spring 1995): 166–87.

11. Arthur Bell, "The Bath Life Gets Respectability," in Karla Jay and Allen Young, eds., *Lavender Culture* (New York: Harcourt Brace Jovanovich, 1978), pp. 78–79.

12. Allan Bérubé, "The History of Gay Bathhouses," *Coming Up!* December 1984, p. 16.

13. Jay Stanley, "Fags Tickle Nudes," *Broadway Brevities,* 23 November 1933, p. 3.

14. Quoted in Allan Bérubé, "The History of Gay Bathhouses," p. 16.

15. Stanley, "Fags Tickle Nudes," 1933, p. 3.

16. Reprinted in Jonathan Ned Katz, *Gay/Lesbian Almanac* (New York: Harper and Row, 1983), pp. 452–53.

17. Charles Tomlinson Griffes, 1914, quoted in Chauncey, *Gay New York,* p. 220.

18. Bérubé, "The History of Gay Bathhouses," p. 16.

19. Bill Willis, from oral history conducted by filmmaker Robert Rosenberg.

20. Richard Goldstein, "A Night at the Continental Baths," *New York* (March 1973), p. 51.

21. Leigh W. Rutledge, *The Gay Decades* (New York: Plume, 1992), p. 235.

LESBIAN PULPS

1. Suzanna Danuta Walters, "As Her Hand Crept Slowly Up Her Thigh: Ann Bannon and the Politics of Pulp," *Social Text* 23 (Fall/Winter 1989): 84.

2. Quoted in Roberta Yusba, "Odd Girls and Strange Sisters: Lesbian Pulp Novels of the '50s," *OUT/LOOK* (Spring 1991): 35.

3. Ann Bannon, "Secrets of the Gay Novel," *One,* July 1961, 8–9.

4. Ann Bannon, *Beebo Brinker* (Greenwich: Gold Medal Books, 1962), p. 41.

5. Artemis Smith, *The Third Sex* (New York: Softcover Library, 1969), p. 13.

6. Ann Bannon, *I Am a Woman* (New York: Fawcett Gold Medal, 1959; Tallahassee: Naiad Press, 1986), pp. 35–36.

7. Ann Bannon, *Journey to a Woman* (New York: Fawcett Gold Medal, 1959; Tallahassee: Naiad Press, 1986), p. 120.

PHYSIQUES

1. F. Valentine Hooven III, *Beefcake: The Muscle Magazines of America, 1950–1970* (Cologne: Taschen, 1995), p. 28.

2. Interviewed in *Daddy and the Muscle Academy.* Written and directed by Ilppo Pohjola, Filmitakomo Oy, 1991.

3. F. Valentine Hooven III, *Tom of Finland: His Life and Times* (New York: St. Martin's Press, 1993), p. 82.

4. Gail Bederman, *Manliness & Civilization: A Cultural History of Gender and Race in the United States, 1880–1917* (Chicago: University of Chicago Press, 1995), p. 15.

5. Richard Dyer, "Seen to Be Believed: Some Problems in the Representations of Gay People as Typical" in *The Matter of Images: Essays on Representations* (New York: Routledge, 1993), p. 27.

6. Tracy Morgan, "Pages of Whiteness: Race, Physique Magazines and the Emergence of Gay Public Culture, 1955–1960," *Found Object* (Fall 1994): 115.

7. Timothy Lewis, *Physique: A Pictorial History of the Athletic Model Guild* (Gay Sunshine Press), quoted in Alan Miller, "Beefcake with No Labels Attached," *Body Politic* (January/February 1983), p. 33.

8. Hooven, *Tom of Finland,* pp. 82–85.

9. Ibid., p. 98.

10. See Allan Bérubé, *Coming Out Under Fire: The History of Gay Men and Women in World War Two* (New York: Free Press, 1990), p. 273, who notes that "physique magazines were developed in part by veterans and drew heavily on World War II uniforms and iconography for erotic imagery."

11. Statistics according to *The Grecian Guild Pictorial* (September 1958), quoted in Morgan, "Pages of Whiteness," p. 116.

12. Miller, "Beefcake with No Labels Attached," p. 33.

13. "The Story Behind Physique Photography, *Drum* (October 1965), p. 11.

14. John D'Emilio, *Sexual Politics, Sexual Communities: The Making of a Homosexual Minority in the United States, 1940–1970* (Chicago: University of Chicago Press, 1983), pp. 115, 133–36.

15. Marc Stein, "Sex Politics in the City of Sisterly and Brotherly Loves," *Radical History Review,* 59 (Spring 1994): 74.

16. *Queers!* Advertisement in *New York Mattachine Society Newsletter,* November 1964, 18.

ORGANIZING

AN EMERGING MINORITY

1. For national "coming out," see Allan Bérubé, *Coming Out Under Fire: The History of Gay Men and Women in World War Two* (New York: Free Press, 1990), p. 6; and John D'Emilio, *Sexual Politics, Sexual Communities: The Making of a Homosexual Minority in the United States, 1940–1970* (Chicago: University of Chicago Press, 1983), pp. 23–24.

2. Lisa Ben, "Commentary Upon a Pertinent Article," *Vice Versa,* February 1948, 10.

3. Letter to the editor quoted in "The Whatchama-Column," *Vice Versa,* November 1947, 12.

4. At least one homosexual organization is known to have existed in the United States prior to World War II, the short-lived Society for Human Rights, founded by Henry Gerber in Chicago in 1924. See Jonathan Katz, *Gay American History: Lesbians and Gay Men in the U.S.A.* (New York: Avon Books, 1976), pp. 581–91.

5. Eann MacDonald [Harry Hay's pseud.], "Preliminary Concepts: International Bachelors' Fraternal Order for Peace and Social Dignity, Sometimes Referred to as Bachelors Anonymous," 7 July 1950, in Will Roscoe, ed., *Radically Gay: Gay Liberation in the Words of Its Founder* (Boston: Beacon Press, 1996), pp. 63–75. Excerpts are quoted in Katz, *Gay American History,* p. 615.

6. D'Emilio, *Sexual Politics, Sexual Communities,* p. 65.

7. Mattachine Society, "Missions and Purposes," 1951, quoted in Katz, *Gay American History,* p. 620. The full document is in Roscoe, *Radically Gay,* pp. 131–32.

8. Henry [Harry] Hay quoted in Katz, *Gay American History,* p. 614.

9. Harry [Hay] quoted in Nancy Adair and Casey Adair,

Word Is Out: Stories of Some of Our Lives (San Francisco: New Glide Productions and New York: Delacorte Press, 1978), p. 242.

10. D'Emilio, *Sexual Politics, Sexual Communities,* pp. 70–72.

11. The Mattachine Society, Inc., "Call to Convention," San Francisco, 1954. IGIC, box 8, f. 1.

12. *One* v. *Oleson,* 355 U.S. 371 (1958).

13. Del Martin and Phyllis Lyon, *Lesbian/Woman* (New York: Bantam, 1972), pp. 238–39.

14. "Purpose of the Daughters of Bilitis," *Ladder,* October 1957, inside cover.

15. Barbara Gittings interviewed in *Before Stonewall: The Making of a Gay and Lesbian Community* (New York: Before Stonewall Inc., 1984). Produced by Robert Rosenberg, John Scagliotti, and Greta Schiller.

16. "Women Who Fall for . . . Lesbians," *Jet,* 25 February 1954, 20–21.

17. "Raising Children in a Deviant Relationship," *Ladder,* October 1956, 9.

18. Kay Lahusen quoted in Eric Marcus, *Making History: The Struggle for Gay and Lesbian Equal Rights 1945–1990* (New York: HarperCollins, 1992), p. 119. Lahusen used the pseudonym Kay Tobin during her years of homophile and gay liberation activism.

19. Letter to the editor from L. N. [Lorraine (Hansberry) Nemiroff] to *Ladder,* August 1957, 30.

20. On DOB, see Martin and Lyon, *Lesbian/Woman,* pp. 238–41. Jim Kepner, "Blacks and Women in the Early Gay Movement," typescript quoted in Martin Duberman, *Stonewall* (New York: Dutton, 1993), n. 42, p. 308.

21. Del Martin and Phyllis Lyon quoted in D'Emilio, *Sexual Politics, Sexual Communities,* pp. 124–25.

22. Barbara Gittings quoted in Katz, *Gay American History,* p. 647.

23. We acknowledge David Gips for coining this most descriptive and apropos term.

24. Robert C. Doty, "Growth of Overt Homosexuality in City Provokes Wide Concern," *New York Times,* 17 December 1963, p. 1.

25. Frank Kameny, "Message to Members of the Mattachine Society of Washington from the President of the Society on the State of the Society," April 1964, quoted in D'Emilio, *Sexual Politics, Sexual Communities,* p. 153; and Dr. Frank E. Kameny, "Does Research into Homosexuality Matter?" *Ladder,* May 1965, 14.

26. "Policy of the Mattachine Society of Washington," adopted 4 March 1965, quoted in D'Emilio, *Sexual Politics, Sexual Communities,* p. 164. Jack Nichols used the pseudonym Warren Adkins at the time.

27. Shirley Willer, national president of DOB, address to the National Planning Conference of Homophile Organizations, August 1966. Published as "What Concrete Steps Can Be Taken to Further the Homophile Movement?" *Ladder,* November 1966,

quoted in Toby Marotta, *The Politics of Homosexuality* (Boston: Houghton Mifflin, 1981), p. 51.

28. Craig Rodwell quoted in Duberman, *Stonewall,* p. 113.

29. Mattachine Society of Washington, Committee on Picketing and Other Lawful Demonstrations, "Rules and Precepts for Picketing," 1964, MSS, Craig Rodwell Papers, box 6, f. "Mattachine Society"; and "Picketing: The Impact and the Issues," *Ladder: A Lesbian Review,* September 1965, 5, quoted in Donn Teal, *The Gay Militants* (New York: Stein and Day, 1971), p. 40.

30. D'Emilio, *Sexual Politics, Sexual Communities,* pp. 190–91.

31. "Now We Are Marching On," lyrics by "Denny," *New York Mattachine Newsletter,* October 1966, 3.

32. Maua Adele Ajanaku interviewed in *Before Stonewall.*

33. See Leo E. Laurence, "Gay Revolution," *Vector,* April 1969, 11; "Gay Rebel Gets Shafted by Uptight Boss," *Berkeley Barb,* 4–10 April 1969, p. 11; "Pink Panthers Gay Revolution Toughening Up," *Berkeley Barb,* 18–24 April 1969, p. 11; "Gay Strike Hits Southern Front," *Berkeley Barb,* 2–8 May 1969, p. 11; and the editorial "A Suggested Policy: Confrontation and Implementation," *Homophile Action League Newsletter* (Philadelphia), February 1969, quoted in Lillian Faderman, *Odd Girls and Twilight Lovers: A History of Lesbian Life in Twentieth-Century America* (New York: Columbia University Press, 1991), p. 193.

GAY LIBERATION

1. Craig Rodwell interviewed in *Before Stonewall: The Making of a Gay and Lesbian Community* (New York: Before Stonewall Inc., 1984). Produced by Robert Rosenberg, John Scagliotti, and Greta Schiller.

2. Psychologist George Weinberg is credited with coining the term "homophobia" and popularizing it in his book *Society and the Healthy Homosexual* (New York: St. Martin's Press, 1972).

3. Dennis Altman, *Homosexual: Oppression and Liberation* (New York: Discus/Avon, 1971), pp. 229, 232–33.

4. John D'Emilio, "After Stonewall," in *Making Trouble: Essays on Gay History, Politics, and the University* (New York: Routledge, 1992), p. 244.

5. Gay Activists Alliance of Brooklyn, flyer, 1972, IGIC, box 58, f. 6; and John D'Emilio, *Sexual Politics, Sexual Communities: The Making of a Homosexual Minority in the United States, 1940–1970* (Chicago: University of Chicago Press, 1983), p. 247.

6. Karla Jay quoted in Steven V. Roberts, "Homosexuals in Revolt," *New York Times,* 24 August 1970.

7. Michael Brown and Don Slater quoted in Roberts, "Homosexuals in Revolt."

8. Frank Kameny quoted in Kay Tobin and Randy Wicker, *The Gay Crusaders* (New York: Paperback Library, 1972), p. 105.

9. For GLF's first statement, see *Come Out! Selections from the Radical Gay Liberation Newspaper* (New York: Times Change

Press, n.d. [ca. 1970]), p. 5. Terence Kissack, "Freaking Fag Revolutionaries: New York's Gay Liberation Front, 1969–1971," *Radical History Review,* vol. 62 (Spring 1995): 108. For "homosexual as a minority group," see Gay Liberation Front, "What Is Gay Liberation Front?" flyer, ca. 1970, LHA, Organization Files/GLF. For a discussion of the movement's general lack of interest in gay liberation, see Kissack, pp. 112–13.

10. Neil Miller notes that Wittman told his friend Michael Bronski that he had written the manifesto in the spring of 1969, before the Stonewall Riots, a fact which makes sense considering that no reference is made to Stonewall or Gay Liberation Front. See Neil Miller, *Out of the Past: Gay and Lesbian History from 1869 to the Present* (New York: Vintage Books, 1995), pp. 384–85.

11. Nonetheless, Huey Newton, in a surprising move, exhorted the Panthers to recognize that the "homosexual movement is a real movement," that homosexuals "might be the most oppressed people in the society," and that "even a homosexual can be a revolutionary . . . maybe the most revolutionary." See Huey P. Newton, "A Letter from Huey P. Newton," *Come Out!,* Sept.–Oct. 1970, p. 12 (first published in *The Black Panther: Black Community News Service,* August 21, 1970).

12. "T.W.G.R. Third World Gay Revolution," *Come Out!,* Sept.–Oct. 1970, p. 12.

13. Sylvia Rivera quoted in Eric Marcus, *Making History: The Struggle for Gay and Lesbian Equal Rights 1945–1990* (New York: HarperCollins, 1992), p. 194.

14. Arthur Evans quoted in Merle Miller, *On Being Different* (New York: Random House, 1971), pp. 37–38.

15. Vito Russo quoted in Arnie Kantrowitz, *Under the Rainbow* (New York: William Morrow and Company, 1977), p. 129.

16. "Cultivating Gay Culture," *Gay Activist,* May 1971, 7, quoted in Toby Marotta, *The Politics of Homosexuality* (Boston: Houghton Mifflin Company, 1981), p. 193.

17. Joan Nestle in David Deitcher, ed., *The Question of Equality: Lesbian and Gay Politics Since Stonewall* (New York: Scribner, 1995), pp. 75–6.

18. Candice Boyce in Deitcher, *The Question of Equality,* p. 78.

19. "An International Directory of Gay Organizations," in Karla Jay and Allen Young, *Out of the Closets: Voices of Gay Liberation* (New York: A Douglas Book, 1972), pp. 375–403.

20. Joseph Epstein, "Homo/Hetero: The Struggle for Sexual Identity," *Harper's,* September 1970, 51.

21. Michael Durham, "Homosexuals in Revolt," *Life,* 31 December 1971, 63.

22. Excerpt from a Student Mobilization Committee Gay Task Force statement quoted in "Homosexuals March for Peace," 1971, flyer.

23. Chicago Gay Liberation Front, "A Leaflet for the American Medical Association," reprinted in Jay and Young, *Out of the Closets,* p. 146; and Gay Activists Alliance quoted in Durham, "Homosexuals in Revolt," p. 65.

24. Kantrowitz, *Under the Rainbow,* p. 131; and Basil O'Brien, "Gay Soirée," *Plain Dealer* (Philadelphia), 3 September 1970, quoted in Donn Teal, *The Gay Militants* (New York: Stein and Day, 1971), p. 59.

25. Morty Manford quoted in Marcus, *Making History,* p. 204; and Leo Skir in *Mademoiselle,* September 1970, quoted in Donn Teal, *The Gay Militants,* p. 24.

LESBIAN FEMINISM

1. Morgan Murielchild, "Shuffle Your Ass and Say Lesbian," *Come Out! Is Dead* (New York), [1972], p. 3.

2. Ivy Bottini interviewed in *Before Stonewall: The Making of a Gay and Lesbian Community* (New York: Before Stonewall Inc., 1984). Produced by Robert Rosenberg, John Scagliotti, and Greta Schiller.

3. Rita Mae Brown and colleagues quoted in Sidney Abbott and Barbara Love, *Sappho Was a Right-On Woman: A Liberated View of Lesbianism* (New York: Stein and Day, 1972), p. 112.

4. Kate Millett, "Sexual Politics: A Manifesto for Revolution" (article written in 1968), in Shulamith Firestone and Anne Koedt, eds., *Notes from the Second Year: Women's Liberation* (New York: New York Radical Feminists, 1970), p. 112, quoted in Alice Echols, *Daring to Be BAD: Radical Feminism in America 1967–1975* (Minneapolis: University of Minnesota Press, 1989), p. 211; and Echols, *Daring to Be BAD,* p. 211.

5. Radicalesbians, *The Woman-Identified Woman,* 1970, IGIC Ephemera/Radicalesbians. This manifesto has been widely published and anthologized.

6. Pat Maxwell, "Lavender Menaces Confront the Congress to Unite Women," *Gay Power,* no. 17, quoted in Donn Teal, *The Gay Militants* (New York: Stein and Day, 1971), p. 180.

7. For the multiple meanings of the term *political lesbian,* see Abbott and Love, *Sappho Was a Right-On Woman,* pp. 152–53.

8. Ibid., p. 124.

9. Ibid., pp. 125–34; and National Organization for Women, "NOW Policy," Lesbian Rights Resource Kit, 1981, pp. 10-1–10-4.

10. "GLF Women," flyer, LHA, Organization Files/Radicalesbians. Published as "GLF Women" in *Come Out!,* Dec. 1970–Jan. 1971. Also in Karla Jay and Allen Young, *Out of the Closets: Voices of Gay Liberation* (New York: A Douglas Book, 1972), pp. 201–202 (titled "Lesbians and the Ultimate Liberation of Women").

11. Jean O'Leary quoted in Eric Marcus, *Making History: The Struggle for Gay and Lesbian Rights 1945–1990* (New York: HarperCollins, 1992), p. 266.

12. Lillian Faderman, *Odd Girls and Twilight Lovers: A History of Lesbian Life in Twentieth Century America* (New York: Columbia University Press, 1991), p. 219.

13. "Salsa Soul Sisters, Third World Women, Inc., . . . where it can all come together," brochure, LHA, Organization Files/Salsa Soul Sisters.

14. Candice Boyce quoted in David Deitcher, ed., *The Question of Equality: Lesbian and Gay Politics in America Since Stonewall* (New York: Scribner, 1995), p. 79.

15. Rita Mae Brown, "The Shape of Things to Come" in *Plain Brown Wrapper* (Baltimore: Diana Press, 1976), p. 114; and Joan E. Biren, Rita Mae Brown, Charlotte Bunch, and Coletta Reid, "Editorial: Motive Comes Out!," *Motive* (Washington, D.C.), vol. 32, no. 1 (1972), 1.

16. Charlotte Bunch, "Lesbians in Revolt," *The Furies,* January 1972, pp. 8–9.

17. Jewelle Gomez, "Out of the Past," in Deitcher, *The Question of Equality,* pp. 44–45.

18. "Middle of the Road," statement by anonymous lesbian from Lansing, Michigan, *Lesbian Connection,* May 1976, 4.

19. Joan Nestle quoted in Rodger Streitmatter, *Unspeakable: The Rise of the Gay and Lesbian Press in America* (Boston: Faber and Faber, 1995), p. 158.

20. Barbara Grier quoted in Mark Thompson, ed., *Long Road to Freedom: The Advocate History of the Gay and Lesbian Movement* (New York: St. Martin's Press, 1994), p. 95.

21. Sue Katz, "Smash Phallic Tyranny," flyer, ca. 1970–72, IGIC Ephemera/Radicalesbians. Reprinted in Jay and Young, *Out of the Closets,* pp. 259–62.

22. Amber Hollibaugh and Cherrie Moraga, "What We're Rolling Around in Bed With: Sexual Silences in Feminism: A Conversation toward Ending Them," *SEX ISSUE, Heresies* (New York), vol. 3, no. 4, issue 12 (1981): 58.

23. Martha Equinox, Eugene, OR, response to "About S&M—Some Feedback Please," *Lesbian Connection,* September 1981, 13.

24. "Petition in Support of the Scholar and Feminist IX Conference," in Carol S. Vance, ed., *Pleasure and Danger: Exploring Female Sexuality* (New York: Routledge, 1982), p. 451.

25. For a discussion on the crucial role of cultural feminism and lesbian communities in the more conservative 1980s and 1990s, see Verta Taylor and Leila J. Rupp, "Women's Culture and Lesbian Feminist Activism: A Reconsideration of Cultural Feminism," *Signs,* vol. 19, no. 1 (Autumn 1993), pp. 32–61.

26. Women's Press Collective, *Lesbians Speak Out,* 2nd ed. (Berkeley, 1974), pp. 139–40, quoted in John D'Emilio, "After Stonewall," in *Making Trouble: Essays on Gay History, Politics, and the University* (New York: Routledge, 1992), p. 254.

GAY RIGHTS

1. John D'Emilio, "After Stonewall," in *Making Trouble: Essays on Gay History, Politics, and the University* (New York: Routledge, 1992), p. 247.

2. Marty Robinson, "Trashing of Intro 475: The Closet of Fear," *Village Voice,* 17 February 1972, p. 18.

3. Maine enacted a gay rights bill in 1997 but it was repealed by voters in a statewide referendum in February 1998.

4. Kathy Kozachenko, elected to the Ann Arbor City Council earlier in 1974, was actually the first openly gay elected official in the country, but her election did not garner the same level of press coverage as Noble's.

5. Virginia Apuzzo, interviewed by Fred Wasserman for the Brooklyn Lesbian and Gay History Exhibition Project, 6 April 1994, Courtesy Brooklyn Historical Society.

6. Jim Foster, "We Were There!" in Mark Thompson, ed., *Long Road to Freedom: The Advocate History of the Gay and Lesbian Movement* (New York: St. Martin's Press, 1994), p. 74.

7. Melvin Boozer quoted in Torie Osborn, "Calm Before the Storm," in Thompson, *Long Road to Freedom,* p. 196.

8. Save Our Children, Inc., flyer, "A Mother's Day wish: . . . That the mothers (and fathers) of Dade County will vote for their children's rights on June 7, 1977." Schlesinger Library, Radcliffe College, Subject Files/Homosexuality.

9. Robert I. McQueen and Randy Shilts, "The Movement's 'Born Again': From Apathy to Anger," *Advocate,* 27 July 1977, 7; and "Out of the Closet," *Nation,* 9 July 1977, 34.

10. Apuzzo interview.

11. Harvey Milk quoted in Leigh Rutledge, *The Gay Decades: From Stonewall to the Present: The People and Events That Shaped Lives* (New York: Plume, 1992), p. 126.

12. Joan Nestle, "Digging In," in Thompson, *Long Road to Freedom,* p. 130.

13. John D'Emilio, "The Supreme Court and the Sodomy Statutes: Where Do We Go from Here?" originally published in *Gay Community News,* 1976, reprinted in D'Emilio, *Making Trouble,* pp. 193–95.

14. Dean Wycoff, quoted in Garrett Brock and Andy Humm, "Right-Wing Group Asks Death Penalty for Gays," *New York City News,* 24 February 1981, p. 2.

15. "Dedicated Christians for the Family Protection Act," fund-raising letter from Edward E. McAteer, President, The Religious Roundtable, ca. 1981. Schlesinger Library, Radcliffe College, Charlotte Bunch Papers, box 3, f. 109.

CONFRONTING AIDS

1. David Black, *The Plague Years: A Chronicle of AIDS, the Epidemic of Our Times* (New York: Simon and Schuster, 1986), p. 40, quoted in Paula A. Treichler, "AIDS, Gender, and Biomedical Discourse: Current Contests for Meaning," in Elizabeth Fee and Daniel M. Fox, eds., *AIDS: The Burdens of History* (Berkeley: University of California Press, 1988), p. 201.

2. Robert A. Padgug and Gerald M. Oppenheimer, "Riding the Tiger: AIDS and the Gay Community," in Elizabeth Fee

and Daniel M. Fox, *AIDS: The Making of a Chronic Disease* (Berkeley: University of California Press, 1992), p. 254.

3. John Rechy, "AIDS: Mysteries and Hidden Dangers," [1983] in Mark Thompson, ed., *Long Road to Freedom* (New York: St. Martin's Press, 1994), p. 251.

4. Randy Shilts, *And the Band Played On: Politics, People, and the AIDS Epidemic* (New York: St. Martin's Press, 1987), p. 110.

5. Larry Kramer, "1,112 and Counting," *New York Native,* 14–27 March 1983, reprinted in Larry Kramer, *Reports from the Holocaust: The Making of an AIDS Activist* (New York: St. Martin's Press, 1989), p. 33. After the first few years of the AIDS epidemic, the *New York Native* lost credibility as publisher Charles Ortleb continued to deny that HIV was the cause of AIDS, subscribed to theories of a government-backed conspiracy, and pursued increasingly eccentric hypotheses about the etiology and epidemiology of the disease. See Rodger Streitmatter, *Unspeakable: The Rise of the Gay and Lesbian Press in America* (Boston: Faber and Faber, 1995), pp. 289–91.

6. Shilts, *And the Band Played On,* p. 143.

7. Vito Russo quoted in Jonathan Mandell, "The Stonewall Legacy," *Newsday,* 8 June 1989, part II, p. 15.

8. Diego Rivera interviewed in the PBS documentary "AIDS: A Public Inquiry," quoted in Leigh W. Rutledge, *The Gay Decades: From Stonewall to the Present: The People and Events That Shaped Lives* (New York: Plume, 1992), p. 262.

9. Padgug and Oppenheimer, "Riding the Tiger," pp. 258–59.

10. People With AIDS/ARC, "The Denver Principles," in Mark Blasius and Shane Phelan, eds., *We Are Everywhere: A Historical Sourcebook of Gay and Lesbian Politics* (New York: Routledge, 1997), p. 593.

11. Cindy Patton, "The AIDS Industry: Construction of 'Victims,' 'Volunteers,' and 'Experts,'" in Erica Carter and Simon Watney, eds., *Taking Liberties: AIDS and Cultural Politics* (London: Serpent's Tail, 1989), p. 118, quoted in Padgug and Oppenheimer, "Riding the Tiger," p. 262.

12. Pat Buchanan column, 24 May 1983, quoted in Shilts,

And the Band Played On, p. 311; and Jerry Falwell quoted in Susan Sontag, *AIDS and Its Metaphors* (New York: Farrar, Straus and Giroux, 1989), p. 61.

13. Allan M. Brandt, "AIDS: From Social History to Social Policy," in Fee and Fox, *AIDS: The Burdens of History,* p. 155.

14. Roberta Achtenberg quoted in Cheryl Clarke, "Spirit and the Flesh," in Thompson, *Long Road to Freedom,* p. 289.

15. Chris Bull, "Peter Staley," [1990] in Thompson, *Long Road to Freedom,* p. 364.

16. Steven Epstein, "Democratic Science? AIDS Activism and the Contested Construction of Knowledge," *Socialist Review,* vol. 21, no. 2 (April–June 1991): 38.

17. *Time* quoted in Rechy, "AIDS: Mysteries and Hidden Dangers," p. 251.

18. John D'Emilio, "After Stonewall," in *Making Trouble: Essays on Gay History, Politics, and the University* (New York: Routledge, 1992), p. 262.

19. Dennis Altman, *AIDS in the Mind of America* (Garden City, New York: Anchor/Doubleday, 1986), p. 94, quoted in Treichler, "AIDS, Gender, and Biomedical Discourse," n. 121, p. 259.

20. Sarah Schulman, "Becoming an Angry Mob in the Best Sense: Lesbians Respond to AIDS Hysteria," *New York Native,* December 1985, reprinted in Schulman, *My American History: Lesbian and Gay Life During the Reagan/Bush Years* (New York: Routledge, 1994), p. 120.

21. D'Emilio, "After Stonewall," pp. 262–68.

THE QUEER NINETIES

1. Torie Osborn, quoted in National Museum and Archive of Lesbian and Gay History, *The Gay Almanac* (New York: Berkley Books, 1996), p. 422.

2. *Romer v. Evans,* 116 U.S. 1620 (1996) (Kennedy, A.).

3. Lambda Legal Defense and Education Fund, *The Lambda Update,* Winter 1997, 5.

4. Urvashi Vaid, Comments at Sager Symposium, Swarthmore College, 2 April 1993.

PICTURE CREDITS

Abbreviations:
(t) top, (m) middle, (b) bottom, (l) left,
(r) right

CB: Corbis-Bettmann
Davies: © Diana Davies, Diana Davies
 Collection, Manuscripts and Archives
 Division, The New York Public Li-
 brary
IGIC: International Gay Information
 Center Archives, Manuscripts and
 Archives Division, The New York
 Public Library
LHA: Lesbian Herstory Archives/Lesbian
 Herstory Educational Foundation, Inc.
McDarrah: Photographs © by Fred W.
 McDarrah from Fred W. McDarrah
 and Timothy S. McDarrah, *Gay Pride:*
 Photographs from Stonewall to Today
 (Chicago: a capella books, 1994)
Manford: Morty Manford Papers, Manu-
 scripts and Archives Division, The
 New York Public Library
MSS: Manuscripts and Archives Division,
 The New York Public Library
NALGH: National Archive of Lesbian and
 Gay History, Lesbian and Gay Com-
 munity Services Center, New York
NYPL: The New York Public Library,
 Astor, Lenox and Tilden Foundations
Rodwell: Craig Rodwell Papers, Manu-
 scripts and Archives Division, The
 New York Public Library
Schomburg: Schomburg Center for Re-
 search in Black Culture, The New
 York Public Library
Schlesinger: The Schlesinger Library,
 Radcliffe College
Wallach: Miriam and Ira D. Wallach Divi-
 sion of Art, Prints & Photographs, The
 New York Public Library
Weeks: Collection of Marshall Weeks

FRONT MATTER AND INTRODUCTION

Title page Davies; **viii** Weeks; **xiv**
NYPL, photo by Bob Rubic.

STONEWALL

"THERE'S A RIOT GOIN' ON"

2 McDarrah. **4** UPI/CB. **6, 7** IGIC, New
York: Flower Beneath the Foot Press
(Steven Watson/Ray Dobbins), 1979. **10,
11** McDarrah. **13** IGIC. **14–15** Davies. **16**
(t), (b) Rodwell. **17** (t) Rodwell; (b)
NALGH. **18** (tl) UPI/CB; (br) MSS:
Gran Fury Collection. **19** IGIC. **20** Wal-
lach: Photography Collection, © Joseph
Caputo, courtesy of Stephen Caputo. **21**
Rick Maiman/Sygma. **22** McDarrah. **23**
(t) © Bettye Lane; (b) Reuters/CB.

SODOMITES, PERVERTS, AND QUEERS

LABELING AND POLICING

26 CB. **28** ©1986 by The New York
Times Company, reprinted by permis-
sion. **30** UPI/CB. **32** UPI/CB. **33** IGIC.
34 MSS: Dorothee Gore Papers. **35** Private Collection, courtesy of the Gay Lesbian Bisexual Veterans of Greater New
York. **36** (t) IGIC, gift of BUREAU, Marlene McCarty and Donald Moffett; (b)
McDarrah. **37** NYPL: Science, Industry
and Business Library. **38** (tr) CB; (bl)
IGIC. **39** NYPL: General Research Division. **40** NYPL: U.S. History, Local History and Genealogy Division. **41** (t), (b)
Schlesinger: Collection MC412. **42**
UPI/CB. **43** IGIC.

SOCIAL WORLDS

EARLY WOMEN'S COMMUNITY

46 Staten Island Historical Society: Alice
Austen Collection. **48** (tl) Schlesinger:
Inez Haynes Irwin Papers. **48–49** Brown
Brothers. **50** Schomburg: Photographs
and Prints Division, © Morgan and Mar-
vin Smith. **52** LHA: Found Images Col-
lection. **53** Schlesinger: Mary Dreier
Papers. **54** Staten Island Historical Soci-
ety: Alice Austen Collection. **55, 56, 57**
Schlesinger: Inez Haynes Irwin Papers.

OUT ON THE TOWN

58 Culver Pictures. **60, 61** Weeks. **62**
Schlesinger Library. **63** Wallach: Print
Collection. **64** The Museum of the City
of New York, gift of Christopher D. Morris. **65** Before Stonewall Collection. **66**
CB. **67** Courtesy of Donna VanDerZee.
68, 69 Weeks. **71** (l) Schomburg: Rare
Books, Manuscripts and Archives Division; (r) NYPL: Library for the Performing Arts, Billy Rose Theatre Collection.
72 Collection of The New-York Historical Society. **73** Weegee (Arthur Fellig) ©
1994, International Center of Photography, New York, bequest of Wilma Wilcox.
74 LHA: Bubbles K. Collection. **75** Culver Pictures. **76** LHA. **78** CB. **79** Collection of David Hibbert.

"I LOVE THE NIGHTLIFE"

80 MSS: Martin Michel Collection. **82,
83** Collection of José Sarria. **84** IGIC:
Tangents, December 1966. **85** Leslie,
Judy and Gabri Schreyer and Alice
Schreyer Batko. **87** © Bettye Lane. **88**
LHA. **89** © Ellen Shumsky/Image-
Works. **90** © Bettye Lane. **91** Davies. **92**
(tr) The Museum of the City of New

York; (bl) IGIC. **93** (tl) MSS: Martin Michel Collection; (bl), (r) NALGH. **94–95** ©1998 Bill Bernstein. **96** IGIC. **97** Collection of Boyd Masten, The Disco Kazoo & Tambourine Marching Band.

CRUISING

98 Private Collection, Europe. **100** (t), (b) NALGH. **101** IGIC. **102** NYPL: Archives. **103** IGIC. **104** Collection of The New-York Historical Society. **105** Collection of Herbert Mitchell. **106** Private Collection, Europe. **107** IGIC. **108** NALGH. **109** © CB, Richard C. Wandel.

LESBIAN PULPS

110, 112, 113, 114, 115 Courtesy of Jaye Zimet Collection.

PHYSIQUES

116 Weeks. **118** Collection of Carl Morse, New York. **119** Weeks. **120** Collection of Herbert Mitchell. **121** (t), (b) IGIC. **122** Schomburg: Photographs and Prints Division, Glenn Carrington Collection. **124** Wallach: Photography Collection. **125** Collection of Carl Morse, New York.

FRIENDS AND LOVERS

126–27 Weeks. **128** (tl) LHA: Found Images Collection; (tr) Collection of Herbert Mitchell; (bl), (br) Weeks. **129** (tl), (tr), (bl) Weeks; (br) Collection of Fred Wasserman. **130** (tl), (tr), (bl) Weeks; (br) MSS: Dorothee Gore Papers. **131** (t) Courtesy of Howard Greenberg Gallery, NYC; (b) Weeks. **132** (tl), (tr) Schomburg: Photographs and Prints Division, Glenn Carrington Collection; (b) Before Stonewall Collection. **133** (t) Collection of Ilana Weinstock; (b) JEB (Joan E. Biren) from *Eye to Eye: Portraits of Lesbians*. **134** (l) © Diana Davies; (tr), (mr), (br) Collection of Donald Vining. **135** (tl) © Bettye Lane; (tr) © Bruce Cratsley; (b) McDarrah.

ORGANIZING

EMERGING MINORITY

138 UPI/CB. **140** MSS: Frank Thompson Collection. **141** (tl) Schomburg: Manuscripts, Archives and Rare Books Division, Glenn Carrington Papers; (br) MSS: Dorothee Gore Papers. **142** (l), (r) Collection of "Lisa Ben." **143** © Jim Gruber,

IGIC. **144** (l), (r) IGIC. **145** IGIC, gift of Randy Wicker. **146** IGIC. **147** LHA. **148** IGIC, gift of Jeanne Manford. **149** IGIC. Matt Bradley, *Faggots to Burn* (Hollywood, Calif.: Art Enterprises, Inc., 1962); Matt Bradley, *Queer St. U.S.A.* (Los Angeles: Century Books, 1965); Doris Hanson, *Homosexuality: The International Disease* (New York: L.S. Publications, 1965); John Barry, *The Militant Homosexual* (North Hollywood, Calif.: Brandon House, 1967). **151** (t) Rodwell; (b) IGIC. **152** (t) Rodwell; (b) Collection of Renée Vera Cafiero. **153** McDarrah. **154** Collection of Randy Wicker. **155** Collection of Renée Vera Cafiero. **156** (tl) Davies; (tr) Collection of Leslie, Judy and Gabri Schreyer and Alice Schreyer Batko. **157** (t) Courtesy of *One Institute/International Gay and Lesbian Archives*; (br) Schomburg: Art and Artifacts Division; (bl) Manford.

GAY LIBERATION

158 Davies. **160** (tl) Schomburg: Art and Artifacts Division; (tr) Rodwell; (b) McDarrah. **161, 162** IGIC. **163** (t) Davies; (b) Schlesinger: Charlotte Bunch Papers. **164** Schlesinger, Su Negrin, graphic designer; Peter Hujar, photographer; Suzanne Bevier, Mandala. **165** (t) Schomburg: Art and Artifacts Division; (b) © Ellen Shumsky/ImageWorks. **166** (t), (b) Davies. **167** IGIC, © Richard C. Wandel. **168** © Bettye Lane. **169** (t) © Bettye Lane; (bl) NALGH; (br) Davies. **170** (tl) IGIC; (br) MSS: Jeanne Manford Papers. **171** IGIC. **172** (tr) Grey Villet, *Life* magazine © Time Inc.; (bl) IGIC. **173** (tr) © Time Inc., reprinted by permission; (bl) Davies. **174** Davies. **175** CB. **176** IGIC, Manford, and Rodwell. **177** IGIC.

LESBIAN FEMINISM

178 © Bettye Lane. **180** Schlesinger. **181** © Bettye Lane. **182** Davies. **183** © Ellen Shumsky/ImageWorks. **184** © Bettye Lane. **185** (tl), (br) © Bettye Lane. **186** Davies. **187** (tl) IGIC, ©1986 by Kitchen Table: Women of Color Press; (br) LHA. **188–89** © Bettye Lane. **190** IGIC (one button gift of Barbara Bergeron), Manford, and Rodwell. **191, 192** (tr) IGIC; (bl) IGIC. **193** (t) © Ellen Shumsky/ImageWorks; (br) Davies. **194** LHA. **195** LHA. **196** (tr) © Bettye Lane; (tl) IGIC;

(bl) Collection of Fred Wasserman. **197** McDarrah; (m) © 1980 Morgan Gwenwald; (br) LHA.

GAY RIGHTS

198 © Bettye Lane. **200** IGIC. **201** IGIC, Manford, Rodwell, NALGH, and Collection of Fred Wasserman; photo by Karen Yamauchi. **202** IGIC, gift of Lambda Legal Defense and Education Fund, Inc. **203** (tl) © Bettye Lane; (tr), (br) IGIC. **204** NALGH, © Richard C. Wandel. **205** © Bettye Lane. **206** Davies. **207** IGIC. **208** UPI/CB. **209** (t) UPI/CB; (b) bumper sticker: Rodwell, button: Manford; postcard: IGIC. **210, 211** © Bettye Lane. **212** UPI/CB. **213** Rodwell. **214** Donna Binder/Impact Visuals. **215** (t) LHA; (b) NALGH. **216** Rodwell. **217** (t), (m) © Bettye Lane. **218, 219** CB.

CONFRONTING AIDS

220 © Bettye Lane. **222** © 1986 by The New York Times Co. Reprinted by permission. **223** IGIC, gift of Joseph Rufa. **224** (l) Rodwell; (r) NALGH. **225** IGIC. **226** © Bettye Lane. **227** © Ellen Neipris. **228** (l), (r) © Steven Meisel, photographs, 1992; © Red, Hot and Dance Ltd., 1992. **230** © Bettye Lane. **231** © Jane Rosett. **232** IGIC. **233** McDarrah. **234–35** © Y. Nagasaki. **236** (tl) © Michael Rohrer, courtesy of Cándido Negrón; (br) MSS: Vito Russo Papers. **237** MSS: David Feinberg Papers. **238** (t) Collection of Fred Wasserman; (b) ©Y. Nagasaki. **239** (tl) Estate of Ronald I. Jacobowitz; (br) The Brooklyn Historical Society. **240** MSS: GMHC Records. **241** MSS: Fierce Pussy Collection.

THE QUEER NINETIES

242 IGIC. **244** (l), (r) IGIC, gift of New York City Gay & Lesbian Anti-Violence Project. **245** CB. **246** (t) IGIC; (b) Jennifer Warburg/Impact Visuals. **247** CB. **248** (tr) IGIC, gift of GLAAD/NY, design by Tracey Primavera and Michael Heitner; (bl) MSS: Fierce Pussy Collection. **249** NYPL: General Research Division, Michael Willhoite/Alyson Publications. **250, 251** IGIC. **252** (tr) © Ellen Neipris; (bl) © Kathryn Kirk. **253** LHA.

283 NYPL, photo by Bob Rubic.

INDEX